Abject Fear

Paul Carro

Tether Falls Press

ISBN: 978-1-7350701-7-9

For more information information on the author and latest updates, visit: https://www.paulcarrohorror.com

This book is horror and deals with phobias, too many to offer triggers for all. If you suffer phobias understand yours may be included in this horror novel. Beyond phobias one characters experiences SA with a non-explicit flashback. Proceed with caution.

If you like what you read, please consider leaving a review. Reviews help authors fins a wider audience. Thank you.

For more information and updates on author Paul Carro, visit paulcarrohorror.com

Contents

CHAPTER 1

Rain pelted the car. Each plop created a concussive boom in the otherwise silent vehicle. Two people sat in the front, quiet as the dead. They stared out into a world obscured by rain pouring down the windshield. Glimmers of neon light broke through the deluge casting purple hues into the Tesla. The female passenger offered proof of life when she crossed her arms and turned toward the driver.

"This is how it all ends, then? The two of us, here in the rain," Wendy asked.

Catching a beam of neon, Wendy's eyes sparkled. The deep blue metallic sheen of her evening dress already made her eyes pop, but the neon pushed them over the top. She understood their strength, kept them focused on her husband Mitch, the dashing man in the suit and tie.

Mitch was in his thirties and fit enough to wear the suit off the rack. The pair made a stunning couple, dressed for an exciting night out, except the man appeared miserable. He kept his face turned away from his wife. He knew better. *Look into the eyes of that beauty and your decisions are no longer your own*, he thought.

"I guess so," Mitch said. "I can't believe Enzo had the baby."

Outside the car, and below the awning of the upscale restaurant, sat a collapsible valet sign. Balloons tied to the sign danced in the storm.

A sheet of paper taped over the sign read: *Enzo had the baby! It's a girl! Street parking, sorry.*

"Can't believe as in we need to buy a gift? Do not dare say unbelievable because we need the car parked. Please do not even suggest you're upset their valet has the night off to be at the hospital?" Wendy asked.

"Honey? I'm a doctor, of course I'm happy for him. And yes, we will get him a present. It's just of all nights."

"Allow me to call Enzo's wife and ask her to suck it up for another few hours so her husband can park our car. Wouldn't want anything to happen to our precious Tesla."

That was all Mitch could take. He turned to face his wife. Big mistake. *Damn, she was beautiful.* "Enzo is not the issue. I don't mind parking the car. I'm simply asking you to get out here."

"And I said no. We do everything together, you know that. Rain or shine, rich or poor. This here is the rain part."

"It will ruin your dress."

"We have an umbrella. And you made me wear this thing. Really? I don't care about the dress. Or the shoes. Okay, rather fond of the shoes, but I'm not getting out. Start the car."

Mitch grimaced and started the vehicle. Its engine remained as silent turned on as it did off, so pelting rain was all the couple heard when they pulled away from the curb.

Wendy grinned in victory. "I'm not that fragile. You think a little rain will kill me?"

"I think you're stubborn. I just wanted to drop you off at the awning and keep you dry, but sure, I'm the bad guy," Mitch said with a smile.

Wendy gripped his leg, and he liked that plenty. He found a spot a few blocks away. Traffic was non-existent because Los Angeles drivers feared rain. Anything beyond a sprinkle and locals stayed home. That made it easier for the couple to find the spot albeit a dark one.

Streetlights were unreliable throughout the city. Several were out along the curb where they pulled up. Mitch parked under the nearest working one, though it flickered like a strobe light. He parked with little effort. The car did most of the work. He killed the engine while his own revved up once he turned back to Wendy.

Her dress was short but not too short, slit at such an angle that one toned leg roamed free while the other peeked out of the material below the knee. He squeezed one of her legs in that certain way. Wendy smiled.

"You start that and we're never getting out of the car," she said in a manner that suggested she was open to the idea.

Wendy kissed her husband. Mitch pulled her closer, needed her close. She was everything. He was lucky. Too lucky. He pulled away just enough that their foreheads still touched, allowing them to stare into one another's eyes.

"If you only knew what I was thinking," Mitch said.

"I have a good idea."

She laughed. Life. So full of life. She was his grace in an un-graceful world. And he needed to be rid of her. He pulled his hand away and looked outside. The storm was not kind enough to stop just for them. Rain cared not a whit for romance, Mitch figured. But he needed to get to the trunk without his wife knowing, because that was where he had hidden her gift.

Mitch knew Enzo well enough to enlist him in a conspiracy. Mitch had Jimmy, his personal assistant, call the restaurant to partner with the now MIA valet. Enzo would retrieve the gift from the trunk after parking their car. Enzo would then deliver it to the wait staff who would bring it out when the time was right. But Enzo had the night off—rightly so.

Enzo's wife must have gone into labor unexpectedly if the restaurant had no time to find someone to fill the shift. Or maybe they tried and failed to find a replacement. L.A. employees were notorious for calling out during rainstorms.

Mitch tried to segue to plan B once he learned of the situation. It should have been easy. Drop Wendy off under the awning to keep her dry before parking the car. (And retrieving her gift.) Most would have jumped at the curbside service, but not Wendy. Mitch and his wife did everything together; it was more than a slogan in their marriage.

Mitch devised a plan C while they sat under the streetlight. He originally placed the gift in the trunk because Wendy randomly touched him so often. When not hugging or acting playful with him, she routinely straightened his clothes. She would have sniffed it out before they got out of their garage. It was the rain in the end that provided the answer. Mitch landed on an idea.

"The umbrella! It's in the trunk. I'll be right back."

Wendy protested when Mitch exited the vehicle and slammed the door. He rushed to the trunk, (his Tesla was not the hatchback version) opened it, then quickly pocketed the box. When he closed the trunk, he yelped. A withered face pressed almost up against his own.

"Spare some change?" the man mumbled.

Mitch stepped back, putting some distance between them. The man wore a hoodie so wet that it molded to his skull. A grizzled beard occupied most of the real estate across the man's weathered face. Mitch patted his pockets, only to remember the box. Earlier, he hoped his wife would not notice the gift but now he hoped the stranger in the street would not.

"Sorry. No cash," Mitch said, upset that he carried none.

With a wave of his arms, Mitch turned away, apologetic, and soaking wet. Wendy appeared, umbrella in hand. She raised it higher to accommodate them both.

"What are you doing? You keep the umbrella in the glove box. Now you're soaking," she said.

Mitch nodded, knowing all along where they stored the umbrella. At six-foot-three, Mitch towered over Wendy, so he took over umbrella duty. As they stepped away from the car, he beeped the locks. Wendy only noticed the man as they walked away.

"Poor man out in this rain," she said.

They moved on and checked for oncoming traffic. They dodged a street puddle then broke into a run, laughing all the way to the awning. Once under the restaurant's canopy he collapsed the umbrella.

"I love you," Mitch said.

"You think I don't know that?"

"I think I don't say it enough."

"But you show it, honey, you always do. Truthfully, I'd rather be at home watching movies, having wine, and then having you." Wendy made certain they were alone before grabbing one of his hands and placing it high on her exposed leg.

Mitch's breath caught. Her skin excited him. He traced his hand even higher. Wendy breathed in time with him, but as she leaned in closer to hide their indiscretion, Mitch pulled away. Their affection would have led to her noticing the gift box in his breast pocket. She moaned in frustration.

"Sorry. I'm starving," he said.

Wendy laughed. "While disappointed, I can't deny I am as well."

Mitch took the hand of the most beautiful woman he knew and led her into the restaurant. Apparently, all the regular employees were visiting Enzo. Mitch recognized no one on the wait staff and had to inform them where their usual tablet was. The server apologized for the soaking incurred from no valet before the conversation turned to how the birth went. Enzo had a girl.

Wendy and Mitch had dried by the time they finished their meal. Mitch cut the last of his steak into small pieces and offered some to his wife. She declined. He happily finished it off. Wendy had half a lobster Cobb salad left on her plate. She flagged down the server and mimed the universal sign for a to go bag.

"A long way from ramen noodles," Wendy said.

Mitch nodded; mouth too full to speak. He sipped the last of his wine to clear his throat. "Agreed. So happy to be past all that."

"You never miss it? Us needing to use the hot pot, because they cut off the gas to the stove when we couldn't pay the bill?" She gripped his hand.

"All that stress? No, thank you."

"But us at our prime? My wearing your dress shirts, and nothing else?" She rubbed her foot against his legs under the table.

"I'm simply glad we made it through. There were times I didn't think we would. You kept me going. Am I thankful to have been with you since college? Yes. Am I fond of how tough things used to be? No. Besides, I couldn't afford things like this back then."

Mitch pulled out the Willington's box. The jeweler was famous locally and competed with Tiffany's in quality and price. Their boxes were pink versus the competitor's blue. Wendy lit up as Mitch handed it over.

"I confess, the box alone is more exciting than our old chilly apartment. Do I thank Jimmy or you?"

Mitch flushed red. Jimmy kept all Mitch's trains running on time, but Mitch had a hand in the purchase. "Jimmy suggested where to shop. I did the rest. With the help of a saleslady."

"I was kidding. I'm grateful. This is too much."

"You haven't even seen it yet."

She opened the box and her face faltered, almost slipping into a cry before she remembered they were in public. An intimate restaurant, but not private. Wendy's eyes connected with a lone female diner who could have been her doppelgänger. The two women traded warm smiles, one stranger sharing in the good fortune of another. Wendy turned her attention back to the gift. It was a necklace comprising two gold circles like wedding rings intertwined at the end of an elegant thin chain.

Mitch moved from his chair to help her fasten it. Once hooked, he kissed her neck and retook his seat. She lifted the charm and caressed the pieces.

"If you thought that buying this would make me want to go home and take advantage of you, mission accomplished."

Her foot found his crotch. He gulped and flagged down the server and mouthed the word check. The server brought it over and Mitch dropped his card. The server also took Wendy's food to wrap.

Mitch stiffened and tapped his foot. The nervous tic spread to his hands as he tapped the table as well. Wendy frowned and followed her husband's gaze to where the server closed out the bill. She gripped his hand, steadied it.

"What is it, honey?"

"Silly thing," Mitch said. "I have the fear."

"Fear?" Wendy asked.

"Not simple fear. THE fear. I'm afraid the card won't go through."

"Seriously?"

"What have we been talking about? Things weren't always this good. I've mentioned my phobia, right? I always feared that if life gets too good, something gets taken away."

"Honey. Don't be foolish. Your credit card is fine."

He nodded, trying to assuage Wendy's desire to change the subject. "They might decline it; I did just buy you an expensive present."

"Yes, you did." She leaned over the table and gave him a quick kiss. Then she looked over to where the server conferred with a manager she did not recognize. "What is taking so long?"

The manager headed their way. A nearby tequila bar wall turned the man purple and green as he passed, carrying the check with a look of great concern on his face. The manager handed over the bill-folder. He stood rigid, but awkward. Mitch and Wendy traded looks.

"Is there a problem?" Mitch asked.

"Yes. It appears your wife is off cake," the manager said.

"What?" Wendy asked. Then her face turned ashen. She shook her head. "Oh, no."

Their server and two waitresses approached, carrying Wendy's leftovers, a tray, and enormous grins. One waitress set Wendy's takeaway down on the table while the other lifted one of two shots from the tray and placed it in front of Wendy.

"Your husband mentioned your cake aversion but never mentioned a tequila aversion," the manager said.

"I have a much greater aversion to tequila than cake. What are you talking about?" Wendy raised the shot glass, anyway. "Honey?" She signaled for him to take the other.

Mitch waved her off and signed the check. "Are you kidding? I'm already terrified of driving in the rain after wine. Add tequila? No thanks. Both are yours."

Wendy downed it, then thrust her arms up in victory. One waitress collected the empty shot glass, while another placed the fresh one in Wendy's hand. The staff started in on *Happy Birthday*. Mitch joined in as did the female diner nearby. Other diners clapped along to the familiar birthday song.

Wendy downed the second shot to cheers. The staff filtered away to attend to their other customers while Mitch and Wendy made their way to the exit. Los Angeles rain was often warm, so neither had bothered with coats. Mitch scooped up their umbrella from the tin near the door and they exited.

Once outside, Wendy looped her hands around Mitch's neck. "Never do that again."

"Buy you an expensive gift? Done. Will never happen again."

"No. Make me feel nervous about the credit card. Honey, we are past all that. We made it."

Mitch nodded, but he did not fully agree. His performance earlier was only partially an act. He distracted his wife with the fear of a credit decline to keep her from noticing the staff prepping birthday shenanigans. But Mitch did fear things going away. That much was true. He found his inability to overcome such fears fascinating, if only because he understood the subject so well.

Many people considered fear an irrational emotion. Not Mitch, who had an affinity for the subject. It was one of his main studies in college. Fear was rational in the correct context. Evolution, for example. Fear was crucial for early humans to avoid danger. Fight or flight instincts allowed humanity to survive. Wendy pulled him tight and leaned into his ear. Her presence always made the fear go away.

She was clumsy as she whispered in his ear, likely the tequila kicking in. "Plying me with alcohol? I think someone is trying to get lucky."

"I am lucky," he said matter of fact.

She shoved him and nipped his ear, a quick snap followed by a warm breath. "Well, you're about to get luckier. Let's go home."

She pulled away, cradling her leftovers. He pulled her into a huddle, opened the umbrella and they dashed out into the still heavy rain. The flickering light pole served as a beacon guiding them toward the vehicle (which he had just washed two days ago!). Mitch turned on the headlights from a distance when suddenly a shadowy figure appeared, backlit by the high beams.

Because of the rain, it took Mitch time to understand what it was they rushed toward. A shadow should not have stood in front of their vehicle. No one should have been out in the storm. As they neared the car, it sank in. The beggar. He who asked for cash. The man inexplicably remained near their car.

Mitch noticed first and stopped. Because of intertwined limbs, Wendy jerked to a halt along with him. She smiled up at her husband, wondering what he was up to. Wendy gasped when she noticed the man from earlier holding a gun.

"Mitch," Wendy whispered.

Mitch stepped in front of his wife. He raised his hand as if it might act as a shield against the weapon.

"Got cash now?" the man asked and emphasized the gun, the enormous gun.

"I swear I don't. I only have credit cards. Here, you can have my wallet."

Mitch pulled it from his breast pocket. Wendy grabbed at Mitch from behind, but he waved her off, trying to keep himself front and center. His hand shook, the restaurant fear coming to life. He extended his arm as far as he dared. The man took aim and fired.

Click!

Mitch jerked in fright, dropping the umbrella, but still holding out the wallet. "Jesus, shit! I'm giving it to you. Stop, just stop."

The man fired again. Click!

Mitch leaped again. The man looked down at the weapon, frustrated. But Mitch relaxed some. No money for bullets. He pocketed the wallet.

"Sorry. I have no cash. But take our umbrella." Mitch leaned down to grab it when it all happened.

Wendy's stunning legs. They rushed past Mitch while he tried to retrieve the damn umbrella. Odd to think of how hot she looked in such a chaotic situation. Maybe it was the rain that made everything slow down. The world stilled as his wife passed him. He wanted to stop her, knew he should have, but the world had slowed. Every raindrop fell one at a time in slow motion. Even Wendy's words dragged. She conveyed a kind offering because that's who Wendy was.

"Food. Here, I have some leftovers. You can..."

Blam!

The explosion caused Mitch to drop the umbrella again. It spun upside down; the rain filling it into a whirlwind of rotation on the pavement. Then something hit the ground with a wet thud. A sack? Sack of what? What made a sound like that when it hit the ground? Nothing should sound like that, rain, or shine. It made no sense. The smell of gunpowder wafted through the air along with another odor, one he recognized from the hospital.

No, wait, what? Mitch thought, his brain scrambled, trying to understand. Something happened. *Did something just happen?* He rose and turned back to the man. The man with the big gun. He was gone.

But so was his wife. Footsteps splashed in the rain, an echo of a man running away without food, or even the expensive necklace around his wife's neck. That gift lay on her chest, atop where her body twitched on the ground.

Wendy's face was halfway gone, taken away by the wicked man with the gun. The cavity in her face spit blood as her body twitched its last.

The rain failed to wash away the blood fast enough. Mitch stood over the thing that could not be his wife, could not be Wendy.

He opened his mouth and choked, unable to find the scream because he could not find his breath. With one more jerk, she fell still. Beautiful Wendy in her last sleep on the pavement in a city where it never rains.

Mitch stumbled back and bumped into something. Down between his legs, he saw another pair. The legs were corpse grey but remained toned. He turned in shock. Standing behind him, minus half of her face, was his wife. She stood there as clearly as she lay on the ground below.

Mitch finally found his voice, and his screams reached the restaurant.

CHAPTER 2

A long queue of cars fed itself into the belly of a docked ferry. The beauty of the Puget Sound loomed in the distance. The size of the Seattle skyline could not compete with the vastness of the ocean at its border. A painted walkway designed for pedestrians remained empty. This ferry boarded only vehicles. Despite the backed-up traffic, no horns blared. There was a sense of normalcy to the procession, a routine for people clearly not working from home. Drivers, riding mostly solo, primped in mirrors, texted, or sang along to the radio as they inched forward ever so slowly.

Above it all rose Mt. Rainier. The majestic landmark came with its own unique optical illusion. The visible base rose above a distant strip of land. Midway up the volcano (a live one overdue for an eruption) its center vanished. A snow-covered peak appeared atop it all, as if floating. In between the landmark's base and top, there appeared nothing but sky. The ocean cast its reflection over the mountain's middle and on days where it matched the sky's color, viola, disappearing mountain mass. The scenery was beautiful enough that some commuters ignored devices in favor of enjoying the view.

A street vendor stood near the ferry selling bags of oranges. Scruffy and in his forties, the man wore a Wolverine tee-shirt. The vendor stood in the otherwise empty pedestrian lane and served a captive audience. A beat-up Pinto stopped, and its driver signaled him.

Yoshi, a sloppy-looking Asian American man in his twenties, manned the wheel wearing headphones. An empty slot in the dash showcased the spot where once upon a time there was a stereo. Plastic sheeting covered one rear window, taped up where the thieves had struck almost two years ago. There was lots of work to finish on the car. Bondo and mismatched paint fought to hold the original frame together. Yoshi rolled down the window manually but stopped halfway to shake out his tired arm.

"How is it I play video games for hours but can't roll down a window? I need to work out," Yoshi said.

The vendor shrugged and lifted the bag of oranges, waiting patiently. Yoshi finished rolling the window down then took one of his ear buds out.

"Five dollars," the vendor said.

Yoshi reached into his front jeans pocket. He was not a wallet guy. As he dug through the wad of bills, he gestured to the man's shirt.

"I see you got the memo," Yoshi said.

"What memo?" the man asked, confused.

Yoshi pointed to his own tee-shirt, featuring the Blue Beetle. "Maybe you don't recognize this one. It's Jaime Reyes, the newest Blue Beetle, except he's been around since 2006, so not so new. He found the scarab of the original Blue Beetle. I loved the middle blue Beatle Ted Kord because he was a scientist like me, but then Jaime came along and wham, the poor down on his luck local kid struck a chord."

"Do you have five dollars?"

"What? Oh, yeah, here." Yoshi traded the money for the oranges.

"I'm just wearing a shirt. I don't know what it is," the man said.

Yoshi started rolling up the window which took forever. Yoshi maintained an awkward smile throughout the ordeal. Once finished, Yoshi glanced back and noticed the gap in traffic he created. The vendor noticed something as well and tried to alert Yoshi. But Yoshi already had his earbuds back in and simply waved awkwardly back and pulled forward to tighten the queue.

Yoshi threw the bag of oranges in the back seat and drove into the ferry's belly with all the other cars. Once inside, a steady stream of pedestrians left their vehicles, heading topside to score some food and coffee. He parked in the first open spot.

Unlike on planes, there was no assigned seating, or parking in this case. First come, first serve with one exception. Doctor Trager always parked near the ferry's entrance in a reserved spot. The car and driver were nothing but shadows from where Yoshi sat. It was an hour-long trip, so he planned to rest and finish his podcast.

The blast of the ferry horn jolted him upright. He laughed (extra loud because of the audio in his ears). The horn announced departure and could wake the dead. Yoshi felt on edge. Had been for some time. Since childhood, he had always remained on guard thanks to a snot-nosed older brother who liked to frighten him routinely. Ironic, considering where Yoshi worked. Or appropriate.

The ferry's destination was a place filled with fear and yet Yoshi looked forward to it. Which created a unique conundrum. He worked in a place where he experimented with fear but fully enjoyed himself there. While back in the real world, he had nothing specific to fear but found himself frequently anxious. Such low-level discomfort while back on the mainland confused him. There was no reason to fear his brother's pranks any longer. How long had it been since he even saw his sibling?

Yoshi avoided thoughts of his family because it made him sad, so he switched to thoughts about his work family. A troubled but brilliant group. Some in that group also happened to be stunning. Okay, one was. He scoured the lot for Elle's car, but it was nowhere to be found, so he leaned back. The gentle motion as the ship moved away from the dock relaxed him. Then a hand thrust just past his face from the backseat!

"Marvel versus DC! What the hell?" Yoshi leaped, ready to jump out of his skin, but the vehicle had him trapped.

"Orange?" Elle asked from the backseat, offering one from her outstretched arm.

Yoshi refused. Elle dropped it in the seat next to him and returned to enjoying slices of her already peeled fruit. Yoshi adjusted his rearview mirror.

"When? How? When did you get in my vehicle?"

"While you were buying this," she said. Elle was Asian with an athletic build and long hair. She wore glasses that flattered her big brown eyes. She leaned forward with great enthusiasm. Her energy was infectious. "I was laying down, planning to nap until someone threw a bag of breakfast at me. Thanks, champ."

She leaned back and continued eating. In that position, Yoshi saw more of her body. She wore an oversize white tee that clung to her in all the right spots. She ate an orange slice and laughed.

"Did I scare you?"

Yoshi nodded. That was why he was on edge. The orange man tried to warn him of a stowaway, but Yoshi drove away too fast. The lingering warning had settled itself in his mind. Yes, she had terrified him. And that was what he hoped to fix when they got to the island, when they got to the lab. Fear would no longer be an issue for anyone if he had his way.

"Stare much?" Elle popped another bite.

Yoshi was staring. Busted. The second Yoshi averted his gaze, Elle leaned back over the seat. "Coffee? Or can you not handle the caffeine right now?"

"Coffee sounds good."

They exited the vehicle and walked away without locking it. There was no theft between coworkers (his stereo was a street parking incident). The pair headed toward a stairwell which brought them closer to a Mustang near the Ferry's entrance.

"Doesn't Mitch usually take the supply ferry?" Elle asked Yoshi.

The supply ferry left an hour before the commuter one and transported supplies via delivery trucks. Employees could ride that ferry if it was not full, but few did. Yoshi took it once. But he thought getting up extra early sucked like the time Doomsday killed Superman. Doctor Trager usually accompanied the supply ferry.

"Guess he was running late," Yoshi said.

They looked over at the Mustang in the distance. It sat ensconced in shadows. Elle waved at the vehicle and its hidden driver, then she and Yoshi went up topside.

Sitting in the car, cloaked in darkness, Mitch gripped the wheel as if his life depended on it. The man had aged considerably since that night on the LA street. A full beard hid some of his grizzled features. The man never flinched when the ferry's horn blasted. It would not sound again until they reached the island. They were on the move.

CHAPTER 3

Quinn felt a storm coming. Gusts from Puget Sound often carried a chill from Alaska or Canada. Her short pixie cut blonde hair barely registered the breeze, but her bones cried out in protest. A soccer injury from college ached in the wind. There was warmth inside the ferry, but it also meant being around people, something she refused to do. There was a reason she insisted on a lab in the dead wing at her workplace.

There was one other who had a lab in the same building on another floor. Mercedette, a Latina hottie, technically too old for Quinn. Age did not matter, Quinn could fantasize. Especially since twenties were for shit in the dating world. Quinn stopped using dating apps months ago. Originally hit or miss, they became mostly miss in recent years.

A fan of traveling, Quinn understood luggage basics. Backpack for camping. A carryon for weekend trips. Twenty-four inches for a week. And the biggie, a thirty-two-inch bag for longer stays. Everyone she met on dating apps carried their own baggage. Once upon a time, she met individuals with backpack sized issues, but recently she only met those carrying the heaviest suitcase's worth of drama.

No more dating apps then. Finished. And she rarely went out. That left coworkers as potential partners. Mercedette was hot, but also a hot mess. There were also rumors Mercedette had an affair with someone on the staff. Both individuals involved disappeared for a few days, so the gossip was likely true. But both returned to work. One was a supervisor, which was why it was even an issue. Normal colleagues had plenty of one and done flings. That Mercedette had slept with a guy stacked the odds against Quinn, but Quinn was not afraid to shoot her shot one on one. Lots of people were fluid. There remained the baggage issue, however. As hot as Mercedette was, the woman was highly anti-social.

The wind whipped harder, interrupting Quinn's hookup fantasy. She cinched her windbreaker, which nearly swallowed her petite body. It was tricky dressing for the weather in Seattle. In Texas, where she grew up, the days often began already warm only to grow hotter with every hour. But Seattle mornings were chilly, especially near the water, forcing people to dress warmly. But as the day progressed, it grew too hot for the same clothes. It was all about layers in Seattle. That grunge phase was not simply for fashion.

She wished it would warm faster. The icy sting of the wind made her increasingly uncomfortable. Perhaps the answer was to go inside. They were all coworkers, every passenger. Not exactly strangers, but not really friends.

A thunderous sound rose above the roar of the wind. Quinn looked up. A helicopter silhouetted against a stunning blue sky flew in their direction. That was not normal. The island was already in view from the ferry, making the electric bird's destination clear.

Their boss was not topside, he remained in the car. He never left his vehicle once on board (in his killer red mustang). Quinn was not interested in Doctor Trager beyond his genius and mentorship, but she fantasized about driving his antique muscle car with a hottie by her side.

The helicopter roared overhead. The ocean drowned out the helicopter's approach. Unless people were topside like herself, they would likely never hear it. She considered informing Doctor Trager. Probably nothing, but certainly unusual.

Another chill whipped by, as if in search of the sore knee. Something about the helicopter worried her. Maybe it tied into her worry about a coming storm. One unrelated to the weather. Change was in the air. Strange to fear something intangible when she toyed with fear on the job.

Trager Chemicals made a drug that induced fear and Quinn enjoyed using it. (If Doctor Trager knew she would be out of a job.) Because it was experimental, she did not know if the drug had flashback effects like LSD. Quinn toyed with their work product often, among others. Not all drugs were equal, and she quite enjoyed certain ones, thank you very much. But something about the early morning helicopter that now faded in the distance worried her. She was about to seek out Doctor Trager when someone leaned on the railing next to her.

"What's all this aboot?" Colt asked, speaking loud enough to be heard over the whipping wind.

He grabbed the handrail that Quinn leaned on and stood uncomfortably close. Quinn shifted a few feet away, signal sent. Colt was an unorthodox scientist. One who appeared more hipster bartender than lab technician. The man was tall and thin, with a mop atop his head that nearly matched her own. His blonde came from a bottle while hers was real.

In his twenties, Colt sported several creative piercings and tattoos. He wore flannel and jeans that were tight enough to advertise his wares. But Quinn was not buying.

"A helicopter," Quinn said.

"What are you talking about? I meant what is this all aboot with you out here all by yourself?"

"Are you new? I am out here near every day."

"Exactly. I finally coughed up the courage to ask why. Hottie like you sitting out here on your own. And you're in that distant wing as well. What gives?"

"I like my privacy,"

Despite the possibility that Colt's hot air could warm her, Quinn turned into the cold, looking out into the sea, wishing the man away. Colt failed to receive the message. He gestured to his own hair, then hers.

"What's wrong with getting to know one another? We could be twins."

"Ya'll are into incest. Is that what you're telling me?"

"What? No. Oh, I get it. You're one of those."

Quinn grabbed the rail, steadying herself for a fight. "One of what?"

"An SA."

Quinn eyed Colt, ready to lash out. Despite an aversion to socializing, she stood up for herself, especially where her orientation was concerned. Though she confronted plenty of haters back in Texas, she still loved her home state. That, despite the number of knuckleheads who made her formative years problematic. Not understanding Colt's acronym, she waited for more information before responding. Her confused look prompted him to explain.

"A social awkward. No shame. I do my best work with bashful women," Colt said.

His oversized grin suggested he believed the conversation was not only going well, but that he was also winning over his prey. *Dead on with that one*, Quinn thought. She was an SA, so took no offense to the comment. But she wanted to make sure her no would take, that their little tête-à-tête would not become a daily routine. She turned to him and flashed a smile. Colt lit up.

"Fine, cowboy, if we're to know one another better, I need to tell you about my condition," Quinn said.

"Your condition?"

"Yes." Quinn looked around to make sure no one was watching, like she was about to share a secret. Colt instinctively parroted her movements before leaning in, waiting for the tea.

"It's very rare. I'm almost ashamed to talk about it."

"No. Please. I'm here for you," Colt said.

"I'm only telling ya'll because I believe you can keep a secret."

"See? It's like you understand me. I am your man. What is it, beautiful?"

"It is a rare condition. Known as Coltitis."

"What? You mean colitis?"

"No. When I meet men named Colt, well, my vag zips right up. Tight, so tight." Quinn raised both her fists and pushed them together hard.

He deflated. "Soorry, your highness, forgive me for trying to be friendly. Your loss."

Colt left her side, vanishing into the mouth of a stairwell. Harsh, but Quinn hoped it would deter the man's outsized ego enough that he did not return for round two. She knew very few unfriendly Canadians, but Colt was one. She understood if she gave an inch, the bombastic coworker would take a kilometer. No, she did not feel bad about shooting him down. If he had character, he would reconnect with her someday but firmly in the friend zone.

The island drew closer. If she was going to alert Doctor Trager, time was running out. She reentered the ship, a necessity to get to the parking below. She passed Colt, already chatting up another woman. His new conquest appeared far more enamored of the Canadian than Quinn. Colt glanced Quinn's way, but barely reacted.

His conquest, on the other hand, laughed at everything Colt said. Quinn assumed the woman would massage his bruised ego in a supply closet once at work. Colt already moved on. A numbers man, she could not fault him. Quinn passed by Yoshi, who sat with Elle. His love or lust for the woman was the worst kept secret at work. Better kept was Quinn's secret connection with the loveable dude. They nodded discreetly to one another. Elle remained none the wiser. Quinn moved on.

On her way back to the parking garage stairwell, Quinn spotted the object of her desire. Mercedette sat stiff, upright, and by herself in a corner booth. The woman's long, flowing hair cascaded over her shoulders. Mercedette was fit, likely a runner though possibly a gym bunny. True to the woman's weird nature, Mercedette even sipped her tea conservatively.

And dressed that way as well. The woman wore a Catholic schoolgirl outfit, despite being in her thirties. Her marriage ring finger remained empty; Quinn checked often. Mercedette also wore a cross around her neck on a gold chain, a permanent part of her look. The Latina woman had brown doe eyes that looked like they were enhanced by an ai app, but no, they were her actual peepers.

A part of Quinn wondered if Mercedette had something to do with the feeling of change in the air. A storm was coming. She did not believe in premonitions, but she felt it in her bones, alongside her injury. Maybe the change would involve her relationship status. Possibly, she would finally get the courage to make a move on her older, seemingly unattainable crush.

The moment Quinn stepped back inside the ferry she unzipped her windbreaker. Not because of the warmth but because it was her chance to show off what she was working with. As coworkers, they usually saw one another in lab coats. The commute was an opportunity to show off. Quinn made sure everything was visible before she waved at the woman. A subtle thing, curled fingers on a raised hand. She got nothing in response.

Mercedette remained still, hands wrapped around her cup. She never even noticed Quinn, never checked out the hot twenty-three-year-old passing by. It was as if Quinn did not exist. Mercedette simply took another sip, locked in a world of her own. Now Quinn knew how Colt felt.

Flushed red, Quinn escaped down the metal staircase leading to the parking belly but froze on the last step. While sunlight glimmered over her shoulder from above, darkness prevailed in the lot. The parking belly lights, like those in their workplace, were motion activated. No one must have come through recently because lights were off. If Quinn waited, an exodus of employees would soon return to their cars. When the ferry next blasted its horns, people would be everywhere.

Quinn wanted to inform Doctor Trager about the helicopter, but she dared not walk further. How many steps would it take to trigger the lights? She waved her arms. Nothing. Silly, but she refused to descend any further without knowing exactly when they kicked in.

Darkness she could not deal with. Worse than her fear of crowds. People she could step away from as needed, but darkness owned her. She could not easily walk away once in its embrace. An absence of light gave shadows great power, enough to interrupt her ability to function. Little by little, her fear would shut down her limbs, her movement, her thoughts.

The dark was where the bad things lived, and where the bad things happened. She stretched one leg out as far as it could reach. Nothing. Where were the sensors?

Stepping onto the ground level might trigger them so Quinn placed one foot on the floor. A chill worse than the wind above rocketed up her leg and into her chest. *No, must not go any further*, she thought.

Quinn turned and ran up the stairwell. Darkness would not get her this day. No bad things. She was back in the bright confines of the ship. Down in the stairwell, darkness crept, chasing after her still. Quinn stepped into a sunny spot and took a seat, breathing deep to calm herself.

At the next booth, Mercedette continued her love affair with her tea, never noticing the antics of the too young girl lusting after her elder. (What was ten years?) While disappointed at being ignored by her workplace crush, Quinn was relieved to bathe in the light. She was safe for now.

The bad things would not get her in the sunlight. She settled in for the rest of the trip, looking much like Mercedette, staring straight ahead, lost in her own world, seeking calm. All thoughts of warning her boss about the helicopter vanished from her mind.

CHAPTER 4

Jimmy ran as if his life depended on it. His slick bottomed penny loafers hindered his progress, sliding out of control with every step. It was unsafe to run in such shoes, but lives were at stake. He needed to warn his boss. *Damn the lack of cell service*, he thought. Once at the twin mid-corridor elevators, he tapped the call button but slid past, unable to stop. Jimmy grabbed the elevator's rim and came to a stop. He hit the button twenty times while fully aware the effort would not make it arrive faster.

Too slow, always too slow. The Empire State Building traveled from ground floor to rooftop faster than theirs managed seven floors. Rather than wait, he ran for one of the stairwells available at either end of the corridor. Jimmy cursed when the elevator finally dinged open at his rear, but he kept running.

The entire seventh floor, (the penthouse they called it) housed the lab and office of their boss, Doctor Trager. But Mitch sat on a ferry, oblivious that he cruised into danger. Jimmy burst through the crash-bar door and took the steps two at a time. Because the building was old, the stairs were of an antiquated design. The stairs wound around leaving a gap between them that ran from floor to ceiling, a deadly drop if one leaned too far over the rails. Each set of steps culminated in a landing with a door to the corresponding floor.

It was dangerous to take the stairs so quickly, but Jimmy did not want to miss his boss. Could not. He had to warn Mitch. Jimmy's pounding footsteps caused a horrible racket, which drew an employee's attention. Derrick, a good-looking black man approaching thirty, opened a door and poked his head out. He looked over the railing until he spotted Jimmy.

"Jesus, Jimmy, what is going on?" Derrick asked.

"Not now Derrick," Jimmy yelled and continued without explanation.

"Sure. The assistant manager is running like there is a chemical spill. No cause for concern, people!"

Jimmy felt the sarcasm drip down like rain. Rightly so, but time was running out. The ferry horn blasted in the distance. His boss was a madman behind the wheel, someone with a death wish. Even now, the good doctor likely pulled into his parking spot. Jimmy ran, hoping he wasn't too late.

The moment the ferry docked on Strode Island, Mitch gunned the engine of his Mustang and sped out of the ferry, across the ramp, and onto the winding road. The dock worker yelled his well-practiced protest and leaped out of the way. With the danger of the menace in the Mustang passed, the dock worker returned to releasing vehicles that belonged to more responsible drivers.

Mitch floored it up the winding road. What began as a straightaway quickly curved. Those who designed the sanitarium made sure reaching the place would be difficult, so they made the only road leading in and out as winding as possible. It forced most to slow their roll when visiting, but more important, slow it during any attempted escapes. Mitch ignored the dangers and sped perilously fast toward the compound.

The road did its part to toss the vehicle over a cliff, especially with roads damp from overnight rain. While the rain gave a fresh burst of green to the lush forest stretching across the entire island, it also made mud of the road's packed dirt. Mitch fishtailed repeatedly. The rear of his vehicle flirted with the possibility of plummeting over the cliff's edge several times.

One side of the road rose with the mountain as cliffs, but the other side offered a freefall back to the beach. A collision with the mountainside was possibly survivable, a drop off the cliff would not be. If the fishtailing worried Mitch, he did not show it. With every precarious drift toward the cliff's edge, he took his eyes off the road to eye the empty passenger seat. Not that Wendy ever sat in the Mustang. The old Tesla brought with it unbearable memories, so he sold it and bought a muscle car.

It was dangerous to drive at such speeds, which was why he exited the ferry before anyone else. Mitch had the luxury of a reserved parking spot in the ferry and at the lab—a perk of being the boss. He hit the road before others even started their cars and his speed ensured no one would ever catch up to him. The dangerous drive was his folly, and his alone. So alone.

Looming atop the hill rose a former insane asylum. The aged sanitarium, once a sanctuary for the suffering, had undergone a transformation of profound significance. A sign reading Trager Chemicals adorned one corner of the roof. The sign's futuristic font and logo suggested the work inside bordered on revolutionary, while the building served as a testament to past scientific achievements.

A seven-story behemoth, the building stood as a stoic sentinel, guarding the secrets of its past while embracing the fervor of modernity. The structure comprised three wings that formed a bat-like shape. The main wing served as the body of the 'bat' while enormous wings branched off on both sides. Light spilled from selected windows in the main and west wings.

The east wing remained in disrepair, a victim of time's neglect. Plywood covered the first-floor windows while most on the upper floors were broken, victims of outsiders with rocks, or perhaps inmates seeking escape. Graffiti marked the walls at ground level. A metal chain-link fence rose around the perimeter of the dead wing, adorned with condemned signs. Grass grew waist high and poked through the diamond-shaped holes in the fencing. The difference between the renovated sections and that of the untouched signified how the world had changed.

The transition from asylum to innovation hub served as a testament to human resilience, proving that even the darkest of places could be reborn. It served as a reminder that the human spirit endured and strove to transform the old into something new and extraordinary. Mitch hoped the grand old asylum could deliver him from his own past.

He screeched to a halt in the parking lot next to a waist-high metal sign bearing his name. The parking lot sat well below the building. From there, one could cross the massive front lawn or use a set of stone steps to reach the building. Normally the first there, Mitch missed the earlier ferry so there would be workers already on site. Lonnie, the groundskeeper, rode his mower in clean patterns across the front lawn.

The scent of fresh cut grass reached Mitch's nose and brought back memories of a hand mower at their first house. The mower was physically taxing to use. By the time Mitch finished half their lawn, he was ready to ditch the gym for a month. Wendy often took over the duties without complaint. Everything together.

A tear leaked from his eye. Allergies. As much as he enjoyed the smell, he needed to flee it. Lonnie waved his cap. Mitch performed a sloppy military salute in reply, then headed toward the building. Two vehicles caught his eye. One a car he did not recognize, but more ominously, a helicopter sat parked on a massive section of the lawn. Mitch increased his pace.

Despite the gloomy exterior of the sanitarium, the main wing opened into a modern, opulent lobby. Immense and inviting, the space emulated a college library. Plush fabric chairs and couches adorned the entrance, creating cozy nooks that urged visitors to kick back and sink in.

An impressive study area awaited those venturing beyond the plush seating space. Like many grand college libraries, mahogany desks took center stage with rows of green lamps lined up like soldiers. The lamps cast a warm glow reminiscent of a bygone era. A few go-getters who caught the earlier ferry worked on laptops, typing away. Even the clicking of keyboards seemed to respect the study zone's silence protocols. Muted conversations between early birds barely rose above a whisper.

Although the surroundings resembled a sanctuary of academia, it was still the lobby of a thriving business. A custodian buffed tile floors within a perimeter of yellow wet-floor signs. The study section sat to the left of the entrance while the lobby itself opened into a sea of tile, culminating in a curved glass and metal security desk. The lobby tightened into a corridor behind the check-in desk and contained twin elevators, public restrooms, and a se-curity office. Beyond that, the corridor branched off out of view, leading to places unknown.

Mitch passed a woman sitting on a couch. She rose but stopped short when he kept going. Though familiar, he could not place the face. His priority was to find the helicopter's passenger or passengers. His head of security, Steve, manned the front desk but was busy dressing down one of their employees.

The conversation, while heated, took place at a respectable volume in keeping with the early hour. Probably a scolding session related to employees partying in the dead wing. Mitch knew Raj as a clean-cut respectful scientist and doubted he was responsible for any such hoe-down, but someone needed to take the fall. The dead wing was dead for a reason. Not safe by a longshot.

Steve grew animated when he spotted Mitch. The security guard raised a finger to his boss to signal he needed only a moment more to close out the tough love session with Raj. But then Jimmy burst through the stairwell doors at the far end of the lobby. The noise startled everyone. Mitch frowned. His assistant's panic was a bad sign.

"Doctor Trager, it's an emergency," Jimmy said.

"Calm down, Jimmy. Given your condition, you should not get too excited."

"Sorry. Can't calm down. It's bad."

Jimmy's outburst drew Steve and Raj's attention. Steve's hand instinctively went to his waist, and he eyed Mitch with concern. Mitch shook the guard off.

"I understand we may have a situation. But I refuse to speak to you until you calm down. Can you do that for me?"

After a deep breath, Jimmy shook his body out. Then he stilled, standing erect, an exclamation point of posture, creating a perfect line for his tie to feed into his sweater vest.

"My apologies, Mitch. You know I'm not normally so frantic."

"I consider you unflappable Jimmy. Now what is it?" Mitch asked.

"New York is in the building."

"Did not expect them until next month," Mitch said.

"Exactly. This visit is different."

"And I will handle it as I always do. They need us more than we need them, do they not?"

Jimmy failed to reply, uncertain how to answer. Mitch patted the assistant on the shoulder before heading toward the elevators. Jimmy stood there, catching his breath, when the woman from the couch brushed past him to catch up with Mitch.

"Wait, who are you?" Jimmy said, but the woman was already gone.

Mitch pressed the call button. The elevator opened immediately, and he stepped inside. As the doors closed, a hand reached in, forcing them open again. The woman from the lobby joined him. Mitch looked her over, confused.

"You're not from New York," Mitch said.

"I'm from L.A. Gillian McCann."

"Names annoyingly familiar."

"I'm a reporter with..." she started and raised her cellphone.

"THE reporter," Mitch said. His demeanor changed to one of outright anger. "I always wondered what I would do if ever I encountered you again."

With surprising speed, Mitch grabbed the woman's wrist. Gillian yelped and dropped her phone. She yanked her hand free, massaging it and shooting him a look, letting him know the move was unacceptable.

"No more recording me," Mitch said.

"I wasn't. I wanted to play a recording for you."

"You ruined my life."

"That was never my intention. I was on the scene and reported what happened. It's been five years, and..."

He turned on her, interrupting. In the tight confines of the elevator, he was close. Too close but moved in even closer. Gillian sought refuge against the wall.

"Every day is the anniversary for me. I relive it every night. That night I was in no state to speak, to process what had occurred. You twisted my words."

"Recorded your words," she said.

And then there is no more room between them. Gillian raised her hands to hold him at bay. She pushed, but it failed to move the man.

"Doctor, you're scaring me," Gillian said.

"This is frightening? This is fear?"

Before she could answer, Mitch slammed the panel. The doors opened back into the lobby. Gillian stumbled out. Despite everything, she reached in and grabbed her cellphone before backing away from the crazed man.

"Steve, please escort this vampire from my island!"

The security guard approached as the door closed on Mitch. Gillian composed herself as employees poured in, finally arriving from the ferry.

"I'm not actually a vampire," she said.

Steve feigned relief and reached for her arm. She twisted her body and squared off against him.

"No. Do not dare touch me. I'm leaving."

Gillian exited the building and raised her phone into the air, searching for a signal. Nothing. She looked back at the closed door. She had so many questions about her encounter with the man five years earlier. The event haunted her more than any other story she ever covered.

But now the doctor who might have answered her questions was closed off in more ways than one. The ferry blasted its horn. From where she stood, Gillian could see all the way to the bay. The blast signaled the ferry's departure. Her trip to Seattle was all for naught. Worse, there would not be another boat until late afternoon. She headed to her car.

She was a woman trapped on an island with unanswered questions about ghosts of the past.

CHAPTER 5

The top floor was where the worst of the worst patients used to be locked up. Patients whose idea of a good time included removing eyeballs or other body parts, their own or those of strangers mattered little. Equally violent guards patrolled the halls, eager for opportunities to punish, to maim, to destroy human will. And when all else failed, lobotomize.

Patients' cries would have carried down the hall, feeding off one another until blending into a cacophony of despair. Not all patients were ill. Some were simply evil and enjoyed the fruits of their labor. Medical files remained on site in some offices when Mitch moved in. Unethical for anyone to leave them in an abandoned hospital, but someone had. Mitch only read so many of the files. The reports were detailed but cold and conveyed horrible people doing horrible things. Mitch understood the nature of such people better than most.

He considered the surroundings as he walked to his office. During the construction of his lab and offices, Mitch insisted half the floor remain untouched to serve as a museum of sorts, a link to the past. (The dead wing served the same purpose but was structurally unsound.) Mitch rode the elevator as far as the sixth floor then took the stairs to the seventh, giving him time to gather his thoughts before confronting his visitor.

A group of visitors would have been preferable to one. There was always one sympathetic member in a group. It was much tougher to bullshit an individual with a mandate. The moment Mitch noticed the helicopter, he understood the situation was dire. Jimmy did not need to tell him that, but Mitch appreciated Jimmy recognized the serious nature of the visit. Smart as a whip, that kid, Mitch thought.

The money to modernize the sanitarium came from military contractors. They had a single interest. Fear as a weapon. Mitch was not opposed to exploring the concept, and made significant strides in that direction, enough to keep the money pouring in, but he had bigger plans in mind, ones unrelated to the military applications his benefactors sought. Or mostly unrelated. Even his employees had no idea what Mitch worked on in his lab. He liked that, let them wonder. Time would reveal all.

If he made it that far. His heart grew heavy. He was ready to take the fight to his visitor except one other visitor threw him a curveball. The woman unnerved him. Mitch already wore the weight of the date before even arriving at work. He understood exactly how many years it had been since he lost everything. The reporter reopened wounds just when he needed to host a financial backer from the opposite coast. What were the chances the financiers flew over to console Mitch about the anniversary? None.

Mitch stopped briefly in front of a former inmate's room. Its door sat open offering a view of a metal-framed bed that had been twisted. One half remained bolted to the wall while the bottom half had been pulled free and bent. It would have taken immense strength to damage that which was designed to be undamageable. Mitch shuddered at the thought of such power in the hands of one who wished to harm others.

Then the pain struck. Mitch grabbed his chest. If it was a heart attack, he welcomed it. Time to visit Wendy. But the raging and intense pain proved short-lived. He breathed, looking at the twisted bed and considered how that was almost the last thing he saw. What had Wendy seen? What did she know in her last moments? Did she understand a monster cut her down? Had she felt pain?

Mitch cried out. The memories of that night refused to die. Time moved on. People were born and died. Buildings as grand as the one he stood in rose and fell in the intervening five years of his wife's death. Yet his pain refused to subside within that same timespan. Mitch twisted hands into fists and brought them to his skull. Not a heart attack. It was the reporter. She brought it back. The memories threatened to bring him to his knees, and while someone from New York waited.

Mitch straightened, regaining his composure. Sorrow would have to wait. Wendy would want him to be strong in the face of adversity. It was not only his life's work at stake now, but that of his employees. That was why he had taken the time to get off one floor below and make the walk.

He moved forward with confidence, back in control. From the elevators on, the floor changed. Unlike the rooms from a bygone era at his rear, the path ahead offered the promise of a high-tech startup. Walls gleamed with fresh paint while metallic accents gave off the pretense of an advanced science center. Artwork from popular local artists adorned the walls. Placards hung below each piece like a museum. The paintings were postmodern, bordering on futuristic science fiction.

Mitch arrived at his door, only to find it open. He entered. His office was a mix of professorial opulence and Pacific Northwest charm. But beyond the large mahogany desk near the rear of the office rose a metal wall which housed a high-tech door. An imposing man in a suit held his hand on the door's palm print reader.

"That won't work," Mitch said, and raised his own palm.

"Yes, well, a call to the board would," the man answered and turned to face Mitch.

Mitch did not recognize the man which meant hired muscle. A messenger. How severe the message had yet to reveal itself. Mitch stepped to an elaborate coffee station while the man took Mitch's seat, eyeing the doctor for his reaction. The man placing his feet on the desk made it worse.

"That room contains my private research. Cream or sugar?" Mitch asked.

"Black. The coffee in Seattle makes the trip worthwhile. Put it up there with our New York pizza."

The 'we' the man spoke of had nothing to do with Mitch, and everything to do with his backers. Puppet masters all. Usually, the visitors rode the ferry like everyone else. Mitch handed the man a cup of coffee and settled back with his own while refusing to sit, unwilling to cede that much authority over the island.

"No internet here. Guess you could not reach me that way. I schedule their Zoom calls from home."

"We are well past..." The man sipped, sighed. "Zoom calls."

Mitch did not bother to ask the man's name. The visitor was a shadow person. Any name he gave would be a cover. The man was a tool to be wielded by his financial backers. Still, the reason for the visit eluded him.

"I am confused. Everything we do here is about to speed up. We just received approval for human trials."

The man sipped again and smiled. Shark teeth this time. "Human trials just being approved. That's the rub now, innit?"

The odd pronunciation. The man was not from New York. His accent was elusive. His size was imposing. The man stood and turned back to the large metal door.

"What are you saying?"

"My job is to protect the board at all costs. Your work is intriguing, but there are other projects we fund as well, projects without the potential for blowback that yours has."

"Blowback?"

The man had a manilla envelope at the ready. Mitch never noticed until the man slid it forward. Mitch opened it, looked inside, and turned white.

"We are on the verge of greatness here!" Mitch protested.

"My job is to protect the board. Your work is done," the man said.

The suit slammed his empty cup on the desk to drive the point home. A picture of Mitch and Wendy during happier times tipped over. Mitch eyed the picture as the suit exited. Mitch reached out and touched Wendy's face in the picture.

"I need you more than ever, my love. Guide me."

Mitch closed the envelope and placed it into his desk drawer. He straightened the picture and returned his desk to the way it was before the world changed. He waited for a sign from his wife. Then Mitch rose and exited his office.

Gillian watched with interest as a man in a suit exited the building in a hurry. He moved at a quick pace despite his imposing size. The man never looked back and headed for a helicopter in the distance. It was not there when Gillian parked. She wondered when it landed. Gillian took the earliest ferry that morning and lied to the guard about working for a University in Seattle. She further lied by saying Doctor Trager expected her. The guard never questioned her. Who would go to a distant island otherwise?

The same man who now made his way to the helicopter arrived about twenty minutes prior to Mitch. The man in the suit seemed to cause concern for a young man wearing a vest and tie. The two rode the elevator together. Mitch arrived about an hour later which turned out to be a bust. Now the man in the suit left by himself. The helicopter started up which meant a pilot remained on board. The big man ducked under the blades, climbed in, and soon they were away. Gillian refocused on her phone. There was no signal, no internet to distract her, but she did have the recording.

She wanted to talk to the doctor, needed him to explain what was on the tape. Gillian had not heard it during her initial reporting five years earlier. There was no reason to listen for such a thing. But when the anniversary of the tragic shooting neared, she dug out the recorder and notes with the plan of revisiting them while also researching whatever became of the poor doctor who lost his wife.

Public records revealed Mitch moved to Seattle after leaving the hospital in Los Angeles. During his time in Seattle, Mitch authored several well-received papers about the mechanics of fear. Periodicals and websites profiled him after the studies and, at some point, he made even bigger news in the business world related to his involvement in a groundbreaking health-industry startup. Gillian found nothing to suggest the doctor ever remarried.

Despite the tragic events, Gillian thought the man would be more open to talking to her because time had passed. Gillian was wrong. And angry. The doctor's behavior was unacceptable. Fine, tell her to fuck off, that was potentially deserved, but to get physical was not okay. Unless the doctor wanted her gone because he knew what was on the tape.

Was there the slightest chance the man knew what Gillian had captured on her recorder that night? Was he intent on avoiding an interview that would force him to lose another job for sounding crazy? If he knew and understood what she had, he might not want others to know. His statements claiming his wife was still alive got him fired.

But Gillian recorded everything that night and had since transferred the file to her cellphone. She now used her phone, but back then had a separate recorder. Five years later, when she listened to the tape uninterrupted from start to finish, she heard it. Did the Doctor know what she recorded? Why else play bully in an elevator?

Gillian adjusted the volume and hit play on the audio file. By now, it was familiar. Sirens whirred in the background while Mitch pleaded with an officer who dragged the doctor away from the tragic scene.

"I swear I saw her, officer; she was right there!" Mitch said on the recording.

"Sir, you are in shock. We need to get you downtown for a statement and..." the officer started before Mitch interrupted him.

"I can't leave her. Wendy, Wendy!"

"Sir, calm down."

"Wendy, Wendy!"

And then the other voice. As if from somewhere else. As if from something else. Gillian kept the section time stamped. She played it and heard a voice answer his cries.

The voice said, *"I'm here."*

CHAPTER 6

G illian played the recording once again. There it was the impossible voice. Gillian had reason to remember that night, even without the tragedy. Her fiancé stood her up for dinner. That boorish move led her to discover he had long cheated. Foolish. A reporter and she never had a clue. And worse, the mistress was Gillian's (former) best friend. The cheaters had since married and were on their second child.

Once Gillian realized he would not show, she ordered for herself. Having braved a rare rainy night, she was not eager to return home. At a nearby table, a couple celebrated an anniversary. In them, she saw what she wanted from a relationship. Commitment. Not just physically, but emotionally, someone Gillian could lean on for anything. Her job led her down plenty of dark roads. A strong support system at home could help lead her back. But she had chosen poorly.

Gillian met the gaze of the woman who was so pretty, so full of life. Just a glance, but Gillian felt the woman's joy. When the wait staff brought birthday shots to the table, Gillian sang along. The couple left soon after, just as Gillian's food finally arrived. She was about to eat when the shot rang out. Diners hit the ground. The blast was loud enough to rise above the storm. Like a first responder, Gillian's reporter instincts kicked in and she raced out the door. People were calling 911, so she did not. It was not only the gunshot that cut through the night, but an anguished cry of despair. No one needed to see the scene to understand a life was lost.

Cops arrived quickly. It was horrible to see that poor woman on the ground, the birthday girl. Not that one could tell by the face. The husband was inconsolable. Gillian always kept a digital recorder on hand, so she captured audio from the scene. It would act as a reference tool to capture details she might otherwise miss. More than anything, she hoped to get a description of the suspect. She wanted that information released immediately before the gunman hurt anyone else.

There was one thing she did not expect. The man who she would later learn to be Doctor Mitch Trager insisted his wife was still there, standing beside him. Absurd. The ramblings of a distraught man.

Gillian wrote up the night's account and mentioned his words in the piece. She attributed his claims to an inability to accept the loss. Gillian believed that detail humanized the poor man. The story went to print after confirming their identities. Doctor Mitch Trager and his wife Wendy Trager, a philanthropist with her own PhD.

Unknown to Gillian, her reporting caused ripples in the man's workplace which led to his firing. Her own paper reported on the firing and mentioned the killer had yet to be found. The follow up story, while adding tragedy on top of tragedy, upset her. The paper's editor should have assigned the piece to her especially because the article referenced her original story.

A young reporter, Justin Mills, wrote it up. She found it unacceptable that he never reached out to her. Forget that she was a reporter at their very own paper, she was a witness. His decision not to interview her was beyond sloppy. After the article went to print, Gillian accosted Justin in the employee restroom. Her presence among the urinals and dirty sinks got his attention. She berated him about poor etiquette before ripping into him for piss-poor sourcing skills. It was during her (justified) tirade that something occurred to her. It was the editor's fault that no one looped her in.

Gillian left the restroom wondering whether she was on the outs with her boss. That worry came into play when deciding to write about the five-year anniversary. Rather than ask for the assignment, Gillian waited to see who the editor assigned it to. Except the assignment never came down the pike. Not willing to let it go, Gillian decided to freelance it. Her contract required the paper would get first look, but if they refused, she could easily sell it elsewhere because of her unique perspective as a witness.

The paper she worked for was old school. There was no remote work unless out on assignment. But she could not get caught researching something on the job that a competitor might publish. That meant all research had to take place on her own time and dime. Gillian researched the project from home (usually with a bottle of wine). The first thing she did was dig out her notes and recording.

She listened to the tape in its entirety that night and almost missed something. But an oddity registered in her subconscious. Uncertain what had caught her attention, Gillian ran the recording back and time stamped the spot where she heard it. Then she listened to it again, and again, and again. It was there. A voice that should not have existed.

Gillian wanted to share it with someone, anyone, to verify that she had not gone batty or drank too much alcohol. But there was no one she trusted to not label her crazy like some had done to the doctor. If anyone heard the voice, they would insist a female was on the scene. A paramedic, a cop, a bystander. Except Gillian knew there were none.

Police let her remain on scene, less because of her credentials, and more because they needed to take her statement. There were limited people allowed through the tape and they were all male. She knew for certain because she forced two unprofessional cops to stop a conversation about the deceased's tits. Sickening that in such an environment they found a way to sexualize the victim. That situation proved there were no women present. She could have used a female friend, a touch of sisterhood, but found none.

And had no sisterhood available after hearing the recording either. She wished she had someone around to listen to it with an open mind. There was one person that would be the best to play it for. Mitch. That was who she needed to talk to which meant a trip to Seattle. The actual anniversary was fast approaching, so she purchased a plane ticket for that weekend. There would be no expense account for the secretive trip to Seattle, but Gillian had faith it would pay off.

Except she hit a roadblock when Mitch turned out to be a tool. Her research had warmed her to the man, but their meet was anything but cute. She kicked herself for not playing it for him immediately. If he listened prior to his meltdown, maybe she would be in his office discussing the impossible. Instead, she sat in her car on an island waiting for a ferry to take her home with no more answers than she started with. She lifted her phone, needing to hear it once again. Gillian hit play.

"*I'm here...*"

Wham!

Gillian screamed when a face slammed against the glass. It happened so fast it was all a blur. A surprise attack on what she assumed was a safe island. She wondered momentarily if the individual intended to finish the job he started in the elevator. It was Mitch at her window.

"Doctor Trager?" Gillian asked.

"Do you still want that story?"

She nodded and exited the vehicle. Mitch apologized about his earlier actions while leading her into the building. She took the apology with a grain of salt. Bruised egos were one thing, a bruised wrist was another. Gillian made her displeasure known, which sent him into round two of his apology tour. His remorse won her over.

She had ambushed the man on a sensitive anniversary. Her replay of the tape while she waited for the ferry reminded her just how horrible that night was. Doctor Trager suffered an unimaginable loss. Then Gillian appeared from nowhere (only because the doctor would not answer her emails or return her calls) and forced him to relive the whole thing over. She played a part in his reaction. Doctor Trager moved briskly and led her to the front desk. The security guard stepped out from behind the desk and joined them.

"I believe you've met Steve," Mitch said.

Gillian nodded. Steve gestured with aplomb, leading the two down the hall to his office. On the way, the security guard mentioned how the corridor led to a receiving dock, and a lab which housed research animals. Gillian did not like that and considered whether that would become her story: a hidden island where scientists performed unethical tests on living creatures.

"What animals?" Gillian asked.

"Sssssss..." Steve began and lashed an arm out at her. "...nakes."

Gillian nodded, relieved to find it was only snakes, nothing cuter. It should not have made a difference, but Gillian had a biased animal hierarchy. They stopped at a door with a security camera above it. Steve punched a code into the trilogy lock, and they stepped inside.

A bank of high-resolution screens rose from a large desk. Three screens stood side by side like wings of the building. One screen showed a single camera feed while the other two showed twelve on each screen, broken down into little boxes. The split screens showed labs, while the main screen focused on the building's exterior.

"What is that?" Gillian asked.

"Calvin's shoulder cam," Steve said, pointing at his own. "We have about a dozen. Cool tool." He gestured to several hanging on a nearby wall, dangling by straps designed to slip over a shoulder. "Do not worry. No filming without consent."

"Why is he outside?" Gillian asked.

"Mounted cameras cover the entire building inside and out, but we can go mobile as needed. No internet but a solid intranet with Bluetooth. It works for us. Calvin is one of our guards. He's investigating something on the abandoned wing."

Steve manipulated the joystick to bring up a split screen. It offered the view of a camera mounted somewhere above the employee along with the man's shoulder cam. Both images focused on the dead wing.

"Investigating for what? Ghosts?" Gillian asked.

"No." Mitch chimed in, almost too quick. "Teens. They come over on their personal boats on the weekends and trash the place."

Calvin steadied himself. An image of a large, spray-painted penis filled the screen. Mitch shook his head.

"That's a new cock," Steve said before remembering the woman in the room. "Still say we should have weekend patrols."

"No ferries Steve. Not going to charter boats to bring your staff out here and back. It's just a bunch of stupid kids with their own boats and too much time on their hands. The main building is secure, and they have not even broken into the dead wing. They party outside and go on their way. Harmless."

"I am not done arguing this, but we have a guest." Steve turned back to Gillian. "This is the hub of our world. One can view any lab from here. Cameras help us monitor our inventory and we have an intercom system to remind people to haul their asses out by end of shift. Miss that ferry and one must spend the night. Need time to get everyone out, lock up, and make it to the ship ourselves."

"Which is why I am here. I know little about all this high-tech stuff, but I need to reach everyone. How do I do that?" Mitch asked.

Steve pointed to a standing microphone that appeared older than the rest of the tech. "Talk. You just press talk."

Mitch pressed the button. "Attention. I need all employees to gather in the auditorium. Drop everything, this is of utmost importance."

Mitch breathed deep. He turned to Steve and Gillian. "That includes both of you as well."

"This story you promised? It's not the one I came here for, is it?" Gillian asked.

"No," Mitch said.

Steve hit a button and the single screen split into a dozen. Confused employees filled every screen as they headed toward the auditorium. Steve eyed Mitch for an explanation but received none. Mitch left the room. Steve shrugged to Gillian, and they followed, locking the door behind them.

Colt and his conquest from the ferry went at it in his lab. The woman lay sprawled across a table lined with test tubes. Colt thrust into her from behind. Their lab coats hid most of the action. Whatever preliminaries got them to the main event, they only disrobed as far as dropped pants. The young workers thrust in synch with great enthusiasm, matching one another moan for moan.

"Attention. I need all employees gathered in the auditorium. Drop everything, this is of utmost importance." Mitch's voice boomed over the speaker.

The intrusive voice startled the couple, who ceased long enough to listen. When Mitch finished, Colt tried to. The woman shoved him off and pulled up her pants.

"Are you serious?" Colt asked, stepping back, his pants still down, anatomy standing at attention.

"Dr. Trager has never called us all together before. Something's up," she said.

"Clearly," Colt said, gesturing down.

"Sorry. Auditorium. I will go first. Do not wish to be seen with you. Someone might tell my husband. Besides, I got mine already," she said, smirking and buttoning up.

"But we were in the moment. It feels incomplete leaving it like this," Colt said.

"Please. Do you even know my name?"

"Jill," Colt said with confidence.

"There are zero letters from that name in my own. See you in the auditorium," she said and left.

The moment she exited, Raj stepped in, wearing his own lab coat. In his twenties, Raj sported a well-groomed beard and bushy hair that swooped high above his head in thick waves. He appeared excited, falling into a slight accent the faster he talked.

"No way! You and Maddy! How did that happen?"

"Maddy! Thank you," Colt said.

Then Raj noticed the state of Colt's undress. "Not cool dude."

Colt pulled himself together while Raj walked over and repositioned the test tubes, OCD kicking in. Colt paid no mind.

"What is going on with that announcement?" Raj asked.

"Let's find out, shall we?"

"Steve busted me for the roof party the other day. I just showed up to make an appearance, How is that on me? Do you think that is what this is all about?" Raj asked.

"If so, be cool and be our fall guy. Respect."

The two men found the auditorium already packed when they arrived. Derrick waved the two guys over and they sat next to him. The trio speculated on what was going on, matching the confused energy of the entire hall. Even the janitors, groundskeepers, and cafeteria staff were in attendance. Yoshi and Elle sat near the front, as confused as the rest of the world.

Jimmy stood on the stage, waiting for his boss. Mitch entered through a side stage door, Gillian in tow. Jimmy looked confused.

"This is Gillian, a reporter. I'll explain later," Mitch said. "The jar is at the podium?"

Jimmy nodded. "And here's the wireless mic. Works with Bluetooth. If your voice cuts out, just move to another position. Best to stand still once you have a good signal."

Mitch clipped the microphone to his lapel, stepped up to the podium, and looked out at the crowd. He pulled a jar out from under the podium and placed it on top so the audience could see. The contents were as dark as tar but peppered with floating silver sparkles. A toxic looking stew. Mitch placed the jar atop the podium.

"Amazing work. The building bears my name, but this product is the culmination of the hard work performed by everyone here. And I mean everyone. Especially those who keep this place running so the scientists can do their work."

Like many workplace cliques, support staff sat with one another while scientists did as the same. Each faction branched into smaller ecosystems of popularity and status. Mitch gestured the support staff to stand. The assembled scientists applauded the employees. The workers performed variations of bows and waves, but sat quickly, wanting to hear what was up.

"Troubled. The press once dubbed our staff troubled. They wrote things I know not to be true. We have press on the premises now. Meet Gillian McCann. I wonder what she might print about all of you?"

All eyes turned to red-faced Gillian. "No comment," Gillian said to some laughter from the crowd.

Mitch continued. "Troubled was inaccurate. Brilliant is the correct word and why I hired you all. The work you have all performed with our core product is remarkable. Given more time, we could have changed the world."

"Given more time?" Derrick asked, surprised.

Amy, a blonde woman in her thirties, sitting next to Derrick, rose from her seat. "Yeah, what are you talking about, Doctor Trager?"

Murmurs filled the hall. Mitch gestured for everyone to calm down. People looked around the room as if there were answers somewhere other than on stage. When they found none, the crowd settled and allowed their boss to continue.

Mitch placed his hand atop the jar on the podium. "We deal in fear. That is what we do. And yet I find myself afraid to share some bad news. The company that finances our amazing work has pulled the plug. The decision is final, and all work is to stop now."

"They just cleared us for human trials," Raj said, standing up, agitated.

"That is why this hurts more. Our benefactors have arranged for today's ferry to return from the mainland early. We have little time to clear our offices of belongings. The New York board will handle final payouts and severance."

Murmurs grew in intensity. Mitch eyed Steve in the distance. The man looked as confused as everyone else. Mitch kept his focus on the security lead while speaking about logistics.

"In order to make certain our fear element does not make it onto the mainland, our security team will search everyone upon exit. I am certain you understand how dangerous it could be to allow our product out into the world. While the ferry will arrive soon, they will not depart until everyone has boarded. Me included. We have empty boxes in the loading dock for your personal items and we will have someone dispense those to you. It was a pleasure working with you all. Truly. I wish it could have gone another way. Thank you all."

A stunned silence overtook the room. Dazed workers dispersed, exiting the room in waves through the rear of the auditorium. Jimmy and Gillian moved to center stage. Gillian inspected the jar.

"What is that?" Gillian asked.

Jimmy answered. "Our reason for being here. It is a chemical that induces fear. A highly potent drug. It is one of the greatest scientific achievements in modern history." He rubbed his hands over his face. "I cannot believe this is happening."

"Something that induces fear? Why?" Gillian asked.

Jimmy continued rubbing his face before throwing his hands up, frustrated. "Why? It should be obvious. What do all humans suffer from? Imagine if we could control fear, change it. Bah! What does it matter now? Years of my life, my life, my life. Years. Bah!"

Mitch had his back toward the auditorium. Gillian looked past Mitch and tilted her head in curiosity. Mitch turned to follow her gaze. Several scientists remained in the otherwise empty auditorium. Steve as well.

"Just like that? They pull the plug and we're expected to bend over and take it?" Elle yelled.

"Yeah, I'm not bending over and taking it either," Yoshi said, standing alongside Elle. She nudged into him as a silent thank you. Yoshi's face turned red.

"What are you suggesting?" Mitch asked.

"Data, doc, we need data," Colt said.

"What data?" Jimmy asked, taking the stage alongside Mitch. Gillian waited in the wings.

Mitch waved Jimmy off, understanding. "Information. About our situation. Our visitor will not make it back to New York for hours or longer, depending on the itinerary. No matter what calls he makes, power must be shut down on site. Electric company would not be out until Monday at the earliest."

"So, we have electricity to keep the lights on," Quinn said.

"And the FDA has cleared us for human trials," Derrick said.

Mitch nodded. Jimmy's eyes opened wide when he realized what the conversation was about. He lit up and stepped forward, absorbing the energy of the room. A hopeful energy. Gillian fought to understand.

Amy asked a question. "Are we losing the interns? I can't finish my experiment alone. I need help."

"Yes. Support staff are all contracted out and not part of research team payroll. To ask them to stay would be unethical. I cannot even guarantee paying any of you beyond today. But any of you deciding to stay differs from them doing the same. You are not breaking a work contract and endangering future employment."

"This is not about money for me," Quinn said. "I don't know about all y'all, but I want a chance to finish what I started."

"Can we do this in three days? Complete our work? I can't, but damned if I'm going to give up this easy," Derrick said. "You need help Amy? I am not above interning."

She nodded and clapped his shoulder in thanks. The mood in the room changed from disappointment to excitement. The enthusiastic crowd vowed to take on the challenge, though one individual remained skeptical. Steve stepped forward.

"Are you talking about people staying here this weekend? I don't like that. Not at all. What if we get dick painters back? What if electricity fails, or plumbing?"

"Let's talk later," Mitch said.

"Sure, why not? We've got about what, three hours?" Steve mimed checking a watch he did not wear and left the auditorium.

"I am game to stay, but no way I can finish by Monday. I am available if someone needs me," Raj said.

"Dibs on the dude with perfect hair," Colt said.

Raj and Colt bumped fists. Then Raj ran his fingers through his locks, smiling at the compliment. The pair turned back to the group.

"We're staying then? And testing on ourselves?" Elle asked.

Gillian looked on in disbelief. "Did you say test on yourselves?"

"Bingo, hot reporter lady. We will test on ourselves like the good Lord intended," Colt said.

"You can't be serious," Gillian said, stunned.

"Please, do you think the scientists who invented Viagra waited for human trials? No way. It was a party in their pants every night," Colt said.

"This is crazy," Gillian said.

A voice sounded from an open doorway. "I will be in my lab," Mercedette said, and then was gone.

"Results. Anything tangible that we can take to the board could resurrect this entire project. Show me what you can do so I can show them. They are misguided. Results are currency. This is our chance to change their minds, make them understand why they should continue investing. I will continue my own work as well. Godspeed to us all. Now, what are you all waiting for? The clock is ticking," Mitch said.

The scientists fled the auditorium. Jimmy and Gillian stood with Mitch. The assistant looked at his boss like a lost puppy.

"Will my services be required?" Jimmy asked.

Mitch placed a hand on the young man's shoulder. "You know I could not do this without you, Jimmy. We need to play it like we are actively shutting down. Start inventory protocols alongside evacuation."

"You knew they would stay?" Gillian asked.

"Hoped they would. There's a big difference."

"And what about me? Do you hope I will?" Gillian asked.

"Yes. What happens this weekend is bigger than anything you came here for. If you cover our hail Mary moment, I promise to sit for an interview about whatever brought you here. We have an office you can use as a home base. We videotaped interviews with our candidates. I will supply our scientists' files for you to better understand them. It will give you something to do while we work. We are here for you, and open to you, but we will be busy."

"Does the office have a couch?"

"Indeed, it does," Mitch smiled. "Jimmy, set her up in the sixth-floor conference rooms while I meet with Steve. We have a monumental task ahead. This early arrival ferry is the last one for the weekend. We need everyone on it. There is much to do to ensure a smooth evacuation."

Mitch gestured to the exit. Jimmy led Gillian away. Mitch lagged, taking a moment to look out into the empty auditorium one last time before turning off the lights and joining the others.

CHAPTER 7

Erik Smith stroked his mustache. The news in the auditorium shook him. It was not fair, and because it was not, he decided to get what was his. But that required stealth and a plan. It would all start with duct tape. Time would not be on his side. The whole building was alive with movement. He needed to blend in with the masses, not be the first or the last to leave. Despite being in his forties, he moved with the speed of someone younger, though without the grace of such a generation. He bumped into chairs, tables, anything within reach of his girth. Each bump aggravated him further.

They can't do this to me, he thought. *Too cowardly to fire me face to face, so they pretend to let everyone go. Bet they all take a long weekend and then come back Monday, all laughing behind my back when I am the only one not to return.*

Erik was not well to hear his ex-wife tell it. And his doctors. And his employer. But Erik knew something they did not. Bad things were under the bed, horrible things. After securing a job at Trager Chemicals, he worked toward alleviating the terror that such knowledge brought. Erik's experiments were geared toward developing a pill designed to allow victims to ignore the dastardly things long enough to fall asleep. As bad as the creatures were, they never attacked once a person slept. Sleep was a shield. His wife did not understand. That was okay. She was an easy sleeper, dropped off the moment the lights went out. His insomnia made him more vulnerable to attack than her.

The man's hair reached for the sky, kept in place by natural oils and dirt. Erik was not a hair washer, nor much of a bather. Too much effort for too little payoff. Einstein wore the same thing every day to save brain capacity. Erik figured grooming was in the same vein.

His unkempt hair was a conversation starter with strangers due to a white stripe running down one side of his otherwise dark hair. Erik had several stories chambered to explain it away, but the real answer was that it appeared after an encounter with the thing under the bed. Erik had avoided the nasty thing for so long as a child but one night it got the better of him, grabbed his leg, and pulled him under the bed where a strange doorway led him and his captor deep into a forest. A feast awaited them but an empty spit over a fire clued Erik in on who the main course would be.

There was not one beast but many in the forest, all drooling with hunger. They tied him to a spit intent on barbecuing him. But his screams roused his parents. When his parents found him, they claimed Erik suffered a sleepwalking episode. But Erik knew better, he had been abducted and almost roasted. Even his parents could not explain the sudden shock of white in his hair (likely born from the fear of the fire). The white stripe never faded.

A horn sounded from the bay. The ferry was close. He looked out the window. Down below, on the lawn leading to the parking lot, employees had already lined up and were moving through a gauntlet of security guards. The guards patted down each person and searched their belongings. Let them search. Erik had a plan.

He stripped off his lab coat (size XXXL) and his shirt. Tearing off a long strip of tape, he placed it sticky side up on a counter. He corked several test tubes filled with black liquid and laid them out on the lengthy strip. The tubes filled the middle of the tape but left space for adhesive flaps on either side. Erik lifted his gut with one hand and the strip with the other.

With some difficulty he slapped the strap of tubes against his lower belly. The vials felt cold against his skin but would warm soon enough. Sweat already beaded on his forehead as he worried about being found out. After pressing the tape tight, he lowered his massive stomach which covered the test tubes.

Contraband in place, he redressed. Guards would only pat so much, and a strip of tape buried under his stomach would be hard to discover. Once back on the mainland, he would secure his own lab somewhere and finish his work.

"No more monsters under the bed for anyone!" Erik yelled across the wide-open lab.

"No more what?" A voice called back from the doorway.

Careless, Erik thought. He let his guard down already, as if forgetting there would be a sea of people converging and leaving. His next-door work neighbor Frank stood in the doorway. Two of the oldest in the Trager joint, they hit it off over music nostalgia during orientation and secured adjoining labs. Frank raised two empty cardboard boxes.

"You left before the handout. One each is the limit. Said we shouldn't have more personal effects than that. Have they seen Yoshi's lab?" Frank asked.

"Who is Yoshi?" Erik asked, sweating.

"Wow. All this time and you still have not met people? He collects things. Lots. Anyway. Do you want the box?"

Erik did. It would help hide his contraband. Worried the tubes might clink, he reached out gingerly for the cardboard, smiling as if he had just eaten a bad burrito. Frank shook his head, noticing for the first time how odd his work friend was. Erik thanked the man and Frank left to pack.

Once alone, Erik fought to calm himself. He quickly packed some things. More than willing to leave it all behind, he boxed items anyway as cover. All he really wanted was what he had hidden at his waist.

It wasn't a shadow, the thing under the bed. That was what his father claimed. Erik knew what he saw. Yes, he had read **Where the Wild Things Are** in bed by flashlight before the incident, but that was coincidence. After the forest incident, his parents routinely checked under his bed for him until well into adulthood. Until he left for college.

Thankfully dorm beds were mass produced on the cheap. The headboard and baseboard served as legs creating a vast space underneath larger than normal beds. The knee high gap from floor to bed allowed him to see underneath from the room's doorway whenever he returned. The design was one he carried into adulthood after graduation. He kept his sheets tucked tight like a hotel so that nothing ever dangled over the edge.

Erik broke up with one girlfriend in college simply because of her bedroom. The woman lived off-campus and owned a four-poster bed complete with a bed skirt! *No thank you, ma'am*, Erik thought and got out quick despite the woman's beauty and brilliance. That was a turning point for him. Erik understood after giving up such a wonderful relationship that something was wrong with him.

But getting hired at Trager gave him an opportunity to make the world a better place. While Erik believed he was possibly abnormal, he was likely not unique, if only because the monsters had to go somewhere on the nights they were not under his bed. If they were not under his bed any longer, it meant they were under the bed of some other poor kid. Erik longed to make a pill to help people fall asleep at night without fear of the foul things.

Sleeping pills already existed, but fear could override such medicines. Adrenaline warded off the drugs' effects. Erik hoped to make a pill that would first reduce fear, then kick in with a sleep aid. Except they shut Trager Chemicals down. How convenient. Right before he made one of the greatest products known to man. Erik vowed to carry on, even if it meant smuggling out samples. Erik leaped when a hand fell on his shoulder.

"Ready?" Frank asked, holding a full box.

"Huh? Yeah."

Erik grabbed his box, and they exited the lab. The two men chit-chatted as they waited for the elevator. Frank went on about the exodus, but Erik was in another world. Two other men stood holding boxes of their own and griped over the wait time for the elevators. The two scientists who Erik did not recognize jointly agreed to take the stairs.

When the departing men turned to walk away, one man's box collided with Erik's. Though his stomach's girth muted the sound, Erik felt a pop followed by immediate pain where the broken glass sliced his stomach. He yelped which caused the other coworkers to give him a wide berth while they headed toward the distant stairs. On their way, they mumbled something about Erik being a freak.

Frank stood up for his friend and shouted smack aimed at the departing duo. The trio went back and forth about manners until the men were too far down the hall. Frank apologized to Erik for the boorish behavior. Frank even made a joke about firing the guys, but Erik heard none of it and never even noticed the earlier slight. He was wounded and needed to check the damage. There was a whole mess going on in Midtown Eriksville, but there was no discreet way to examine himself until seated in his car. The elevator arrived already full. Erik ignored it and stepped forward only to have passengers yell him off.

Even Frank sided with them and pulled Erik back. Moving brought with it new problems. Erik felt a fresh jab in his folds, one that threatened to puncture his gut if it had not already. His natural padding acted as a barrier of sorts, but all flesh cut under the right circumstances. At the least, the glass had scraped skin.

Then he saw it. Dots of red and black on his shirt. He was cut and liquid from at least one tube had spilled. The jig was up if anyone noticed the stains. More employees flooded the hall to wait for the elevator. Then he glimpsed something out of the corner of one eye.

The thing under the bed!

In his peripheral he glimpsed what at first appeared to be another scientist in a lab coat, but the face betrayed its true nature. It was a thing from under the bed! Ebony fur lined the monster's face like a lion's mane. The skin at its center approximated a human face but the features were harsh and sharp. It had a pug nose with mouth too wide for its face. Tiny dark horns jutted out through the fur atop its head. The creature's skin had a shiny dark sheen like bell peppers cooked on a grill.

Erik held his breath. It could not be. Surely a trick of the light but then the thing stepped into plain view. It was real! The thing under the bed stood there amidst a corridor full of employees. Posed as one of their own, the creature wore a lab coat and held a box. But the disguise was flimsy. Its face and hands were in plain view.

Their overall appearance was the whole poo inducing package. The beast's countenance and sharp teeth suggested they were always ready for a meal. But what unnerved Erik the most was the weird configuration of their hands. It was not that they had only three fingers and an elongated thumb on each hand, nor was it how sharp talons capped off every twisted digit. The oddity that disturbed him so was that in their natural state, one palm faced up while one palm faced down. The strange anatomy only emphasized they were not from this world.

Erik turned to the crowd to see if anyone else noticed the beast and a gasp died in his throat. They were all monsters! His coworkers were creatures in disguise the entire time. Erik had been so worried about the smuggling that he failed to notice the poor disguises.

The monsters roamed freely, coming and going, as if they were on the clock. Trembling, Erik eyed them all, so many, more than he had ever seen before. The ones closest to him, those waiting for the elevator, faced him and hissed.

Erik launched his box at the assembled horde and ran down the hall. They must have learned it was Erik's last day and made their move. He looked for Frank, hoping to get some help, but failed to spot him in the sea of creatures. A collective growl gave wings to Erik's feet. Never the fastest amongst his friends, he found a gear previously unknown to him while sprinting down the corridor.

He burst through the stairwell doors and leaned over the railing. The staircase rose in a square pattern, with a floor to ceiling view if one leaned over the railing. Erik feared the pair who bumped him earlier remained in the stairwell, but a glance down showed the stairwell was empty. Across the landing was the door to the next wing. It was probably safer there than in the main wing.

Before he could approach the other door, a clack of claws on metal sounded overhead. Erik looked up and saw a pair of monster hands grip the rail. One hand curled over the railing while the back of its other one rested atop it. Such a strange thing, their hands!

It was too dangerous to cross the landing without a weapon, so he rushed down the stairs. He reentered the facility one floor down.

Monsters filled the corridor there as well. They all hissed at him. Erik dashed into the nearest lab in search of a needle only to find dozens of injectors which had tiny needles designed for wimps of the world. Everyone had gone soft, Erik thought. He needed the real thing.

And there it was. On the wall in a glass case hung a syringe and lobotomy spike, staged like a museum display. He elbowed the glass and cried out when a shard buried itself into his flesh. It was not like the movies. Erik pulled the large piece free from his elbow causing blood to spurt, but adrenaline muted the pain. He grabbed the obscenely long needle and headed back to the stairs.

"Y ou have an overnight bag in your vehicle?" Jimmy asked, surprised, while escorting Gillian back to her car.

"Yes. Many reporters have them," she said and opened her trunk, retrieving a backpack.

"I'm impressed. I try to be prepared, but then, who was expecting all this?" Jimmy took the bag for her, and they started across the massive green lawn.

"The closure was a surprise?"

"Absolutely. It makes no sense. We just got cleared for human trials. We were showing incredible progress, solid results. It is highly unusual for funding to be pulled at such a delicate time."

Gillian spotted Mitch in the distance saying goodbyes to those lined up on the front lawn. "How long have you worked for Mitch?"

"I worked for him since Los Angeles. Mostly virtual assistant until after the tragedy when he needed someone to look after his home affairs. A broken man back then. I had issues of my own as well…"

Jimmy stopped himself. "Sorry. Not about me. I helped him leave his old life behind and build this one from the ground up. He's brilliant. If he asks me to follow where he goes next, I will."

"Did he ever mention anything to you about that night in Los Angeles?"

"I don't follow."

"A voice? Did he mention a voice?"

Jimmy tilted his head. "What are you probing for? Either be more direct, or I cannot answer. We all hear whispers of our past, especially when violence has played a hand in our lives."

Gillian knew the two men were close. If Mitch confided in anyone about that night, it likely would be his assistant. Gillian wondered whether to come right out and ask the young man about it. Despite the potential story of a scientific breakthrough, Gillian could not purge the original reason for her visit from her mind. Before she could push Jimmy harder for an answer, cries rang out.

"Hey! Stop!" a guard called from the front doorway of the company.

A heavyset man burst through the door, shoving the guard aside. He ran across the lawn and reacted to the assembled group. The runner appeared terrified or intoxicated. Or both.

Jimmy called out and approached the employee. "Erik, what is wrong?"

Security guards working the line rushed over but Jimmy got there first and noticed the needle much too late. Jimmy raised Gillian's overnight bag to ward off the oncoming attacker. Erik raised the needle and stabbed Jimmy. The needle dug into the bag approximately where Jimmy's heart would have been. Jimmy met Erik's gaze, stunned by the attack. Erik was not done. He yanked the bag which spun Jimmy around. Erik freed the needle and placed the point against the man's throat. Erik raged to the monsters on the grounds.

"You won't get me. I'm an adult now. I always check under my bed!" Erik yelled.

Mitch moved in with arms raised. "Erik, stop this craziness. Don't hurt him. Take me instead."

The crazed employee shook his head and, in a flash of recognition, saw Mitch for who he was. Then Erik spotted something else. Or someone. Over Mitch's shoulder. Dead Wendy stood there scowling, her face mostly gone.

"The woman. I have seen her with you before. Who is she? Why is she always near you? Does she know the monsters?"

Sweat from all the running dripped into Erik's face. He closed his eyes and shook his head to clear his vision. When he looked back, Dead Wendy was gone. Gillian stood in her place. Erik struggled to recognize her. In a moment of lucid confusion, he shoved Jimmy away.

The guards moved in along with Mitch. Mitch shoved Jimmy further back. Gillian placed a hand on Jimmy's shoulder.

"Are you okay?" she asked.

"Y-y-yes. I g-g-g-got t-t-t-too close."

A gauntlet of security guards moved in on the dangerous man with the needle.

Why did he refuse to help me? Erik wondered. Doctor Trager was right there and did nothing. Maybe, like Erik's parents, his boss refused to believe in the things under the bed. Wives one and two left Erik for that exact reason. Wife three hid her lover under their bed once when Erik arrived home earlier than expected. Erik noticing motion beneath the bed, lashed out with a pen, destroying the man's (monster's) eye.

The cheating Erik could have dealt with, but the indignity of hiding a lover under a bed was a bridge too far. He left Sandy that night, never to return. He was better alone; it was harder for the monsters to find him.

Except now they had. He searched for an exit and found no good options. Three converged toward him while dozens of others stood around baring teeth and drooling while holding those stupid boxes. They were everywhere. He ran, threading the needle of the trio behind him. Talons brushed his coat. Had their weird opposing hands saved him? All teeth and no gripping action?

Crying out in victory, he raced toward the distant cliffs. From there, he would scale down to the shore. If he could catch his breath, and if he had it in him. Climbing stairs was one thing, descending a cliff was another, but what choice did he have? After descending the cliff face, he could enter the ocean. If they followed, the beasts' fur would drag them under. He was almost free.

Almost. A glance over one shoulder showed how resourceful the Godless monsters were. One creature extended an arm and black tendrils shot forth from its hand. Fire filled his veins. His muscles seized, and he fell face first into the grass which promptly vanished.

Familiar scents reached his nose. A chewed wad of gum stuck to a bed post, ready for a re-chew, dirty sneakers, soiled tube socks filled with sexual energy. Without looking up he knew where he was. His childhood bedroom. Stretched out on the floor like Superman, Erik's body seized as the fire spread, causing total immobility. When did they develop stinging tendrils?

Once the fires in his veins subsided, he lifted his head which provided a clear view directly under the bed. Ironically, it was all clear. Fur rustled somewhere at his rear, and claws scraped the floorboards as something approached. The underside of the bed suddenly appeared as the safest place in the room. Erik crawled toward it, finding strength in his limbs once again. The Star Wars bedsheets, the ones with the Millennium Falcon, hung loosely over the side of the bed. Once underneath, he would pull the bedding down and hide there. He moved swiftly, wondering whether he would fit in his current size. Erik slid one arm under the bed. it vanished in shadows. With a violent hiss, a face suddenly broke through the shadows under the bed. The thing grabbed his hand.

The monster. It was there with breath like spoiled meat. Its teeth bleeding red from some previous meal. Its eyes reflected an image of the two monsters that gripped his legs from behind. Those beasts pulled him away from the bed and rolled him over.

Erik screamed, not sure when he dropped the needle. He was without a weapon. he covered his face with his hands, but they were not interested in his head. They tore into his stomach, digging deep. He looked down at his torso and felt a tremendous rip. The hands playing with his insides yanked up and out. The motion tore his gut open, exposing muscle and freeing ribs that sprung open once relieved of their fleshy cocoon. Blood spurted almost to the ceiling.

The jagged talons tore at his insides, seeking to do as much damage as possible. His tormentor pulled strings of intestines and internal organs out. The hands made no sense before, but he realized they were designed to shred. Their positioning of claws was the perfect vessel for violating flesh. Erik screamed as the beasts hollowed him out. He grew dizzy and weak. Before his world fell dark, he had one last thought.

"I want my mommy..."

CHAPTER 8

After the Taser brought the man down, Erik attempted to crawl away. Mitch turned the man over, hoping to reason with him but Erik kept fighting. And now Mitch knew why. A combo of blood and chemical stains covered Erik's shirt. Mitch tore the shirt open and discovered duct-taped contraband. When Mitch yanked the strip away, Erik screamed then passed out. Mitch avoided contact with the spilled liquid. Only two tubes had broken.

The man suffered lacerations from the glass, creating a perfect gateway for the tube's contents to enter his bloodstream. That would cause immediate symptoms and explain Erik's mania. There was no simple way to identify his level of exposure. Their company developed the fear element in many forms, from oral to topical. Each version had vastly different potencies. The strongest versions were liquid. The fallen scientist also had a sliced elbow that looked like it needed stitches.

"Where are the medics? Where is Steve?" Mitch yelled as both appeared.

Though a doctor, Mitch did not have what the two medics did—gloves. Mitch stepped aside and allowed them to work on the patient. Steve slipped on gloves as well and bagged the strip of test tubes. One medic gave a thumbs up on Erik's vitals. Steve ordered the assembled crowd to get back in line, announcing the show was over.

"Stitches, then once you bring him around, make sure you have cuffs handy. Hold him in a private room on the ship," Mitch said to the medics.

"Are you arresting him?" Gillian asked.

Jimmy answered for Mitch. "No. But he will be a danger to himself and others until the effects wear off. He should be fine by Seattle."

Then what the man said struck her. Gillian remembered her tape, the reason for being there. "A woman. He mentioned a dead woman behind you."

"You stood behind me," Mitch said.

Gillian nodded. "Yes, I suppose I was. But I don't understand. What was all that?"

"That was our product at work in an uncontrolled environment," Mitch said.

"And your team is going to use whatever that was on themselves?"

"Yes. That is the actual story this weekend. Have no fear, I will update you on Erik's health if you choose to write about this unfortunate event. And no matter what, I will sit for an interview about the anniversary of my wife's death. I have already lost everything; a little more ink cannot hurt me anymore than I already am. I promise nothing but transparency this entire time. Our operation and personnel are open books for you, but I hope you will keep your eyes on the bigger picture. We could make history this weekend. Wait and see everything before you settle on an angle." He turned to search for his assistant who was already there. "Jimmy, please escort Ms. McCann to her quarters."

Mitch handed the overnight bag back to Jimmy then turned away to attend to the injured man. Gillian pressed her finger against the bag's new hole. Jimmy shrugged an apology then led Gillian inside. They rode the elevator to the sixth floor where the doors opened to darkness. Jimmy stepped out of the elevator and waved his arms until lights came to life, spreading down the hallway like a virus.

"Motion sensor activated. This floor appears a bit off. I'll look at it later, but not sure I can do anything. Our engineer is already on the ferry. Steve fixes things where needed but after they finish the personal belongings checks, he and his team will leave as well. This floor was originally our admin offices. It has gone unused for some time because they moved the HR offices off site. It is all yours now."

He escorted her to an office near the end of the hall beyond which stood double push doors. Crash bars lined the doors, offering entry to the other wing with a simple push except handle-shaped bars were welded midway up the doors surfaces. A chain ran through the welded bars and were secured with a padlock. Gillian eyed the ominous sight which stood out from the balance of the corridor lined with artwork and fake plants.

"Those doors lead to the dead wing. This is the only internal access point. The stairwell on this side of that building is damaged. Only the fifth-floor landing is intact. No one should enter but people do."

"Why?" Gillian asked.

Jimmy mimed drinking a beer. "We have a perfectly good roof overhead, but no, they like to party where they might fall through to ground level. Go figure."

Gillian nodded. "I saw the security guard discussing that with a scientist this morning."

"Yes. It is Steve's job to play bad cop. Now, let's show you where you will hole up this weekend.

Jimmy led her into the human resources suite. The offices were modern, antiseptic with fabric chairs and still smelled of newly laid carpet. A small waiting room greeted them with a couch and chairs. Past the waiting area, a tight corridor fed into a row of offices. They stopped at a sizeable conference room, where the chairs changed from fabric to leather. An oval conference table centered the space. An alcove on the far side of the office led to a unisex bathroom. A large screen TV hung on one wall, designed for presentations for those seated. A laptop sat open at the head of the table. Jimmy leaned over the device and typed.

"No internet here and no phone lines to the mainland. There is an intranet that you might find handy. It is a significant resource, but the data set leans toward scientific research. I set the laptop to guest credentials. You can set your own password. It has writing software already installed. Be mindful to save your work, there is no auto-save without the internet."

Gillian nodded, grateful for the important tech reminder. Jimmy spun the laptop, and she typed a password. Jimmy set her overnight bag in a nearby chair. Gillian looked around.

"Couch and bathroom. I've had worse."

"Allow me to give you the basic tour before cutting you loose." Jimmy escorted her back into the hall. "The dead wing remains undeveloped. They planned for it to be the processing plant for our product until permits fell through so they opened a manufacturing facility on the outskirts of Seattle instead. We ship the chemical over from there."

"Is that what was on the ferry I rode over on this morning? There were lots of trucks."

Jimmy nodded as they walked along the corridor. "Yes, that and many other necessities. Each scientist has been prepping for upcoming experiments, so they have had all sorts of equipment shipped over. Not to mention food and other supplies. Each wing has a stairwell on either side. The one furthest from your office leads to our west wing that houses only two scientists. Let us introduce you to them first."

Once they passed the elevator banks, the corridor transitioned from developed real estate to undeveloped. The floor was a mix of asylum patient rooms and larger common areas. Gillian poked her head in the first they happened upon.

The space was filthy. Torn sheets covered the bed and hand-drawn pictures lined the walls. A clown's face scrawled in crayon stood out from the other pictures. As Gillian studied it from a distance, the picture seemed to take form, becoming more than a scrawled image. The shadows surrounding it looked as if the face grew a body. A loud flapping noise from behind startled her.

Jimmy stood nearby holding open one half a set of swinging doors that opened into a gym with a small basketball court. Past the court was an open room with some cardio machines and weights. A jaundiced overhead light flickered at random intervals. A ball station made of PVC pipe stored exercise balls and basketballs.

"They renovated your end of the hall, completely modernizing it but this gym and the cafeteria down the hall are holdovers from days of yore. The contractors freshened them up but left them mostly in their original state. The cafeteria has free snack machines for your convenience."

Further down the hall they passed a closed metal door with a machine room sign. Jimmy moved opposite the hall and pushed open another set of double swing doors to show off an antiquated cafeteria stuck in the fifties. Anchoring the hall were doubles doors matching those near Gillian's office. They lacked the chains of the dead wing entrance.

Gillian crossed her arms. "You don't find this place totally creepy?"

"What? Oh, yes, once upon a time. Now none of us give it much thought. The real estate was dirt cheap and allowed us to pour money into high end equipment rather than the high rent of a more desirable location. And the setting it is appropriate considering what it is we do here."

"And what is that exactly?"

Before he could answer, the doors at the end of the hall burst open. Quinn stepped into the hall like a rogue tornado. She almost collided with the duo.

"Ooh, my bad," Quinn said. "Sorry. Hit the doors hard if you want the motion sensor lights to turn on quickly, my grandmother always used to say."

"Quinn, this is..." Jimmy started.

"The reporter, I know. I was in the auditorium. Late. I'm late for a very important date." Then the young woman was gone, tapping elevator buttons in the distance.

"Let's go meet Mercedette. You just met Quinn."

"Would not call that a meeting," Gillian said.

"It might be the most you get from some. Everyone has work to do. While Mitch promised full access, interviews will be on the scientists' timetables. Their work comes first." The pair navigated across the stairwell landing into the next wing, a twin to the one they just left. "Quinn's lab is straight ahead while Mercedette works two floors down. There is one stop along the way," Jimmy said.

They descended to the next floor. Once there, they walked about halfway down the corridor and stopped at a door painted black. Jimmy led them into a dim room lit by tiny LED strips. Three tight rows of pyramid style seating ran high to low culminating at a glass wall which overlooked a lab below.

An impressive one. Gillian took criminology classes in college, so she knew her way around a lab, but the space below appeared far more advanced than anything from her alma mater. A woman in a lab coat moved about below. Gillian recognized her from the auditorium. The woman had appeared in a doorway then vanished. Jimmy waved his arms, proud of the show.

"State-of-the art. This was once upon a time a teaching facility in the sanitarium, where new employees could watch doctors treat patients. We repurposed it for the same thing, but there is no need for the space until at least a second round of human trials, so Mercedette uses the space in the meantime. Mercedette and Quinn both leaped at the chance to have privacy. Mercedette is brilliant if not troubled."

"Troubled?" Gillian asked.

"Many employees here are," Jimmy said, matter of fact.

"Including you?"

In lieu of an answer, Jimmy opened a black door that had remained hidden alongside the viewing window. "Let's go down and visit, shall we?"

The doorway led to a black carpeted spiral staircase. They descended into the lab where massive high-definition screens lined the entire perimeter of the room near the ceiling. The lab's center contained an ergonomic 'floating' chair. It rested atop a metal pole which provided the illusion of floating. Various equipment and wheeled medical trays circled the chair. A smaller high-definition screen sat on one cart.

Mercedette worked nearby, fiddling with something in a waist high plexiglass box. Two holes with built in arm coverings allowed her to work inside the box like building a ship in the bottle. Her gloved hands handled a device the size of a spray paint can. Jimmy and Gillian moved closer. Bent over as she was, Mercedette should not have noticed their approach but she somehow did.

"She's not corporate," Mercedette said without looking up.

"You must have arrived late to the meeting. Our guest is..."

"Gillian, I'm a reporter. Never seen a cross on a scientist."

"Must be your lucky day then. Maybe you will spot bigfoot later. We are deep in a forest after all."

"Please forgive the stereotypes, but I never considered scientists as overly religious."

"All scientists are religious. We have faith in constants."

"Like mathematically?" Gillian asked.

Mercedette nodded. "Or those used in experiments."

"Believing in constants is hardly the same as believing in God," Gillian said.

"No? In the absence of constants, order would collapse and give way to chaos. Bad actors could use such chaos to tailor any scientific studies to deliver predetermined outcomes. This already happens. Large corporations and politicians pay to get the results they desire and then gaslight the populace. Universal constants allow for peer reviews that can expose such liars. Other scientists can duplicate the studies minus the influence of financial donors. During the peer review process, the truth shall come out. We can offer truth versus preordained results."

"Preordained? Are we having a fate versus free will argument?" Gillian asked.

Mercedette stopped working long enough to glance back at Gillian. "Are we arguing? If so, for the sake of the argument, what would you make of an individual placed in a commune? Too young to be on their own, they are at the mercy of their surroundings. And what if they are taught coercive tactics designed to believe certain falsehoods? What if those lies are harmful to the very people who believe in them? If one believes they deserve the punishment and abuse they suffer daily, then do they have free will any longer? Would they not feel they were at the mercy of a horrible fate?"

"That is a highly specific example, but yes, I could see such a person believing in fate. I have covered stories of people who deserved much better than what life visited upon them. But those of you who remain here are testing an unknown product on yourselves. I've seen the drug commercials with a laundry list of side effects up to and including death. Knowing that in advance, if any tests result in tragedy, would that be free will or fate?"

"Maybe both. I have developed a device designed to protect a person's free will in the face of one wishing to take exactly that away."

Mercedette pulled the trigger on the canister. Black liquid sprayed, followed by an explosion of pink paint. Gillian leaped in surprise. Mercedette removed her arms from the container.

"I will see this experiment through no matter the cost. If it is my fate to suffer because of self-testing, then so be it," Mercedette said.

"Her device combines the fear element with a mace variant. We have yet to aerosolize our product, so she used a globular liquid stream," Jimmy said.

"And the pink?" Gillian asked.

"Why not mark the bastards for the police?" Mercedette said.

Mercedette walked over to the pod chair in the room's center. Along with the machinery and monitors, a wired mesh skullcap sat on a medical tray. Mercedette placed it on her head. The screens on the cart showed a 3D image of a brain. The brain model flickered in and out. She pressed the skull cap tighter.

"Good, the brain imaging program works. I am afraid there is much more equipment for me to test before I get started."

Before Gillian could ask about the equipment, Jimmy stepped uncomfortably close to Mercedette. "If you need help, someone to test on."

"We've talked about this," Mercedette said.

Grimacing, Jimmy stormed off, through a different door than the one from the viewing booth. It opened out into the hall. Mercedette removed the skullcap followed by her lab coat. She walked to the exit and threw the coat over the camera above the door. Underneath the coat, she wore a businesswoman meets Catholic schoolgirl outfit, down to man-tailored shoes.

Mercedette returned to her workstation and grabbed a tablet. With a few swipes the screens lining the top of the lab came to life with images of a burning fireplace. The smaller screen at ground level still showed the earlier brain image even though she ditched the cap. Mercedette then moved to a box full of candles. she started standing them up throughout the room. Gillian furrowed her brow, confused.

"All for ambience, to lower my heart rate before I begin while simultaneously testing my equipment. The images you see will change drastically. As will I," Mercedette said.

"Change how?" Gillian asked.

"Even off the record I would prefer not to say. Now if you will excuse me. What I am about to face, I would prefer to face alone. It was... interesting talking to you."

"Thank you for your time," Gillian said and exited into the hall.

Jimmy had wandered to the end of the hall where he waited for Gillian. Once she caught up to him, they returned to the conference room, walking mostly in silence, Once back inside, she took a seat at the laptop while he vanished down the hall to offices she had yet to explore. Gillian logged in, checked the writing software, and tested the intranet. It acted much like normal internet. Gillian leaped when a stack of files dropped on the table. The deliveryman did not look happy.

"What is all this?" she asked Jimmy.

"You will meet everyone in time, but until then, we need to get you up to speed. The questions you were asking Mercedette…"

"I'm a reporter. It's what I do. I was just curious about science meeting faith."

"The questions were button pushers to someone with her psyche profile," Jimmy said and tapped the pile of folders.

"You keep files on employees?"

"Like many other diseases, someone experiencing cancer will be the one to cure it someday."

"What is it you all are here to cure?"

"Peter Piper picked his peck of pickled peppers."

"You stuttered when outside earlier."

Jimmy twitched at the reminder. "I did, but it was situational, fueled by adrenaline. I no longer suffer from that ailment."

"So, you cure stuttering?"

"More than that."

Jimmy leaned over and pushed a flash drive into her laptop. He grabbed a remote and turned on the TV. The screen matched the desktop on her computer. Clicking on the flash drive storage, he brought up the contents on screen. The screen showed individual folders labelled with employee names.

"Watch the videos and you will understand. For the record, I am opposed to sharing this information, but Mitch wants you to have total access. Employees signed consent forms for the dissemination of these files when hired. I believe Mitch intends all of us to be part of a broader study of fear. The information contained in the interviews and the other files could help with that. But you are not here in a scientific capacity which is why I am hesitant to share this access."

"It is in good hands. I would not use names from such files without permission of the individuals themselves. But why am I here, really?"

"We believe one of the greatest scientific breakthroughs in modern history will occur this weekend. If we are wrong, at least you can cover our mission."

"And what is that?" Gillian asked.

"We hope to eradicate fear."

CHAPTER 9

Jimmy left without saying another word. Gillian eyed the stack of file folders. She spread them out to view the names. The first was Amy's. Gillian lifted it from the pile and set it aside but did not open it. She clicked on Amy's digital file. It contained a few PDFs, jpgs, and a video file. She double-clicked the video file. An empty chair filled the screen, going in and out of focus as someone off-screen adjusted the camera.

"There we go," the voice of an unseen man said after solving the technical issue.

A female walked into view and leaped into the chair. Once settled, Amy locked directly at the camera. She appeared a bit nervous.

The off-screen interviewer asked, "Do you know what this is all about, Amy?"

"Yes. Answer the questions and maybe get hired. Refuse to answer and guaranteed not to be hired," Amy said on the screen.

"Something like that," he said off-screen. "We are seeking individuals with certain skill sets that one cannot get from a lab, only from life."

"Yay me. Trauma," Amy answered.

Gillian laughed. She appreciated the woman's honesty and scribbled a note. She wanted to make sure she remembered to interview the firecracker.

The interviewer continued. "Are you up for speaking about it? Your phobia?"

"Would way rather not. Hey, what happened to that poor woman you all dragged out before me? I think her name was Mercedette," Amy asked.

"Let's keep this about you, shall we?"

"Sure, doc. You all delayed my slot while someone on your staff came to clean this room of blood. Let's ignore all that. My newest fear may be people developing obscene apathy."

Gillian scribbled a note on her pad about Mercedette who apparently had some sort of accident during the interview. Even unaware of the circumstances, Gillian found the idea unnerving. Amy's sarcastic response to the interviewer was spot on. The man sounded robotic with no vocal emotional tells, but then Gillian could not see him. Maybe he looked disturbed when they discussed Mercedette, but somehow Gillian doubted it.

"Let's stick to the fear that brought you to this seat. Your records show..."

"If you have my info in front of you then why all the questions?" Amy waited for an answer that never came. She fidgeted then spoke again. "Add uncomfortable silences to my list of fears. Okay. Understand I am a professional. I am good at my job."

"Which is why you are here."

"But we all start somewhere and for me it was in grad school. There were many avenues of study in my field but the trip had little to do with mine. I am ashamed to admit that I followed a man into the jungle."

"Tell me more."

"He was a professor, and sometimes the age gap between the students and the teacher are minimal. I was twenty-two, he was in his late twenties. I knew he led expeditions into the rainforest. Not my exact area of expertise, but it would round out my thesis."

"You're stalling."

"Fine. I am. Turns out the dear doctor had the hots for a different student, and by the time we made it to base camp, I knew I would sleep alone."

A my, even younger than in the video, walked with a group of grad students through a lush jungle. A thin, bespectacled man led the charge but stopped to talk with a machete wielding guide who chopped a path for them. Two more guides, locals to Brazil and carrying enough gear for the whole group, brought up the rear. Animals and birds of unknown origin chirped, squawked, and yelped. The group was so submerged in green they could have been navigating ocean waters.

A female student in cutoff shorts (fashionable but jungle inappropriate) stumbled on a tree root. She fell into the arms of the professor. Amy witnessed the whole thing and thought it looked staged. The man pulled the injured student off to the side of the trail and sat her on a rock. From there, he examined her leg. A guide stopped to help, but the professor waved him on. Most students (a dozen in all) marched past without concern, but Amy stopped.

"Need help professor?" Amy asked. The man's gingham shirt stuck to his chest, damp with sweat in the heat.

"No. Checking for a sprain," Professor Parks said.

The shorts-wearing coed (Holly something or other) noticed Amy and frowned. They had indeed staged it. Amy studied medicine. If there was any swelling at all, it was in the professor's pants. Holly gestured toward the path.

"I will be fine, no need to tally. Join the others. We'll be right along," Holly said.

The professor nodded in agreement. The two guides bringing up the rear bumped Amy, urging her forward. She moved on and they followed. The guides shoved one another and looked back, the universal language that said they knew what was going on.

While attempting to catch up to the group, Amy occasionally looking back for the professor. Each time the guides grinned, a shared secret between the three. Amy frowned each time in return. They eventually emerged into a clearing where the guides transitioned from machete swinging to base camp setup. One guide climbed a tree while the other handed off a bundle of canvas. With practiced precision, the group set up the first pod tent quickly. The teardrop shaped tent hung twenty feet off the ground and dangled from a tree branch.

Dropping to the ground, the guide asked Amy for her bag. "Higher is better. Yours."

Amy handed off her backpack. He climbed back up and dropped the pack through an opening at the top of the pod. The tent sagged at the bottom when the weight hit. Crunching footsteps from behind caught Amy's attention.

Her newfound rival emerged from the forest, sweaty from the jungle heat or something else. Probably something else. Holly fussed with her clothes while trying to blend into the crowd as if nothing happened. Professor Parks stopped alongside Amy, testing the waters, seeing if anyone noticed their absence. Amy served as the man's canary in a coal mine. He gestured to the scene and asked Amy a question.

"Ever slept in one of these before? Lots of critters out here," Parks said.

"You don't say," Amy replied.

"Does the job, will keep us safe while we sleep."

"Sleep? Is that what we're calling it?" Amy said and walked off to join those readying the fire, making sure he understood the canary was dead.

The professor reached out, but she brushed him off and kept going. He looked around to see if anyone else had noticed before joining the party. Despite Amy's disappointment, she spent the night laughing with her classmates over a meal. The guides were skilled cooks. The grunt work of navigating the rainforest gave way to a celebratory mood. Together, they had navigated a very difficult path into a world most would never see.

Nightfall soon set in. Where sunlight had filtered through during the day, starlight failed to do the same, too distant, and diffuse. Starlight could not penetrate the thick foliage that blanketed the sky above them. The group carefully extinguished the fire and switched to flashlights before securing anything that had touched food into plastic bags. Stateside they used bear lockers when camping, but they needed something more mobile for such a treacherous hike. Plastic bags it was.

The guides had their own shelter at ground level where they planned to sleep in shifts, with one keeping watch for wildlife. Though having reason to be more tired than the students, the resourceful workers helped students who struggled to reach their pods. The group was young and determined, so most ascended on their own. Except for Holly. Parks held her butt, pushing her cushion to get her into the tree. Amy wondered how long before the professor entered the tent of his new favorite student. Letting it go, Amy climbed.

Hers was the highest of the tents, but she grew up a tomboy. She easily made her way to the top. From there, she lowered herself from a branch into the opening. After she adjusted to the strange flexible flooring, she reached up to zip the top closed. Mesh airholes provided necessary air, but their diminutive size worried her so she unzipped a small section at the top of her tent to allow more air to circulate.

Amy stripped naked, packing her outfit in her backpack, and pulling out underwear and socks for the next day. She would wear roughly the same clothes. The air remained warm but moist and felt good on her skin. They packed light, so her only bedding was a thin blanket in place of a sleeping bag. The tent floor served as her bed. She rolled a shirt into a pillow and covered herself with the blanket which she would likely kick off during the night because of the temperatures. But modesty made her cover herself. No telling if guides would climb branches and peek through airholes to make sure everyone was okay.

After the strenuous day of hiking, Amy quickly drifted to sleep on her side. During the night, she shifted, rolling onto her back. The rollover caused the branches to shake. The pod rocked like a cradle. A strange mass loomed above the tent (squirming?). A tiny black limb broke through the large mass that resembled hardened cotton candy. A second leg followed, then another, until the whole thing tore free from the inside out. The side broke open and black balls fluttered down.

Inside the tent, something plopped onto Amy's face and scrambled away. She swiped at her forehead and woke as another landed. The object that struck was sizeable enough to elicit a gasp, but not large enough to identify what hit her. Then another plopped, and another. The drops fell like hard rain, but she could not identify what they were. She switched on her flashlight and screamed. Masses of the deadliest spiders on earth poured in through the opening. A wave of black orbs landed on her face, hair, and chest, where they unfurled from cannonballs to spiders. Amy kicked wildly, sending the covers flying. A black wave covered the tent's floor even as more fell from the sky.

Amy cleared her face long enough to spot a massive leg as large as a king crab dip through the opening in search of its babies. Its head appeared. The horrendously large and frightening spider caused Amy to scream, which was a big mistake. Spiders fell into her mouth. She choked and spit, and scrambled for her backpack, no longer even trying to fight the tide of arachnids raining down.

The mother spider leaned over the edge of the opening and bared fangs, Amy grabbed her knife and slashed the bottom of the pod. Her weight helped the fabric rip once she sliced. The floor vanished and she fell.

Amy spun in a cartwheel and thudded onto the ground. Grunting in pain opened her mouth once again. The spiders refilled her open cavity. She spit until her mouth cleared, and then she screamed anew. She pounded her head, trying to loosen those tangled in her hair.

They crawled over her, raining down from above. The guides lit Amy up. Their beams revealed the enormous number of arachnids covering her nude body. In her panic, she ran deep into the jungle, screaming and swatting creatures off herself. Soon the jungle swallowed her in darkness.

Gillian gasped and hit pause. Amy's face filled the screen. The young woman looked white as a ghost after sharing the horrifying tale. Gillian opened the manilla folder containing Amy's file.

The first picture caused Gillian to leap from her chair. A picture of a massive spider greeted her. Gillian turned the image over and moved on to the rest of the folder's content.

It pleased Gillian to find there were no medical records, though extensive notes were in each file. It appeared to be the notes the interviewer referred to at one point. No medical records meant the interviewer was likely not medically licensed. A corporate headhunter perhaps, fishing for information. There were handwritten notes in the margins of the typed notes, likely jotted down during the interview process. The interviewer noted the demeanor of applicants before and after the interviews. Gillian wondered what Mercedette's would say, but figured she would read all about it after getting to that video. There was no reason to view in a specific order, Gillian planned to watch the videos in the order the files were delivered.

Still uncertain of what to expect for the weekend, Gillian at least had a treasure trove of research materials available. Amy's file was like a dossier. It had information about her studies, home life, a lot about the woman. The spiders Amy encountered were apparently a deadly species. Had they had time to develop their venom, the woman would possibly be dead. Terrifying. Gillian shivered, then leaped. Something sounded down the hall.

"Hello?"

No one answered. She shrugged and returned to the next file in the pile. It was Derrick who she remembered speaking up in the auditorium. Something about helping others rather than finishing his own project. Good-looking and kind. She looked forward to talking to him. But until then she hit play and watched his file.

Onscreen Derrick fidgeted in his chair. Gillian settled back in hers. It was time to play voyeur.

CHAPTER 10

Mitch sat kicked back behind Steve's desk while the head of security worked the surveillance system controls. Steve grunted in frustration upon noticing Mercedette blocked her camera. Steve remote controlled a camera located within the viewing booth above her lab. A quick adjustment and he had the woman on screen. Steve smiled, proud of himself for finding a workaround for a woman trying to hide. Steve turned to Mitch, disappointed that his boss failed to register his tech prowess.

"Are you paying attention to all this, Mitch?"

"Not at all."

"You need to take this seriously. You have a scientist trying to avoid detection."

"More like trying not to be spied on. Kill that feed. Watching her after she starts her drug regimen will have nothing to do with surveillance and everything to do with voyeurism," Mitch said.

"Look, I understand the smallest part of my job is to make sure that our workers do not steal product. I trust them. I know most of them, but times have changed. What if Mercedette plans to hoard the fear element? What if she plans to bring it to the mainland?"

"Are you listening to yourself? Everyone here is focused on one goal. To eliminate fear. These are people who have suffered life altering phobias. They are here to cure the cancer, not spread it."

Steve nodded, accepting the sentiment, but steepled his fingers. "So much could go wrong. I think I should stay."

Mitch pushed away from the desk and leaned forward. "Hate to break it to you, but they fired you. All of us."

"Yet a bunch of you are staying."

"For a single weekend with a single goal. I dangled paychecks for those who report to me, but I do not know if I still have access to company accounts. We are staying hoping to bring all workers back eventually. Frankly, I do not need to learn about these cameras because I won't have time to view the feeds. As for you, if you stay behind you might face trespassing charges if my former bosses get a bee in their bonnet."

"And you won't face the same?" Steve asked.

"Almost certainly. But my career path is not in security. A trespassing charge would damage your job prospects more than mine. Are those of us remaining behind sacrificing for the greater good? Yes. We might make a breakthrough in this artificial timeline that would otherwise never have happened. If we get stiffed on pay or get arrested, so be it. At least we took a shot. Our experiments might change our entire situation, which makes it worth the possible consequences. There is no upside to you remaining behind."

Steve cycled through more feeds, stopping at Elle's lab. The man breathed audibly when he spotted her. Not once did he stop on a male's feed.

Mitch noticed as much. "You are a family man. The dissolution of our company gives you the chance to leave mistakes behind."

Busted. Steve rose from his chair and coughed away the suggestion. "Who keeps the lights on, the air running? What if another employee dabbles too much and freaks out like our friend on the front lawn? What if Vincent Van Penis shows up this weekend?"

"Then we'll have more dick pics on the dead wing."

"What if they break in?"

"They never have. They come, they party, they prank, they leave. It's difficult getting here without a ferry. It is not an everyday occurrence."

Steve nodded, giving in. He pulled a weapon from his hip. "This is a company issued gun. Extra ammo is in the cabinet over there. Safety on, safety off, point and shoot." Steve showed Mitch how to use it, keeping the weapon pointed away from them both. "At least take this. I'll feel better if I arm you for the weekend."

Steve held it out, butt toward his boss. Mitch backed away. "No guns, Steve. Never any guns. I have seen what they can do."

Steve jerked back, awkward, forgetting Mitch's past. He circled around Mitch and placed the weapon in the desk drawer. "Sorry. I forgot. But in case of emergency, it is there."

"Won't need it," Mitch said. He noticed something else at Steve's hip.

Steve lit up. "Taser. We had to use these today. Can take down a rhino. You never know. Let me show you how to use this, at least."

Mitch sighed and nodded. Steve handed the weapon over and began a tutorial. On one screen behind them, neither noticed Quinn darting down a corridor. Onscreen, she searched for witnesses. Spotting none, she slipped into a lab that was not her own.

"N o, no, stay!" Elle said, gripping Yoshi's arm.

"I can't. I have my project that I need to finish." Yoshi answered, checking the time on his phone.

"Come on, work here. It's going to be a long weekend."

Yoshi suddenly lit up. "But we would have to sleep somewhere."

"A sleepover. Perfect," Elle said, bouncing with enthusiasm adding a flirtatious pout for effect. She knew which of Yoshi's buttons to push.

He checked the phone again and frowned. Elle grabbed his phone. "What are you doing? We don't get a signal. You're not hooking up with another woman, are you?"

"What? No. I mean who? Everyone left. Who would I hook up with?"

She handed the phone back. "Kidding. Just checking to see you didn't have some secret internet connection. You are wonky enough. Besides, who is going to sleep with you?"

Yoshi deflated at the casual slam, but quickly refocused on his phone. "I told you, just time. Time that I get some stuff from my office if we're going to work here."

"I'll go with, help you."

"What? No. My place is all kinds of a mess. I'll be back. Soon."

Yoshi exited. Elle moved some beakers around on a shelf, trying to find something to do. Then Claudia, one of Elle's neighbors, stepped into the doorway.

"You are staying behind Elle?" Claudia asked.

The woman held a box of personal items. Elle grew excited and leaped toward the door. Claudia stepped aside as if expecting the woman to rush through, but no, Elle retrieved a binder from Claudia's box.

"Yep. Mad scientist, that's me. This binder looks heavy, let me help you to the ferry."

"I'm good," Claudia said.

"I insist."

Elle followed the woman to the elevator. Down the hall, Yoshi burst into the stairwell. Elle watched Yoshi go. Claudia watched her watch him. They stepped into the elevator which had a few other scientists inside.

"Would it kill you to tell him how you feel?" Claudia asked.

"It might," Elle said as the elevator closed.

Yoshi raced up the stairs and exited on his level. He powerwalked toward his lab where he discovered the door wide open. He entered and screamed.

"No. Stop!" he yelled. "Put down the Shadow Trooper!"

Quinn held the small square box in her hands. It was one of many filling a floor to ceiling shelving unit. Yoshi leaped forward and took the Funko Pop from her.

"Do you know how much this is worth?"

"Not enough to leave at home. Instead, it sits in an accessible office," Quinn said.

She smiled; point made. Yoshi placed the box back where it belonged. His collectible wall emulated those of a comic book shop. Quinn reached a hand into her lab coat and pulled out a test tube filled with powder. She opened it and poured some out on a nearby desk.

"Wasn't sure you would show for our normal time with everything going on," she said, pulling out a credit card to shape up some lines.

"Doing it here, are you crazy? We need to go to our normal place," he said.

"Stairwell, where there are no cameras? Those days are over, pal. Security has left the building in case you haven't noticed.

Yoshi looked up nervously at the camera, then turned to the black lines of powder. Quinn gestured for him to go first. Yoshi leaned down and snorted a line. He rose back up and gasped while looking straight at Quinn.

The world went red. Quinn smiled obscenely as one by one, teeth fell out of her mouth in spurts of blood. Each tooth plinked onto the floor. In the abscesses, new teeth grew, all in seconds. The fresh teeth comprised razor wire that jutted out at crazy angles, mangling her gums like out-of-control braces. Blood drooled from her mouth.

Bloody Quinn walked toward him in herkie jerky steps. She moved quickly, too fast for Yoshi to process. He stumbled back and then she was on him, leaping with inhuman speed. She snapped her mouth open and closed, the razor wire teeth banging with the metallic clang of heavy metal machinery. Yoshi screamed and swung at her. Mistake. His arm swung too close to her face and the razor wire teeth severed his hand at the wrist. Blood gushed from the stump, shooting several feet in timed pumps.

"Yoshi, stop, chill!"

Yoshi shook his head and saw something at his feet that brought him back. Not a severed hand but a Funko Pop with a damaged box from where he knocked an entire shelf's worth over.

"Whoa. You've upped the potency," Yoshi said.

Quinn smiled for real, her teeth flashing back and forth between her perfect ones and the razor wire braces version. Yoshi focused on the fallen toys to sober himself up. He shrieked when he noticed the fallen and now damaged Green Lantern toy.

"Aw, man, this is the Ryan Reynolds version."

Quinn eyed him with interest. "You freaked. How was it? Did you see whatever phobia brought you through these doors?"

"What? No!" Yoshi snapped, bordering on anger. Off her surprised look, he settled down, spoke softer. "I mean, it's not a real thing. How could I see something that wasn't real? No, the effects enhanced things in this room." He looked at her and she got it.

"Oh, you enhanced me! Did you make my boobs bigger? Witch hair? Did you give me witch hair? Unshaved armpits?"

"Yeah, let's go with that," Yoshi said.

"My turn."

Quinn leaned down and snorted. Her body shook from the effects, but her head remained low to the table. She raised it slightly only to slam her head back down. It cracked hard against the table. Despite the pain, she grabbed her forehead and came up laughing.

"Crap. Going to feel that for a while. Yoshi?" She looked around but could not find him. The lab was empty, untouched, nothing out of place. The black lines even remained right where she left them. "You got the good stuff, Yosh—wherever you are. I got nothing."

Then she felt a tug. Quinn glanced down and saw one of her legs stretched out to the side, being pulled by something not there. Then her other leg shot out. She gripped the table to keep from face planting as both her legs extended into the air like someone had grabbed them to wheelbarrow her. Only her tenuous grip on the table kept her from falling face first.

The invisible something in control of her legs yanked with greater force. Quinn screamed when it pulled her free of her mooring. Rather than hit the floor, her legs shot toward the ceiling where she landed in an upright sitting position. Her hair spilled past her face, trying to reach the floor below.

Only her legs remained firmly in place. The full weight of Quinn's torso dangled toward the ground, eager to follow laws of gravity. Then invisible hands grabbed her breasts and pulled her flush against the ceiling. Once flat, she spun one hundred and eighty degrees where she found herself in a psyche room one floor above.

Medical equipment filled the room. Quinn fought to move, but found herself still held in place. The invisible force from earlier took on the form of three female nurses in obscene outfits. They wore sexy versions of nurse uniforms like every Halloween costume but with sections cut away as if by scalpel. Each woman displayed a sheer bra encased breast poking through a strategically cut section of the outfit.

The nurses held her tight while an ancient female doctor entered. Very old, a walking prune. The doctor's smock appeared made of the old woman's actual flesh but with a slight color variant compared to her exposed skin. A long tongue dangled from the doctor's mouth, slipping in and out of the crevices on her cheeks.

Quinn struggled not to gag and turned away which was when she realized where she was. On a medical gurney. The old woman retrieved a lobotomy spike and hammer from a nearby medical tray. The woman placed the spike's tip against the edge of Quinn's eye. The doctor raised the hammer and swung it down on the lobotomy spike!

"My eye!" Yoshi screamed.

Quinn came out of it and saw Yoshi holding his eye and herself clenching a fist so tight it hurt. She shook out her hand. Yoshi rubbed his eye and blinked a few times. Red but okay.

"You clocked me."

"Oh shit! Did I? Sorry. Yeah, this was way stronger than before." Quinn leaned on a lab table to support herself when something occurred to her. "Hey, you said the drug enhances our physical surroundings."

"Correct," Yoshi said.

"Well, this Elvis left the building. Not the building, but the room. I was in one of the psyche rooms."

"Really? That should not be possible. I've never left the confines of a room. But you stayed in the building. You walked past the rooms on the way, they creeped you out, it stayed in your head. I guess it is possible to roam under the influence."

"Not to trash your theory, but if recent memory can be influenced by the drug, then thinking about our wort fears beforehand would do the same. No?"

"Hell no. Do not even raise that issue. All this time and we could have experienced our greatest fears? Now I am nervous about this stuff," Yoshi said.

"Calm down. Only a working theory. We should probably call it a day. I'm sure your girlfriend is waiting."

"Please. Elle does not know I exist. She forgets I'm there like we all forget that we breathe."

"It's a long weekend. Don't count your chickens before they cross the road."

"That's a pep talk?" Yoshi asked.

"Hey, single here. I do not have my ten thousand hours of relation-ship experience in. I am no expert. Well, the drug got me pumped. Same time tomorrow?"

"Yeah. Elle would be upset if she knew I toyed with this stuff, but it helps me think. Too strong by half, though."

"Agreed. Too strong."

Quinn lingered in the doorway. She and Yoshi both looked back toward the table.

"One more?" Quinn asked.

Yoshi nodded and met her at the table.

"Same time?" Yoshi asked.

She nodded in return and they both leaned in, snorted, and went to deep dark places.

CHAPTER 11

Death Metal blasted at an insane level, making the already inde-cipherable lyrics even more unintelligible. Colt head-banged while playing drums on the edge of a lab desk. Using rulers as drumsticks he displayed significant skill. The song slipped into a drum solo when suddenly the music changed to a pop song.

"Jesus Murphy! What the hell?" Colt rushed to the speaker and tilted it as if that would explain anything. "Stop this blasphemy!"

Colt pretended to like pop if it helped him get into a woman's pants. But left to his own devices, he would rather shove pencils deep into his ears than listen to such garbage. Yet there it was, an autotuned princess of pop singing about lost lust.

While he appreciated the sentiment of the song, Colt long ago stopped feigning innocence with any women. Put it out there up-front was his motto, which worked well enough. It was all a numbers game. Colt planned to focus on his work for the weekend, ignore his other base impulses, but the song put thoughts in his head. Amy stepped into the doorway. The nut he could never crack. (Well, her and Quinn.)

There was also the reporter. The thought of banging one was excit-ing. He had never done that before. There was an author or two, plenty of podcasters, but never a reporter. The night was young, though. He ran through the index in his head of who remained an islander for the weekend.

Colt nailed Elle once and wondered if Yoshi knew. The poor guy had the droopy goopy love bug for that chick. The man's infatuation was the worst kept secret in the lab. Then there was the Mercedette hookup. A major Latin hottie who unnerved him with her sexual aggression, while somehow remaining clinical through it all. And seemingly religious. Weird chick. But Amy? Never Amy.

"Oops, I did it again," Amy said, holding up her phone. "Blue tooth hijack. Seriously, I cannot think while you blast music so loud. Just because we are the last two on the floor does not mean work courtesies have gone out the window." Amy entered the room, Derrick in tow.

Though busted, Colt played it cool. Amy was less than a decade older than him, but that made her the closest thing to a mom in the place. A hot one in the MILF zone. Despite that, she remained the one person beside his boss who could order him around.

"Soorry." Colt said. "How about you, Derrick? Let's hold a vote on a playlist. Two against one?"

"Leave me out of it. Besides, my vote would be classical."

"You disappoint me, my man," Colt said.

"What are we talking about?" Raj asked, entering the room and fray.

"Voting on music for the weekend," Amy said.

"I like this song," Raj said.

Amy high-fived Raj, who awkwardly missed the strike. Then Amy turned the music off. "Or silence? Does silence work?"

"Golden," Colt said, deflated. "Now, if you will all stop chirping, I have work to do now that my brilliant assistant is here."

Raj beamed. Amy shook her head and headed back toward the door. Derrick stepped out first.

"We both got lucky with our assistants. But did they get lucky with us? Good luck with this one, Raj." Amy slapped Raj on the shoulder and exited the lab.

"Did you see that? Heavy flirting, right?" Colt asked.

"None whatsoever," Raj said.

"I think she was smitten,"

"She is disgusted by your very presence."

"Yes!" Colt pumped his fist while Raj scrunched his face in confusion. Off the look, Colt answered. "That is how it starts with all of them. I am halfway there."

"Well, I am here as a different type of wingman so, what are we doing?"

"Injections."

Raj waved his hands. "No, no, no. I know we have some oddballs who use around here, but I am not one. No drugs. Alcohol is bad enough. I am up for helping, but if you think you are going to inject me, then the deal is off."

"No. You are going to inject me."

"Oh. Cool!" Raj shrugged.

A bag of oranges from the street vendor sat on a desk. Raj reached for one, but Colt slapped his hand away.

"Don't touch those. They are part of the experiment. Now help me gather everything."

"Where are we going?"

"To the snake pit," Colt said, grabbing the bag.

"Snakes? I used to like you, Colt."

Colt grinned and they went to work grabbing what they needed.

Derrick's interview was on par with Amy's and Gillian wondered if all the employees had such traumatizing backgrounds. She would find out eventually but had watched only the two videos so far. Onscreen, Derrick held his hands against his face. The man stopped speaking some time ago after sharing his story. Derrick finally lowered his hands and stared straight at the off-camera interviewer.

"Are you okay?" the voice asked.

"No. I have not thought about that for years. Is this ethical?"

"It is a requirement of this particular..."

"Stop with the HR garbage. It is unethical the questions you are asking. I am more than qualified. I do not see what dredging up old fears does to..."

Now the interviewer cut Derrick off. "It informs us, rounds out your profile. Some employers ask for social activities, hobbies, and such. All meaningless. But your deepest, darkest fears mean something to us here at Trager Chemicals."

"Means you are sick individuals. Did I get the job or not?"

Something clanked down the hall. Gillian froze the frame on an agitated Derrick. His fear bothered even Gillian, made her nervous. She understood why the man would be so upset. Many people developed fears at young ages, but most grew out of them. To revisit such a thing from his childhood must have been difficult for him, Gillian thought.

Another clank sounded. "Hello?"

No answer. She exited the conference room and leaned her head out into the hall. Something sounded in the distance. A hum? She called out. When no one answered she headed toward the source of the noise. A hum for certain, growing louder after passing the elevators. Arriving at the gym doors, she heard the pok-pok-pok of a slow bouncing basketball. One rolled through the double swing doors, coming to rest at her feet. She picked it up.

"Hello? Loose ball means jump ball," she said and stepped inside.

The gym was empty. A distant ball caddy had an empty spot for the basketball. Gillian shrugged, assuming it came loose from its storage point. She lined up a shot with the nearest basket. Her form suggested she played before, as did the nothing but net shot. Gillian raised her arms in victory and exited the gym.

The hum remained present, still further down the hall. Before she could investigate further, something touched her foot. Impossible. The basketball sat at her feet. She never heard it roll up, but she was focused on the original hum. Gillian picked up the ball and returned to the gym. She opened one swing door and called out anew.

"Hello? Who is here?"

Silence. Gillian launched the ball toward the furthest spot in the gym. It careened off a wall and disappeared somewhere beyond. Clang! A loud bang drew her attention back to the corridor. She released the gym door, which swung open and closed. With her back turned, Gillian failed to notice a woman appear in the gap of the doors in between swings. Dead Wendy watched Gillian leave. Sensing someone watching her, Gillian turned back. The swinging door stopped moving. Nothing was there. Gillian continued walking until arriving at the machine room, the door of which sat open.

The electric hum filled the corridor. What began loud grew deafening when she stepped inside the dark space. The metal door was there for a reason to contain the noise behind it. But why was it open? She stepped further into darkness and cursed when she banged her head.

Foolish to wander in the dark. She grabbed her phone and turned on the flashlight. While not up for the job of lighting much, it revealed the low hanging pipes that had introduced themselves to her skull. A note taped to a section of pipe read: *be careful.*

"Yeah, thanks," Gillian said.

Moving slowly, Gillian maneuvered through the maze of plumbing and machinery. Who was inside? Her reporter instincts led her forward. Never become the story was her profession's mantra, but Gillian was always quick to rush headlong into the unknown. If she took time to search herself, she might recognize how foolhardy such confidence was. The universe cared not for press credentials. Yet something about being with the press made her feel as if she wore a bullet-proof vest.

She waved her light back and forth and caught someone in the beam. It took a moment for her to sweep it back to where the man stood, hunched over.

"Hello?" Gillian asked.

The man spun and pointed a powerful flashlight at Gillian who raised her arms to block the light. There appeared to be something in the man's other hand, but it was hard to tell around the halo of light.

"What are you doing here?" Mitch asked, yelling to be heard above the noise.

"I could ask the same of you. I heard a noise and saw the door open."

"Checking the air is on for the weekend. Place is being held together by duct tape!"

"By what?"

The sound was too much. Mitch waved the roll of duct tape in his hand, then tossed it aside. It landed on a duffel bag. Gillian eyed the scene. Though the area was foreign to her, something felt out of place, but she could not put a finger on it. Mitch gestured to his ears, then pointed toward the exit. His moving toward her blocked the view behind him so she could not investigate any further. In a few steps he was on her, and with the walkway was too narrow for him to pass, she had to move or become intimate. They exited into the hall. Mitch laughed once they cleared the room.

"What is so funny?" Gillian asked.

"Silly, but that volume level reminds me of restaurants today. So loud. Leaving one after dinner is like exiting a rock concert."

Gillian played along. "How was the fish!" she yelled.

"What? Yeah, I agree, the bathrooms were really clean!"

They laughed, both on the same page with the humor. Gillian relaxed, finally finding some levity for the first time since her visit. She was happy to see the doctor maintain some sense of humor after all he went through. Humans were nothing if not resilient, she thought.

"I don't know what I was doing in there, but everything looked okay. Machines were machining. If air shuts off on a timer this weekend, I think I located the overrides," Mitch said.

"Even if the central air turns off, can't people just open windows?"

"No. The labs need a controlled environment. Too many contaminants if a window is opened. Most labs do not have windows by design. We have more than normal here because of the building's layout."

Gillian gestured to the eerie corridor. "I guess it would be a shame to shine sunlight on this bright and welcoming environment."

"You get used to it."

Mitch turned to close the door when something clanged inside. Gillian eyed him with concern. Mitch aimed his flashlight into the void. He appeared on the defensive, surprised to find someone inside.

He waved Gillian back. "Stay here."

"What? Why?"

"Just. Please," he said.

Before Mitch could enter, a dueling flashlight beam matched his own from inside the room. Mitch stepped back while Jimmy stepped into the hall. They extinguished the flashlights.

"Jimmy? What the hell were you doing?"

"I saw the open door and checked it out," Jimmy said.

"How did we not see you?" Mitch asked. Before Jimmy could answer, Mitch grilled him some more. "What did you see? What were you doing?"

Levity left the building while Mitch grilled his protégé. Jimmy cowered under the questioning. Gillian watched closely, surprised by the accusatory nature of the conversation. Jimmy closed the door then eyed Gillian before gesturing to his boss for a sidebar. They left Gillian and fell into a whisper.

Gillian coughed to get their attention. "You promised full access this weekend. What were you doing in there, Jimmy?"

"Doctor Trager supplied you with unprecedented access. At your disposal is more than enough to write a hit piece of some sort..."

"Jimmy," Mitch said.

Jimmy turned innocently to his boss. "What? You called it a hit piece, the one she wrote about you."

"Wait. What?" Gillian asked. She eyed Mitch, ready for a fight.

"That is history, Jimmy. Me and Ms. McCann discussed our differences."

"Apparently not entirely," Gillian said. "I do not write hit pieces."

"Ms. McCann. Gillian. I have an experiment underway that I need to get back to. We may never see eye to eye about the past, but this weekend is about the future. And you are correct. We are hiding something. We believe we might have a stowaway this weekend," Mitch said.

"What do you mean?" Gillian asked.

"Our head of security. After everyone left on the ferry, we did a head count on the cars in the parking lot to make sure someone was not inadvertently left behind, but we found Steve's car," Mitch said.

"I spotted his car in the lot," Jimmy said.

"Why would he still be here?" Gillian asked.

"The man was hesitant to leave. Such loyalty tells you something about the special place we have here. How much like family we are."

"Then why am I nervous having a rogue man roaming the grounds?" Gillian countered.

"You should not be. If here at all, he wishes to keep us safe. Steve has foregone pay and risked his future employment ventures," Mitch said. "Though his concerns are overblown. Silly, even."

"Sometimes teens explore the island on weekends. They know the place is unstaffed. They party, drink, do drugs, and have sexual relations," Jimmy said.

Gillian frowned at his odd attribution to what even she, as a somewhat conservative person, called screwing. "Even if he stayed, why can't you find him then?"

Mitch answered with confidence. "Steve likely escorted Erik, our injured scientist back to the ferry. He could Uber home once in Seattle. Or…"

"Or?" Gillian asked.

"Steve insisted on staying despite my demands for him to leave. I assumed he did leave but I was not there when the ferry departed. If Steve ignored my suggestions then he will pop up at some point with an absurd excuse for why he stayed. He knows we will all be too busy with experiments soon, which is the perfect time to come out of hiding. Not that it matters. I am not his boss any longer. Or anyone's."

"Ahem," Jimmy said.

"You were there before this, Jimmy, and you will be after. If you stop skulking around. I do not want to find you popping up in places you should not be like this. Just do your inventory of our chemical stores and check in on Gillian and our remaining employees to see if they need anything. Nothing else. This is not a video game. No side missions, is that clear?"

"Mercedette is asking for the prepoxyhydrazone."

"What is that?" Gillian asked.

"Essentially female Viagra." Mitch reacted to Gillian's surprised look. "Promised full disclosure. She needs it for her study." He turned to Jimmy. "It should be in the receiving dock in one of the medicine coolers. Find it and bring it to her. But get in and get out of her lab. Do not be there after she takes the drug. Do you understand, Jimmy?" Mitch said, as if scolding a child.

"Understood," the red-faced assistant said before heading to the elevators.

Mitch turned to his guest. "Are you hungry?"

Off her nod, Mitch led her down the hall toward the cafeteria. As they walked away, neither noticed a black mist escaping through the bottom of the closed maintenance door.

CHAPTER 12

The immense cafeteria was a ghost town until Mitch and Gillian entered. A row of empty buffet tables lined one side of the room. The cafeteria only served lunch because breakfast was available on the ferry. With the company's sudden closure, the dining room staff left before finishing prep. Empty holes in the tables awaiting food trays only highlighted the building's desolation. Sneeze guards seemed pointless in the absence of people. Gillian crossed her arms, uncomfortable in a place know for serving comfort food. Mitch noticed her demeanor.

"A touch of agoraphobia?" Mitch asked. "Fear of open spaces?"

"What? No. Only fear of this one specific place. Creepy when empty. This building felt relatively warm during the exodus. But now, absent people, eerie. Is this an old cigarette machine?"

Gillian examined the antique machine that now housed cups of ramen. Faded stickers with cigarette brands lined the bottom of the vending machine below each pull button. Mitch pulled twice and retrieved the cups of noodles from the drop spot.

Only one half of the large space served as a functioning cafeteria. The other half was a more traditional corporate lunchroom that with its microwaves, refrigerators, and sink with a water filter attached. Mitch filled the ramen containers with water and placed them in the microwave. A cup filled with plastic forks sat atop the microwave. With a ding, Mitch opened the door and handed her a steaming cup.

She grabbed two forks and smiled. "Thank you. Haven't had this since college."

Mitch took a fork as well. "World's best sodium delivery system."

They sat at the nearest table and removed the paper tops completely. Gillian blew on hers while Mitch dug in. Testing the heat with her tongue. Gillian used the back end of the twin forks like chopsticks and slurped noodles. Mitch grinned. She touched her chin.

"Something on my face?"

"No. Sorry for my reaction. Your makeshift chopsticks? That's how... Well, I knew someone who used to eat ramen that way."

"Your wife. How did the two of you meet?"

"We almost didn't. I was head over heels for her best friend."

"Sounds romantic."

"It was in college. I was eighteen and became infatuated with a young woman I met at orientation. Her name was Katie, and she was loud and outgoing but had a quiet friend always tagging along."

"Wendy?"

Mitch nodded. "I read in the college paper that our football team was going to host a game against a team from Katie's home state. It was the perfect in. I invited Katie and to be polite, I invited Wendy along. We set the date for that Friday."

"Isn't college football on Saturdays?"

Mitch raised a finger to emphasize the point—exactly. "I didn't know sports enough to catch the typo. I couldn't afford a car yet, so the plan was to meet at the bus stop. The stadium was quite far from the campus. While waiting for the bus, I received a text that Katie could not make it. She had been trying to get into a certain class. Someone dropped it so she was in which meant she could not make the game."

"So, what happened?"

"I was not too bummed. The game was merely an excuse to get together with her. I was never really into sports. There would be other opportunities to get together, or so I thought. I decided to head back to campus when Wendy showed up, picnic basket in hand. She had made food for the game. I couldn't back out at that point; it would be rude. We hopped on the bus and headed to the game. Except..."

"There was no game?"

"Exactly. Not a soul in the stadium. We chose the best seats in the house and held a picnic in the stands. Without looking at Wendy through the prism of her friend, I discovered what was under my nose the whole time. She was intelligent, beautiful, thoughtful. Hopeful. I found her more exciting than any woman I had ever met and knew then that I would marry her someday."

Gillian awkwardly slurped noodles as Mitch reminisced about love. The sloppy act brought him back. He looked at Gillian in a new light as well. She returned the gaze and smiled. A different time, maybe? Gillian finally saw Mitch for who he was, a wounded warrior who suffered lost love. She understood where his earlier anger came from. While not okay she at least understood.

"What about you? Is there someone?" Mitch asked.

"If you think I'm going to follow that story, you're crazy."

"I will confess more later," Mitch said.

"Excuse me?"

"Whatever you were originally here for. I promise I will share every-thing. But for now, can you please focus on the work we are doing? It would mean so much to Wendy."

"Would have meant," Gillian corrected.

She turned red over the insensitive but accurate comment. The man only nodded, lost in the reminiscing. Then his eyes met hers again.

Another time, another place, why not now? *Nope, all kinds of nope,* she thought. Her relationships all withered and died. The man had been through enough. She straightened, gulped the remnants of her soup, and returned to work mode. Break over.

"I am concerned by your hiring practices. You required psyche profiles from damaged people?"

"You are quite single-minded. I like that. Focus on the story. You like to be in control. Is that your fear? Losing control?" Mitch asked.

Gillian did not back down, though she wondered if that was a proposition or a question. "My fears are not your concern. Are you obfuscating my question?"

"Not at all. Occupational hazard to wonder. The road to beating cancer is riddled with failures, but someday there will be a cure. But that cure is likely to come at the hands of someone who has suffered loss from the disease. That is a truism of many a scientific break-through. Science and art intermingle in the fight against diseases. The elusive intangible that produces success is sometimes as simple as the drive behind the researcher. The search for any cure is almost always enhanced by someone who has lost someone to a disease."

"Having phobic employees is your plan?"

Gillian retrieved her phone and began taking notes. She remem-bered a similar sentiment from Jimmy earlier. The two men were on the same page. Belief, or talking points?

"We built phobias into the business model. And to be frank, it helped secure funding. It was one intangible."

"Except they pulled funding."

Mitch winced. Yes, yes, they did. "Visionaries do not concern themselves with money. But hedge funds do. Results were not to their satisfaction."

"That is why they pulled funding?" Mitch did not answer, so she asked another question. "Jimmy said he used to stutter. You cured him? How?"

Mitch collected their finished cups and dropped them in a nearby bin. "Mercedette cured him. She is brilliant, but troubled."

"So, I have heard. And one of the tapes I watched suggested as much. There was an incident during her interview?" Gillian eyed Mitch who did not answer so she continued. "Having said that, I met her. She seemed okay, perhaps antagonistic. I feel my presence unnerved her." Gillian rose to meet Mitch, and they stepped out into the hall.

"Bothered. You bother her. Mercedette does not like your presence."

"She told you that?"

"Roughly. Do not take offense. Mercedette is here to do her work. She was excited more than most to learn our testing would begin soon. Sadly, the plans have changed. And for that reason, I need to check on her."

"I already spoke to her and now you are telling me she does not want to see me? Is this a good idea, then, our visiting?"

"Not visiting, checking on her."

Mitch led Gillian through the doors to the next wing and then to the viewing room where they watched Mercedette work diligently, prepping various laptops and workstations. The large seat in the center of the room glowed with soft blue hues of hidden LED lights.

"Certain events in my life led me to study fear. But to study fear, it needs to be present in more than short bursts. I developed a fast-acting nerve agent that induces intense feelings of fear. That fight-or-flight response you have likely heard of throughout your life? I needed to duplicate that in a lab. With hard work and determination, I succeeded."

"The liquid on the dais. That is your product."

"Correct. The fear element. We have so far made the central ingredients into powder, pills, liquid. Each version is designed to act with varying intensities. We have a factory near Seattle where we make the drug. Once processed, we ship it here. But our investors were only interested in aerosolizing the fear agent."

"Why?" Gillian asked.

"Military. They wished to use it as a weapon on the battlefield. Or I should say, they were interested in collecting government money to sell it as a weapons system. My intentions were more mundane than what they wished for. I wanted to help people control their fear. We were going to use the abandoned wing to produce the product, but besides permit issues, the space was not large enough for the equipment needed to weaponize the product which was why we purchased the Seattle factory. I thought the mere presence of a building designed to their specs would keep them happy. But it was not enough. Had I focused more on aerosolizing and testing we might have kept funding."

"And your benefactors finally had enough of altruism? They cancelled because a future gold mine had yet to be mineable. Is that what I put in the story?" Gillian asked without disguising her doubts.

Mitch smiled, busted. "No. We would have supplied them with a weaponized variant. I am not that altruistic. We need to pay the bills, or they shut us down, which happened. I simply wished to point out my intentions. Mercedette reverse engineered my product, creating an anti-version. Hers blocked the same receptors we used to induce fear. Brilliant piece of work. She designed a pill form that helped Jimmy with his stuttering. There are plenty of anti-anxiety mediations on the market, but ours is different. The main version induces fear so we can better study it, while the antidote if you will, stops biological routes for fear to take hold. Not all anxiety is stress related, some is fear related. That is where we fit in."

"Is Mercedette the brightest student, then? The one I should focus on?"

"No. I would ask you to stay away from her. While everyone here has their own issues, Mercedette is unique."

"As in, you allowed her to develop a pill for a member of your staff, obviously well before human trials were in place?"

"You picked up on that. Yes. And you can use it in your next hit piece on me."

"I was at the restaurant that night. Mere chance. I reported your words."

Mitch waved her off. "I was making light of Jimmy's slip earlier. When he mentioned the hit piece, that was how I phrased it to him to explain your presence and who you were. I was concerned at the time over our other guests. I did not mean it. Just as I did not mean to react the way I did in the elevator. My apologies again. What we are embarking on this weekend might end up with me facing charges more severe than a hospital administration believing I lost my faculties. There are real world repercussions that will arise from this weekend. I only ask that you focus on the big picture and wait until it is all over to determine an angle for your story. Our benefactors already prejudged this project. Will we change their minds by the time we are done? I believe so. I ask you to wait as well. Facts on the ground today will be different by Monday."

"And if you fail?"

Mitch shrugged. "I already failed five years ago. I understand failure. But fear has always affected my life. That makes me and the others here the perfect candidates to cure it."

Before Gillian could respond, Jimmy entered the lab below and handed Mercedette a package. The assistant talked animatedly, as if pleading. Mercedette appeared to rebuff Jimmy, but Gillian found it impossible to know for certain. Mitch frowned throughout the interaction but remained otherwise silent.

Jimmy gestured to the camera hanging near the door and pulled the coat off. Mercedette scolded him while shoving him out of the lab. Once Jimmy was gone, Mercedette tried to toss the coat over the camera once again. It missed and fell to the floor. She ignored it and moved to a sink. She filled a cup with water, took what looked like several pills from the package Jimmy handed her and downed them followed by water. Then she set about lighting the candles she staged earlier.

"Why did he want the camera unblocked?" Gillian asked.

"No good reason I can think of," Mitch said. "She can cover it again and should. Mercedette will be baring more than her soul this weekend."

Once the candles were lit, Mercedette moved to a laptop that appeared to control the room's environment. She dimmed lights and the sterile environment took on a warm glow under the candlelight. With a few more taps, the room burst to life with motion on massive screens lining the entire perimeter of the lab. The big screens hung at angles where walls met ceiling and angled such that the screens were best viewed from the lab floor. They came to life with images of scantily clad men and women. The images flashed fast and furious, skin taking front and center, shy of pornography by an inch. Simply everyday advertising in a super cut of the most enticing shots.

"What is she watching?" Gillian asked.

"A mashup of ads and adult videos. The goal is to induce sexual arousal through visual stimuli. She will use a rudimentary brain scan to determine the subject's arousal levels. This is in conjunction with a revolutionary drug that also causes arousal. Once the subject has reached peak arousal, she will test her self-defense device on them."

"She is the subject?" Gillian asked.

"Yes. A unique situation. The medicine Jimmy delivered is in its own trial. Mercedette and I coordinated with another lab to study their product alongside her test. We ordered the supply some time ago. It was never intended for her to use it, but circumstances change."

"She is horning herself up with chemicals, then using yours to stop the effects of the first. And both drugs are on trial, so either one can produce devastating health results. This is insane! This is what you asked your people to do?"

"Excuse me? You were there. They volunteered."

"*Voluntold* is more like it. You are their boss. They look up to you. Who is to say whether they are testing to help people or simply trying to impress their hot professor?"

Mitch turned, surprised. Gillian had let out a slip. Before he could speak, she went rigid, suggesting her raised topic was off limits. Mitch avoided the bait and continued their conversation.

"Not a professor, a mentor. Out of everyone, Mercedette was one I could never control. She is going to do what she wishes. I admit hers is the most extreme test of anyone here this weekend. But if Mercedette succeeds, people will have something stronger than mace but less lethal than..." Mitch stopped, not wanting to say it.

"A gun."

"You may interview Mercedette regarding her results, but for some time, she will remain in a fragile state. That is why I urged Jimmy to stay away. I ask the same of you. We do not know the nature of the pills she is taking. Even if we fail this weekend, her use of the stimulants can help a separate trial elsewhere in the country."

"What about you? Will you interact with her?"

"Yes and no. Someone needs to make certain there are no adverse reactions to the drug. We already planned it out. I do not need to go down because she already initiated the protocol. See that green paper on the wall down there? If it remains there, she is okay and I have no reason to invade her space. If she removes it, then she is concerned over her vitals. If removed, I will step in. Please remember, I am no one's boss. I am available to you if needed, otherwise you and the others will not see me. Once my own tests are complete, I promise to share the results with you."

"I will stay clear. This wing creeps me out, anyway. But I am thinking I may have stumbled into something much larger than I expected."

"That's the spirit," Mitch said before escorting Gillian from the room. Once they left, Mercedette looked toward the glass, as if she knew they were there all along. Then she unbuttoned her blouse.

CHAPTER 13

The grand departure was long over, the ferry nothing more than a dot in the distance. Isolated. They were all isolated now. Wacky, wacky weekend time stuff. Yep, nothing but one big party, Elle thought. Except where were the partygoers? No one anywhere. Even the yard crew was gone. Elle missed their constant mowing and leaf blowing. She was the outlier. Elle found comfort where others did not. Engine noises meant people were nearby.

Now they were gone. Everyone was gone. Even her boy-toy Yoshi. She liked him plenty, and since she was not an idiot, she was aware of his infatuation. But she also understood if she gave in, then there would be no reason for him to linger, to hang on, to always be there. Too many men scored and moved on, ghosted her even. Elle could not fault them. She had done the same. The difference was, Elle wished for someone to always be there. She worried if she gave in to Yoshi, he would no longer be omnipresent in her life.

With no company available, she busied herself by gathering up the product and prepping her station. She worked her way through college as a line cook. The skills carried over to working in a lab where prep was crucial. If one did not have the correct supplies on hand at the correct moment, it could derail the experiment. Lab assistants were a thing for a reason. Strange how there were none left on the island. (Raj and Derrick did not count. They were scientists as well.)

Dr. Trager was a brilliant man with a brilliant plan. Assemble people with specific phobias to cure their own issues. Elle had no desire to seek a cure for her ailment because it was the rarest of mental hiccups. She decided to work for the greater good and develop something useful to the masses. Very few needed a cure for autophobia.

Never a fan of needles, Elle carefully filled a dozen injectors. The devices were a variant of pediatric needles used to immunize children but designed to deliver larger payloads. Harmless, almost like feeling nothing at all, Mitch assured them. The knowledge did little to comfort Elle, who was phobic about needles. Some employees toyed with the chemical but needle usage when not sick never made sense to her. Besides, Elle never did drugs of any type. Oh no, not her. Mother would not approve. Mother would be furious.

Elle's mother had very specific ideas on how to assimilate when they arrived in the states. It started by her mom marrying a man who walked away before Elle's pre-frontal cortex had developed enough to store memories of the man. Life became taking care of mother and mother taking care of Elle in a symbiotic but unhealthy relationship. Elle's hands tremored at the memories. She shook her head to clear her mind.

She stopped what she was doing and studied her hands. Odd. Normally it took a long-time wallowing over the past before her hands shook and her tears flowed. There were no tears yet, but the hands did a hearty version of a jig. Perhaps it was not only remembering her past, but remembering how alone she was.

With no cell phones, she could not even reach out to Yoshi. Where was he? Off with another woman? Cheating? Except they were not a thing, so how could she call it cheating? And most of the staff knew of his obsession with her. Elle could not think of anyone who Yoshi would hookup with. Wherever he went, he must have had his reasons.

Elle searched her surroundings, hoping to discover why she felt so on edge. The prep from her cooking days was spot on. She had everything in its place and was on schedule. Or as scheduled as she could be. They were no longer on an eight to five. Things were good to go, yet she felt out of sorts. Out of the corner of her eyes, she glimpsed something.

Was that smoke? A burst of black particles seeped through an overhead vent. It happened frequently in the early days when construction workers remained on site and shook things loose all over the place. Doctor Trager swore he kept some sanitarium rooms intact for historic preservation, but Elle always believed the construction crew missed their deadline. Trager Chemicals needed to open; the startup was all over the news.

Dust and dirt would not contaminate anything in her study except one important thing. Allergies. When testing on people (in this case herself) it was important to identify which medications they were on. The fear element came with a warning list of which other medications to avoid when taking Ink. Ink was the slang that many employees referred to the fear element as. Mitch did not like that nickname, so it was used sparingly. Elle felt those who routinely called it Ink were likely users themselves. Yoshi called it that often, but he was a nerd, not a drug user.

If the dust in the room caused her allergies to flare up, Elle would have to take allergy medicine. It was important to note any medications someone was on to ensure there were no adverse reactions, and if there were, to note it on the study (after getting medical help if one were in distress). She was also on birth control. Elle preferred to keep it at that and not add an allergy medicine into the mix if she could help it.

Elle wondered whether there was anyone on site to fix the vent problem. Doctor Trager made it clear he would be busy on his own experiment all weekend. She did not wish to disturb him. That left Jimmy. Except he gave her the willies, always had. Elle was not above one-night romps. Preferred them, despite having made some dubious choices in men, but she drew a line somewhere.

Creepy party of one your table will never be ready because I'm not taking the date, Elle thought where Jimmy was concerned. Predatory. That was the word. She drew the line at predatory behavior. Elle was fine with boldness, directness, and even disgustingly direct booty call requests. But Jimmy gave off true crime vibes. Rumor had it there was something between him and another scientist in the building.

With no one to call, Elle took matters in her own hands. It would give her something to do while she waited. (Where was Yoshi?) She grabbed a hand-held vacuum cleaner from a cabinet. But she needed a ladder or stable chair to reach the vent. Elle turned it on to check if it was charged. It burst to life as someone burst through the door. Elle shrieked in surprise. In her fright, she jerked her arms and the vacuum sucked in her hair.

Elle's initial cries turned to yelping as she blindly fought to free her hair. Yoshi dropped his box on a lab table and rushed to the rescue. He turned it off and helped her pull it away. The fiasco left a section of her hair reaching for the ceiling. She blew some stray hairs out of her face and burst into laughter.

Yoshi laughed along until she hugged the air out of him. Yoshi's glasses slipped, and he shoved them back up his nose with one hand before reaching down to hug back. She clung to him and felt his body responding downtown. She knew is she held him much longer, he would have some explaining to do so she let him go, just happy to have the company.

"Sorry, I didn't mean to startle you," Yoshi said, readjusting the glasses once more.

"No. I knew you were coming. Just surprised me is all. Let's see what made you vanish so long., What is your mysterious experiment?"

Elle dug through the box, lifting various food items. She said yum on a few and gross on a couple. She dropped each back after checking them out. Halfway through the box inventory it hit her.

"Snacks? You went to your lab for snacks?" Elle asked.

"You said sleepover. I don't know how you do it, but this is how I roll," Yoshi said.

"But your experiment? Please tell me you are not going to work out of your lab? I'm not a truck stop. Sleepover suggests we work in the same lab, not just sleep and/or do other stuff," Elle said, throwing out a lure.

"About that. I think I'm like Raj and Derrick. Much better if I help you."

Elle leaped up and hugged him again, tighter than before. "For real?"

"If you need a helper," Yoshi asked, face buried in her neck.

She released him and led him over to a desk against the wall where her laptop sat open. She dropped onto a desk chair and patted the armrest. Yoshi leaned on it and vacillated between watching the screen and trying to look down her shirt. Elle typed away.

"Everyone's working on something related to their personal phobias, right? That is why most of us rarely talk about our research with one another which is weird. We are coworkers trying to get results in a shared field. We could all greatly benefit from one another's research but most of us keep things close to the chest, too worried to give away our deepest fears. Hella personal, all this. Except I'm not doing an experiment related to my personal phobia."

"What is your phobia?" Yoshi asked.

"Uh-uh, tut-tut, not kind to grill a lady. That and my favorite sex position are off limits. You can tell me yours, though."

"Any that involves someone other than just me," Yoshi said so innocently that Elle snorted a laugh.

Elle refocused on the pitch deck on her screen. Yoshi nodded in appreciation over her next level prep. Elle let the slides play out and spoke over them, an enthusiastic spirit taking over for the formal presentation.

"All of us are going to die, right?" Elle said.

"Not today, I hope."

"You never know. But eventually. A fact. We also dream. What do you know about lucid dreaming?"

"Isn't that the dreaming that is like virtual reality?"

"Except better. VR is a closed system with limits to even the grandest world building. In lucid dreaming, one can travel anywhere, go anyplace. There are no limits. Lucid dreaming also provides physical stimuli. One does not simply watch themselves fly in a dream; they experience it."

"I might have done it before. I never remember my dreams, only nightmares."

"You haven't then. The sensation would stick with you. The experience of lucid dreaming is so real that the brain can write some dreams into memory."

Yoshi grew excited at the possibilities. "If piloting a spaceship in a dream seemed real enough, I would have the memory even though I know starships do not exist?"

"Sort of. If the memory wrote itself into your lived experiences, it would also convince you that starships exist. There are theories that people who claimed to have had alien abductions were simply under the influence of an LD."

Yoshi turned suddenly pale and stepped away from Elle before wiping his forehead with his sleeve. Yoshi shook out his hands. Elle turned to him, confused by his actions.

"Are you okay?" she asked.

"Sure, just my butt falling asleep. Forgot to set the alarm."

His joke fell flat, a cover. Elle eyed the slide on the screen and could not find a possible trigger that might have set him off. If it was something she said, she was long past that thought, too excited to share the concept of it all. She continued with her presentation.

"In a world where anything is possible, imagine reconnecting with a lost loved one."

That notion brought life to Yoshi who spun and sat his ass on the edge of the workspace and looked down at Elle. "You are on to something. My research suggests fear can induce hallucinations. What kid hasn't seen a coat in a chair turn into a creature in the dark?"

Elle fed off his excitement with more of her own. Lab work was a lonely affair, but now she had someone to share her workspace with. Yoshi's enthusiasm was genuine beyond his desire for her. For a moment she was a scientist, a teacher, lecturing a student rapt with attention. She stood up, too excited to sit any longer.

"Exactly. Monsters in a chair. Not real, but close as can be. Fear can alter a person's mental state, make them see things that are not there, were never there."

"You plan to induce hallucinations?" Yoshi asked, disappointed. "Are we down to parlor tricks?"

Elle shook her head. "No. There will be hallucinations of course. We know they are a common side effect of the drug based on anecdotal employee information. You know, the stoners." Elle laughed but Yoshi remained quiet, too quiet. She continued. "I intend to push well past those boundaries to a point where the subject experiences a lucid dreamlike state while still awake."

"How do you plan to get someone into such a state?" Elle moved opened a nearby cabinet in which hung IV bags of black liquid. "Holy Image Comics! This is the mother lode of Ink! I wish I had this much," Yoshi said.

"Why? We receive exactly what the specs of our experiments require. Or so I thought." Elle searched Yoshi's face because of his odd response.

"Yeah, well, my plans were in flux, so I did not get very much up front. They inventory weekly and you need to account for it all. I might have spilled some of mine that I could not account for and was afraid to ask for more," Yoshi explained it all much too fast.

"Spilled some? Really?" Yoshi simply nodded and Elle thought for the first time he might be lying to her. Rather than probe, she continued with her plan. "My original goal was to introduce the solution via an IV drip overnight during a subject's sleep cycles and then wake them while they are deeply medicated. But given our current circumstances? I think to get lucid while awake, we simply need to take a shit-ton of this stuff."

Elle grabbed a nearby injector and showed it off. Yoshi looked as happy as Elle looked nervous.

CHAPTER 14

G illian poured a second cup of coffee. Colt remained frozen on the big screen in her conference room office. The young man was full of himself. It showed through in his tape and lined up with his casual sexist comments in the auditorium. But he also carried his own demons. Apparently, everyone in Trager Industries did. After having watched his video, Gillian went to the coffeemaker for round two. She stirred coffee while thinking about the diverse group unified by a common element. Fear.

When Mitch escorted her back after their noodles (only to vanish quickly off to work on some top-secret project) he described more potential benefits of the fear element. It had never occurred to Gillian that a single medication could serve multiple purposes. But she had recently read an article that proposed people would someday have medications tailored to their own DNA.

That made sense because common medicines that worked for some did nothing for others. In the new scenario, sick people could get individualized treatment. The medicine at Trager seemed to fall into such a category. Induce fear in some, reduce it for others. All to mitigate anxiety or strengthen one's resolve to face a daunting task.

The milk industry had already diversified, why not the biopharmaceutical industry? Trager Chemicals (or Jimmy) stocked the office with every type of milk imaginable in a dorm style fridge. The choices included her preference—oat milk. A top for every pot in the dairy field. Why not for drugs?

She added a splash to her cup along with two sugar substitute packets. As a reporter, she was adept at mainlining coffee. But Seattle was renowned for its superior brews. Maybe the strength of their coffee explained her edginess. Gillian felt as if on a sixth cup. But in true coffee addict fashion, she prepped a fresh cup.

Gillian had minimal vices. Her world revolved around the written word, and for that reason she lived out other people's vices through words on the page. She frequently interviewed people who lived lives much different from her own. Gillian never shied from entering any situations where police were on scene. She would visit any neighborhoods with nothing more than a press pass for a shield. But to go to a bar on a Saturday night after work? Or a nightclub? No, thank you.

Besides, who was there to get crazy with? There were her coworkers, but she kept up some level of guard to maintain professional relationships. Gillian rode the coattails of her college friendships as long as she could, but they slowly faded over time as each person married. Gillian was estranged from her own family for years.

While attending college a mere three hours away from home, Gillian had limited travel options to travel home during breaks. Unable to afford a car or even a bus ticket during peak travel times, her only option was for her parents to drive and pick her up. Except they never did. Somehow, they could not be bothered to drive the three hours which became the basis for future therapy sessions.

Gillian never faulted her parents for not sending ticket money because they struggled financially. But to avoid the drive made little sense. They routinely made three-hour trips to go sightseeing or leaf peeping. Their refusal to pick her up made her feel unwanted and left her embarrassed around friends. Classmates wondered aloud why Gillian was always the last to leave campus.

College closed during those breaks, and the campus forbade students from staying in the dorms during the holidays. A friend offered Gillian an off-campus apartment to stay at during the break, but it was without heat. The combination of roomies shut off their electricity and gas to avoid extreme heating bills while on vacation. That left Gillian wrapped in blankets through a New England winter where temperatures dropped below zero every night. During the days, she parked herself in coffeeshops and nursed a solo cup of coffee for hours to enjoy the heat.

The long, cold winter months during what should have been the most exciting years of her life taught her an important lesson. Never count on anyone to look out for you. Not even family. There it was. The source of her edginess. She had not thought of those troubling days for years. Gillian owned her own home with heating available in a climate that rarely required it. Los Angeles was a weather oasis compared to where she attended college.

Gillian finished stirring and sipped. Though an unfamiliar brand, the coffee was spectacular. She sipped again. The warm liquid was as comforting as it was tasty. Then she spilled.

Just a tiny slip, enough for her to instinctively leap to protect her clothes. The splash landed on a carpet wisely designed to camouflage such drops. A spill was unlike her and resulted from something else uncharacteristic. Her hands shook.

Too much, or too strong. Caffeine alone explained the hand tremors, but there was more to put her on edge. She had about a dozen people to interview over the course of only a few days. That would not give her much time with any of the subjects. But the Monday deadline had her concerned. She had to get Doctor Trager to commit to an interview no later than Sunday night.

When Mitch dropped her back at the office, he suggested he would not see her for the duration of the weekend. Despite her initial reasons for visiting the island, Gillian had some new questions to ask when she finally got his ear again.

The first question would be what his project was. Couched in secrecy, it left her curious. Then she would press him on the true reasons behind the financing cuts. A fear element appeared groundbreaking, so shutting off funding made no sense. Mitch hinted they were close to the financier's goal of weaponizing the product (a terrifying thought).

But not as terrifying a thought as the tape that brought her there in the first place. The voice on the tape. She wished to ask Mitch if he recognized it. Ask if he heard it that night. Except she did not hear it back then. There were so many people on the scene. Surely it was an officer responding to another officer's question. Except she saw no female officers that night. Gillian remembered standing out as the lone female. Who was the mystery woman? Did her voice come over an officer's radio? If so, where was the static?

Enough! Gillian shook her arms and hands out. Ridiculous, being so unnerved. Maybe it was being alone in such a big place. Except she was not. She had an entire staff on video ready to talk. That was it. She needed to get back to their stories, take her mind off the creepiness factor of the old sanitarium.

But first, heat. A carryover from those college days. Always at the back of her mind was the need to know her surroundings were safe. Safety included warmth. She found a temperature controller on one wall and slid the knob two degrees higher. Her fingers came away dirty. She rubbed them together and her fingertips turned black. She used a napkin from the coffee station to wipe the remnants away.

The doctor had turned the air back on. That had to be the cause. A reboot of the central air system. She worked in a similarly old newsroom. Nothing out of the ordinary there. They would suffer their own dirty particulates until maintenance finally changed filters. It was only a weekend. She would have to deal with it.

She sat down, prepped a pad and pen for notetaking, then pressed play on the next video. Raj appeared onscreen. She noticed him earlier in the lobby arguing with the security guard over something. She paid it no mind, too busy watching the entrance, awaiting Mitch's arrival.

Now Raj appeared on the TV, asking questions of the interviewer. The question-and-answer section was unintelligible because Raj was too far from the mic, but he appeared distrustful of the process. He finally took a seat. A lock of hair dropped over one eye with a bounce as he plopped into the chair. Raj wiped the hair away with practiced precision.

"Tell me about your father," the out of frame interviewer asked.

"Why would I want to do that?" Raj asked.

"Because in the pre-interview, you mentioned him repeatedly. He must hold great significance to you."

"What are you, a shrink?"

"No. A corporate recruiter."

"Right. Well, leave my so-called father out of this. It's easy to leave him out of things. Graduations, birthdays, sporting events."

"Are you sure your father has nothing to do with this?"

"Other than how he was not there to protect me when the thing happened? And that we would not have been there at all were my mother not left alone in America."

"Do you dislike America?"

"What? No. I fucking love this country. This country took better care of me than my absent pop. I can love India and love America as well. Combined, those experiences got me where I am now."

"But something frightens you, otherwise I would not be interviewing you. We have screened all the candidates that have made it this far. I see in your pre-interview…"

"I'm shooting my shot for a dream job if I can get past these weird questions. You are here. I am here. Stop looking at that piece of paper and talk to me like a human being."

"Does my reading your file make you uncomfortable?"

"No. It makes you look like a murkha."

"Sorry, I do not understand."

"A jerk."

"Okay, no more paperwork. I'm putting your file down. But it is difficult to ask pertinent questions without my notes," the interviewer said.

Raj leaned forward in his seat. "Look, do you want to hear about the witch or not?"

CHAPTER 15

Raj shivered while his mother dragged him through the mostly abandoned city. His discomfort arose less from the chilly night air and more from the scenery. Metal bars covered every window in sight for all the good it did. Many of the same windows had broken panes. Metal drop doors covered all the shop entrances on a street where businesses closed at sundown, except for a lone liquor store. Even that establishment had bars on the windows. Its half-lit neon sign advertised that they sold 'liq.' Two different crowds held court near the building. One a group of teens riding bicycles, the other men tossing dice in the alley.

The teens yelled crude remarks aimed at Raj's mother. Though Raj did not understand the words, he felt their weight. They meant harm. Raj's mother simply moved faster even as the teens circled closer.

Laughter erupted from the alley in between healthy bouts of trash talking. It sounded like a good time and Raj wished those older men noticed the younger ones hassling his mother. Maybe they would do something because Raj could not. Petite for his age, Raj regularly suffered beatings, wet-willies, and wedgies at school. His tormentors there were smaller than the kids on the bikes. Raj understood he stood no chance if the riders got more aggressive.

And they likely planned to. Raj's mom made a strange noise, an involuntary one that spilled forth from her throat signaling a worried concern. Raj's mom was dowdy compared to those of his friend's mothers, but her matronly appearance failed to dissuade the bikers, whose catcalls included one word Raj understood. Tits.

Raj's mom cinched her shawl tighter and walked faster, pulling Raj along. The disgusting word set Raj off. He wanted to fight despite the odds. But the teens amped up their movements on their bikes, making them appear more dangerous than they already were. The teens weaved back and forth like sharks.

Something about the way the boys pumped hard before rising high off the seats made the threat real. They were not only predators, but ones with all the time in the world. Police were nowhere to be found. And who could blame them? There were not enough shadows to disguise the dangers lurking in every direction.

An odor of piss emanated from a nearby alley, one without a dice game. Rats scurried about as if keeping a schedule. Someone had tagged most of the buildings, but not with the cool names of street artists (like those in the school restroom). These were all territory markers.

The catcalls grew closer. One boy swooped in a wide circle, pulling ahead of them. Raj's mom gripped Raj tighter and walked them to the other side of the street, as if that would work. Once they turned a corner, a strip mall came into view. The main draw of the run-down property was a bodega. Its closed pull-down door was covered in graffiti.

They had traveled far enough from the liquor store that they no longer heard the dice men. The isolation gave the boys renewed courage. The bikers circled Raj and his mom, hooting, and hollering, promising that his mom was about to have a good time.

Raj waited for his mom to yell back, but she only kept her head down and kept walking. Then the strangest thing happened. After passing the strip mall parking lot, the boys hit their brakes. Their mouths went as silent as their tires. His mother faced the boys and smiled a wide grin that surprised Raj. The boys looked at her and trembled.

No. Not at her. Past her. Raj followed the group's gaze to a house behind them where candles flickered in the window. The boys sped off into the night. Raj's mom led him up the small rickety staircase of the home and knocked. A woman answered the door. She was somewhere between seventy and five hundred years old. Raj could not tell. The two women exchanged greetings then they entered the warm and damp home.

Besides a crocheted shawl, Raj's mother wore traditional Indian clothes. It was somewhere in the folds of her Kurti that she pulled out a jar filled with liquid. An egg floated in whatever brine the jar held. The ancient woman took the jar and vanished through hanging beads that led to a kitchen. Once the beads settled, a hand thrust back through and a finger beckoned Raj's mother.

"You must not move, not even an inch," his mother said to Raj, crouching down to plead with him.

"Why? I don't want to stay here. Can I watch TV?"

Raj pointed to the floor model TV in the adjoining living room. It looked as old as the woman, which made it cool. Raj imagined it played only old monster movies in black and white.

"No. We are not guests here. We are customers."

"Customers of what?"

"Do not concern yourself. I am only looking out for us. Understand?"

Raj lied by nodding. His mother had that faraway look, which meant she was not talking to him, not really. She was talking to herself or about adult things he had yet to understand. His mother was superstitious, that much he knew.

Once his mother beaded herself into another universe, Raj took in the surroundings. Candles were the only source of lighting, but it served its purpose. In the living room with the cool TV (it had wooden legs and was as large as their dishwasher at home) bookshelves lined the walls. The odor of ancient pages rose above the scent of candles. It reminded Raj of libraries back in India.

From Raj's experience, old people's homes reeked heavily of curry. Though accustomed to the spice (it was his favorite), older people built such a tolerance they cooked with more of it than even Raj could take. Visiting an old person's home could result in burning eyes. And the aftermath of cooking could lead to a sour stomach as the heady scent lingered like over-sprayed cologne. The same spices in moderation, however, caused his stomach to gurgle with hunger every time, even if he already ate.

A single electric lightbulb in a home seemingly containing none, caught his gaze. The lone bulb showed through the window of a back door at the end of a long hallway that bisected the house. Two closed doors in the hallway likely led to a bathroom and bedroom.

The exterior light calmed Raj, serving as a totem, a sign of electricity that showed they still existed in the present day. The two women spoke in hushed tones beyond the beaded barrier. Unable to contain himself, Raj spread open a small section of beads to spy.

The old woman placed the jar on the table, opened it, and retrieved the egg. Brine soaked her arm like slime. Candles flickering off the liquid made it appear she was melting. The woman smacked the egg on the table. The heavy sound startled Raj, causing him to shake the beads. How could an egg sound like stone on stone? The woman opened the egg over the small white bowl. Acrid smoke rose from the eggshell and swirled around the woman's face. Something small and chunky dropped into the bowl.

Raj's mother turned her head away when the stench of sulfur mixed with eggnog filled the room. Raj scrunched his nose at the odoriferous onslaught. The woman bent down and retrieved something from the floor. (From within a cage?)

She retrieved two things: a live chicken, and a butcher's knife. The old woman swung the blade. It hit the counter with a thunderous thunk. The woman turned and aimed a rotting smile at Raj who became tangled in the beads. A feathered body fell off the counter and onto the floor.

The decapitated body ran!

The headless chicken bolted for the exit, straight toward Raj. He screamed and tossed the beads aside. He sensed his mother rising, yelling, trying to stop the bird from reaching him, but she failed. The fowl scrambled through the doorway, brushing past Raj's feet.

He figured the bird had the right idea. Run! While the bird sought the living room, Raj bolted down the hallway, toward the modern-day light bulb at the back. But as he neared the first door on his left, an arm reached out from within, grabbing at him.

Impossible. No way the woman could be that fast. How did she get ahead of him? He narrowly avoided the flailing limb and kept going. The youth picked up the pace, running through a hallway which seemed to stretch into oblivion the further he ran. But finally, the back door neared. And burst open on its own!

No, not on its own. The bruja opened it from outside. Again, how did she get ahead of him? She blocked the doorway, stopping him in his tracks. The old woman suddenly tilted to one side as if into a lean.

For a moment, Raj worried she suffered an attack of some sort the way she wavered to one side, up and down, her legs bending sideways at the knees.

Did the legs leave the ground? She continued to lean as if falling except the legs lifted from the ground even while she remained upright in the doorway. Once her feet were entirely off the floor, the woman's legs swung in a strange jerky movement. Her body rose slowly at first before accelerating until rising out of sight.

The legs bounced against the top of the doorframe as though the woman scaled the side of the house onto the roof. Raj raced out and glimpsed the woman's silhouette in the sky. A small woman crouched as if riding a broom and disappearing over the rooftop.

Raj's mother stepped through the back door and grabbed his arm, leading him away, across the mostly dirt lot and back to the city streets. Raj searched the sky as the dirty city beckoned. His mother's grip felt cold, and she refused to speak.

Her silence unnerved Raj. He searched the streets for the hoodlum teens on bicycles. They would be his new totem, the proof that he was back in the real world, in a place where brujas did not take to the skies on brooms. But the streets remained silent, there were no bullies to guide their way home.

CHAPTER 16

Amy opened a cabinet filled with baby food sized jars. Derrick stood by with an empty plastic tub that Amy filled with jars. With society's fixation on charcoal enhanced products, Derrick felt the jars looked ready for sale at any boutique beauty store. Once Amy filled his tub, she filled her own with jars from a different shelf. Once both had loaded up, she led Derrick to a nearby workstation where they unloaded the jars. Amy smiled warmly at her helper.

"Thank you. I can't tell you how much it means to me to have your help," Amy said while emptying her tub.

"No problem. Does Gwyneth Paltrow know she has a competitor?"

Amy laughed. Derrick examined one of the jars more closely. His batch had red dots on the tops of the jars, hers had green.

"Red, green, a stop start situation?"

"Precisely. Not going to lie, the start part worries me. I am ashamed to admit that I had no hesitancy over this experiment when I planned to test on strangers, but now that I am the test subject, my stomach is doing flip-flops. Have you experimented with this stuff before?"

Derrick shook his head. "Just say no to drugs."

"I have. Once. Just a taste."

"Like when cooking a meal?"

"Yeah, let's use that analogy."

"And?"

"Not good, Derrick. Not good at all. This stuff works. This is extremely effective medication."

"Medication, is that what we are calling it?"

"Yes. A topical treatment. Not all medicine comes in pill form, you know that."

"Many of the Biggest scams out there are topical. If developers label it as a cream versus medication it allows them to avoid regulation. People can put anything in creams and such and call it a cure all. Snake oil comes to mind."

"Wow. Someone is biased against what form medicine takes. Vaccinations or nothing? Or is it pills only for you? How about cough medicine? Do liquids pass your scrutiny? Originally you had a plan, what form was your medicine going to take?"

Derrick eyed Amy. The woman was brilliant. He enjoyed their occasional talks in the time they worked at Trager together. Her serious demeanor aligned with his own. The word poised came to mind. She seemed trustworthy, but to tell her everything? Nah.

Derrick shrugged. "Trade secret. Can't say a word. Patent pending."

"A mysterious man. I like it."

Derrick glanced around the room. "It does not seem real."

"What?"

"That they shut us down. We could have helped so many people. Why cease operations when we were so close to significant achievements?"

Amy adjusted her glasses and stepped away from the table. "I have some idea. Did you know I won my local science fair in ninth grade?"

"Sure. I am so enamored of you that I followed your socials all the way back to when you were thirteen," Derrick said.

"Smartass. And don't knock Myspace, I had a killer page. Point is my project went on to states. *Digital Photography Filters Recalibrated for Imaging Diagnosis of Populations in Impoverished Communities.* That was my project's title. Did you grow up poor?"

Derrick took a breath and crossed his arms. His breath hitched before shaking his head. "Poor? No. Dad was the head of a tech startup. He had madness money."

"You mean mad money?"

"Yeah, sure," Derrick said.

Amy removed her glasses, set them on the table. "Showing my age, but the iPhone was not quite a thing yet when I created my science experiment. But digital cameras were. I was an avid photographer and a science nerd. From a young age, everything about life excited me. I had a thirst for knowledge. What I loved about digital cameras was their ability to manipulate images."

"I am only a few years behind you and share a similar fascination with digital. I have often pondered the dichotomy of digital. On one hand, it can last forever, but on the other, how often has someone manipulated the original file? How far removed is it from the original creation? Any changes would be invisible. If we extend the same process to humanity, the advancements in plastic surgery may reach the point where what God created may be lost to that which man created." Derrick was on a roll, excited, in his element, but realizing his tangent, he steered the conversation back. "But as for photography, I spent my youth trying to get photos with myself and certain girls."

"Player," Amy said. "Filters fascinated me, and I quickly learned how some highlighted people's skin flaws. Armed with that knowledge, I tested whether digital cameras could identify skin cancer."

"Wow. Using digital cameras? Brilliant. What are you doing here?"

Amy tilted her head slightly, unnoticeable to most, but not to Derrick who spent his life trying to read body language and facial expressions. His suggestion that she was bigger than her current job offended her. Derrick had not meant to, after all they had the same job. Excitement over her youthful ingenuity got the best of him. He should have simply said she was brilliant and left it at that. Derrick fought the urge to apologize but he learned long ago that groveling after social miscues made things more awkward.

"I am slumming with the best of them here I guess," Amy said.

It took Derrick a moment to realize Amy had made a joke. He laughed. Probably too hard. Laughter was not his thing. Derrick hated being in his head. He made calculations and deductions all in the time Amy took a breath. She continued while he tried to shut off his brain.

"If my science project worked back then it would have helped a lot of people. Digital cameras are cheap. Even the most impoverished communities could screen residents. Spotting skin cancer early is key to beating that disease. Certain big name medical and pharmaceutical companies learned of my project."

Derrick leaned against the counter, drawn in. "What did they do with the information?"

"They sought ways to monetize it. Even if they could diagnose people, was there a way to make money if patients were uninsured? They could not. And for that reason, they bailed on the project. That is my point. Because of Doctor Trager's inability to mass produce a weaponized aerosol or gas version, or his refusal to do so, my guess is the higher-ups lost patience."

"Seriously? With so many of us is working on different treatments for fear, there must be multiple revenue streams that would pay off. The investors are horribly short-sighted. Look at this place. We are wandering the halls of potential modern miracles. I sometimes roam the halls of the closed wing which is like a fossil preserved in amber. It is a place where patients suffered abject horrors. Sad because many of the patients were as likely misunderstood as they were afflicted by madness."

"You appear fixated on duality," Amy said.

Now Derrick tilted his head. Did he feel insulted? That was unlike him, but her intelligence made him more invested in her words than the average person. Such judgement was a flaw of his character. A mechanic performed tasks Derrick might never understand without further study. Why did he not attribute intelligence to mechanics in the same way he did to people in lab coats? There Derrick was again, in his head where all the guilt and doubt lived.

Amy waited for an answer. Like a filter identifying skin cancer, Amy seemed able to spot hidden things as well. Things inside him. She understood him too well.

"Interesting observation deserving of introspection. I never noticed before."

"Sometimes we cannot see the forest if we are the trees."

"I stayed behind not for my own glory. I did so because I understand what is at stake. The innovations happening in this once bleak medical facility offer the chance to provide help for so many. Imagine how many lives we could change for the better. We only need one scientist to succeed, one project to be deemed financially viable, for the rest of us to stay. The place will reopen, and all will be as before. I want to finish my work. If that means helping you succeed first, then that is exactly what I will do."

"Thank you, Derrick."

Amy moved to a microscope. As she leaned into the device, he realized he had yet to learn what the woman planned to do. He was a lab assistant in a foreign lab where he did not speak the language. Until receiving instructions, all he could do was twiddle his thumbs.

What did twiddling thumbs mean? Derrick understood the phrase but did not know how to twiddle a thumb, not to mention what twiddle meant. If their cellphones worked, he would have looked it up on the spot. *Mechanics probably know how to twiddle thumbs,* Derrick thought and felt bad once again for earlier denigrating the common man. Ugh, in his head again.

Desperate to change the subject in his mind, Derrick wandered the lab, looking for clues, hoping to find answers rather than simply ask what they were about to do. He approached another metal cabinet. At his height, he noticed the dirty top of the cabinet. Unnoticeable to those shorter than him. He swiped a finger which came away black. Experiments were to be performed in sterile environments. Circumstances changed all that. They were half-assing everything.

Once Derrick opened the cabinet, all became clear. Rows and rows of much larger jars lined the shelves. Now was the perfect time to ask Amy what she planned. He walked a jar over and tapped her on the shoulder. She leaped to her feet and shrieked.

Inside the jar, a massive spider attacked the glass, hoping to get to the woman. Amy scrambled back, knocking over the chair. Derrick made things worse when he thrust the jar in her face while reaching out to help her.

Amy froze in place, staring at the jar in Derrick's hands. A splash sounded. Then a puddle grew at her feet as Amy wet herself where she stood.

CHAPTER 17

Something was wrong. Quinn examined her shaking hands. The tremors made no sense because she was not only accustomed to the effects of Ink but it excited her. She loved the discreet meetings with Yoshi, her powder snorting bud. She considered him safe company because of his infatuation with Elle. Never once had he made an awkward pass, not even when the drug's effects visibly turned her on and she got flirty. Quinn considered Ink non-addictive fun. Well, the studies were not out on that yet, but Quinn had not tried to take any home with her. She did not share the drug with outside of work friends. Not that she had many.

Done in the light of day, she thoroughly enjoyed the nose powdering. But hand tremors were new and her inability to stop the low-level shaking made her wonder whether she took too much. Maybe she and Yoshi should have stopped a bit sooner. Weird unidentifiable noises echoed everywhere. A brewing storm outside had already made the room grow prematurely dark. Seattle was notoriously cloudy and the day was fading fast.

It even appeared as if the clouds outside had moved inside. A layer of black mist floated near the ceiling. Stupid. It was in her nature to seek darkness even in its absence. Not that people around her would know that about her. Most considered her a bright but unserious individual. Quinn embraced such impressions. When not wallowing in life's heaviness, she could be a fluffernutter. Everyone had two sides, and she was no exception. Quinn sought lightness and fun where she could because of how much time she hid from darkness. Literally and figuratively. One she could manage, the other she could not.

Tiny sprinkles of rain pattered against the lab window. The glass was a lifeline in the event of power outages. They were on a ferry schedule so the job never allowed them to stay past sunset even if they wished to. That meant the window always kept her lab partially sunlit. Until today. The last vestiges of sunlight caved into the maws of the oncoming night. Any power failure now would thrust her into darkness. Though the lights in her lab remained on, electricity in the old space was fickle. The building was old, maintenance staff were already back in Seattle.

Night also meant time to consider sleeping arrangements. It would have to be alone (unless Mercedette was finally agreeable to a little romp.) The things in the dark only came around when Quinn was alone. A partner in bed made sleep easier. And the part leading to sleep was so much more fun. But she had no partners on the island.

It was likely the thought of sleeping in the asylum that had her on edge. After all, the drug itself had been nothing but fun since day one. A small dose of the fear element in its purest form was terrifying. It shook her knees with terror and created visions of things that should not exist. But the rush never subjected her to the creatures in the dark. Had it done so, she would have ceased using Ink immediately, but Ink proved more entertaining than frightening. Yoshi once turned into a full-fledged vampire with double rows of sharp teeth, pointed ears and a snout. That was cool and exciting.

An unexpected side effect of the drug was how it turned her on. Losing control, letting go, it did something primal. She longed for sex when she took the drug. Left on her own, her choices of women were specific. She had a type, or at least needed to feel a vibe. While on the drug, she was less selective. It was about an urge, a sudden rush that could be enhanced with good old carnal fun behind it which excluded Yoshi despite how good a friend he was.

Now, as she watched her hands dance a jig, she felt all the symptoms with no drug behind it. Hand tremors? Check. Desire to get a groove on with someone? Also check. Quinn heard of LSD causing flashbacks. The fear element was new enough that they had yet to identify all side effects. They would identify most during human trials. For some reason Quinn felt as though she had recently done a line.

Mercedette was a floor below and, given their current weekend situation, was possibly available. It thrilled Quinn to think of visiting and flirting with the object of her affection. Their circumstances at their workplace had changed. Sleepovers would be a thing. Did anyone want to sleep in the asylum alone? Even the elusive mad scientist Mercedette? There was one way to find out. Glass front cabinets lined one wall of her lab. Inside several of the cabinets she kept baseball sized plastic balls.

Quinn opened a nearby cabinet, grabbed one, and headed to the door. She hit a button and small LED lights came to life, circling the circumference of the orb. She rolled it into the hall where it triggered the motion sensor lights. Quinn stepped out and retrieved the kid's toy that served a very adult purpose. It kept her free of shadows. She headed for the stairs. The lights in the stairwell came on with a hand wave, so she held the ball, ready to use it in the next dark corridor. She descended to Mercedette's floor.

Despite Mercedette's anti-social tendencies, Quinn often barged in to see if Mercedette wanted anything from the cafeteria. It was the polite thing to do since they were wing mates. It took a long time for

Quinn to realize she always visited Mercedette. Never once did her neighbor visit her. It stung when Quinn visited the cafeteria once and found Mercedette there. Apparently, it never occurred to the woman to return the favor. Deep down, Quinn understood Mercedette had no interest in her. Moments like that made it clear.

Yet Quinn longed for the woman. There was at least one competitor for the woman's affections. Jimmy routinely hovered around Mercedette and there was talk of a torrid affair between the two. Quinn was perhaps barking up the wrong tree. But additional gossip labelled Mercedette pansexual, so there was that.

Fantasy. It was all fantasy. Quinn had the hots for those unavailable. Plain. Simple. It happened to the best of people. Who did not have crushes on teachers, professors, or people of authority from time to time? Somehow Mercedette fell into all three categories in Quinn's mind despite them being peers. After emerging from the stairwell, Quinn rolled the ball to trigger the lights, picked it up, and walked to Mercedette's lab.

Quinn threw Mercedette's door open and gasped. Naked men and women cavorted throughout the room. More accurately, across the top of the room, on immense screens lining the lab's perimeter. Quinn noticed the screens in past visits, but they were never on. Now images of mostly naked males and females pranced about in high-definition glory.

The images created an erotic visual stew. A blend of lingerie and cosmetic ads, reality TV, and Pornhub clips. Quinn recognized more of the source material than she was comfortable with. The audio itself was also enticing but did not line up with the video. Speakers blasted a blend of ASMR and carnal moaning.

Quinn looked away from the ceiling and caught something more stimulating. Mercedette moved about the lab, wearing only a sports bra and panties. Quinn gasped, stunned by the woman's beauty. The Latina woman was always hidden behind a coat or at least skirts and blouses. The scientist noticed the intruder.

"I'm not hungry," Mercedette said.

"What?" Flustered, it took Quinn a moment to remember their routine. "Oh. Yes." *I am, though*, she thought. "That's not why I am here. What is all this?"

"Visual and audio stimuli. Soon I will transition to a VR experience."

Mercedette gestured to the spa style chair in the center of the room. A medical tray sat stationed alongside the chair. The setup looked like a spa experience from an overpriced resort. A VR headset rested atop the tray, along with a skullcap that Quinn recognized as a neural net. High tech. A metal pole connected the chair to the floor, which gave it the illusion of floating. The chair's fabric looked like memory foam and rested in a recline.

"A neural net? What is all this stuff?"

"Test subject has taken sexual stimulant enhancers. Medical grade, not available to the public. While still under review, they are proving highly effective," Mercedette said.

Quinn noted the pills nearby and read the packaging. Her eyes grew wide at the implications. Mercedette approached Quinn and yanked the pills away. They brushed against one another and Mercedette gasped.

"Please do not touch things in my lab," Mercedette said.

The odd way that Mercedette mentioned testing on a subject finally sank in for Quinn. "Subject? We're testing on ourselves!"

"Was that not clear?"

"But..."

Quinn looked up, overwhelmed by the sensory overload. The entire thing sank in. Mercedette appeared more robotic than normal. Now Quinn understood why. Mercedette fought to maintain control after juicing up her libido. Mercedette gripped the edge of a nearby chair.

"Your presence is becoming problematic," Mercedette said.

"How can you do this to yourself?"

"I need to know if I can stop this in its tracks. The skull cap will partially image my brain. The sexual arousal center concentrates in the hypothalamus. Once the scan shows that portion fully in the red, I will expose myself to the deterrent. I need to learn whether my formula can immediately stop desire in its tracks and determine how quickly t transform that sexual energy into desperate fear."

"Flee or fuck? Those are the options?" Quinn asked, stunned.

Mercedette gripped the chair tighter and nodded. "As mentioned, your presence is interfering with my work. Unless you wish to stay. To help me. I am warming to the idea."

Mercedette looked at Quinn the way Quinn always fantasized about. Hungry. Mercedette broke into a sweat. The woman was battling for control. Doctor Trager had warned everyone off from Mercedette's lab. Quinn did not understand then but understood perfectly now.

Quinn had long fantasized about the woman and, mere moments ago, had hoped for a tryst. Now the moment had arrived. Mercedette was not asking only for help with an experiment, but something more. Quinn knew an invitation when she heard one. It was mostly in the eye contact. Mercedette held the gaze, awaiting an answer. There was only one answer to such an invitation. One obvious, unequivocal answer.

"Hell, no. This is crazy. I want no part of it. This is far from okay. Manipulating desire?"

Mercedette turned away from Quinn, seemingly angry. "But we can test on others? That is the line which makes it ethical? Experiment on innocent subjects, make them do things? Dirty, awful things. But not ourselves? As scientists, are we to lord over others? Make others do that which we do not dare? When did the word scientist become synonymous with cult leader?"

"Cult leader?"

Mercedette's hair had spread when she turned on Quinn. The woman was wild, not a person of science, but something else. An individual wrestling her demons while experiencing the effects of whatever drugs were in her system. Quinn wanted to help but felt unequipped.

"Sorry. I cannot be any part of this," Quinn said. "And your experiment has a major flaw. You are trying to stop attackers? That is about power, not sex. Unless you have it in that brilliant brain of yours to harm people, you are not the best test subject. It is not about stopping sexual arousal. One has nothing to do with the other."

Mercedette stormed forward, pressing up against Quinn while pointing past her, gesturing to the exit. "Out! Get out!"

Quinn exited into the hall, leaving behind a woman damaged by a mysterious past. The lights in the corridor remained on. For that, Quinn was grateful. Quinn rubbed her face and took a deep breath. Out of control. Quinn felt out of control. Mercedette was as well, but Mercedette had a reason. Whatever those pills did, they affected the woman in a dangerous manner. Quinn approached the stairwell door. It burst open in her face.

"Shit donkeys!" Quinn screamed.

"I'm sorry. Did I scare you?" Gillian asked, emerging from the stairwell.

"No, I use that phrase as a matter of course. Yes. I'm on edge already, and then you pop out of nowhere."

"Sorry. I was hoping to interview you. I went to your lab. You were gone but lights were on in the corridor and you did not pass me. I followed the trail of already turned on lights. It led me here. I was told to steer clear of Mercedette though."

"That is great advice," Quinn said, looking back at the woman's lab. Light from the flashing images on the screens leaked through the door's window. "I should have taken it. We should talk somewhere else."

Gillian nodded, and Quinn led the reporter to the stairwell. Quinn explained her encounter with Mercedette as they climbed the stairs. Gillian reacted much as Quinn had, with shocked revulsion. But as they talked through it, Quinn realized Mercedette was correct about one thing. If Mercedette did not test on herself, it would be someone else. Was that fair? Was it okay to subject those not in lab coats? She kept those thoughts from her stairwell buddy.

The two women emerged from the stairwell to a darkened hallway. Quinn hit the button on her ball then rolled it until lights flickered on. Gillian watched with amusement.

"Neat trick," Gillian said.

"They placed the sensors in this wing poorly. One must walk quite far down the hall before they kick in. I improvised a solution."

The pair caught up to the ball just outside Quinn's lab. Quinn lifted the ball with a swift motion, upsetting the low-lying dusty air which spun in a dark cyclone before vanishing. They entered the lab. Quinn opened a chiller cabinet that contained bottles of the fear element alongside some other bottles. Quinn grabbed one out and offered it to the reporter.

"Yoo-hoo?"

"No thanks. I'll stick with coffee. And probably need to stop where I am at. I am rather jumpy, likely not used to such strong caffeine."

Quinn shrugged, then grabbed a tube of almonds from a nearby snack shelf. She leaped onto the edge of a table, legs swinging. She shook the bottle, popped the top, and took a swig. *Yeah, that's the stuff.*

"Okay. Ask away," Quinn said.

"First, are you aware that Doctor Trager has given me access to all of your records, including the interviews required to land the job?" Gillian asked.

"No. Weird, but I guess I get it."

"You do? You have no problem with it?"

"Have you watched my interview?" Gillian shook her head. "Nyctophobia. Fear of the dark. Clinically diagnosed at a young age. Big whoop, right? Mundane compared to others here."

"I would not say that."

"Then you haven't watched Mercedette's file?"

"Not yet."

"Please give me the deets after that one. I would love to know where her behavior originates from. A little inside scoop."

"I can't do that. Despite my access to the files they serve as background for my work. I would not divulge such personal details without permission. And if I needed to divulge anyway for purposes of the story, it would be anonymously unless the individual granted me permission to use their name alongside the information. If Mercedette chooses not to share, then I will not betray her right to privacy. She does not strike me as the agreeable type."

"Lame. Fine, I'll read it as a blind item, not too hard to figure out." Quinn rolled her eyes. "If Mitch gave you access, it's because he..." A whir interrupted Quinn's thoughts. She eyed the camera in the corner. Had it moved? Zoomed? Gillian followed Quinn's gaze. Quinn shook her head to signify it was nothing. The young woman continued her train of thought. "Mitch knows results might save us. You appear focused on ethics while we are all focused on results."

"Ethics?"

"Like a commitment to keep files privileged. Though noble, you work under criteria that none of us are limited to this weekend."

"Are you suggesting we barge back in on Mercedette? Ignore whatever concerns you had over her? Is she the actual story?" Gillian raised her eyebrows.

"Dang. Smack my argument down. Okay, yes, there are still lines that we should draw on a professional level, but there is no need to hold to every rule of our occupations. What I am trying to say is if you focus on only ethics violations this weekend, you might miss the bigger story."

"There is no story yet. While I have you, tell me your goal. What do you hope to achieve?"

"This." Quinn pulled an almond from the single serve packaging. "Amygdala. The word means almond, which is appropriate. It is an almond sized organ at the base of the brain which stores awareness of life's dangers based on prior experience. It is the part of the brain which starts the fight-or-flight instinct."

"And what do you hope to do?"

Quinn squeezed the almond between her fingers. "I intend to crush it." She pressed harder. The almond shot out, flying across the room where it pinged off a chair. "Or at least ricochet it around a room."

The offhand joke caused Gillian to laugh but Quinn had not intended for the little nut to fly from her grip. It shot from her hands because she could not control them. The tremors lingered which meant she and Yoshi had taken too much Ink earlier. Yet somehow, she wanted more. She did not suppose the reporter would wish to partake. Quinn tried to conceal the quiver in her voice.

"My intention is to dampen that instinct into non-existence."

"Don't we need that? Is not that an important part of our DNA?"

"Absolutely, but not needed during sleep, mostly. Fires or intruders at night are cause for concern, and a portion of the brain remains on alert even while sleeping. But my product will not keep people asleep, it will simply allow them to sleep in the first place by removing fear of the dark. Mileage may vary."

Another joke to cover an outright tremble in her voice. Quinn was talking about the dark. She knew what lingered there. She knew what hid there. Quinn desperately needed her own cure.

"How do you intend to accomplish such a thing?"

"A bit of reverse engineering with a variant that minimizes fear versus inducing it. Unlike many here, I am a perfect test subject. After setting up a makeshift bed, I'll remain still until the lights turn off. If I cannot handle the dark, I will wave my arms to trigger them back on. From there I can up the dosage continuously until I no longer need to wave hands. That is how I will know it works."

"Interesting. Allow me to get out of your way so you can start. I wish you well. Good luck."

Gillian exited the room. Quinn examined her hands again. The tremors had worsened, along with the nagging fear tickling the back of her brain. It made no sense but would serve her experiment well. Earlier she fantasized about finding a bed buddy, but minus an assistant participating in her experiment, Quinn needed to sleep alone. That was likely part of her extra dose of nerves. The decelerator medication would hopefully work its magic.

She opened a drawer and pulled out a generic pill bottle (*hey kids, our drugs look official!*). The label read: *fear element deceleration*. The company would eventually give it an unpronounceable name. That was how the pharmaceutical industry worked. Make it hard to pronounce and harder to afford.

Though dark out, it was not late enough to sleep. And since Quinn was inexplicably scared, she decided she might as well continue her voyage on the fright train before throwing it all into reverse. She grabbed a vial of the powder, dusted some across the table and snorted. She shot her head back with a gasp. Monsters danced in every corner of the room. Even Yoshi the vampire made an unexpected appearance despite his being elsewhere in the building. She shuddered as much with excitement as fear.

A momentary burst. Intense, but quick. The world would return to normal soon enough. She took in the images for what they were. None as scary as what waited in the dark. But something felt wrong, more intense than usual. She waited for the initial buzz to die down but it did not. If anything, it Increased.

Yoshi the vampire attacked. How dare he! She hit the ground and came up laughing, embarrassed over having leapt away from a non-existent drug buddy. But then something unprecedented happened in slow motion. Darkness crept in along the peripheral of her vision. Shadows closed in. Never once had the fun little drug induced her own phobia. At least not until now.

"No, no, no!" Quinn yelled.

But it was too late. With a thump of defeated electricity, all the lights turned off. The world went dark.

CHAPTER 18

"**N**o, no, no, No!"

Complete darkness. Quinn suffered through a power outage her first week on the job. Too many new employees setting up labs all at once overwhelmed the system. When it happened, she freaked out with a capital F despite sunlight shining through her window. The outage made her fearful it would happen again. What if it occurred while in an elevator, restroom, or anywhere else where ambient light was scarce? Once the power returned that day, Quinn stormed into Mitch's office to complain.

Her reaction was so over the top she feared Doctor Trager might fire her, but she let it rip anyway. Midway through listing all the reasons that power failures were amateur hour, Quinn finally realized she was yelling at her boss. He took it in stride and encouraged the articulation of her phobia. Strange reaction she thought then, but it made sense later when she learned everyone on board the S.S. Trager Chemicals Company suffered from their own issues. After the incident, Quinn set up contingency plans, which included purchasing LED balls.

But how to find the balls in the dark? This was the first time the power failed after sunset. Normally she kept her cellphone (and its flashlight) nearby, but with no service on the island she had set it down somewhere in her lab. As well as the ball she used on her way back to the lab. They were such a routine part of her life that she did not remember where she set it down when she returned with Gillian. Not that she would find it in the dark anyway without knowing exactly where she stood in the room.

"Blink, don't think," she said. "Blink, don't think."

She repeated a childhood mantra from the child psychiatrist who treated her phobia. The doctor reminded Quinn that all humans blinked, so technically, for nanoseconds at a time, everyone was in the dark. The argument was sound. Never had the things in the dark appeared in the time it took her to blink.

Quinn found some comfort in the theory. (Theories carried weight with her even as a child. She was likely always fated to become a scientist.) Under the doctor's care, Quinn developed a mantra which she carried into adulthood.

"Blink don't think. Blink don't think," she said and blindly waved arms.

She sought an anchor in the room, something that could orient her. A sudden collision of hip against a counter's ledge gave her hope. Glass front cabinets hung above the counter and somewhere in there she had some balls. She just needed to find them blind.

Ting. Ping. Ting.

Something sounded in the exposed ventilation ducts lining the ceiling. When she first moved in, she thought the exposed pipes gave the lab a steampunk look. But the initial charm gave way to fear as something crawled through the overhead expanse. Probably a rat.

"Blink don't think. Blink don't think. Blink, don't think."

She returned to the task at hand, seeking the safety of the LED lights. The first cabinet contained no orb. She cursed when her hip hit the ledge again. Despite having oriented herself Quinn still stumbled blindly. She moved to the next cabinet.

Ting. Ping. Ting.

What was in the ducts? Multiple rats, Quinn decided but kept searching. The third cabinet proved a charm. It contained a ball, but like the almond earlier, it rocketed from her grip, bouncing somewhere across the room.

"No, no, no!"

Her entire body shook, signaling that she had made the leap to that almond sized lobe in her brain. Once that portion took over, she would ride a wave of instinct. Not much of a fighter, to flee would be the move. Unwise in a place filled with hidden obstacles but fear drove the car now. Once she got moving, she would not stop until something forced her to.

She needed out! Not from the lab but from the dark. Without illumination, the swimmers would appear soon. Terrifying things, but as bad as they were, they were only heralds. They paved the way for the Whispering Man. She tried to block the memory. It had been a long time since an encounter. She controlled her environment as an adult and minimized their ability to find her. But now she was trapped in their world. Quinn roared hoping to establish a sense of strength. It failed.

Ting. Ping. Ting.

"Stop! Please stop! What is that?" Quinn spun, looking up toward the air ducts.

A foolish move. Investigating the vents was pointless because she could not see the piping anyway. Worse, the attempt to find the source of the scraping caused her to lose contact with the counter that served as a GPS. She was a woman at sea with nothing mooring her to land. The night was as vast as the ocean in the Puget Sound.

Ting. Ping. Ting.

The sound reoriented her. She turned to face the cabinets and shrieked. Blazing red eyes reflected off the cabinet's glass front. A thing from the dark! It was the source of the pinging metal. Claws versus metal would create such a sound. And where the things went, the Whispering Man followed.

Stealth was a limited option for the things in the dark as their eyes blazed like fire. Despite the reflection of glowing eyes, the presence of a creature inside the air ducts made little sense. They were massive beings. But perhaps they started small and grew after feeding on their victim's fear.

Quinn wished not to feed the beast, but a scream built in her throat. She clasped her hands over her mouth, aware that any sound would only draw others out, and worse, would give her location away. Quinn's almond-shaped portion of brain decided it was time to flee.

The thought arrived too late. With concussive force, the vent system exploded. The thing dropped from above and landed in a crouch before rising to its full height. It towered above her. They were unsightly things, as abhorrent as they were frightening and harder to look away from than a car crash.

Its facial skin, if one could call it that, was made up of bone and fossilized rock. Eyes shimmered like burning coals within deep eye sockets on its oversized football shape head. Two cavities opened on either side of its head. If they served as ears, they were cavernous.

Its face skipped a nose, going straight from eyes to teeth. If the beast had a lower jaw, it remained hidden behind the curtain of oversized massive upper fangs. The sharp teeth appeared made of fossilized rock like its head (Or coral? Were they truly swimmers?), and extended from its upper lip down into points well past its beefy neck. Its teeth were sharper variants of walrus tusks.

Its bony arms stretched past its knees. The clawed hands were as sharp as its teeth. Sinewy strands of meat and fluttering tentacles made up the base of the thing's body below its torso. Wing bones extended from each shoulder rising high above the creature's head. They looked like skeletal remnants of angel wings, minus any feathers or piety. The wings' tips ended in sharp hooks. Fluttering insect setae covered its torso and shifted rhythmically as it moved. The fluttering made the creature appear as if it floated underwater.

Because it was, Quinn thought. They swam in the dark. The shadow realm was their ocean. She finally found her feet, ran, and tripped over a chair smashing her face against the floor. Quinn's teeth clacked painfully together. Pain would have to wait. She looked up from the ground. The beast now stood sideways, floating in mid-air. Darkness gave it freedom of movement.

Then it struck! One featherless wing tore through the air. With a fleshy thunk, the wing-bone impaled Quinn's shoulder, pinning her to the floor. Quinn spasmed in pain, fought to rise but could not. She knew what was coming. The thing would not kill her, at least not immediately. Its drool signified its hunger, its desire to finish her, to make of her a snack. Yet it did the bidding of another. A voice echoed through the overhead vents.

"One potato, two potato..." the voice whispered, but the metal amplified the words.

Quinn panicked. The Whispering Man was on his way! Worse, because she was not in bed, she was unable to hide under covers. With her good arm, she searched around the floor. The movement prompted fresh agony from her fileted shoulder. The pain of the puncture was like fire. She reached anyway.

"Three potato, four..." the voice whispered.

Quinn feared monsters from a young age. For that reason, her parents bought sheets of glow in the dark star stickers. Quinn applied them liberally around her room, but the glow only lasted so long. When they lost their strange white/green glow, she would hide under covers if still awake. Once the night extinguished the universe that was her room, the swimmers came.

It started with a creak from the closet door. Though silent during the day, the hinges announced the presence of visitors at night. Like clowns exiting a car, the creatures would emerge from her tiny closet.

Despite plentiful opportunities, the creatures never chomped on her with their nasty teeth. As hungry as they were (always drooling), they avoided making a meal of her. They served the Whispering Man. And there he was.

The Whispering Man peered down from within the mutilated vent. Unlike his monster heralds, the Whispering Man took human form, but was no less scary for it. Obscenely tall, with a gaunt, lanky frame, and wearing a bowler hat, the Whispering Man moved unnaturally, in fits and starts. He too was visible in the dark, but not because of fiery eyes (his were as dark as obsidian). What made him visible was the number of glowing stars covering his body. Glow-in-the-dark star stickers covered his face as well as parts of his hands, arms, ankles, and neck. The bowler hat sat midway down on his forehead. The stars filled his face just below the brim.

As a child, when Quinn first encountered the Whispering Man, he threatened to harm her parents if she said anything. For that reason, Quinn never told anyone about him, not even her therapist. Impossible to treat one who keeps secrets, but Quinn had no choice. There was only one thing that made the Whispering Man vanish. Turning on lights. No adults could help her as a child, only the wonderful hum of electricity or a sunrise could accomplish that.

The herald that had her pinned down shifted its stance which induced a new round of agony. The Whispering Man reached for Quinn from the ruptured air duct where he sat perched in the opening. His arm stretched, extending beyond human limits. It grew to ten feet, twelve, and would reach her soon.

That was new. Mercifully, she had not encountered the Whispering Man for years. Apparently, he had developed new terrifying abilities, confirming he was not human. Covering the entire stretched arm were glow-in-the dark stars. His hat remained firmly atop his head despite him looking down from a steep angle.

Quinn swung an arm across the floor, searching. She did not want the Whispering Man to touch her again. He took great glee in causing despair. The swimmer studied her as if entertained by her effort to escape. Its eyes reflected off something. The LED ball she dropped!

Wishing she could stretch like the Whispering Man, Quinn struggled until her fingertips touched it. Miraculously, the ball rolled toward her. She turned it on, and the beast vanished. Was that all it took? Was she in the clear?

Quinn gripped the ball so tight it hurt her hand. Not as much as her shoulder, though. She slowly turned to examine her surroundings. The orb's light provided a tiny cone of comfort, not enough to spot the room's borders, but it was something. She had created a rip current in their ocean. Her toy was a beacon, a buoy in the night.

She rose and ran into the hall. There, just beyond the reach of the orb, was another harbinger, the same red eyes, but dangling upside down from the ceiling like a bat. Its tentacles rippled as if swimming through opaque water. Its eyes cut through the murkiness.

The orb's light only reached so far. Beyond that, shadows ruled. It was their world; she was merely navigating through it. She had staged flashlights strategically throughout her lab, but it was too late. Quinn had already entered the corridor.

She placed her back against the wall to minimize her exposure. Meanwhile, the upside-down closet monster moved closer, treading dark instead of water. Quinn wondered if rolling the ball closer to the beast would make it vanish again, but she was not about to test her theory. *Leave that to other scientists. Thank you very much.*

She needed stairs. One floor down for an exit to the other wing. Two floors down to Mercedette's lab. The main wing had backup generators, so one floor it was. Get back to the main wing. But the monster blocked the nearest stairwell. That left the stairs at the opposite end of the hall. She ran for them, vaulting down the steps once there.

While Quinn never spoke of the Whispering Man to her therapist, she had mentioned the night swimmers. Her therapist had professionally scoffed at the idea. But night swimmers were real. Quinn nicknamed them that because of their fluid movements. With no feet touching the ground they technically floated but appeared to swim because of their fluctuating tentacles. They hunted children in the dark and trapped them until the bad man came.

Overhead, one of the swimmers gave chase, bursting through the door with such force that the twisted metal door rocketed past her, clanging on the railings as it fell to the first floor through the stairwell gap. Quinn put her pedal to the metal and escaped through the door on the next floor down.

And the world changed. Trager Chemicals had vanished. In its place was a familiar child's bedroom. Quinn gasped in a voice not her own. Well, not hers anymore. The gasp took the form of a stunned child. She knew every poster on the wall and the constellations built of glow stars on every wall and ceiling.

She glanced at a wall mirror in which the reflection showed a six-year-old. But how? She had little time to think. The desk lamp near the bed flickered, ready to go out. The pink bedspread served as a haven. If she stayed under the covers long enough, the bad things went away. The Whispering Man would still whisper, but the blanket acted as a shield.

In the past, (currently her present?) when the Whispering Man tired of his inability to draw her out, he usually faded away, returning to whatever hellscape he resided in. His servant monsters would follow. Except now a swimmer was somewhere at her rear.

Quinn ran and leaped, suddenly aware of how small she was. As she flew toward the bed, it dawned on her that she was always six, had never moved past that age. Technically, she was an adult but never moved beyond the fears birthed at that age. Being in the room brought everything back.

The light bulb popped when she landed on her bed in a bounce. On the upward trajectory, she yanked the top blanket free and slide beneath it on the way down, a magic trick of efficiency. She practiced it hundreds of times. The swimmer had been in the stairwell at Trager, but now she knew where it lurked. The closet.

Sure enough, hinges squeaked, the same ones that remained silent when opened in the light of day. Quinn sometimes wondered if it was not the hinges at all but merely the creatures making the sound to further terrify her. They were not stealthy beasts, they cared not for subtly. Scare the victim, find the victim, eat the victim was their goal.

And only the terrifying man overseeing them all kept them from satiating their hunger by feasting on children's bones. The closet door opened. Her L.E.D. ball? Where did it go? Maybe it remained in the present, inaccessible to her while she slipped into her own past.

Squishing tentacles made obscene sounds. Despite the lack of any water, the fluttering of their tentacles sounded moist.

She shivered and kept the covers over her head only to realize she missed the other blankets and had only covered herself with the comforter which was old and filled with holes. Her parents wanted to get rid of it, but she loved it. Now it betrayed her. The ratty comforter barely shielded her. Red eyes of multiple beasts appeared, forming a circle around her bed. She could see them through the worn fabric.

The beasts stood as sentries. She could not wish them away. Quinn understood what they waited for. A second creak as the bedroom door opened, followed by footfalls on the carpet. At that moment, she was six again mentally as well as physically. Doomed to experience that first time all over again.

That first night a thump from her closet startled her enough that she sought refuge under the covers. Before long, her bedroom door opened. She prayed it was her parents checking on her, but an unfamiliar lanky figure leaned next to her bed. The Whispering Man spoke. It was not her parents. A stranger stood in her room!

"One potato, two potato, three potato, four. If you raise your voice, I will bury your parents under the living room floor."

The words sent a chill through the already terrified girl. Quinn wanted to scream but worried the Whispering Man might hurt her parents. He spoke again.

"Five potato, six potato, seven potato, eight. You should have locked the door, but now it's too late."

Back then, six-year-old Quinn had to know the face of terror. As frightened as she was, she flipped the covers down, just for a second. There he stood, grinning through the glow-in-the-dark stars stuck all over his face. The bowler hat made him look like something from time gone by. She could not determine his age.

But a sudden breeze at her feet made her forget that horrific day and remember her horrible current situation. Though still in her childhood bedroom, she had returned to adult size which meant the comforter no longer comforted. It covered only neck to knees. The transition from youth to adult left her head and feet exposed.

A swimmer dangled upside down directly above her. Reaching down, it lifted her from the bed as if she weighed nothing. It lifted her past its own upside-down face. In its upturned position, the bony, spiked teeth pointed toward the ceiling. The night swimmer tilted its jaw forward at just the right angle, then dropped Quinn. The underside of her jaw caught the upturned teeth impaling her. Its lengthy fangs clacked against her own teeth in her mouth.

Though petite, Quinn felt every ounce of her weight while sliding down the impossibly long fangs. One jagged tooth pierced her tongue which brought pain far worse than biting the tongue on her own.

Only after she settled into place and dangled above the ground (where had the bed gone?) did blood finally spurt. It gushed around her mouth and jaw. She hung there kicking and flailing. Quinn coughed, trying to clear blood from her throat while struggling to breathe. Sparks of light danced in her vision as she fought to maintain consciousness.

Then, like a bullet striking her shoulder, another swimmer jabbed her good shoulder with a winged talon, tearing through her flesh with efficiency. The talon struck her from behind but exited through the front, a full impaling. Then a second wing bone pierced her other shoulder entering roughly through the hole of her previous wound. Quinn dangled limply, impaled at jaw and shoulders.

A door opened and slammed in the distance. The weight of the closing door suggested she was back at Trager. She was no longer in the bedroom if she ever was. The Whispering Man entered like so many times before. He was so tall that he looked down on her, even from her elevated position. Without saying a word, he studied her face. Then something novel occurred.

One of the many stars covering his face fell off. Then another, and another. More and more detached from his face. They became a cascade of falling stars. Some hit Quinn's face, but most fell off to either side. Some shot past like falling stars in a night sky. So many fell that it emulated the sensation of looking skyward during a snowstorm. Quinn felt as if she were flying. It was beautiful.

But there were only so many stars in the sky. The wave slowed and the Whispering Man turned away. She could not follow his movement because of her impalements. The man whispered in her ear.

"One potato, two potato, three potato, four. It is long past the time we redecorate the floor."

Quinn understood his intentions and shook her head the few inches her situation allowed. The wings at her back shuddered, a warming-up flap. The movement brought such agony that her voice froze, unable to scream. He desired her silence, for how else could she hear his whispers if she screamed? The Whispering Man stepped back into view and the stars were gone.

This was it. She would finally see the face that had tortured her since youth. Who was responsible for her lifetime of worry? Who kept her from living a normal life? She first glimpsed the bowler hat, then looked down at his face.

Her laughter erupted from somewhere she did not understand. The cackles rocked her body and magnified the pain in both shoulders. Her tongue wiggled around the tooth it was stuck on. She could not help it as laughter coursed through her even though it came out as snorting gargles.

Years of fearing a mystery man were suddenly answered. All became clear. The bowler hat sat atop a head alright, but not a normal one. The Whispering Man's face was blank, or more accurately shiny like her orbs. The face was rounded like a motorcycle helmet, but entirely mirrored. Below the bowler hat, the face that revealed itself was her own. In reflection. With the stars gone she could finally see her true tormentor, the one responsible for a lifetime of fears. The realization caused her to laugh uncontrollably.

"Five potato, six potato, seven potato, eight. You figured it out much too late!" The Whispering Man whispered.

But the words were in her voice. The Whispering Man (woman?) raised arms like a music conductor. Her own face stared directly back at her, capped off by a bowler hat. The Whispering man acted as a music conductor, directing his swimmers as if they were an orchestra, ones playing instruments of pain. They performed their parts perfectly. When the Whispering Man waved his arms, the swimmers spread their wings wide.

A symphony of torn flesh and cracked bones harmonized alongside an all too brief scream that quickly turned into something once alive murmuring 'ugh.' The violent motion of spreading wings tore Quinn's body in half. A sludge of gore slid from between the body halves and squished into piles on the floor. With a shake of the wings designed to free their load, the twin pieces of what used to be Quinn dropped into the bloody mess on the floor.

Her head remained attached to the upside-down swimmer's teeth. But with a spit, Quinn's head joined the fleshy puzzle pieces on the floor. Then the Whispering Man's face went blank once again, and he led the army of night swimmers away to terrify other victims.

CHAPTER 19

*S*tupid, *stupid, stupid,* Derrick thought as he mopped up his scientific partner's mess. Amy, she of the accidental pee, was in a nearby shower washing up. OSHA required labs using chemicals to have onsite emergency wash stations. Chemical exposure information sheets lined the wall just outside the shower stall. The chemicals they used were mostly benign. Exposure to the fear element could cause powerful LSD style effects (or so he heard), but chemical burns were non-existent. The company produced the drug off site and trucked it in.

Showers were most often used by employees to freshen up after workouts or pickup basketball games. Many kept sweats on site to change into for the gym. He hoped Amy had some because her clothes were soiled. Bummer how he charged in like a bull and frightened the poor woman.

Obviously, the spiders were her fear which was why she had them on site. The spiders were kept in mini terrariums hidden where she could not see them. Until Captain Bringdown sprang into action and made the woman who he respected above all others pee herself.

Derrick was over women romantically. A bad breakup left him devastated years earlier, and he had yet to move on. Did not wish to. He saw what happened to his parents and the science side of him decided his relationships would go as south as theirs, so why bother? But he missed female companionship, especially that of highly intelligent women. Amy fit the bill and he hoped by helping her he would make a good friend.

There was no ulterior motive. If he desired her as anything other than a friend, he would lean his head into the shower station housed at the rear of the lab. She was beautiful, period. Was sexy. Period. She was damn intelligent, and he was—not interested. That was likely why she felt comfortable around him. Little did she know he was a creep. Who else but he would put a speed bump on her experiment?

They should have been knee deep in work already, but Amy lost time because of his goof. Derrick mopped up her pee in a flash. The filthy water in the bucket revealed the floor had been covered in heavy grime. Derrick went the extra mile and mopped the entire floor. By the time he finished, the bucket had seen better days.

The dirtiness surprised Derrick. Labs were supposed to be sterile. He had considered his own lab clean, never noticed a dust or mold problem. Derrick considered suggesting they take the party back to his place, but he worried the suggestion would offend her. And it would mean more delay. No, he would keep his mouth shut.

They were all on the same ticking clock. Only one weekend's worth of work could make the difference between defunding and re-funding. Derrick hoped Amy or anyone else might make a breakthrough, no matter how small. Nothing had to be concrete, just promising enough to warrant further study.

The sudden closure made no sense. Unable to even begin to start testing on his project, all he could do was assist another scientist. His experiment was going to involve kids. Last he checked, there were no kids on the island. Even if he could assemble a test group of teens or pre-teens, he could not test on them until well after the adult human trials panned out.

It was appropriate that he wished to help children because thanks to his earlier actions he felt like one. Or a bumfuzzle. That was the word he and his D&D friends used to curse in the presence of parents, leaving adults none the wiser. The lingo served as a substitute for asshole. Goofy things like that made childhood fun, but the younger a person was, the greater their fears. While most of his colleagues worked on curing adult phobias, Derrick focused on a demographic mostly ignored. Kids.

Scientists generally focused on adult problems because that's where the money was. But kids needed help as well. Children with healthy families and a solid support system could likely weather any number of mental challenges and probably be okay. But what of shitty parents like his own? How many kids grew up like Derrick?

On paper, all looked swell. Wealthy parents? Check. Private schools? Check. The Jones' that everyone fought to keep up with? Check, they were that family. But protect your kid? Keep them safe? Nah, his parents were not down for that part of the job. They screwed him into existence before screwing over his peace of mind. All by age eleven. Yay!

Derrick fell on the reverse side of most scientists at Trager. Like Trix being for kids, he felt anxiety reducing medications should be available for kids as well. As for adults, he had a built-in bias. He believed adults should get over their issues. At a certain age people should no longer suffer phobias. A hypocritical thought because he clung to his childhood trauma like an old teddy bear.

He pushed the mop bucket back to its spot alongside the washbasin near the shower room. So much for his trustworthiness. Derrick noticed movement behind the distant shower curtain. The curtain was not fully drawn which left small gaps on each side. Derrick glimpsed Amy's ass through one opening. It was spectacular. He was no voyeur, but he called them as he saw them.

Guilt overcame Derrick. Not over ass glimpsing but over biases. It struck him that he was way off base with his beliefs that adults should man up against their phobias. What were adults if not grown children? Why shouldn't they still suffer fears over a variety pack of life's horrors? Amy was in a shower because he induced in her an uncontrolled bodily function. Humiliating for both. Did he wish to be there when she got out? Wouldn't she prefer a moment to gather herself, dry off, pretend things were normal?

For once, Derrick thought straight. Women needed their space, and he was happy to give it to her. Her ass was nice, but he was one, a king sized bumfuzzle. Derrick searched the lab for pen and paper and wrote a note: 'Quick trip to my lab. Back in five.'

Give her time. Let her return to the role of a professional. He would go, waste some time somewhere, and then return as if nothing happened. He wasn't hungry, at least for ramen. Then it hit him. Beer sounded better. He knew just where to go. But as he walked down the hall, he wondered why his eye twitched. Guilt or something more?

Fear could make eyes twitch; he knew that much from when his dad used to scream at him. He rubbed his eyes. Nope, still twitching. He continued down the hall and figured the beer would help.

"Are you sure about this?" Yoshi asked.

"Yes. And consent is key. Every single shot we must ask for from the other."

Yoshi postured, offended. "You think I would drug you without your consent? If you think that of me, then why don't I leave you alone and go back to my experiment?" He headed toward the door.

Elle realized her mistake. Her words came off rude regardless of his crush on her. She knew Yoshi better than he realized. Elle was a good listener and remembered minor details of most conversations with men in the off chance that her eternal wandering eyes decided to settle on monogamy someday. Yoshi was a decent dude. Cute even. The male version of the movie trope wherein taking glasses off a nerd resulted in a hidden hottie underneath.

Yoshi exited the room leaving Elle alone. That was not good. She ran out into the hall and slammed into someone. Elle yelped and struggled to break free. An overwhelming mixture of an unfamiliar cologne and body musk frightened her further. The man was solid and powerful, there was no moving him. He gripped her shoulders, limiting her ability to move or fight back. She finally looked up.

"Jimmy?"

Jimmy nodded, bow tie askew. "My apologies. I intended to knock, but you vaulted at me,"

Vaulted? Elle considered the word. Was she so desperate to bring Yoshi back that she vaulted into the hall? Yes, yes, she had, but it worked. Yoshi was back at her door investigating the brouhaha.

"What's going on?" Yoshi asked.

"Ask him," Elle said.

Jimmy still held Elle firm. Why had he not let go immediately? It took a confused cough from Yoshi for the man to release her. *Did Jimmy want to hurt her?* Elle wondered.

Jimmy released her and straightened his bow tie, turning mild-mannered. From Superman to Clark Kent. Or in this case, Superdouche. There was something scary about the man. This one was trouble. She never noticed before.

"I am making the rounds to let everyone know I sorted through the cafeteria and filled one refrigerator with food. It is the fridge labelled good. Mostly vegetables, fruit, yogurt, and such. Also, while searching for Steve, I brought his fancy espresso machine from his office to the cafeteria as well."

"Searching? Didn't all of security leave?" Elle asked while instinctively glancing at one of the overhead cameras.

"Yes, of course. Poor choice of words." Jimmy said.

The man placed his hands behind his back and strolled off toward the elevators. Yoshi and Elle whispered simultaneous WTFs to one another. The elevator dinged and Jimmy was gone.

"Dude's close to our age, and he acts like a boomer. What's up with that?" Yoshi asked.

"Yoshi. I am sorry I offended you, but Jimmy weirded me out. Do you mind hanging out for a while longer?"

"Huh? Yeah, sure."

They returned to the lab. Elle immediately turned to him and apologized. "I said something that came out bad. I want to apologize. What I failed to articulate earlier was that asking was important not for trust, but for experimental purposes. If one of us does not agree to the next shot, it could mean we already leaped into a lucid dream state. In that case, we should stop the injections and treat one another like sleepwalkers. Deal?"

"Deal. And apology accepted. We are recording this, correct?"

Elle nodded and produced a tablet. She opened a program and started to record. Once set she set the device down.

"Audio only. No need to see us getting goofy," Elle said.

"If you think it gets goofy, you might not know what is in store. I will not pretend to be an expert, but this can get intense. Since I have used the product before, you should start with me."

Before injecting him, she prepped herself by taking off her lab coat. She wore a tank-top underneath. Yoshi rolled up the sleeve of his tee shirt. She pressed the injector against his arm then spoke to the recorder.

"Subject A, female, is about to inject subject B, male. Do you consent, Yoshi?" Elle asked.

Yoshi nodded as Elle squeezed the trigger. He gasped and jerked his head back, lashing out at something only he could see. Elle gave him room, but Yoshi quickly recovered and laughed.

"How this stuff works immediately I do not know, but wow, that was intense."

"Because me no likey needles, I asked Mitch to help secure a highly potent strain. I figured the fewer shots it takes to get there, the better."

"Mission accomplished," Yoshi said and placed a bullet into a second injector. Yoshi struggled with the device because of trembling hands. "That's weird. No matter how strong, I would not expect it to affect me physically so soon. Let the record show, the initial dose resulted in immediate hallucinations. After one dose, subject B suffered hand tremors. The tremors are a first for the subject who has limited experience with the drug. Tremors suggest a high potency or an unknown variable. About to inject subject A. Do you consent?"

Elle gulped. "Hallucinations?"

"You like horror movies, right?" Yoshi asked.

"Sure?"

"Then strap in for some fun." He pressed the injector against her shoulder. "Do you consent?"

Elle nodded. He pulled the trigger just as Elle cried, "Wait!"

Too late. The effects hit instantly. The speed at which the surroundings changed shocked Elle. Everything turned red, including the ceiling, which dripped liquid. (Blood?) With her attention turned to the ceiling, she noticed the air vents feeding clouds into the room. The inkiness stood out against the otherwise red background.

Then she looked down and saw Yoshi sitting on a stool, facing away from her. When had that happened? She called out his name, but he did not respond. Elle walked around him trying to get to his front, but she could not get around to his other side. Odd.

She ran trying to get around him, but she saw only the back of his head. Eventually, she abandoned the chase. She stared at the back of Yoshi's head, and he suddenly stared back when his eyes opened in the thicket of his hair.

Elle screamed while Yoshi's head turned forty-five degrees in a quick jerk. Though shifting his head to a profile position, the head remained covered in hair, though a nose broke the surface of his locks. His head jerked another forty-five degrees which should have snapped poor Yoshi's neck. A mouth. A mouth appeared at the bottom of the hair curtain. Would the next turn reveal ears? Would there be a next turn? There was.

With a violent jerk, Yoshi's head spun again. The hair remained in place, but a face showed through his thick strands. Not Yoshi's face, one with intense green eyes. Its nose was pug, like a bat's. The mouth housed long crooked sharp teeth, the longest of which cut through his upper lip. Yoshi thing hissed and spit.

Then it leaped at her!

She tried to escape, but the creature caught her by the shoulders. Elle struggled to get away, but the grip grew tighter. The familiar touch caused Elle to focus on her captor. It was Jimmy in the nude. He stood tall and erect in more ways than one.

The man stared her down. "I've heard things about you. I know you sleep around. Well, guess who is down to fuck? I'm done with Mercedette. Now I'm going to take you. And when I finish, I am going to murder you all, including your little boy toy, Yoshi."

Blood. There was so much blood. It had pooled from the ceiling until she stood ankle deep in it. Then, with a flush, the blood receded as it poured down an invisible drain. Jimmy noticed and cried out angrily.

"No. I haven't f-f-f-ucked you y-y-yet!"

The drain came into view sucking out the last of the blood then took Jimmy with it. The nude man hit the drain on the floor and came apart. His body split into strands of spaghetti matching the width of the drainage squares. Play Doh going through a presser as a kid. Someone gripped Elle's shoulders. Was it starting all over? No. It was Yoshi.

"Are you okay? You were totally freaking."

"What? Yeah, sure, I'm okay," Elle said.

She wiped her brow, overcome with sweat. She looked around the room. The black clouds still fluttered in the air, but the rest of the world returned to normal. She blinked and even the dark clouds vanished.

"Are you sure you want to do this again?" Yoshi asked.

Elle surprised herself with how enthusiastically she answered. "Hell yeah!"

Yoshi had to remind her to record her experience on the tablet and then prepare his next injection. She went through the motions but was eager to take another shot. She never knew how amazing the drug could be.

Once lucid, she could enter the strangest of worlds and find her way around, and be with people, all the people, never alone again. She would be the star in her new lucid film. Until arriving at the desired state, she planned to ride the terrifying yet exhilarating rush of fear. She loaded the injector and fought the urge to inject herself. Barely giving Yoshi time to consent, she injected him, then watched in wonder as he went somewhere else.

Next, it would be her turn.

CHAPTER 20

G illian paced the conference room. Something was wrong. The nagging edginess from earlier had only grown worse. Flashes of the murder in LA haunted her. But the intense flashes were more than simply memories. Details from that night changed the more she relived it in her mind. Like a reboot of a movie franchise, unfamiliar images took place of the old ones while maintaining some similarities. Gillian saw herself in the restaurant, miserable in the face of her fiancé ghosting her.

Ghosts. Gillian crossed her arms to ward off a chill. There she was in the restaurant, deciding what to do. She remembered worrying that something bad happened to the man she loved, perhaps an accident. Then a squeal of delight drew her attention. A woman at an adjacent table chirped with glee over a birthday gift. Gillian noted the color of the box. Pricey.

The man was handsome and the woman stunning. Gillian fought to hold on to that portion of the memory. Seeing the pair gave her hope that love could prevail despite feeling in the pit of her stomach that *a change was gonna come*. Watching the couple interact warmed Gillian's heart but she could not hold the thought while pacing the conference room.

Gillian sang along to the birthday song that night. Another warm thought interrupted when the conference room TV blitzed, moving in and out of static. A burst of signal noise startled her. She had left the screen paused on one of the employee's interviews. Gillian grabbed the remote but could not stop the splurge of static.

And then it was static no more. The restaurant from Los Angeles appeared on the screen. No more interview tapes. Someone subjected her to the mother of all pop-up ads. *Want to know all about tragedy? We have got your number! Now offering tragedy 24-7, join today! Wait, our records show you are already a member. Congratulations.*

"What is this?"

The ad could not be on the screen, only in her mind, so she rubbed her eyes. But sure as shit, a scene played out with her as a guest star. All the other birthday voices fell away, leaving only hers. Gillian murdering notes embarrassed her as much as the scene frightened her. She worried whether she was experiencing a stroke. Pinching herself to check for dreaming did nothing but hurt. She was awake.

Except she could not be. It had to be a dream or a trick. Maybe Mitch, in his anger over her visit, set her up. He could have gotten footage from the police or the restaurant itself. But to what end? To shock her? Remind her of how horrible that night was?

She understood how upset he was over her showing up to relive that night. She did not wish to see anything else on the video. One thing to remember, another to see it. Then everything changed. On the screen, the birthday girl rose from her seat and approached Gillian in the restaurant, something that never happened in real life.

"Hello. My name is Wendy. Thank you for the birthday wishes," the woman said.

"Absolutely. My pleasure," the on-screen Gillian answered.

"Such a wonderful husband. He spoils me so. Do you like it?" Wendy leaned over and showed the necklace.

"It's beautiful," on screen Gillian said.

In the conference room, Gillian reached for the screen as if she could touch the jewelry, but the screen was too far away. Gillian plodded forward numbly, stunned by the footage of such clarity that it had to be real. Yet was not. How? Why? On-screen Gillian looked non-plussed.

"He wants you to have it," Wendy said.

"Who?"

"My darling husband. He wants inside of you," Wendy said.

"What?"

"We want inside of you. It is my birthday; it would mean so much to me."

On-screen Gillian appeared as confused as the off-screen version. Both Gillian's spoke simultaneously. "I don't understand."

Then it happened. The awful thing. Half of Wendy's face fell off and into on-screen Gillian's lap. On the TV, Gillian screamed and batted at the chunk of flesh while a half-faced Dead Wendy stood by and laughed.

"So sorry. This happens all the time," Dead Wendy said.

On-screen Gillian stood, and in doing so, the fleshy treasure flew from her lap. The object flew toward the screen, then through it where it landed on actual Gillian's foot. She stared in disbelief at the half a face resting on her shoe. The partial face blinked its one eye. Gillian screamed and kicked the face across the room. It splatted against the wall in a wet gush, sticking briefly before sliding down somewhere behind the coffee maker.

Gillian cupped her mouth to stifle her screams. She did not wish to announce her newfound insanity to the residents at Trager. It was not real, could not be. She was a reporter who dealt in facts. Faces did not fly from television screens. She closed her eyes.

"It's not real. It's not real."

When she opened them, an interview tape was back on the screen. Gillian used the moment of sanity to grab the remote. She aimed and pressed a button. It worked. The TV turned off, but she yelped when the reflection on the blank screen showed Dead Wendy.

Or she thought it was at first. A closer look revealed it was merely her own reflection. The frantic overreaction to her imagination running wild left her looking a mess. Her hair and clothes were out of sorts from dancing around in fright. Gillian fixed both and checked her reflection again. A door slammed outside. Gillian raced into the hall.

"Hello?"

The sound was not that of an office door slamming. It had the telltale crunch of heavy crash bar laden double doors closing. Someone had entered the dead wing, the wing that remained an insane asylum.

Book me a room, Gillian thought. She remained uncomfortable over her earlier experience. Unless Gillian fell asleep on her feet in the conference room, it was not a dream. So, what to make of it? A vision? She did not believe in that woo-woo stuff. No. Merely the effects of inhabiting an unfamiliar place and watching too many people's phobias.

She approached the chains designed to secure the dead wing. They were pulled aside. The padlock hung from a chain link but was unlocked. Someone had gone through. Gillian opened the doors and yelled. No one answered. There were no automatic lights inside, so she could only see as far down the corridor as the ambient light at her back allowed.

From what she could see, it remained a sanitarium. Padded cells lined both sides of the corridor. She called out once more. Something sounded far away, a clang like a metal pipe bouncing down some stairs. That was enough for Gillian.

"Nope. All kinds of nope."

She slammed the door. Once closed, she loosely reattached the chains. Not enough to keep someone from returning but enough to ensure they would fall away if someone came back, it would serve as an alarm to alert her to their presence. She could simply enter and catch up to the person so she knew who was skulking about, but something kept her from doing so. It bothered her that the thought of exploring the wing frightened her.

Why be so afraid? Rubber rooms, a sanitarium, the voice on the tape. Then the face on the floor. Gillian could not explain what she witnessed minutes ago, but clearly it never happened. It was all a figment of her imagination, something to do with bread pudding like Scrooge. There was one way to make sure. Gillian re-entered the conference room and pulled the coffeemaker stand away from the wall. Not far, just a couple of feet. That would be good enough. She looked down.

Nothing. Simply a carpet, slightly brighter than the section surrounding it. The table had been in place since the remodel. There was no fleshy half-face. Gillian pushed the table back. Against her better judgement, she made another cup of coffee. As nervous as she was, she did not wish to sleep for fear her dreams would be worse than what she already experienced.

She fixed her cup then sat and hit the remote. Outside she swore she heard the doors to the dead wing open once again, but she no longer cared. Let the spirits roam was her new motto. To forget it all, she watched the TV where one of the scientists shared their deepest, darkest fears.

The chains holding the dead wing closed were for show. Trager employees kept a key taped to one end of the chain in case someone accidentally padlocked them. If anyone every did lock the chains it was before Derrick's time at Trager. After removing the unlocked lock and sliding the chains to one side, he entered the dead wing. Pushing the doors open caused a flurry of black dust to circle like a tornado, spinning either into the dead wing or out of it. He could not determine which. That made him think of the dirty floor in the lab, which made him think of Amy. The thoughts combined made him more eager than ever to get to a quiet space.

Getting there was anything but quiet. Entry was loud, everything dangled and clanged, as the doors shut behind him. Once inside, he grabbed one of the staged flashlights. There were four total. The place was so dark no one would know where to look for them without prior knowledge of their existence. He turned it on and walked the corridor. Employees usually visited in groups of two or more because of how creepy the old place was. But Derrick mostly visited alone. It allowed him a serene place away from others where he could think. And get a beer which was the target of his current mission.

Derrick never did drugs, nor hard alcohol, but college taught him socializing was easier with beer in hand. As he grew older, he developed a taste for craft beer and appreciated how so many breweries sprung up all over the city. Moderation still guided him. He almost never mixed brands when drinking but did enjoy tasting flights when available.

Flight. Just the idea made him shiver. Why had he thought of that? Because of the beer. He was on a mission for beer, and that made him think of drinking a taste of each style offered by a brewery. Usually laid out on a wooden plank, bars called those a... Derrick abandoned the thought, unwilling to even think the word again. The abandoned sanitarium's surroundings never frightened him, yet Derrick found himself uncomfortably edgy.

The stairwell at the main entrance had fallen into disrepair and no longer reached the roof. To get there, visitors had to cross the entire corridor to the second stairwell. Derrick pointed his flashlight into every padded cell that he passed. Shadows took menacing forms under the influence of his flashlight beam, but they did not bother him. He did not believe in ghosts. Derrick subscribed to the philosophy that everyone was future worm food. No afterlife, no heaven. Life consisted of a one and done actual YOLO situation. The odds that life developed from a big bang (or some other theory du jour) already defied the odds. The chances that the same species defying the odds would get a round two via reincarnation or an afterlife sounded absurd. He often wished others felt the same. Maybe people would be kinder. Too many were assholes, like his parents.

Ugh, why bring them into this? Derrick wondered. But how could he not? They set him on his current course. They raised Derrick in a manner that he wished to protect other children from. The same people who acted as jerks their entire lives believed a deathbed apology earned them a ticket to an all you can eat afterlife buffet. Those same misguided "souls" often damaged children the most while offering the least affection and guidance.

His parents were such people. Highly religious, highly conspiratorial. An awful combination. God looked out for their family what with them being the chosen ones. Yet the government was out to get them.

They lived in an elegant home in a pleasant neighborhood. Derrick attended private school from pre-school through senior year. Despite being well off, his parents constantly railed against their perceived enemies. The worst beating Derrick ever received happened when he innocently asked why if God was all powerful, then how did the government get the upper hand?

Derrick's mother put a stop to the beating but not out of the kindness of her heart. Through all the screaming (Derrick's), and the yelling (his father's), his mother only demanded the beating stop to avoid charges. Never once did she ask the man to stop hurting her baby.

On Derrick's eleventh birthday, rather than get the new skateboard he asked for, his parents separated. Derrick spent his birthday in a motel. His mother used to gripe about such places whenever they drove by one. She often groused how they drew undesirable characters and crime into neighborhoods. Interestingly, his father would only shrug his shoulders and mention they served a purpose. His parents would then fight. Derrick never understood why. (Though later learned his pop met his mistresses in such places.)

His father worked for a pharmaceutical company and quickly moved up the ranks. The higher they promoted him, the better the amenities around their house became. They even got a housekeeper for a while, Andrea. Derrick liked her a lot. But one day Derrick's parents fought louder than normal. During the fight, Andrea entered Derrick's room and apologized to him.

"I'm sorry, kiddo. I made some mistakes and won't see you anymore," Andrea said.

Derrick did not understand. He hugged the woman and cried. Derrick's mother stormed into the room and screamed for Andrea to let go of her child and leave. Andrea did as Derrick's mother said.

Derrick begged his mother to let the woman stay, but his mom refused. The one person who showed him kindness was gone.

Amy reminded Derrick of Andrea. Those feelings likely influenced his desire to assist her. By helping Amy, Derrick could thank Andrea for being there when he needed her. Yes, he was a kid then, but she treated him as a person, not an unwanted problem. Derrick always assumed the woman slept with his father, but when he ran into Andrea at a supermarket years later, he found out what really happened.

Derrick outright asked if she slept with his father. Andrea laughed, which brought a smile to Derrick's face. The laugh that comforted him as a child had not changed. Andrea was forthright. Yes, his dad was a shit who groped her regularly and tried to have sex, but she rebuffed him. The poor decision she made came down to selling pills for the man. She needed money and Derrick's dad had an endless supply of opioids that he sold through various people.

The revelation rocked Derrick but explained so much. When he went to the motel with his mother, she insisted they stay until his father took care of some business. The government people that were out to get them were planning something nefarious. Derrick did not know then, but his parents were on the run.

But the motel would not be far enough. Before long, they sent Derrick away. That led to his greatest fear. That was what made him want to help children. It resulted in an incident which forever shaped his life. His parents' horrible life choices made him turn his back on religion. How to believe in something where the practitioners were so cruel? And if the big guy upstairs did not exist then ghosts did not either. That was why Derrick did not fear such things while walking alone through the dark asylum. The only ghosts that existed were those from his past. He walked faster, hoping they would not catch up to him.

CHAPTER 21

Raj and Colt exited the upstairs lab, each holding a box of supplies. Raj repositioned his load while trying to close the lab door. He struggled with the task. Colt whistled. Raj leaped and almost dropped the box.

"What are you doing?" Colt asked.

"We're not coming back, right? I should lock the place up."

"What? Why?"

Raj eyed the door and grimaced. "To help ease my OCD?"

"Nope. Nobody here to steal, nobody cares. My lab assistants don't worry about open doors, only closed ones," Colt said.

Raj nodded and they walked to the elevators. They entered and hit the lobby button. Once inside, Raj studied his friend, seeing him in a new light.

"That was inspiring about closed doors. I did not know you revered you coworkers so much," Raj said.

"I do not. That TED Talk was for an audience of one to get his butt in gear. But I can't thank you enough. This experiment is all aboot my fear and I truly could not do it alone. How can I repay you?"

"Introduce me to Maddy?"

"Who?" Colt asked.

Raj burst out laughing, too loud, too long. He was quick to laugh but found it embarrassing in mixed company or on the job. Both situations were in play. It was the confused look on Colt's face that caused Raj to cease laughing.

"You truly do not remember?" Raj asked.

Colt shrugged. Raj shifted his box to one arm and used his other to make a fist. He moved it back and forth. Colt rolled his eyes.

"Someone I banged? You can't say banged in your country?"

"This is my country. I am simply being polite in front of a coworker."

"Fuck that, Raj. I'm from another country. Where I'm from, we say what's on our mind."

"What country?" Raj asked.

"I recently said aboot, did you not get that? Canada."

"Aren't people from there supposed to be nice?"

"I get that a lot," Colt said.

The elevator opened on the ground floor. Raj leaped at the ding, confused to why it unnerved him. Colt paid no mind and exited the elevator. Raj followed him down the hall.

"Why Maddy?" Colt asked. "She's married,"

"Then you know who I was talking about."

Colt swung his box and walked backward while chatting. "I'm a bad person, Raj. Though I refuse to work on it, or myself, I am at least aware of that shortcoming. Instead of working on my flaws, I have been trying harder to remember people's names."

"But you failed to remember. I had to prompt you," Raj said.

"But I remember now. See? progress."

Raj shrugged, unable to debate such sound logic. "How many women are there in your life that you cannot remember their names?"

"I don't know, Raj. I'm a scientist, not a mathematician." Colt continued backward and sized up his lab partner. "You must kill it with the ladies. You're fit, you've got hair for days. That's movie star hair, my friend."

Raj blushed and laughed the goofy laugh again. Flattered as if complimented by someone he desired. Colt stopped walking and the two bumped boxes. Raj's laughter settled into a snicker before fading.

"Okay. Now I understand why," Colt said.

Raj deflated. He longed to fit into *cool kid* crowds, except he was not a kid any longer, even though he still lived at home with his mom. She relied on him to be there. As for his father, well, never let it be said that absence **always** makes the heart grow fonder.

There was no love lost between Raj and his absentee father. Last Raj heard; his father's employer fired the man for cause. Big surprise. The man was seriously flawed. Yet somehow such flaws looked cool on Colt.

"You need to look outside these walls for companionship, Raj. What if something goes bad? Do you want to have workplace issues because you had an affair with someone?" Colt asked.

"Not issues, but yes, I would very much like to have an affair. Besides, you have managed not to create a stir."

"Because people like yourself are cool and say nothing. And because the women I hook up with are in relationships, so they keep quiet." Colt stopped and tilted his head. "Wait. I have banged a lot of women here, right?"

"Is not that exactly what we are discussing?"

"I thought we were discussing your lack of love life, but sure, it started with me banging Melissa."

Raj did not correct Colt. Colt stacked his box on top of Raj's, freeing his hands. Raj grunted, already struggling. Colt church-steepled his fingers, bringing the two index fingers to his lips as he thought out loud.

"Mercedette got suspended for an affair with someone. Rumor was that it involved Jimmy. He was missing for some time as well. The cover story was that Jimmy went to supervise the chemical plant.

"So?"

"So? It's well known around here that I'm a little loose with the zipper. What must have happened that they were booted while I bootied?"

"Yeah. You do not even avoid the cameras."

Colt gestured back toward the security office. "Hey, he wants a show, so be it. I don't care. But something big must have gone down. Quinn should know. They share a wing. Let's pay her a visit after our experiment. Come on. The sooner we start, the better."

Colt hurried down the hall, leaving Raj to struggle with the dual load. Raj called out to Colt. "Hey that thing about you being a dick?" Raj said. Too late, Colt was gone.

Raj lowered the boxes to the ground. While bent over, a shadow passed the gap under the security office door. The lights were on inside. Why would the lights be on if no one was home? Raj rose and shook his arms. He would catch up to Colt later. Raj knocked. No answer. Someone moved inside moments ago. Why would they not answer?

Raj leaned his ear against the door and heard rustling. Someone did move around inside. Everyone on the job was friendly. Someone staying silent made no sense. He sensed someone leaning their own ear against the door from the other side. Raj tried to brush it off. That made no sense. If someone was in the office, they had camera access. Why press up against the closed door?

Then it began.

A bowel clenching feeling overtook Raj while he listened. He sensed the person within knew where Raj was, was watching and listening. For a moment, Raj was the young child in the old woman's home again. The woman had an advantage over Raj then by knowing her home's layout. Surely that was how she got to the backyard before him, despite his youthful feet being faster than those of an octogenarian (or centurion?). At least that was what Raj convinced himself over the years.

As for Raj's mother, she never spoke of that night. She rambled some on the way home, said some things as if trying to manifest results. The gist was that the bruja's ceremony should have cured Raj's father of his excesses and make him return to his family. That never happened. Raj often wondered what part he played in the ceremony's failure. Was his father destined to live a life of addiction and bad choices because a frightened child interrupted the bruja's work?

Raj was a frightened child that night. Though finally an adult, he could not help but feel the same vulnerable worry while listening at the door. The person on the opposite side of the barrier matched his movements, mimicking him. Raj closed his eyes and listened, truly listened. There was no way to know for certain, but he believed it was the bruja. As sure as she had lifted off into the night on a broom, she somehow existed in the security office. Though he escaped from her once, the old woman apparently still had plans for him.

A hand landed on Raj's shoulder. His scream came out as a shrill whine. One more indignity, one more uncool thing to add to his repertoire of nerd-like indignities. All in front of the buddy he wished to impress.

"Are you okay?" Colt asked, still gripping Raj's shoulder.

The man's look was sincere, as were his words. Raj nodded. "Sorry. Thought I heard someone inside."

"Yeah, that would make me wet myself as well," Colt said, searching Raj's eyes.

Though the man followed through with a joke, Raj appreciated Colt's concern. The sentiment, while not well spoken, was well meaning. Raj shook off his nerves, happy to have someone act as a friend. Colt apologized for being a douche and leaving Raj to carry both loads. They picked up the boxes and moved down the hallway. Raj turned back and glimpsed movement under the door again. In his mind. All in his mind. He had made a friend; he tried to focus on that. *Bros before brujas*, Raj thought and slipped into one of his laughing jags.

Colt glanced back, appearing ultra-concerned. Raj zipped it and tried to act like a normal human while following his new friend to the mysterious lab just past the receiving dock. Colt burst through flimsy double swing doors into the room. The lab's vastness suggested it too was once a receiving area as well. Compared to the more luxurious spaces on the higher floors, the place served as a throwback, as dated as the cafeteria. Touched up a little, but not much. Even the few chairs in the room were wooden versus cookie cutter wheeled spin chairs. Colt dropped his box on the nearest desk.

Raj did the same. "I never asked. What is it you are afraid of?"

Colt gestured toward a door on the farthest side of the room. A chicken-wire lined circular port window at face height took up space near the top of the door. Just below the window hung a sign that read: 'Snake pit. Enter and you're hissssstory.'

The window's interior dripped with moisture. Raj pressed his face to the glass, hoping to see through the wet drops. He isolated a clear spot through which he saw a narrow corridor that led to another door. Floor to ceiling snake terrariums lined both sides of the tight corridor.

"You're afraid of very long penises?" Raj asked.

Raj turned away from the window, proud that he did not laugh at his own joke. He was evolving. He failed to notice the face of Dead Wendy staring at him from the other side of the window. Sensing being watched, Raj glanced back, but the window had fogged over entirely.

"How are you with snakes?" Colt asked.

"They were a thing where I grew up. I'm fine with them."

"Well, I am not. Terrified. Even the thought of them. Being this close to them makes me want to run."

"But you're going to test on yourself?"

"Right as reindeer, my friend. While it would have been easy to find people with severe snake phobias, we are in a different world right now. Was waiting for human trial approval, and here we go. Tag, I'm it."

"What is the plan, then?" Raj asked.

Colt pulled a bullet dose from the box and showed it to Raj. "This variation is a highly concentrated extract. Fast acting with a major kick. I plan to inject myself with a large dose of the concentrate formula. Once I achieve a state of fear so great, a fear dysmorphia if you will, my brain will attribute that fright to the nearest object on hand."

"Making your new phobia override any other phobias?"

"Exactly. Snakes will be a walk in the park compared to my newer fear. I'll know it works if I can waltz through the snake pit without a second thought."

"Have to admit, this sounds interesting. So, what are you planning for a replacement phobia?"

Colt lifted an orange purchased from the street vendor earlier.

CHAPTER 22

G illian leaped when the room went dark. With a wave of her hand, the lights flickered back to life. She reached for her phone, the same one with the mysterious voice at Mitch's crime scene. She considered listening to it again but remained too freaked out. Gillian felt she should have long ago regained control of her senses, but apparently not, and she could not fathom why.

Raising her hands, she noticed subtle tremors. Attempts to still them failed. Calories. Lack of calories combined with too much caffeine. Already a bad combination but throw in video files of everyone's personal scares, and it made sense why she was nervous. She had yet to watch all the interviews because she took took extensive notes during and after each viewing. While taking notes on the last watched video, the motion sensors decided she was no longer in the room.

It was only when the lights turned back on that Gillian noticed how dirty the conference table was. She entered the restroom, wet some paper towels, and came back out to wash the table. The wad was filthy when done. She kept her house immaculate, and while she slept in many a cheap hotel for her job, the griminess of the old building had her longing for the ferry on Monday. But it was not only the dirt that had her eager to leave. Her inability to focus bothered her.

Dumping the wet paper in the trash, she struggled to remember what she had just been doing. Notes! Yes, notes on the last interview. She shook her head as she tried to understand her fuzzy headedness. The unexpected stay on the island played some part. But a gnawing doubt about why she was even there contributed to her confusion. Gillian was unmoored, sitting in an office watching videos with no known purpose. The tapes were very interesting and intimate, but why watch them? Would they even be used in a story? Would her editor care?

She needed to determine her reason for being on the island. She came to interview Mitch, so why did she allow her subject of interest, well, change the subject? What story was more relevant than the five-year anniversary of a tragic unsolved murder? Rogue scientists playing God? Rogue scientists saving mankind? She struggled to settle on a headline or an angle to the story.

A fear inducing drug was newsworthy, but it was stopped before ever going to market. Depending on who the financiers were, there could be a David versus Goliath angle. A rag-tag team of scientists taking on big pharma and finishing work designed to benefit citizens rather than shareholders. That begged the question of why a company would shut down something serving the common good? On its face, a drug designed to temper fear could bring in huge money. Heck, Gillian would use such a product herself.

Foomp!

The air turning back on startled Gillian. It cycled on and off frequently and brought with it the dust she had just cleaned off the table. The sudden noise startled her each time, but this time it was worse. Her edginess was peaking. Thinking of the voice on the tape made her shiver further.

Mitch had earlier inquired about her fears. Gillian had some, but none as deep-seated as those of the individuals in the videos. Fear of heights and such were helpful, part of the evolutionary progress of keeping humanity alive. Gillian's fears were common ones, with one lone exception. The voice on the recorder.

Whose voice was it? That was still the story. Maybe that explained everything about her low level fear. She was so intent on finding a new story that she ignored the most important one. Gillian stayed for the weekend to appease Mitch, but in the end, she wanted what she came for. She wanted to play the voice for him.

Except Mitch had vanished along with his second in command. The building was only so large. They were avoiding her. She needed to speak with them again. Even innocent conversation could reveal details that someone wished to hide. Consciousness of guilt was a legal term that revealed how a person's words inadvertently confessed guilt. It was useful in reporting as well. Not everything was a crime, but people could confess to facts they wished to keep hidden.

What was Mitch hiding? Why did the company in charge shut everything down? She decided to focus on two angles for the weekend. Who was on the tape, and why was the company shut down? Any other questions were tangential to those. Deciding on her key avenues of inquiry relieved her. She felt less frightened.

Until the face. Gillian gasped when she turned to the TV and saw Mercedette's face. The woman stared at the camera as if looking through it. Maybe there was a third story lurking. Mercedette was an interesting woman on the surface, but there was something more going on with the scientist. Coworkers spoke of her as if she were as fragile as a Faberge egg. Gillian could politely call Trager employees damaged based on the videos alone. But as collectively damaged as they might be, many still singled out Mercedette. Something more was going on.

Gillian sat and pressed play. On the screen, Mercedette stood behind a chair. The camera zoomed in and out, trying to frame her before she finally leaped over the chair's back into the seat. Mercedette was athletic and a bit more playful in front of the lens than she showed in real life. Or perhaps it was nerves. The woman (younger in the video) could not seem to sit still. The camera operator tried to frame her while she rocked back and forth. The camera eventually settled on a medium shot from her waist up. Mercedette looked pale as well as jumpy.

"Do you know why you are here?" the now familiar interviewer's voice asked.

Mercedette simply nodded. "Are they here?"

"Is who here?"

"Them. They."

"I am sorry. Is this a pronoun issue?"

"What? No. I have no problems with identifiers. I was asking if *they* were here. As in multiple people. Some like to watch," Mercedette said.

"You understand this is merely a job interview? There is no one here but me. You met Doctor Trager during orientation. He is not here, for example. I am tasked with recording your fears or phobias so that we can best match you with lab partners and or projects in your field."

"Yeah, sure, sure, an interview."

Gillian fast-forwarded the video, watching at an increased playback speed. Mercedette's face danced between variations of anguish. At one point the screen went to static. When the image returned, Mercedette sat upright, more in control. The shot had tightened so that Mercedette's hands remained out of view. Gillian returned the video to normal speed.

"Now that we have established this is merely an interview process, we can proceed against my better judgement," the interviewer said.

"I can do this," Mercedette replied.

"Tell me your name and your greatest fear," the interviewer said.

"My name is Mercedette. You have my work history in front of you. My fear is..."

"Mercedette. It is fine. Not everyone can articulate their fears. That is why we here at Trager are doing what we do. We want to help people like you."

Mercedette laughed even as her face tightened until she glowered at the interviewer. "Help people like me?"

"Yes."

"Help me? You want to help me? Then where were you?"

"Excuse me?"

"Where were you? Because you sure as fuck weren't there that day, were you?"

"That's enough..."

"No! You sit down!"

A shift in shadows suggested the man had risen to his feet but took her up on her suggestion and sat back down. Mercedette rocked in a fluid motion, though her hands remained out of view.

"It is too late to help me. Once their faces turn upside down, they have chosen you."

"Upside down?" The interviewer asked.

Mercedette leaped from her chair and vanished from the camera's view. The screen remained empty for a moment until Mercedette's face returned to the frame, upside down. It filled the screen.

"Holy Christ!" Gillian yelled and leaped back.

A back bend. That was the only way Mercedette could have managed her face upside down short of a broken neck. As fast as Mercedette assumed the position, she vanished from the screen and retook her seat. Her frazzled hair stood as a testament to her mania.

"Upside down. Understand?" The interviewer's silence suggested no, but Mercedette kept going. "That is how you know they have chosen you. Once they choose you, you must do their bidding. It is the law of the Three."

"Look. We needn't finish. This is enough. There are some people I can direct you to for guidance," the interviewer said.

Mercedette laughed, subtle at first, then shifted to a cackle. Then fell silent. She stopped laughing so suddenly the interviewer gasped.

"Guidance? They supplied it. That of the Three—the trinity," Mercedette said, as if the interviewer were stupid.

"The Father, the ghost, and the holy spirit?"

"Openings. How many openings do humans have? Sorry. Trick question. How many openings do they have before being sliced? That is the trinity of the Great One. The trinity of flesh. Three serviceable openings before being sliced, after which there are more. But you talk of a different trinity, one of a flawed religion."

"Flawed? How so?"

"In the religion you speak of is a conundrum. His existence proves He does not exist. His existence proves HE does not exist! For how can darkness walk the earth without an absence of light? His existence proves He does not exist," Mercedette said.

"I am not sure I understand the argument. Because evil exists, God does not?" the interviewer asked.

"Yes. I have sought comfort in my new faith, but I know God was not there that day. They used me to open a portal, to welcome the Great One in, except he never arrived. All that pain and he never came.

But through me, they opened the portal. Since then, I can only wait for a day when the Great One finally walks this earth. But God? Feh, nothing but an absent parent. God was not there that day, he was not there that day, he was not there!"

Mercedette raised her hands. Her arms had been in motion off screen the entire while. The results of her actions became clear when the hands came into view. She had dug nails so deep into the palms that blood ran down them in thick rivulets.

"Good lord! Nurse, we need the nurse!" the interviewer yelled from off camera.

A bang sounded as his chair hit the ground off-camera. A shadow danced around in the frame, casting itself over the woman. The video lighting made the shadow loom large over Mercedette, who pressed her hands to her face and smeared the blood.

"His existence proves He does not exist!"

Gillian realized Mercedette was talking about two different beings. God, and someone, or something else. On the screen Mercedette laughed despite her blood-stained face. The shadow kept moving and for a moment, however brief it seemed to take shape. The shape? A hoofed devil with enormous horns throwing back his head in ecstasy. Then a nurse appeared and the recording stopped.

Gillian cried out, stunned by the video, and surprised by the abrupt cut to black. She dropped the remote and searched the room. Though spooked, nothing stood out as dangerous despite the oppressive silence. Everything in its place. She could not leave the remote on the ground.

Crouching on all fours, Gillian reached under the table for the remote and screamed. A shadow shaped like a devil charged at her. She scrambled away as the black figure dissipated into mist. The remote lay where it fell. Gillian grabbed it and quickly stood. She placed it on the table.

Fresh air sounded good. It was time to visit a scientist. Any of them. She simply needed to talk to somebody to get her mind off the darkness invading her mind. Left to her own devices, Gillian was slipping into a hysterical fugue. Everything caused her to jump, to see shadows, to imagine the most disturbing things.

But asking questions gave her control. That would steady her hands. That would get her back to her proper level. She would interview the first person she came across, even Jimmy, if he was wandering the halls. And if she ran into Mitch, she would gladly have another lunch date with the man. Anything to get out of her temporary office for just a little while.

The only person she would steer clear of was Mercedette. Out of all the other tapes, none showed a person more traumatized than that poor woman. Gillian had unwittingly asked questions regarding consent and religion. Now Gillian felt the need to apologize. To Mercedette's credit, when the two women spoke. Mercedette never showed the depth of her tragic past. Despite being a reporter, Gillian had no interest in digging for details. If Mercedette had moved on, then who was Gillian to set her back?

Gillian left the conference room and into the hallway. She never looked toward the defeated chain and the dead wing. Had she done so, she would have seen Dead Wendy standing at the end of the hall.

Mercedette rocked back-and-forth on her knees. She gripped the cross dangling from her neck and mouthed a silent prayer.

Brought up religious before taken in by the cult that would change her life forever, she had returned to the tenets of her former life. The life she had before everything fell apart. She found some comfort in the memories of her life at age six. That was the end of her innocence. Mercedette was never the same after betrayal by those she trusted most.

She rubbed the cross while trying to forget the past, but she never could. Flashes of a certain evening came to mind. The night of pain. She remembered the upside-down faces. Though seeking solace in her necklace, she understood it was time to let go. For her experiment to work, she needed to abandon fears, morals, and control.

If she was ever to stop certain predators, she needed to think like them. Thanks to the experimental medication, she felt her needs rising. Meanwhile, the overhead images helped stoke her sexual desires. Soon she would be like the upside-down men. Not enlightened beings, but animals. She planned to become a beast herself, a devourer of flesh. Once amped up enough and hungry like the wolf, she would then attempt to stop herself. The attacker and the force majeure that stops animals in their tracks.

Mercedette removed the necklace out of guilt. Rising from the floor, she hung the jewelry on a microscope. She then placed the skull cap on her head which generated an image of her brain on the nearby screen. Calibrated just so, it showed a portion of the brain in red. The brain section housed sexual desire but it was not completely red. Once she felt more animal than woman, she would test her personal protection device. For if she could kill the inner beasts, she could finally kill her past.

CHAPTER 23

"I want to go on record as being opposed to your current course of action," Raj said.

"Noted, dad," Colt said.

Raj deflated. Relegated once again to the role of the adult in the room. He was used to such a role. If his father was not an adult, then someone needed to be. Sometimes Raj wished he could let go and lighten up. But become too frivolous in all matters and he would become his dad. No, he would be the stick in the bum as the Americans saying went. The pooper at the party.

"I just..." Raj started, trying to weasel out of the dad role.

"Ball busting, you my friend," Colt said.

The comment lit Raj up. He was in with the cool kid. Colt loaded one injector and placed it in a holder much like a holster which sat atop a medical tray. Colt launched an orange through the air. Raj bobbled it before finally securing it.

"Not one much for cricket, are you?" Colt asked.

"You know about cricket?"

"Every sport, my friend. Great equalizer of society. Might not have toys growing up, but most neighborhoods could wrangle a stick and a ball or a soccer ball," Colt said.

"Or basketball."

"Ah, a basketball fan?"

"Yeah, sorry to disappoint. I know little about cricket. Never understood the rules by the time I left home. Golden State Warriors fan here," Raj said.

"Don't mention that to our Seattle hosts."

"Are you kidding? I rub it in when I can."

"Come on, use real trash talk. I rub that 'shit' in!"

"I rub that... No can do," Raj said, unable to cross the Rubicon.

Colt laughed off the failure. "Good for you. Your parents brought you up right."

Raj fought the urge to reply 'mother.' He remained silent while Colt explained the details of the experiment.

"The testing room contains a chair with arm restraints, one of which is on a timer that will release me at a designated time so I can get my ass out of there. You cannot remain in the room because, God forbid, I glance at you and fear lab partners for the rest of my life." Colt grabbed a second injector and three bullets.

"Restraints?"

"Yeah, you're my BDSM partner today. I'll just call you daddy for the rest of the day."

"Please do not," Raj said.

Colt laughed again and grabbed a large towel from the box and draped it over his head but left his face clear. "My prizefighter outfit. Are you ready to lead me into the ring?"

"I am more than ready to lead you away from metaphors."

"Hey, that's why I'm a scientist, not a writer. You lead me in, and I will take it from there."

Colt stepped to the door with his gear and draped the towel over his head. Raj set the orange down and approached Colt, taking an arm to lead him through the door and past the snake pens. The reptiles hissed and struck at the glass as the pair walked through.

The two men stepped into a tiny room at the end of the hall. The small room was painted black and centered around the chair, which Colt mentioned. It sat bolted to the floor, a holdover from the sanitarium years. One restraint cuff had wires running into the leather padding along with a digital readout. A medical tray was stationed behind the chairback. Directly across from the chair was a metal pole topped off with what appeared to be an upturned claw from an arcade claw machine.

"I am still freaked out, knowing we walked by the snakes. Lead me to the chair. I need to lower my heart rate while we set up. Leaving my face covered for now, to help chill me out," Colt said.

Raj led him to the chair and took in the view. He felt like he was forgetting something but shook it off. It surprised him to see Colt so nervous, especially since they had not injected him yet. As if reading Raj's mind, Colt chimed in with how he was feeling.

"Breathe. I need to breathe. Don't know why I have felt on edge all day. Must have been walking past the snakes that freaked me out. Even though I could not see them. Weird, how that works. We cover a horse's eyes to calm them. Guess we're nothing but animals ourselves, huh?"

"Some are," Raj said, uncertain of why he kept thinking of his absent father. Why was he suddenly living in the past?

"Or it is simply nerves. Chalk it up to the fear of what we are about to do."

"We? You are the one who is about to make himself afraid of breakfast fruit," Raj said, taking the injector and bullets from Colt, and placing them on a medical tray behind the chair.

"Roll up my sleeves and secure them with the restraints."

Raj rolled up Colt's first sleeve and found a surprise, and a matching surprise on the second arm. Twin cobra tattoos ran the length of each of Colt's arms.

"Seriously? You get those before or after your phobia?"

"Way after my phobia. I got the tattoos when I was fourteen," Colt said.

"But?" Raj failed to articulate a follow up question, unsure whether to ask why snakes, why tattoos at fourteen, or how young was he when he developed his fear.

Colt saved him the trouble of asking. Colt turned his head toward where he thought Raj stood and shared the story of where it all began.

Seven-year-old Colt stood in a field with his mom at a time when men considered her pretty. That would not last. She sported multiple tattoos long before it was cool to do so, and her frame was so skinny a breeze could blow her away. But breezes were hard to come by in the hot city summer. Colt poked around in the grass with a tree branch and noticed something slither by.

"Mom, it's a snake?"

"Do you like it, honey?" Colt answered with a nod, so his mother gestured to the ground with her head. "If you like it, then it likes you. Pick it up, don't be a coward."

Colt was too excited and loved his mother too much to pay attention to her harsh assessment of his bravery, or lack thereof. Colt picked the snake up by the tail. With startling speed, the snake coiled around his arm and bit his wrist. Colt shook his hand but could not dislodge the reptile. His mother stood by as Colt screamed and struggled. Finally, he tore it off and tossed it aside. The snake slithered away while the boy cradled his bleeding wrist.

"It bit me!" Colt cried.

His mother laughed. "Guess you learned your lesson. Welcome to life, kid. Wait here."

She walked away to greet a human snake nearby. The large man looked dirty and dangerous. His mother traded bills for a small bag. After the exchange, she kissed the disgusting man. Throughout the entire interaction, Colt could not help but notice the snake tattoos lining the man's muscled arms, matching the ones he would get later in life.

Cord spoke through the towel. "Thought if I could be as tough as the guy in that park, I'd never be afraid of anything. No luck. I was afraid of snakes from that day and never outgrew it, even after I got my own tats to try to prove to myself that I was not afraid."

"Wow. Your mom should meet my dad."

"She might have, cowboy. We could be brothers. Brothers from a stoner mother."

Raj liked the idea. The only thing better than cool friends was having a brother. Raj grew up alone. Very alone. Colt adjusted the towel.

"Key is for the drugs to max out their effects. Twenty minutes should bring me to peak."

"I would feel better if Doctor Trager were present," Raj said, slipping back into adult mode.

"Maybe I call you pa instead of daddy. You're not enjoying this enough. If I was watching someone get so jacked up that he craps twinkies over a navel orange, I would have a ball. You need to live a little, my friend. But since you cannot, let's get back to the details. See the timer?"

"Check," Raj said.

"Same guy who built the snake pit built the timer for me. The restraints ensure I remain here long enough to feel the effects of the drugs. The timer will pop the restraint free at the designated time. It pops, I free my other hand, then pull the towel, see the orange, and casually walk through the no longer terrifying snake pit. Understand?" Raj nodded. "You're nodding, aren't you?" Colt asked.

"Sorry," Raj said. "Secure the arms?"

Now Colt nodded. Raj guided the man's hands into the restraints one at a time. One side secured with a thick leather strap and heavy buckle. After pulling it tight, Colt confirmed it held. A bell jar style lock apparatus secured the restraint with the timer attached. A wire ran between the timer and the latch.

"Set twenty on this timer after you inject me. Do the same on the timer in the lab so you know when to expect me. The metal latch should pop free when the timer hits. But that's where you come in. If I am not through those doors within minutes, it means the latch did not pop and I need help."

"Got it," Raj said and latched the cuff tightly. "Did you even test this thing?"

"No. never expected to use it this soon. That's why you are the backup. My being freaked out enough to bypass the reptiles is the plan but have the counter agent injector ready when I make it back. I may not be the most coherent or cooperative person at that point."

"Scientific diva, got it," Raj said.

Raj placed the injector against Colt's arm and pulled the trigger. Colt reacted quickly and pulled against his restraints. The sudden movement startled Raj, who dropped the empty bullet after ejecting it from the device. It shattered on the ground.

"What was that?" Colt asked, his head darting around under the towel.

"An empty, we're good."

Raj kicked the shards to the side. Loading the next bullet, Raj noticed his hands shaking. Food, he needed food. To shake was unlike him. He was nervous and could not understand why. He administered the second shot. Colt cursed and pulled harder against the restraints.

"Jeez, twenty minutes of this?"

Raj loaded the last one and gave Colt the third shot. Colt screamed underneath the towel. The intensity worried Raj.

"Are you okay?"

"No! I am way not freaking okay. Now get out. Make sure the orange is in place and get out!"

The orange! That was why Raj was so on edge. He forgot it in the lab. It explained the nagging sense that he forgot something important. But the problem had an easy solution. He merely needed to return to the lab, grab the fruit, then sneak back in and quietly place it on the pedestal. There was plenty of time.

Or not. Before Raj could open the door, Colt continued screaming. Raj wondered if his new friend would even last the twenty minutes. With a newfound sense of urgency, Raj raced to retrieve the killer orange.

CHAPTER 24

It was too good to be true, Yoshi thought, while cradling Elle in his arms. The results of the injections so far left both sweaty. Elle's shirt clung to her breasts leaving little to the imagination. Stunning, so stunning, he thought. Deep down, he knew she was out of his league, but he only needed to be one of her stopovers. A poor decision in the night. That's all he wanted. Yoshi had learned to dream small his whole life. His older brother and his brother's friends always left Yoshi behind on their adventures. Worse, his cooler brother scored all the women, including those from Yoshi's age group. Somehow his brother's three-year advantage acted as a passport to traverse any female body in Yoshi's radius. Frustrating.

Yoshi focused on books, toys, and tech, which carried him through most of his life. Until meeting Elle. She was the first woman who never griped about his choice of wardrobe, or the cowlick rising from the rear of his head. No matter how much product he used, the little strand reached for the sky (which is why he tufted most all of it toward the sky, so the cowlick would blend in). She even feigned interest in his office collectibles, though he knew she was simply humoring him.

But feigned interest meant she cared about him. If she lied to spare his feelings, it meant she was concerned about them to begin with. The two sat on the floor leaning against the side of a desk. She was curled in his arms and reaching out, grabbing at things that were not there.

Under the influence of Ink, both went to their own places in their respective minds. Elle laughed or shrieked at things invisible to Yoshi. Her laughter brought him great joy, but her screams unnerved him, and they were increasing. Through it all, Yoshi acted as her rock, the guide through her trips. In lieu of payment for his services, she allowed him to hold her.

Yoshi believed humanity existed as a simulation, and finally whoever his game player was gave Yoshi a shot at the woman of his dreams. He would take it while it lasted. The problem of living in a simulation was that it could change at any time. The Mandela effect proved the simulated world had changed many times over.

Some conspiracy theorists believed the Mandela effect was a sign that time travelers changed history. In the old timeline, there was a movie called Shazaam with Sinbad. Then someone screwed up the timeline and that movie was gone. Why did some remember it and not others? That fell more cleanly into Yoshi's theory of simulation versus time travel. Yoshi believed glitches in the matrix resulted from someone rebooting the game. Soft reboots would not wash every avatar's memory, only hard reboots would.

If someone tripped over the cord and plugged it back in immediately, then most would remember things as they were. The matrix would lose some minor data. But a hard reboot would wipe the collective conscious when the system turned back on. Yoshi and his brother constantly remembered the same events differently. Unless his brother consistently lied, the two had split memories. The Mandela effect.

Even the Blue Beetle shirt Yoshi wore lent itself to the theory. Yoshi's older brother could not remember Ted Kord ever being a Blue Beetle. His brother only remembered Dan Garrett. Yoshi Googled it to confirm there was a Blue Beetle named Dan Garrett but that would have been well before either was born. There was no way for his older brother to remember Dan being the original when it was always Ted Kord in their lifetime until Jaime Reyes.

The simulation theory made sense until Yoshi tried to explain it to others. (Many suggested his brother simply read old comic books online, before Yoshi was old enough to share in the experience.) Moreover, the Blue Beetle reference fell flat because most never heard of any iteration of Blue Beetle. It would take a movie being made to get more people to know the character. Yoshi could not help but like his version best because the character shared his brother's name. His long-lost brother Jaime.

Yoshi's parents eventually held a funeral for Jaime, but Yoshi always held out for a body. Characters in comic books were not dead if the artist never showed the body. That extended to simulations as far as Yoshi was concerned. One day someone would reboot the whole thing and his brother (as big a jerk as he was) would reappear in Yoshi's universe. In the current simulation, Yoshi was seventeen when his brother vanished.

"Ready for another shot?" Elle asked.

"Or we could stay like this for a few more minutes, or a year or two," Yoshi said.

She smiled but the grin quickly turned to a frown, a jerk, a twitch, a tick. That was what the drug did. One second Yoshi would go from prince charming to prince not so charming—now with more teeth!

Elle rose and helped Yoshi to his feet. They came face to face and he gasped. Elle looked at him with great curiosity, holding him in place so he would not run.

"What? Tell me. What did I look like?"

"It was like someone took your face and pushed it into a deep fryer, like at the state fair? You were extra crispy, with your hair molded in place, splayed out above your head."

"That is awesome! You had a second set of eyes earlier, and then for a moment looked like one of my exes, a psycho one. It was uncool, and then each of your body parts fell off you."

"Speaking of, have you seen my arm anywhere?"

Elle punched him. Yoshi made the joke to cover his disappointment. She so cavalierly threw out an ex that it suggested he remained firmly in the friend zone, despite their earlier cuddling. They had only ended up in that position after he corralled her when she freaked out after her last shot. He held her on the ground where she fell until she stopped shaking.

Still, it was a cuddle. She was beautiful, even though her smile was now fang-filled. Chunks of flesh dangled between her sharp teeth. Apparently, she was a cannibal now. Yoshi leaped when she growled, but her words brought him back. She was back to herself and looked distraught.

"Why isn't this working?" Elle asked.

"It is working. Deep fried Elle, remember?"

"Yeah, that is fire. But I mean lucidity. Why are we not slipping from this state into that?"

"Well, it is only a theory," Yoshi said. Off her frustrated look, he raised his hands in surrender. "A valid theory. An intriguing theory, but gravity theories still have not panned out either."

Elle cut him off. "No need to gaslight me on my brilliance. It was not my theory. A lucid state is one effect of the drug over extended use in short periods of time according to tests by Doctor Trager himself. I did not make up the theory, only latched onto it for what I hoped to perfect with my study."

"How would he know that?" Yoshi asked, confused.

"He invented it. He's done his own studies, obviously. The initial product had to go through other regulating agencies before we started experimenting with it. Who knows how long he was at it before we all came aboard?"

"But human trials just got approved."

Elle squinted, considering, but the drug kept her anything but clear. "All I know is lucidity is one side effect, so why aren't we there yet?"

She raised the injector and loaded it again, ready for another go. Yoshi looked at his clawed hands and flexed them. An idea struck him.

"There is a chance we are already lucid. I have a theory."

"Here we go," Elle said.

"If we exist in a simulation, then we could be one version of many from different dimensions. In this dimension I am a charming, dynamic, brilliant Asian scientist."

Elle laughed. "One who collects toys. Go on."

Yoshi was too excited to acknowledge her burn of his current "avatar," so he continued. "But now I have clawed hands. In another simulation, I could exist as a clawed creature. If we find ourselves looking different, it could mean we are elsewhere and not here at all."

"So deep fried me was not me from here. You were exploring another place and met that version of me? Possibly a lucid dream." Elle said.

"Exactly. But we remain so focused on one another's changes in appearance that we are not exploring the surrounding realms. We are serving as anchors to one another. You said as much before we began. Once one gets there, leave them alone. We should split up. Maybe we need to be alone to explore other places in our minds, to experience the drug's full effects. How will either of us encounter a lost loved one if we focus only on changes in one another's appearances? We need to go solo for this."

"No!" Elle yelled.

The intensity behind her shout shocked Yoshi. She noticed his reaction and pressed her hands against his chest, then gazed into his eyes. He met her gaze, and it struck him there was something different there. Yoshi could not explain it other than she looked at him with need.

"I can't do this alone. We can figure it out together. There must be a way to know when we get to lucidity. We can stop looking at one another," she said, suddenly excited. "Yeah! That's it. We can just ignore the other person; pretend they are not there. But they are, but not really, and..."

Yoshi deflated. Her supposed desire for him was gone as quickly as it arose seconds ago. She was now pitching a plan to ignore him. She kept on, but he was no longer listening. Yoshi felt foolish. He was a lab assistant, nothing more. A test tube mook who she would refer to as *subject B* in her study report. He meant nothing to her. It was time to wake up to the realities of every single universe he existed in with her.

With hopes of intimacy dashed, Yoshi defaulted to his scientific side. They had not taken enough, which was why they remained stubbornly stuck in place. They were likely anchors to one another as he suggested, but with enough of the drug, those same anchors could disappear. But how much was enough?

He worried he had a long way to go because of built up tolerance. He needed to find a way to leapfrog her, get ahead of her consumption. Yoshi squinted when something caught his eye. Dark smoke filtered through the vent near the rear of the room.

"I see a black cloud! This is what we've been looking for. Rather than noticing changes in you, I see a change in the lab itself. A changed environment suggests we are further along than we thought. Assuming that cloud is not real, and the lab has not changed, it means I have slipped into an altered state. Things are different but the same."

"Except I see the cloud as well," Elle said.

"You do? Bummer. Ink does not induce group hallucinations which means the cloud is real," Yoshi said.

Before he could investigate further, the door blew off its hinges. A massive arm so large it filled every inch of the doorway reached into the room and grabbed Elle. The monstrous hand squeezed until Elle's head popped open in a shower of blood. Her body flopped lifelessly in the giant's grip; her innards oozed out like toothpaste from a tube.

Now it was Yoshi's turn to scream.

CHAPTER 25

Raj panicked. The orange, where was it? Foolish, so foolish. He had to find the thing, then sneak back in and hope he did not freak Colt out. The poor man was suffering the full effects of the fear element. Desperate not to be the fool, the gum in the works, Raj wondered if he was under the effects of the drug as well. He experienced a contact high from his cooler friends in the past. Though Raj never actively took part, he hung around people who used. Maybe they would have accepted him in their group had the secondhand pot smoke not brought out his foolish laugh. Despite being stoned, the group roasted him over his goofy laughter. He distanced himself from substance users ever since.

After eliminating a subcategory of people from his life, finding new friends became difficult. Seems everyone was on something, even more so as he made his way through college and into the working world. Coworkers often wore sunglasses to disguise their condition, which fooled no one. But since the higher ups wore the same, there was no one to complain to. Not that he wanted to be a snitch. At an employee gathering for a medical start up, he made an off-the-cuff comment when a certain odor wafted through the bar they gathered at.

"Remember when everyone did not smell like pot?" Raj mused. He said what he was thinking, not meaning to say it out loud.

Oh boy, did the group run with it. To those coworkers Raj was brown skinned, and they did not have it in them to notice when he blushed with embarrassment. His face reddened then, and he wished for someone to come to the rescue. Raj searched coworker's faces in the crowd looking for one person who understood his discomfort, who could gently steer the conversation to something else. He found none.

Genuine friends would have noticed his discomfort. The coworkers often called themselves family, but Raj was not. It served as an awakening. They were all employees for hire, nothing more. His newfound belief bore fruit when the company started layoffs. Families might grow estranged, but they did not fire one another. Raj made it through the first round of cuts. Former family members left in tears, and those remaining talked crap about those let go as if doing so elevated their stature. Raj was happy to take severance when his time came.

Now at Trager, Raj found a friend whose biggest vice appeared to be women. A vice that Raj shared (if only in fantasyland). Colt seemed genuinely interested in Raj and appreciated their new partnership. But Raj was about to screw the whole thing up. Friendships at Trager could grow if the place remained open. Raj did not wish to be the reason that they failed.

It would be a simple fix. Grab the fruit, sneak in, and place it on the pedestal. Mission accomplished. But he could not remain focused on even the simplest things. In the back of his mind, he kept thinking back to that day with his mother. Those thoughts overwhelmed him to the point where even finding an orange felt like too much work.

Somehow, he must have been exposed to the fear element. It was the only thing that made sense. There was no reason for him to be frightened at all. But he was and recognized it. There must have been a leak in the injector bullets. A contact high of a different type. Raj decided to fight through it so he could help his friend. If Raj felt frightened from minimal contact, he could only imagine what his poor injected friend was going through. The least Raj could do was get the orange.

Then he spotted the fruit on the lab table where he left it. But something was off. When had someone peeled the darn thing? Raj blinked and for a moment the fruit appeared whole again before it returned to the peeled version. The remnants of the thick skin lay scattered about the table like a debris field of a downed plane. Worse, there were slices missing. Someone had eaten sections of the orange.

The fruit leaned on one side, settling on the groove of where someone had taken slices out. Raj lifted it, yelped, and threw the orange across the room. Maggots devoured the fruit's flesh. Orange had become the new black, covered in rot below the maggots.

How? Who? They were not in the backroom that long. Had a snake gotten out? That had to be it. Raj knew they ate mice; people treated snakes with cautious respect where he grew up. Though some were deadly, residents never killed them because they kept certain other pests at bay. Did snakes eat oranges? Well, one apparently did.

Maybe venom turned the fruit's skin black. The arrival time of maggots was a head scratcher. Plus, snakes could eat fruit but could not peel it. He needed to figure out the mystery later as time was running out. There were more oranges up in Colt's lab. Raj raced to the door and sensed something behind him.

Dead Wendy stared through the snake pit porthole once again, but now a snake slithered out from her open eyehole on the destroyed side of her face. Raj leaped, but with a blink the image was gone. Proof of accidental exposure. There was a counter agent. He would use it when he returned from getting another orange. He could not rest until he made things right.

Raj raced down the hall and clenched his bowels while passing the security office. The place gave him the creeps even before his exposure. Or was he already exposed and that freaked him out earlier? Shadowy movement at the base of the door suggested someone inside again. The telltale whir of a camera zooming in and out sounded from the camera above the security door. Someone was watching.

Great. They would capture an epic failure on camera if he did not get another orange in time. Colt remained unaware of the situation, so Raj could make everything right if he hurried. He chose the stairwell over the elevator. The elevators took forever. Stairs would be faster, and he could hopefully sweat out some of the drug while climbing. The stairs wrapped around themselves in rectangular fashion from ground level to the building's top floor, giving an open view of how far he had to go. The sight was dizzying.

He set one foot on the stairs but startled and slipped when something crashed loudly behind him. The door. He turned to check why it had closed only to find it locked. He would have to take the elevator back down once he got to the lab. He ascended the stairs.

The first and second floor doors were both propped open as was the norm. He must have disrupted a door stop at ground level. That would explain why the door closed behind him. It had nothing to do with whoever was in the security office. When Raj reached the third floor, a loud metal clang sounded. A door below had closed as well. How? Raj leaned over the rail and called out.

"Hello? Doctor Trager? James? I'm using the stairs."

Someone cackled in response. But the voice sounded from above, not below. What was going on? Raj looked up toward the top floor from where the strange laughter had emanated. He called out again and climbed to the next level.

Wham!

The door of the floor he just left suddenly slammed shut. Were the doors on an automated weekend lockdown? Nothing else made sense. Not wanting to be trapped in the stairwell, Raj stepped toward the nearby door only for it to slam closed as well. He yanked the handle. Locked! He needed to reach an open door before they all closed. Raj took steps two at a time and cried out to alert whoever was locking the place down.

"Hey, stop closing the doors! I'm in here! Hello?"

Security. It had to be security. He saw movement in the room downstairs. Steve had given him grief that morning about beer bottles left out on the roof and cigarette butts. Why the man blamed Raj, Raj did not know, but he suffered the heat. He had no idea who had been up there. Maybe Steve was locking the stairwell down to drive home the point to Raj.

There were only two more floors left. However Steve was locking the doors, Raj needed to get there faster. If security was not proving a point and simply following procedure, then who knows how long Raj might be stuck. Racing to the next landing, Raj rushed the door which slammed closed on him while he was at a full run. The door struck him with such force that it propelled him backward. As he stumbled he thought of how no one was on the other side of the door but it closed with more than mechanical force, like someone pushed it closed but no one was there. And then he was not there either, his feet left the ground.

Raj windmilled his arms and tumbled over the railing! He grabbed the rail as he fell. His arm twisted painfully but he had a grip. The bottom floor loomed far below, a straight shot to a melon splitting. Raj screamed for help even as he kicked to reposition himself, spinning until he righted his arm and gripped the rail with his other hand. Someone cackled overhead.

"Help me! I need help!"

Raj calculated if he could land on the next level landing if he let go. Negative. The angle seemed off. A face peered over a railing on the top floor. The bruja! Her laughter filled the air.

"No!"

A quick glance down toward his doom and then back up. Legs, the strange dangling legs which appeared to have no weight, slid over the railing above. Her face was no longer in sight, but the cackling persisted.

Adrenaline gave him the strength to pull himself up and over the railing. The effort taxed him, and he fell onto his back, breathing in relief. The position on the floor gave him a clean view up to the distant ceiling. A dark figure suddenly flew across the top level, moving from one side of the stairwell to the next so fast it was a blur. Raj tried to comprehend the incomprehensible.

The motion repeated, one floor lower, flying from one side to the other. At the speed the woman (thing?) moved, it would be upon him in no time. Raj shot to his feet and raced down the stairs to the next door. Locked! One floor above, the woman crossed again, a black form against the white stairwell paint. The cackles grew closer. He panicked and refused to let go of the door handle, though it would not budge. The cackling grew so close he felt breath over his shoulder.

"Let me out! Let me out!"

The door suddenly creaked open which made little sense, but he rushed though, stumbling. When he regained his footing, he noticed Trager Chemicals was gone. He stood in the bruja's house from when he was a kid. Except the place appeared even more menacing than he remembered. Blood-smeared satanic symbols covered the walls. A scream sounded nearby. It came from his younger self. Young Raj ran by him, screaming.

Impossible. Raj shook his head, and the surroundings changed. He was back in the corridor of Trager. At the end of the hall, a woman tilted on her feet as if drunk. He looked closer, and it sank in. She lilted to one side because she hovered rather than stood.

The woman lifted her head. It was not the bruja but a face unknown to Raj. The half-faced woman with the snake in her eye back at the snake pit. The woman grinned with a smile of half exposed teeth and gristle. Raj jerked backward in fright only to find himself once again in the bruja's house.

Murmurs sounded in the kitchen. Raj looked inside where his mother sat in a chair. The bruja, looking like a normal old lady, held a butcher knife in one hand and chicken's head in the other, the deed already done.

Raj's mother turned to him. "Oh, hi, honey..."

She failed to finish her thought. With a ferocious swing, the bruja decapitated Raj's mother. Her head rolled to his feet and blinked several times before realizing she was no longer among the living.

Raj glanced back up at the bruja whose features aged until her skin threatened to slough off from drooping. The woman's eyes sunk into pools of jet black. Even her clothes went to rot, barely clinging to her thin frame, looking more like strands of spaghetti than a gown.

Transformation complete, she charged him, blade raised. He glanced while running and saw the blade turned into a broom. Raj suddenly hit a wall. Confused, he looked around and found himself back in the Trager corridor. Airborne on the broom, the woman closed in on him. The elevators were close. He made a run for them. One opened and Raj leaped inside. The doors were taking too long to close. He cried out for them to hurry up.

A thump sounded above. The ceiling vent shook, jostling loose particles like earlier in the lab. With a crash, the vent hit the floor.

The bruja's head and torso lowered down. She grabbed Raj's shirt and yanked him into the shaft. Her cackles drowned out his screams. The doors finally closed, and a wet splotch cut off his desperate cries.

Outside in the hall the elevator closed. A torrent of blood washed over the elevator doors painting them red. The numbers ascended as the elevator took Raj to a higher place.

CHAPTER 26

T he hallway to Mitch's office was quiet, too quiet. Gillian coughed to make certain it was not her ears, that she had not fallen into another dream like fugue. One of the first things she planned to do was tell Mitch about the face, or half a face with a blinking eye. Disgusting. But it was her imagination, so the manifested images gave her pause. Who came up with things like that? Daniel, a friend of hers and a fellow reporter, authored horror novels. The gory gooey stuff. She wanted to support him, but those kinds of books were not her jam. She never understood how people could freak themselves out at will. Worse, she wondered how such normal people (Daniel was a mensch) could come up with such twisted stuff.

Gillian was her own answer. Earlier, she created with her mind the most grotesque thing. With sleep deprivation, calorie deficits, and isolation, apparently imaginations ran wild. She vowed no sequels to her crazy waking dream. She would share every detail of the strange vision and Mitch would laugh, and she would pretend to laugh. After sharing, Gillian planned to move on. There were plenty of other fears in the building to deal with besides fanciful imaginary ones. Gillian arrived at his office and found the door partially open. She pushed it the rest of the way.

"Dr. Trager?"

Mitch was not there. His absence was a mixed bag. As a reporter, she relished the chance to examine the man's office without supervision. Observing a person's natural environment was a great way to learn about someone. But she also longed for company. Rather than dwell on the good doctor's absence, Gillian went into snooping mode.

The office included a traditional mahogany desk and an impressive espresso bar. A massive steel door rose from floor to ceiling behind the desk. It was there that the feng shui of the room took a turn. The door looked like something out of *Star Trek* and appeared as impenetrable as a bank vault.

Gillian placed her hand on the palm reader. How many people had done the same? The urge was irresistible. It failed to open when she touched the cool pad. She was no King Arthur. The sword remained buried to the hilt in the stone. Proximity to the palm reader brought her to his side of the desk revealing a framed photo of his wife. Five years on and he had yet to let go. If the good doctor had moved on, wouldn't he have a photo of his new paramour?

The picture showed why it would be hard to move on. They looked perfect together. Gillian knew of such couples, but never found the same in her own life. Then the strangest thing occurred. The picture danced. Not the couple in the picture, but the image itself. The picture jiggled like an earthquake had struck the office, but the framed photo was not on a desk riding out the storm—it was in her hand.

Jitters had returned. Why could she not escape them? The same nerves that struck her in her temporary office had found her while she stood in what was likely the most inviting space in the building. It made no sense until the eyes in the picture followed her. She moved it side to side. Wendy's gaze followed her like some creepy painting in a wealthy estate. Wendy was subjectively beautiful, a stunning woman who oozed confidence and vitality. Gillian noticed as much at the restaurant when the two women exchanged smiles.

A brief interaction. The two women shared a mere moment in time, and yet somehow, five years on and in a different city, Gillian held a photo of that woman in her hands. Strange how it all came around. The article Gillian wrote in the murder's aftermath was almost as brief as her interaction with Wendy. Gillian wrote about the murder and mentioned Mitch's mental state, thinking it humanized the man. Never did she believe it would result in Mitch's firing.

A five-year follow up made sense. Such articles were easier to write because most of the details were already in print. It was simply a matter of adding fresh details. Research revealed where he moved to. The man's career trajectory was interesting on its own outside of the tragedy. If the doctor refused to participate, her paper would not run the story. Gillian left many messages for Mitch but never heard back. There was zero chance the paper would pay her to fly to Seattle without first securing the interview, so she took it on as a freelance project. But that meant going to Seattle to find the man.

It also gave her reason to dig out her notes and recording which is when she heard the voice for the first time. She enhanced the audio to make sure it was not an anomaly and transferred the recording to her phone for easy replay. No mistaking it, Mitch screamed for his wife, and a female voice answered. Then another voice spoke in Mitch's office.

"I'm here," it said.

A reflection of Dead Wendy appeared in the picture frame's glass. Gillian dropped it and spun, but no one was there. Only more imagination figments. It needed to stop. *And take the jitters with it as well,* she thought. Gillian looked down at the desk and gasped. The glass on the frame had broken and tore a portion of the picture, slicing into Wendy's smiling face, tearing it roughly in half.

Horrible. She had defaced an important part of the man's life. First the hospital firing, showing up at the man's office during the demise of his new business, and now this. Gillian shook her head. How could she cause so much trouble?

Not wanting to leave Mitch to discover the damage without her around to apologize, Gillian opened a drawer and placed the picture inside. Surely the picture was digital, and he could easily reprint it. But until she was certain she would suffer in silence, feeling like the foolest fool who ever did fool. A manilla envelope sat in the drawer, its flap unsealed.

The reporter in her wanted to open it and look inside, see what it was. But she had done enough snooping and enough damage. Besides, she was seeing things. With her luck she would pull the half face out of the envelope. Despite being torn down to one eye, the picture of Wendy still appeared to gaze at Gillian.

Gillian slammed the drawer. She needed company, needed comfort. Then it hit her. Gillian knew exactly where to go next. She left Mitch's office, taking with her more guilt than when she first walked in.

CHAPTER 27

"**E**nough!" Colt screamed.

He yanked at the straps holding him in place. While having toyed with Ink, Colt had never used the variant supplied by Doctor Trager. The procurement process for the specific version was more rigorous than for the core product. Now Colt understood why. The old psyche hospital restraint chair did not help matters.

Colt experienced flashes of being a patient, one misdiagnosed then restrained. In one moment of panic his mind even went to the idea that he had never been a Trager scientist but was always a patient at the hospital. Maybe they never shut the place down and he was delusional. He needed to shake off those thoughts, as they freaked him out too much.

That was when he latched onto Maddy. He remembered the woman's name from earlier, could still smell her. The world was not a figment of his imagination. He was a rockstar scientist and banged women ceaselessly. Not proud, he could not help himself but think of the recent conquest to ground himself. But as his fear grew, he cried out for her. He could not think of anyone else to ask for help. She was as intimate with him as anyone. Would there ever be anyone for him when he needed them? Because he needed somebody now.

"Maddy, help! Maddy, please!"

She would not be there, of course. The only women who could even possibly be there for him were those he screwed over. Colt was not one man; he was the man every woman wanted him to be at any moment. Once he conquered them, he moved on. A lonely existence? No, that was what the next conquest was for. But what happened when the defecation hit the oscillation? Who would be there for him?

"Maddy! I'm sorry, babe. I'm a piss-poor boyfriend, but I could use your help, sweetheart!"

The towel would have flown off long ago were it not plastered to his face with sweat. Colt looked to his lap, and though he could not see, he could feel. Colt giggled and soon that turned into a guffaw which segued into a maniacal laugh. How could it be? Mitch laughed. He could not stop. Despite his situation, despite having already had sex earlier, he sported a full-blown erection. He stopped fighting the bonds at his wrist long enough to wrestle with those in his mind.

"What the fuck is wrong with me?" He looked to the sky, still blind. "What did ya do to me, ma?"

She did not molest him, nothing of the sort. But something, some-thing made him like this. There was plenty of other crap. But how? How had he ended up the way he was? The drug faded into the background as his heart pounded with sorrow. Colt mourned. He felt a loss. It was him. He had lost himself somewhere along the way. The thoughts took hold in his mind.

"Ungh! No. Ah. Stop! I don't want to think about this now. Sorry Maddy. I'm sorry, Maddy. You deserve better. You all deserved better." Colt choked on a sob. "I'm nothing but a tramp. A bum. I'll never amount to anything. Yeah, I know ma."

Then the tears and fear turned to rage. He yanked at the restraints. Something inside his arm popped. He did not care. He pulled and pulled. The bonds were too strong, maybe given power by his faults and misdeeds. If that were the case, he might never break free. Colt screamed until running out of breath.

Where were the monster movies? Where was the creepy pasta crap? Why, when scared off his rocker, did Colt revisit his past? Was his mother responsible for his inability to commit, or to seek stable relationships? He tried not to think about it, but his mind traveled back in time to that day on the field. There was no crying when the snake bit him. His mother would have laughed had he cried. Young Colt learned that by age five. No crying in front of Mom. It only made him feel worse when she mocked him. The one that bit him was not the real snake, though. The true one was the man with the tattoos.

Then a pop and tension released one of his arms. The timer! It worked. He had not set a volume on the digital device, for the sound alone might have become the focus of his terror. As it was, the slight pop caused him to squirm in his seat in fright. He was afraid to remove the towel, was afraid to look at anything because he understood whatever it was would scare the Twinkies out of him. Even the towel had to be tossed aside so it would not inadvertently become an object of his phobia. Until he was fully ready, he kept his eyes pressed tight.

After removing the towel, it would take him time to loosen the restraints. That was by design. He needed to ensure he was trapped long enough to view the orange. The thought of the fruit frightened him in advance, which was irrational. That was what he found himself suffering from. Irrational fear.

The drug was more powerful than anything he ever imagined. But had it done the job? Was he only going to reassign his original fears to an orange? Would he now be frightened of snakes, personal debauchery, AND citrus? He hoped not. Replacement theory was the goal.

With head bowed, Colt dangled the towel low enough to pull it free while keeping his eyes closed. He sat up straight so that when he opened his eyes, the object would catch his sightline. But he feared opening them, too worried something bad would happen. It was his experiment though, he had to look sooner than later. Colt readied to release himself, (and run after viewing the object). He opened his eyes and screamed, letting out all the built-up terror. Nothing was there!

The scientist in him urged him to shut his eyes and wait for Raj to rescue him. Though closing them anew could result in an irrational fear of the dark. Besides, introspection waited in darkness. Then something moved along his arms. He felt cold scales against his flesh. Snakes! Had they escaped? One crawled up each arm. Then he realized where they came from.

"Raj, my tattoos, I forgot about my tattoos! Raj, help!"

The cobras wrapped tight around his forearms, holding them in place tighter than the chair restraints. Their heads danced before him, hissing, and spitting. One lashed toward him, and he jerked his face away, barely escaping the bite.

"Raj! Raj!"

The snakes danced in synchronized fashion and hissed in harmony. Then the sound transformed, becoming something different. Colt glimpsed a flicker in one snake's glassy eyes. Light? The snake turned its head and a beam of light shot toward a sheet dangling in the distance—the cheapest of movie screens. Snake hisses morphed into the clicking of a projector rolling film.

A film played on the unclean sheet. Urine, sweat, and even spaghetti sauce defiled the white fabric. It could have been his bedding growing up, Colt thought. His mom washed it about once every six months. The state of the makeshift screen was the same state of the slum apartment shown in the movie. A home movie.

On-screen, younger Colt watched a monster flick on an old box TV. The antenna was wrapped in tinfoil. He sat with his back resting against a futon couch, the only piece of furniture in the living room. The carpet underneath him was threadbare, worn so deep that some tufts crusted into points sharp enough to cut skin. The actors screamed about a rubber suited monster on the TV, but louder screams elsewhere in the apartment drowned out those of the actors.

Young Colt followed the sounds to his mother's cracked-open bedroom door and pushed it open further to make sure his mom was okay. Inside, a greasy man stood on his knees on a filthy mattress. The spindly naked form of his mother, mostly out of view, rested her head near the man's lap. The stranger smiled at Colt with a mouthful of silver-capped teeth.

Colt called out. "Mom?"

She quickly covered her body with a sheet. A snake dangled from her mouth and slowly slithered all the way in. Once it vanished inside her, his mother smiled, and a snake tongue flicked out. Young Colt bolted back to the living room and covered his ears. His mother never checked on him.

Back in the chair, the older Colt had enough. A tear ran down his cheek. The movie ended with a title card which read '*Fin?*'. The snake stopped projecting film, and both faced him but no longer in synch. They individually lashed out.

Colt freed his arm from the popped restraint. He reached for the other and struggled to unbuckle it. Drawn by his movements, the reptiles snapped at his free hand. After unbuckling the second restraint, Colt pulled the slithering creatures off his arms and tossed them into the shadows. With them temporarily out of sight, he tried to gather his thoughts and navigate through terror.

The experiment worked. The drug brought him to a state of irrational fear. And as planned, he attached that fear to an object. The problem was it was the wrong object. His fear imprinted on his tattoos. Colt inadvertently engaged in operant conditioning, reinforcing his reptile phobia.

Colt understood there were many more reptiles waiting in the snake pit outside the door, but he needed to escape those in the room. He rushed through the door mindful that glass prisons encased those in the tight corridor. Except glass crushed underfoot as soon as he entered the snake pit. Shards covered the floor in piles from broken enclosures.

Thick steam filled the area. What had happened to the place? Only the nearest containers were visible. A wall of steam hid the rest. Snakes lunged through broken glass of the nearest enclosures. Colt raced into the unknown. Steam parted like a curtain as he ran, revealing snakes of various types trying to bite him.

They were everywhere! He screamed and leaped into the lab. It was filled with fog, so dense it hid the entire floor. Raj was nowhere in sight, but the antidote remained on the tray. The antidote would take time to work, but he hoped it would start with a placebo effect.

As he reached for the injector, a cobra (from his tattoo) lashed out and knocked the injector away. The instrument vanished into the fog, clanging near his feet. Colt reached down to retrieve it when a snake erupted through the fog, launching through the air, its body stretching from coiled to uncoiled as it shot into a full leap. The large fangs and open mouth went for his face. Colt turned in time, so the snake barely connected with his nose.

The aborted strike still stung, but a scrape was preferable to a bite. Despite Colt's fear, he understood he was hallucinating under the effects of the drug. Except the pain made it real. If he were hallucinating, would he feel pain? No.

That meant the snakes had escaped somehow. It explained Raj's absence as well. Phobia or not, Raj would have run away in the face of a swarm of snakes. A snake lashed out from the fog as he neared the exit causing him to stumble through the exit. He landed face first in the corridor.

And started drowning!

His face rested in water. He coughed, spit, and came up soaking wet. Mud sucked at his knees, soaking through his pants. What happened to the concrete floor? Colt rose to his feet and turned to find the lab door gone, along with the rest of the building. A dense jungle surrounded him. Something rustled in the nearby brush—the mother of all snakes. Colt froze as the massive monstrosity slithered through the underbrush. It seemed to go on forever. Colt estimated it to be forty feet long. While that monster snake moved through with quiet grace, angry hissing sounded from somewhere nearby.

The trees! Dozens of snakes slithered in branches overhead. One dropped toward his face, and he batted it away. But then another dropped. He ran. As he sped off, snake after snake dropped in succession so that he dodged a phalanx of falling reptiles. Colt cleared the trees and emerged into a clearing. The area, while still thick with green, was so marshy that water rose to his knees. The gigantic snake moved past once again. He escaped to an area thick with vines and brush.

Nothing made sense. There was no way he was in a jungle. And what was that enormous snake? Colt fought to remember the layout of the hallway back when it existed. He should have passed one of two supply closets, the one used by housekeeping and the other by the gardening crew. Past that would be the security office, followed by the elevator bank and lobby.

He spotted the elevators. Though surrounded by vines, they were visible. One carriage sat open. Colt leaped in and pressed buttons. The doors closed and the numbers on the panel ascended. Colt breathed in relief until a hand tussled the hair on the back of his head. He spun and came face to face with a sickly, stick-thin woman. Her shorts and tank top threatened to fall off because there was so little to cling to. Colt froze as the woman spoke.

"Look at you, you're all growed up."

"Mom? How are you here? You're dead."

In a flash, she was in his face, rotten teeth bared, snarling in response to the insult. "How dare you speak like that to your mother!"

With a ding, the elevator door opened. He staggered out into more jungle while seeking to put some distance between his mother and himself. Hissing filled the air. A mass of writhing snakes stood between mother and son. His mother pointed at the pile of reptiles.

"Go ahead, pick one up."

"No, Mom, please," Colt said, tears welling in his eyes. Less from her demand than simply seeing her again.

"Pick it up little sissy!"

"I won't, you're not real."

"Oh, that hurts, son. Mommy's just a little sick is all, you know that right? That Mommy's sick?"

With that plea she changed into the occasionally clean version of his mother, the one who made appearances far too rarely. Colt always lived for those days when that mother would appear and laugh, and smile, and be a mom. Colt held onto those rare memories.

"I know Mom, I know."

Colt stepped forward, and the pile of snakes vanished, leaving only a boy and his mom. And the boy needed a hug. He reached for her with a desire to tell her he made good, that he became a scientist. One who made good money and lived in a nice place in Seattle, but who also frequently visited Canada. Now he had the chance to tell her everything.

Without warning, the massive forty-foot snake struck and took the woman down like an offensive tackle destroying a quarterback. The woman vanished from sight in the blink of an eye.

"Mom!"

He splashed through swampy waters, chasing after the evil thing that stole his mom's innocence, but only got a few yards before the massive snake rose high above him. Its tongue slithered out with a deafening hiss. Visible in its gullet was his mother's shape being swallowed feet first. From inside the snake's belly, the woman reached for her son.

She was too weak to break through the beast's skin. She was always too weak. The snake paid no mind to its partially swallowed meal, instead it danced back and forth, trying to hypnotize Colt into submission. It failed.

Colt turned and ran. In the distance, he spotted a lifeline. One of the supply closets. The snake's shadow cast over his shoulder and grew to an impossible size. He leaped into the closet, turned, and pressed against the door just as the snake rammed it. The beast hit with such force it launched Colt back into shelves, dislodging supplies. The snake outside prepped for another strike.

He attempted to close the door, but it stopped short. A bottle of cleaning solution had caught between door and jamb. The snake struck. Colt threw the bottle aside and slammed the door just in time. The snake made contact, but the door held up. A gentler thumping sounded in the hall as the beast slithered past. Its length rocked the door where it touched, but it moved away. Slithering off until all fell silent out in the hallway.

Colt breathed in relief. He hoped his fear would soon subside enough to think clearly. His experimental days were over. He vowed never to subject anyone to such a drug. If the financiers had not already shut everything down, he would have fought to do the same. Colt had never known how dangerous the drug was. As his heart rate neared normal again, something hissed.

He rose to his feet and pressed his ear to the door. He waited for the big mother-effer to pass. But he soon realized the hissing came from inside the closet! He spun. Nothing. More hissing to his left. He spun. Nothing. Then he felt the writhing on his skin.

His tattoos. He raised his arms. The snakes danced in formation. The twin cobras flared their faces open and struck his eyes. Colt dropped to the floor with both snakes still attached to his eye sockets. Once on the ground, Colt tremored violently for some time before finally going still.

CHAPTER 28

Two women kissing threatened to push Mercedette over the edge. The scientist rested in her contoured chair as the world around her oozed sex. The brain scan registered her arousal as almost fully red. Ninety-nine percent was still shy of a hundred, so she continued watching the videos. Mercedette did not believe the one percent would make a difference, but she needed a level set for her experiment. The highest level possible was what she wished to test against. Stop people at that level, and her personal protection device would stop anybody.

It took great willpower not to relieve herself. Though it would have been easy. She was alone (the viewing booth remained empty), and she was already half naked. She considered tracing a hand down and... That thought pushed her closer to one hundred.

But she refused to give in. This was one instance where self-care would sabotage her greater interest, that of stopping predators in their tracks. Predators were monsters who sought power over victims. But sexual arousal often grew in the bastards as they took control over their victims. What Mercedette really wished to develop was a guillotine that fit a different sized head. But driving predators mad with fear and marking them for the police would have to do.

Mercedette had a healthy sexual appetite, even without libido drugs. She left a trail of broken hearts behind since college. There was only one thing in mind when she hooked up with someone—gratification. Others controlled her for far too long, so she avoided long-term relationships. As a scientist, she understood biological needs, so engaged in routine sexual relations, but any connections ended there. Relationships were societal constructs which she had no time or desire for.

She was too busy working on creating a powerful self-defense deterrent. It was not sex she wished to stop; it was those who would use it as a ruse to prey on others. Not all Trager employees had prepared for future testing, but the scientists who wanted results the most certainly had. She was one.

The FDA had a process and a timeline for clearing drugs for human testing. Mitch kept the employees in the loop on which stages had already passed and which were forthcoming. Once human trials were imminent, the most forward-looking scientists of the bunch expensed their required equipment. Those individuals would hit the ground running on day one. Once the FDA cleared them, each scientist could test up to seventy-five subjects.

Phase one of trials tested for safety and generally lasted a year. Phase two concentrated on effectiveness. Normally, the staff would have had to wait for the original fear element to go through all the trials. But by modifying the chemical component, each variant earned its own trial.

In Mercedette's case, she wished she could jump straight to phase two. Her study was all about effectiveness. She cared little if it was safe. If an attacker got a face full of some unknown side effects all the better. She hated to waste a year on safety (but she planned to, there were rules), but on the first day she could, Mercedette always planned to be her own first subject. By testing on herself, she would fully understand if the device truly worked. Through experience she would learn if it shut people down enough to keep them from further victimizing someone.

Her plans to self-test from day one was why she had the fore-sight to reach out and become part of a study on another drug making waves in the pharmaceutical industry. The drug was in its own human trials. Mercedette applied and was selected as a trial subject. The drug was a variant of Viagra for females. Originally it was tested as an anti-seizure medication but the odd side effect of arousal caused them to study it further and perfect a variant. It induced physical symptoms of arousal, but that was not enough. Men experienced erections during their sleep cycles. That did not mean they were aroused. The drug could only do so much in the way of stimulation, there needed to be other mechanisms to feed into the physical stimulation.

Mercedette needed to induce a heightened state of arousal in the test subject. (Herself in this case.) That required adding visual stimuli into the mix. Designed as a teaching lab, her workspace contained large screens when she moved in. She hired someone to make the stimulating video loops. VR goggles stood ready as a further stimulant. If Mercedette felt her arousal was close to stopping at a certain degree (or worse, declining), she would introduce VR. The VR had its own videos designed to act as if one were taking part in an actual sexual tryst. Those videos already existed on the market (so many of them), so she purchased several for her experiments.

Mercedette hoped her dispersal device would be effective because it was not an aerosol. It sprayed liquid. The payload was more super soaker than pepper spray. The fear element induced fear topically through skin, but if a predator swallowed, all the better. Taken internally, it would hasten the drug's effects.

She shook her head, trying to get out of her own way. Her body screamed with arousal, but her mind kept thinking about the experiment itself. An assistant would have been useful. They could have done much of the work while she simply focused on her building desire. Except she might have engaged in sex with someone in the room. That was the problem built into the testing process.

The chair! Mercedette leaped from her own contoured one and removed the brain imaging cap. *Stupid, stupid, stupid*, she thought. The tablet would fire the weapon, but human instinct would make subjects dodge any oncoming spray. To avoid that, Mercedette planned to sit in a chair which would limit her ability to dodge the stream. But she forgot to put the chair in place.

Not wanting to lose too much pent up arousal, she tried to hurry. She rushed to a large supply closet at the rear of the lab. In its face-high rectangular window, she studied her reflection. For a moment, there appeared a strange variant of herself, one where half her face was missing. But upon closer inspection, all she saw was a woman who looked horny as heck. Good, she thought and opened the door. She grabbed a hardback chair and rushed over to the dispersal device and positioned it.

From there she raced back to her experiment chair, the fantasyland place. Except something was wrong. She placed the imaging cap back on and found herself down to eighty percent. She still felt obscenely aroused, yet she was losing ground according to the imaging. Then it hit her. The chair. Moving it brought her back somewhere else. She had long ago blocked out those memories, but now they threatened to come flooding back. She closed her eyes and tried to clear her mind. And failed.

The act of placing the chair was a painful reminder of the days when the commune tasked teens with setting up the banquet hall for father-daughter dances. Once women reached a certain age in the commune, they attended the dances. Never were they allowed to invite boys of their own age, rather they attended with the male adults living in the commune.

Daughters in the commune had to set up for their own dances. Mercedette was strong, so often set up the chairs. In charge of everything was the Elder who lived in a massive home atop a hill while the rest of the commune lived at the base of the same. The residents farmed their own food and worked hard every day to serve their own closed community. The Elder (whom Mercedette never met) lived above it all and made rules (often arbitrary) that were to be followed without question.

When Mercedette's parents moved there with her in tow, it initially felt like a wonderful place. One that was a far cry from the hustle and bustle of the city they left behind. She quickly learned that things were far from ideal. The Elder declared her parents' marriage an unsuitable match. The Elder declared the two divorced and assigned each a new spouse, that of another married couple.

Dan became her new father. The community forbid Mercedette from referring to Dan as anything other than Dad, or some variant. If she called him Dan, there were repercussions. Mercedette's mother acted as if nothing was wrong, appeared happy even. The two certainly sent her to the fields often so they could have time alone. Eventually, every wife in the compound had to visit the Elder. The women who went were normally gone for days at a time and when they returned (tired and haggard) they were pronounced wives of the Elder. Never mind that they already had assigned spouses.

Mercedette was young enough when they first moved in that it was years before she finally attended a father/daughter dance. The rule was the daughters could dance with any father except for their own. Maybe because she was new and there for the first time, she received much attention. Men came up to her with dizzying speed, speaking in rushed tones about things she could not fully understand.

It was when she finally had a break from the action that she noticed a man standing alone. It was her biological father. He saw her, took her hand, and they went to the dance floor and danced to a slow song. It took most of the song for her to realize he did not even recognize her. Mercedette cried there on the floor in the arms of the man who birthed her but did not know her from the next daughter in a row.

Her crying brought tears to her father as well and he wept along, mourning something different. They danced until the tears dried, and Mercedette let the man go for good, only to be invited to the floor by others, men who groped and grinned and made innuendos.

Later in life, well after leaving the cult, Mercedette better understood the machinations of life in the compound. Had teens been allowed to interact, they would have explored their sexuality together. But they were kept from doing so. Natural sexual energy that came with a transition into adulthood became focused in one direction. To explore such things, one needed to become a bride of the Elder. Or a ward. That was the designation of the men taken to his palace.

Stories about the man (they knew that much, that He was male) spoke of an individual so startlingly beautiful that none could resist Him. For that reason, Mercedette had to forgive her mother for abandoning their father. She was under the sway of the man, as was her original dad. They made their choices. Mercedette had not.

Mercedette shook her head, trying to erase the memories of her past. She checked the tablet. Red was quickly receding from the arousal center in her brain. She decided it was time for the VR. So slipped the headset on which almost dislodged her imaging cap.

She did not know in advance which videos would play on the VR, but the first showed a forest which looked familiar. The forest quickly vanished, and a sex scene surrounded her. She was a voyeur so far; her avatar was not taking part. A man took a woman from behind. The woman's curvy body excited Mercedette, the VR experience was working. Until she looked at the man.

His face was upside down! Mercedette tried to take off the VR headset but could not. The man continued having sex but turned to Mercedette and smiled upside down. Everyone in the camp understood what that meant. If one saw such faces, it was time to see the Elder. Mercedette had recently turned eighteen in the compound when it became her turn.

Until that night, Mercedette thought she might escape the situation because other adult residents had identified Mercedette's aptitude for science. Mercedette landed a scholarship at a prestigious college. Rather than forbid college attendance, the compound directors insisted she attend. The compound administrators identified certain individuals as well suited for further education. The plan was for those members to get degrees and bring the skills back to the collective.

Believing a trip to college would bypass a trip to the Elder, young Mercedette assumed she might avoid the ritual many others experienced. Until Dan roused her in the dead of night and led her to the forest's edge where a line of tiki torches stretched up the hill. Other teens marched the path ahead of her. She was not to ascend alone. Rogan, a gentle soul with a pleasant smile, was there as well. He looked nervous when his mother took his glasses off. Dan asked Mercedette to take Rogan's hand, as he could not see without glasses.

Running was not an option. The torches were not unmanned, each was held by robed figures with upside-down faces under their hoods. The upside-down faces were upturned masks of an identical but unknown male face (that of the Elder?). How they could see through them was a mystery.

The marching line of teens consisted of equal amounts of males and females. It was too dark, and the others were too far along for Mercedette to identify anyone. She and Rogan climbed under the watchful gaze of the upside-down men. Once they arrived at the end of the path, they reached a gate adorned with sculptures of mythical creatures. Beyond the gate was an opulent palace rising high into the night sky. The gate opened silently and despite Mercedette's nervousness, she marched forward with some sense of awe.

Grand oversized doors stood open. Rogan gripped her hand too tight on the climb, but she allowed it. She was afraid, too. But the enormous structure evoked memories of the grandeur of high rises. Once upon a time, such structures were routine. She often thought of them, but over the years, her memories faded. Stepping through doors twice her height reminded her of those days, and she fought to remember innocence.

A symphony of sights, sounds, and scents overwhelmed her upon entry. Sparkling chandeliers adorned a grand foyer. Their crystal facets cast shimmering patterns of light across immaculate marble floors. A delicate aroma of fresh flowers filled the air.

One upside-down man in the grand foyer gestured for them to follow. The man led her and Rogan through a labyrinth of chambers, each more resplendent than the last. Lavish tapestries, hand-woven with threads of gold and silver, graced the walls. The ceilings were impossibly high and adorned with breathtaking frescoes that depicted celestial scenes.

There were too many sights to absorb them all. Rogan, he of the diminished eyesight, missed out on the awe inducing scenery. For that reason, his fear remained on the surface while Mercedette distracted herself with the scenery. Until they arrived at the stone staircase.

The stairs were made of large rough-cut stone. Small torches hung in wall mounts the length of the stairwell. The light at the base of the stairs gleamed red, as if the path led to Hell. (Little did she know.) Mercedette finally gripped Rogan hard enough for him to yelp. Their guide whisked them down the stone steps. She heard cries of pain somewhere below, mixed with grunts of pleasure.

Once they reached the bottom step, two upside-down men forced her and Rogan to strip. Nervous and shamed, she saw a penis for the first time. Rogan was hard and flushed with excitement. No matter what awaited them and how little he could see, he fixated on her naked form. It would not last. The lights (emanating from somewhere unseen) were so deeply red that her nude body could have been bleeding and she would not have known.

The upside-downs led the teens through a velvet curtain to a grand ballroom made of more stone where many teens were strapped into numerous restraint devices. Though she knew many of the residents, she had never seen any nude before. She struggled with desire, all while experiencing a growing sense of dread. They led her and Rogan over to matching devices where they were forcefully strapped into place.

Mercedette cried out in the lab and fought to remove the VR headset. It was real, too real, and why images from that night? An upside-down man in the VR world struck young Mercedette with a cane. Adult Mercedette cried out, feeling the pain anew. The younger Mercedette in the virtual world cried out for mercy. There would be none.

Different men with the upside-down faces appeared as one and threshed her. Those in her sightline disrobed until naked. They were all erect, excited by her pain. Many branched off and used the other trapped bodies in the room. Mercedette had a limited view but could see the suffering of some of her peers. Each upside-down man, nude except for the masks, used the nearest body they could to satiate their twisted desires.

The men closest to her soon moved beyond her sightline. She awaited their touch, but the creeps first assembled around Rogan. Her poor friend fell into a confusing series of cries, screams, and groans. His innocence defiled; his world forever changed. Then, like that, the world fell silent. A hush fell over the crowd and footsteps evacuated the room.

All was silent except for one set of footsteps. Supposedly, the Elder was an angel. But she never got eyes on the man. He circled behind her. And when the man spoke, it was not the voice of an angel. It was the voice of a demon. And soon the pain began.

Adult Mercedette wanted to watch the VR long enough to spot the face of the evil man, but she could not take it, could not relive that night. She finally ripped the headset off and threw it across the room. It landed with a crack. She cared not if it broke. She sat up, rubbed her eyes, and sniffed. Impossible!

Whale oil. They used it for the torches. It had a very distinct odor, and it lingered in the air in her lab. The sexual enhancement drug was untested. Did it influence her memory centers? Mercedette needed to shake off the memories if she wanted to continue with her experiment. There was not an ounce of arousal in her now. She did not need a brain scan to know that.

She focused on her transition from the compound. Once at college, she never returned. The collective sent people to abduct her, but she worked with college police to have the men arrested. (The same who were there that night? She never knew because they wore masks.)

From there, she worked jobs to pay for college and started a new life. Eventually, authorities raided the compound. Mercedette was unaware if they scooped up her parents in the raid. She never sought the information because she never planned to speak to them again. Let her forget them the same way her original father had forgotten her.

The memories sapped her sexual energy. Mercedette ignored the warnings of the trial drug and took three more without water. It would take time to get back into the red. (Wasn't the torture room red? Hadn't she just remembered that?) Mercedette instinctively rubbed her lower back tattoo. She got the intricate tattoo to cover the branding she and the others received that night.

In defiance of the monsters, she had since reclaimed pleasure. She refused to let them take that from her. She had separated sexual acts from that of her encounters with the upside-down men and the Elder. Mercedette understood pleasure existed separate from pain. She just needed to remember how.

Looking at the video screens, she understood that would not be enough. As much as it frightened her, she needed the stimulation of VR. Head clear, she picked it up off the floor and found that it still worked despite the abuse. Mercedette settled into the chair and slipped it on. The man and women were normal actors this time. Taking in the virtual debauchery, Mercedette fought to put memories of the past aside. Unable to stop monsters in her past, she was ready to test her device on them now.

CHAPTER 29

Derrick stood on the roof of the abandoned wing. Condemned signs hung everywhere. Little did the people who posted the signs know, but the rooftop became a gathering place for Trager employees. If Mitch knew about the building's designation he never objected. Jimmy may have known, but that was unlikely as the creepazoid would have shut the whole thing down. A fan of true crime media, Derrick long ago noticed something about predators' eyes.

In mugshots and other pictures, those who committed heinous crimes had a weird eyeball thing going on. One eye always looked straight at the camera, while the other drifted so far in another direction it appeared to stare into another dimension. Jimmy possessed such a look. That was probably why the man usually avoided direct eye contact.

Not wishing to waste time thinking about the authority figure any longer, Derrick looked to the night sky. The fresh air reinvigorated him. He felt stifled inside after the spider incident. *The Spider incident* did not have a nice ring. He needed another name. The *tinkle incident*? That was better, but he would workshop it with Amy if she ever spoke to him again.

A cooler nestled in a nearby nook beckoned. It rested alongside two collapsed lawn chairs that were folded down so the wind would not blow them away. Derrick opened the cooler and found several beers and cans of soda floating in watery remnants of melted ice. Gross, but Derrick wanted a beer so grabbed one.

Opening a lawn chair, he set it up with a clear view of the distant ocean. He lined up the bottle cap along the chair rail's edge and slammed down so the top popped off. He took a refreshing sip and looked out into the bay. Soon they would all ride the ferry one last time and land—where? Derrick was uncertain what the future held if they failed over the weekend.

Unlike the others, Derrick did not believe that the dream would live on minus funding. Money ruled everything in society. He understood that well from his father's time managing an innovative pharmaceutical company.

The view of the sky was stunning from the island. Stars ruled the sky. Where he grew up, light pollution drowned out the stars. The bright lights made him think of his father. One night, while standing on their massive lawn and looking up at the sky, Derrick's dad stepped up to his son. Derrick asked his father why they could not see stars from their home.

"Because man shines brighter than the stars. Their creations are as beautiful as anything in the heavens," his father said.

Such a sentiment made Derrick long to become a man who made things as bright as the stars. But months after inspiring Derrick with those words, his father began using the product his company produced. The pills left the man listless and different.

Another night (after the change) when Derrick was on the lawn again, his father ventured out to smoke (another recent habit). Hoping for another round of inspiration, Derrick asked the same question about the stars.

"Light pollution," his father grunted.

The man then wandered away, bumping into a wall on his way into the house. His mother had already started the same drug regimen as his father, but functioned worse than he did. She spent most of her days in bed. Derrick's father was less Jekyll and Hyde than he was Jekyll and Checked Out Jekyll. The man was simply lifeless. Violence when it struck came in short bursts. His father always wore himself out quickly.

That was why Derrick refused to test the fear element himself. When trials were ready, he planned to use volunteers chosen through a normal vetting process. (Mostly college kids are down on their luck and needing money.) Derrick was a lifelong tea-totaller thanks to his parents' sad shenanigans.

Eventually his parents split up and during that time his mother regained some clarity. People called all the time and with each call, Derrick watched his mother grow older. He thought they were in a motel because of the split, but it turned out they were on the run. (Whether from tax people or more dangerous people, Derrick never learned.)

His mother made them change motels several times which made no sense to Derrick. One night he made a stand, refusing to leave. His mother grew angrier and more frantic than he had ever seen before. In the end, his mother moved him, got him in the car, but she had enough. The next day she put him on a plane. At eleven, his mother sent him on a cross-country plane trip by himself to visit grandparents he barely knew.

Derrick shivered despite feeling no breeze. He gulped the balance of his beer and rose to grab another. Why think of planes? Derrick was careful not to mention his fear in front of others because it meant reliving the terrifying night when he was young.

He never flew since, not even during Harvard. He drove cross-country each semester. Planes were a no go in his life. It had been so long since he flew it made no sense to think about it. So why was he?

Something had to have brought the memory to the surface. Maybe his boneheaded move in front of Amy. He looked at the dazzling stars he normally could not see and blinked. Was one star moving? It was. But the angle was off, the item was too low to be a star. Whatever it was, it moved fast. He rose to get a better look and dropped his bottle. Glass exploded at his feet, but he barely noticed it, too fixated on the horrible realization.

It was a plane! One dropping fast. As it drew nearer, he saw why it flew so low. Flames covered one engine. Derrick knew firsthand that screams inside the cabin likely exceeded those of the screaming engine.

His feet would not move. It was happening too fast and appeared the plane might hit the building. And then the wind shear hit. The violent draft caught the lawn chair, spinning it around and whipping it across the roof. The roar grew so loud Derrick covered his ears. A mistake. With his hands occupied, nothing held him in place. The wind caught him full force and pushed him back. He fought to remain on his feet and failed. With a sudden burst, the force knocked him off his feet until, like the chair, he slid on his back across the rooftop.

The burning plane flew low over the building and the burning wing exploded, sending shrapnel all over the rooftop. Smal fires erupted atop the building, burning bright in the night sky. Derrick cried out as the plane roared by, seemingly inches, but likely yards, above him.

It passed quickly. Derrick scrambled to the back of the roof where he watched the doomed flight. The plane crashed on the back half of the island. Though the dense forest swallowed the plane, a fireball rose above the trees. A thunderous explosion shook the foundation of the sanitarium. Fire spread to treetops where orange flickered in the night even as smoke rose above it all. A strange silence descended over the night.

"Oh, my God. Oh my God. No! Hey!"

Derrick yelled toward the main building, hoping others heard it, hoping someone was trying to get help. What help? They were it. No one else was on the island. Derrick rushed through the rooftop door and skidded down the steps, grabbing the metal rail to keep from falling the entire way. He burst into the hallway and kept running until the ground shook. He stopped to recover his balance when a voice cried out.

"Sir! Sir! Sit down! The seatbelt sign is in place. What are you doing?"

He turned, looking for the source of the voice, and froze. It was a woman, one who should not have been in the deserted corridor of a sanitarium. And he instantly wondered if he belonged in one. She was a flight attendant, strapped in tight near the rear of a plane.

It could not be. No way was he on a plane. He did not fly anymore. With tremendous force, the plane shifted, throwing him into the lap of a very concerned trio crammed into their seats like sardines. They pushed him aside with a yelp. Derrick flew back and fell into the opposite row of seats, where passengers manhandled him again, crying for him to go away.

"Get in your seat asshat, are you crazy?" a gray-haired man screamed.

Yes, crazy as the stereotypic cuckoo, Derrick thought. "I'm so sorry," is what he said. Before anyone could accept his apology, the plane jolted, and Derrick made a quick trip to the ceiling. Gravity returned, and he fell in a heap on the aisle.

"Sir, please, you must sit. We are experiencing severe turbulence," the flight attendant pleaded from her seat.

"I'm trying," Derrick said. "Where's my seat?"

"Take any open one, dumbass," the charming gray-haired man yelled.

Derrick bounced up again. Nothing made sense. How? How was he on the plane? While understanding it was impossible, he could not find his footing, which kept him from finding his mental balance as well.

When he fell back to the floor, he grabbed the nearest arm rest and rose to his feet. People screamed, prayed, and cried. Through it all, Derrick gave everyone something to watch. All eyes were on him, the idiot too stupid to fasten a seatbelt.

He locked eyes with a kid that could have been him once upon a time. But that kid was not young Derrick because young Derrick had wet himself when the plane dove after jumping around in the sky. This kid was dry, except for tears.

Like a bouncy house, Derrick thought of it at then, the night the plane threatened to go down. Like the entire plane was in a bouncy house. How could that happen? Derrick wondered then and now. Planes rode air. How could air manhandle a massive metal tube in the sky?

Derrick better understood the concept of turbulence once he grew older, but he never bothered becoming an expert on the subject. His inquisitive mind stopped short of learning about something that terrified him so. At Trager, Derrick planned to develop drugs that could relieve anxiety and be safe enough for children to take. He never intended to use the product himself, even if it was successful. Derrick was done with flying, period.

Until now.

There was no time to consider the circumstances. The plane kept him in a constant state of motion. He glimpsed an empty row several feet ahead and made his way toward it. If he could strap himself in, it might give him time to figure out what was happening. He was not on a plane, would never enter one.

But even the odors from that day as a child checked out. Smells and sounds from that day stuck with him over the years, haunted his dreams. An overweight man with body odor. The smell of vomit from someone two seats away. The smell of Derrick's own urine (his pee incident that he would never share with Amy). A woman whose perfume was so heavy it made him sick.

As bad as it was back then, they had landed safely. The current turbulence felt worse. Despite being an in-shape adult, he could not keep his feet on the floor. There would be no rescue from the airline steward who remained strapped in. A victim of gravity, she could not rise if she wanted to.

His ears popped. The whine of an engine took on a strange tone, like a blender underwater. The world became muted. Even the old man swearing at him lost clarity, became a mumbled mess. Clogged ears served as one more sign he was airborne.

"I don't understand..." Derrick started before another jerk sent him straight up to the ceiling.

Derrick grunted in the face of such force that held him aloft for what felt like an eternity. The plane descended so fast it glued him to the roof. Then, without warning, the ceiling released him, and he fell once again to the ground. His ribs caught an armrest on the way down.

The pain was real, which meant the plane was real. He rose again, determined to get strapped in. The ceiling threatened to make his acquaintance again, but he grabbed the headrest of the nearest seat so that only his feet reached for the sky. While he struggled not to take off like superman once again, he noticed a teen filming him, some jerk kid who documented every moment of life. A sudden tilt to the right caused the young man's phone to rocket somewhere across the aisle.

Derrick rose and staggered down the aisle in a lean. The plane was at a sharp angle, there would be no walking straight. No one watched him anymore, too scared about their own situation. Many tried to call loved ones on phones but struggled to keep the devices pressed against their ears.

He neared the empty seat when the plane rocked, straightened, then turned hard in the other direction. He flew against a window and landed in the lap of a new trio. They pushed at him, but the efforts were lackluster.

"Please!" one woman underneath him screamed.

Without time for an apology, a sudden drop from the plane forced him back into the ceiling. Overhead bins opened. Passenger bags and other items rocketed through the cabin. One carryon flew across the cabin and struck a man's face. The man's head snapped back, then settled into place, looking straight ahead, blood pouring down his nose. He did not appear conscious (or living) any longer, despite the open eyes. Derrick dropped back into the aisle, facing the strapped-in flight attendant.

"Sir. Take your seat!" The woman found her voice.

Derrick took that as a sign the turbulence had settled to a level where she even noticed him again, so he ran for the seat. He neared it and tripped, falling face first toward the armrest on the aisle. His jaw clacked hard against it, causing him to bite his tongue. Engines announced they were giving up, they had nothing left. Derrick grabbed a seatbelt and held on as his feet flew into the air. They swung right, then up, then left, before smacking down into the aisle.

He refused to let go and pulled himself into the empty row. Another jolt sent him sprawling face first against the window. Once there, he righted himself and strapped in.

Whoomp!

Loose luggage and debris rose to the ceiling at once before thundering back down onto passengers. The seatbelt kept Derrick from taking that ride again. The plane tilted into a dive. Everyone screamed in harmony as oxygen masks finally dropped from the ceiling.

Derrick panicked anew. He was not on the flight when it departed, so had missed the instructional portion of the ride. He was not on the plane because he never boarded. How was he there? He grabbed for the mask and placed it over his face, as did others. He watched a couple across the aisle. Place it on, tug at the tube and he felt the rush of cool air.

The plane jerked, and they fell into a dive. Derrick vomited into the mask and yanked it off. In the distance, an island rose from the sea. They were going down! With a loud pop the engine burst into flames. The burning wing was on the same side of the plane as the one he witnessed while standing on the roof earlier. A familiar ferry landing came into view followed by a sign blazing in the night sky. Trager Chemicals.

It couldn't be! But turbulence had given over to an impossible speed as they descended out of control. When they roared low over the building, Derrick glimpsed a man standing on the roof. It was too quick to know for sure, but it looked very much like himself. In a blink, his doppelgänger vanished from sight. A treetop ripped off the wing on his side. It bounced off, igniting sections of the forest.

Derrick suddenly understood his unwillingness to fly kept him from seeing his parents over the years. He had avoided them for multiple reasons once he left for college. But as the ground came on fast, he thought of only one thing. *I want my mommy*!

The remaining engine exploded on the opposite side of the plane, and shrapnel ripped through the cabin. A large chunk of metal landed in the face of a man across the aisle. The struck passenger ceased becoming a person and instead turned into an object. That of a fountain squirting high into the air, except the water ran red.

The man's wife found a higher level of scream and then, with a strange, muffled ear thump, a section of seats ripped away and flew off into the night sky. The fuselage popped and crackled, and a treetop appeared in the plane's new hole.

Derrick watched in awe as the plane segmented and spun off, as if becoming two different planes. Each half competed to see which could crash more violently into the ground. The impacts set off spectacular fiery explosions that reached high into the sky. The debris field stretched for miles and started fires in the forest.

Something in Derrick thought of how beautiful the aftermath might be, how the flames would perform a dance to celebrate the dead. But he never got to see it, for within seconds of the plane splitting apart, his thinking ceased.

CHAPTER 30

The elevator doors opened into the lobby. Gillian stuck her head out, searching. For what? Anything unexpected. Coast clear, she stepped out, only to leap in fright as the closing doors dinged. Out-of-control nervousness and rampant imagination made her abandon the videos. The walk was intended to shake off her fear-based fugue, but apparently her nerves came along for the ride. During the elevator ride, Gillian tried to identify the nature of her growing unease.

Besides the waking nightmare earlier, she had developed a case of permanent gooseflesh from something she could not shake. *A walk on my grave feeling*, she thought. But why feel that way? It made no sense. Perhaps it was because no one knew where she was. Gillian signed in at hiking stations when she planned long treks as a safety measure and carried a GPS device in case she got lost or hurt. But now she hiked through a former asylum without notifying anyone where she was.

Intent on selling the article even if it meant going outside her paper kept her from informing her coworkers. She was simply on a normal weekend off as far as they were concerned. And there was no one in her life to share the trip with. Gillian grew distrustful of relationships after losing her best guy to her best gal.

In and out would have been fine, but circumstances led to her spending the weekend. Had she known that was the plan she would have reached out to someone, anyone, to let them know where she was. But she stayed and cellphones did not work. All that was enough to explain her unease.

Gillian made poor judgement in not planning better. That unease combined with the uniquely creepy environment was enough to put anyone on edge. Research was the most boring part of her job, so watching the videos did not take her mind off her situation. But investigating always did so she decided it was time to investigate a missing person.

Steve gave Gillian the creeps from the get-go and now the man was missing. One who considered himself the de facto manager of an island made an unlikely abductee. Someone like that might go underground. But to what end? Was he disgruntled? Mitch testified to the man's loyalty, but where did the guard's true loyalty lie? What if the guard knew in advance about the shut down? Was he working for the financiers who pulled funding? Mitch did mention Steve and other service workers were paid directly from New York. Even in the mob, true loyalty belonged to the paycheck. Mitch and the ragtag crew remaining behind could be trouble for Steve. With no way for Steve to reach the mainland, the best he could do was sabotage the work of the scientists who stayed behind. Or at least gather incriminating evidence on them.

Okay, there it was. Her churning brain shook off some of the jumpies. Mere moments ago, she had contemplated making zoomies like dogs. She never understood why they did it, but it was likely to release pent up energy. She needed that to shake off the *why am I so freaking scared* vibes. But now she found a release valve in theorizing about the security guard's disappearance.

Gillian looked around the immense lobby and a thought struck her. She was all alone, absolutely no one in sight. That made sense with so few people in such a large building. Yet she encountered two individuals in the machine room. That had to be more than coincidence.

Mitch had a valid excuse to be there, possibly. What did he really know about engineering? If he was there for the stated reason, then fine. But why Jimmy? She investigated an open door. But why was Jimmy there to begin with? Mitch appeared as surprised as she. He also exited behind them. Was it possible Mitch and Jimmy arrived together to search for Steve?

After they all converged in the hallway, the two men navigated around an argument in front of her. Mitch only confessed their concerns about the "missing" security guard when she confronted him. Why there? If Steve planned something nefarious, what could he accomplish from the machine room?

The easiest answer was to ask the missing person, so she walked to the security office. A familiar whir sounded overhead as the mounted camera focused on her. The dark bubble casing kept her from seeing where the camera pointed, but what else would it focus on? She was the only thing in the hall. Did motion activate it, or did someone inside control it? The camera outside her office had whirred as well. She knocked.

"Hello? I know you are in there."

She knocked again. Nothing. Something caught her eye further down the hall. Was that a shoe? She approached and picked it up. Size ten. Why would a shoe be in the hall? It felt warm, as if recently worn, but the bright lights might have warmed it as well. A worker likely dropped it during the exodus. It was a Van's, which was not standard security guard material.

To make sure the shoe's owner was not injured, she continued down the hall, passing storage areas and a loading dock. She poked her head in each but was not sure where the light sensors or switches were located. Illuminated exit signs hung at the rear of the dock, but the place was otherwise dark. The last stop on her tour was an empty lab with lights still on.

The room's condition set off alarm bells. The lab was in shambles. Someone had tipped over stools and a medical tray. The tray's contents lay spread across the floor. A door in the distance drew her attention. She moved toward it and scrunched her face at the snake pit sign before sticking her head into the cramped space. The air was damp, a different environment from the dry, temperature-controlled lab.

Something hissed nearby. Snakes. The sign was accurate. Glass containers lined the shelves on both sides of the tight space. Snakes struck the glass, trying to get at her. Gillian returned to the lab. There was another room at the end of the snake pit, but she did not care to explore it. *No sir, thank you very much.* She spotted an orange on the floor and retrieved it.

"Score!"

She sniffed and squeezed it. Fresh. Still, it had fallen on the floor. She went to the nearest wash station and ran the fruit under water then patted it down with paper towels. A worker must have dropped it when they exited. Better for her to get the fruit than critters finding it. Though she imagined the snakes would not mind a few rat visitors.

Gillian dug a nail into the soft flesh when something sounded in the hall. A series of heavy thumps. Gillian exited the lab and rushed toward the ruckus. Someone wrestled with the security office door. The individual wore blue latex gloves and had his back turned toward her. Then, as if sensing her presence, Mitch turned around.

"Orange. I stole an orange," Gillian blurted out, holding up the fruit. She feared getting busted. Why?

"What?" Mitch asked, looking disheveled in his lab gear.

She tried to explain her outburst. "The fruit was in a lab."

"Are you hungry? We have more than noodles. Jimmy assembled a refrigerator's worth of good food in one of the cafeteria refrigerators," Mitch said, catching his breath.

Or trying not to breathe? Something was off about his demeanor. Gillian could not place it. Fear? Was he also suffering from what shook her earlier? (And now. She was frightened to admit she was an orange thief.) Gillian reverted to reporter mode to regain control.

"What are you doing here?"

"I am failing to enter the security office," Mitch said.

"You're the owner. Don't you know the code?" Gillian asked, referring to the trilogy lock on the door.

"Somewhere. In an email, on a piece of paper. Beyond kids using the island to party occasionally, there was never much to deal with security wise here. Steve ran the show and had the codes. I think it was his espresso machine in the cafeteria as well, placed after you and I were there so Jimmy likely has the code."

"Why are you trying to get in? Do you think Steve is in there? Is he in medical distress?" Gillian asked.

"Well i did not think that until now. Never mind. I still do not. The man left. He did everything he needed to do. Steve offered me something in the room earlier. Things plural."

Mitch's hesitancy did not go unnoticed. Gillian studied his face. Shy of an outright lie, it was too late for the man to back down.

"Objects I am uncomfortable with. It is nothing. I hoped to make sure the items were still secured. I am not looking for Steve because I am confident that he is not in his office."

"But he never made it to his car. Did something happen to him somewhere else?"

"Look, he likely rode with the medics to the ferry to help oversee our injured employee. That would give him an excuse to return here for his car on Monday and check on things. It is the best explanation. He is a stubborn and proud man."

"Stubborn men can get injured. But you do not believe that to be the case?" Mitch's non-answer was an answer. She pressed him on it. "You think he might be here for other reasons? Nefarious ones?"

"Steve is a good man."

"You're avoiding the question. If he were doing something improper and hiding out, what would be the reason? And what is it you are worried about in his office?"

Mitch raised his hands and tilted his head. Reluctantly, he spit it out. "Defensive items. Just being cautious, but mostly spot checking for our product."

"The fear element? You think he stole some? How does he plan to get away with no one noticing?"

"He can't. As much as I trust this group that stayed behind, I will insist on searches when we depart on Monday as well. What I said about Steve is just a theory. Please, it is not of your concern."

"No? If someone hopes to smuggle drugs from here, aren't we in the way of such a plan?"

"Theoretically..."

"Then, theoretically, what would a person like that do?"

"Our inventory shows no sign of depletion."

"Inventory?"

"We control the product and have built in inventory procedures. Any sizeable missing quantities we would know about. Jimmy conducted the inventory. Place is large but only so large."

"That is why I haven't seen him around."

Mitch frowned. "No? I instructed Jimmy to check on you regularly to see if you needed anything."

"Well, the night is still young."

"Except it is not. It is getting late, and his inventory rounds should be long finished. He only had to verify quantities, then lock up the storage cabinets." Mitch's face soured in frustration before refocusing on the issue at hand. "I understand Steve's presence on the island might concern you, but please do not worry. Even if he is here, then he is only helping to keep the facility running. There is no ulterior motive. Nothing is missing."

"Besides Jimmy and Steve?"

Mitch shook his head. "No. My time like the other scientists is precious. I will not spend the weekend worrying about where everyone is. Also, I refuse to let an outsider influence my trust in my coworkers."

"Outsider?" Gillian asked.

"No offense. Look, am I concerned about Steve's wellbeing? Yes. But that is not why I am here. I was not looking for him. And never mind what was stored in the desk inside, it is of no consequence, just paranoia on my part. Truthfully, I was after the intercom system. I hoped to unlock the door, leave it open and allow anyone to use the intercom as needed. We do not have a way to reach one another easily otherwise. But, because Steve was doing his job, he secured the office."

"I thought I heard someone inside."

"No one is inside."

Gillian looked at the camera above but chose not to share her secondary concern of being watched. Until she learned more, she changed the subject herself. "I saw a snake pit back there."

"Yes. We have arachnids and snakes on site. It was Steve who demanded the snakes remain on the first level. If they escaped, they were more likely to escape to the island on this level whereas upstairs they could have got into the plumbing. Colt and Amy's videos explain their phobias."

"I looked at some files but have yet to complete them all. But why was a snake pit prepped prior to human trials?"

"Wow. A true reporter," Mitch smiled while Gillian frowned. "I meant that as a compliment. I've already promised to hide nothing. The pharmaceutical industry and those who oversee it are quite incestuous and notoriously greedy. There are few companies of note that do not get a heads up when an approval or denial was on its way."

"Good old lobbying?" Gillian punched a fist in the air.

"Exactly. Average Joes are not on a level playing field against large corporations. I get it, lobbying is legal bribery. No argument here. But it is how the world works. We prepped for all this over a month ago. Arachnids arrived first. Snakes came later because we had to build an enclosure. Without the prior prep work and advance notice, we would not be here right now. No one would have been ready to give this weekend a go. Even with the advance notice I forecasted to staff, most were still not prepared to move ahead with their plans. Not everyone is a Mercedette. She immediately got the ball rolling with a secondary drug. Impressive."

"Her video was..." Gillian began.

"Please. Her background is tragic. Beyond the events that led to her on camera breakdown, being roped into a cult at a young age and raised in questionable circumstances would damage anyone. I took a chance on her. She is brilliant and belongs here."

"Why keep Jimmy away from her?"

Mitch's enthusiasm faded. "I am an open book, Ms. McCann. I intend to share every detail of this weekend and the background of all those who are here trying to make the world a better place. Isn't that enough?"

"Offer me full disclosure except for this one thing?" Gillian asked.

"Fine. Mercedette hooked up with Jimmy. Look, we work on an island. People hook up in various places. Colt is insufferable that way. But there is a power dynamic between those two I was not comfortable with. Further, they were of two minds on where they stood with one another after their act."

"Act? Hooked up? To clarify, they screwed?"

"Once," Mitch said.

"You know the exact number? And how is that a problem?"

"Because Mercedette was done with the man after they hooked up once. Jimmy did not take the rejection well. His awkward attempts to rekindle the relationship were unsuccessful and unwelcome. We suspended both while we investigated. Eventually they both returned with demands they keep things at a professional level."

"Except now they are facing one last weekend together."

"Not ideal." Mitch tried one more code on the trilogy lock, but it failed. "There is no reason to believe Jimmy is doing anything untoward. He is a professional and the entire thing embarrassed him. When I finally find him, I will re-emphasize my instructions to check in on you more often."

Mitch started off but continued past the elevators. Gillian stopped there and hit the call button. She also called out to Doctor Trager.

"I recorded a voice!" Mitch stopped, turned, intrigued. Gillian continued. "The night at the restaurant. I recorded a voice. I want to play it for you to see if you recognize it."

"Whatever happened that night has led me here for a reason. All that matters now is our work. Let me finish mine in peace. When this weekend is over, I will talk about that night, but right now there is nothing more important than my work."

"Then why are you not returning to your lab?"

"I need some fresh air. And you made me paranoid about Steve's absence. I plan to walk the path back to his vehicle just to make sure he is not in some type of distress, as you called it. Save your tape. We will talk when all this is over."

Mitch stepped out into the night. Gillian entered the elevator, regretting ever bringing up the recording. Not because she did not want to talk to Mitch about it, but because the thought of it frightened her so. She had yet to play it for anyone. Maybe it was all in her mind, a ghost of her own past. It was no longer simply a voice that was a secret. Gillian also saw a partial face drooping over her foot earlier. Crazy. Was Gillian going crazy?

At least going scared, she thought. If that was a thing. With Mitch gone and no one left to distract her, Gillian felt gooseflesh rising again. She refused to look at her hands and did not need to. She could feel the tremors. They were back and once again Gillian felt impending doom closing in on her, and an inexplicable certainty that something was wrong, very wrong.

Whatever the cause, she would not find answers in the lobby. The elevator doors finally opened, and she stepped inside, never noticing the wisps of black smoke swirling out of the elevator carriage at her feet. She rode back up into the asylum.

CHAPTER 31

Blood and gore flew everywhere. Elle's body dangled from an impossibly large hand that squeezed the life out of her. Literally. Blood gushed like a fountain from her neck. Yoshi fought to push the liquid back in. It was a losing battle. His hands were not a dam, he could not stop the flow. He was not a doctor and even if he were she was no longer Elle, simply a meat sack. He cried out over his inability to help her.

"Stop! We need to put this back. She needs this!"

Yoshi fought to stop the jet of gore, tried to push it back as if it could go into a body no longer breathing. A cry sounded out above his own whining failure.

"Yoshi, stop!"

A voice, strange, slow, sounded somewhere close. The scream swirled around his brain, sounding familiar.

"Are you okay, Yoshi?" a second voice said.

Another voice, less familiar, more masculine. The world went from red to normal. He wiped the tears from his eyes. Elle! He held Elle in an awkward position. Awkward because she fought to free herself from his grip. He was tripping. So was she, but they were at different stages of the journey. A giant hand had extinguished Elle (that was the most appropriate word he could think of). Except there she was, accompanied by Jimmy.

"Please release your coworker," Jimmy said.

"What? Oh, sorry. I am so sorry, Elle." Yoshi said.

Coworker. Jimmy put it out there so cold. Never mind how the couple recently cradled one another. Goof. What a goof. Yoshi should have known he meant nothing to Elle. His "coworker" was only along for the ride because of the drugs. Mystery loves company. Nervous about experimenting with the drug, Elle sought refuge in Yoshi's arms. If Yoshi were not around it would have been someone else helping her with the experiment.

Jimmy even. Word was Jimmy slept around the office. Did so with impunity because he was the boss' bestie. Yoshi had not hurt Elle just now but did refuse to let go. Worse, his faux pas was in the presence of a company executive. Once free, Elle stood, disheveled. She straightened her clothes, but the tee still clung to her. Jimmy leered at that which Yoshi did earlier. Yoshi fought to regain his composure and not fight his boss over checking Elle out.

"What are you doing here, Jimmy?" Elle asked.

"Doctor's orders," Jimmy laughed awkwardly, an old joke that he used often around the place. "As in Doctor Trager?" It did not land with the pair, so he kept on. "I need to complete a thorough inventory of our chemical supplies. We were current through last weekend so please bring this week's l-l-logs current by Monday."

"Who cares? Why do inventory? They shut us down," Yoshi said.

"Exactly. None of this belongs to us anymore. All contents besides personal b-belongings are now the property of a certain hedge fund in New York."

"How can you say that?" Elle snapped. She spread her arms, angry.

Jimmy jerked his head back, surprised. "Excuse me?"

"You heard me. Why are we doing all this then if we are giving up? I'm shooting up for no reason? Just for fun? Who would do this for fun? Who would expose themselves to something so terrifying for no reason?"

Yoshi looked away, guilty. He reached out. "Elle, it's only Jimmy." She waved him off.

"I know. And he was here earlier and could have told us all this then,."

"I was here to tell you about the food and the inventory but you were rather upset, so I t-t-thought it best I return later," Jimmy said.

"Not upset, creeped out. If you want to storm in here then it should not be acting on behalf of corporate. You should be cheerleading us. Encourage us to believe our results will change investors' minds. Isn't that what Mitch said?"

"Mitch?" Yoshi asked, uncomfortable with the familiarity.

"I have merely b-been instructed..." Jimmy started.

"To take away hope? Because that's what you're doing. But thank you. I was nearing the point of giving up. I'm taking shot after shot and seeing stupid things fluttering around the room. Black freaking smoke everywhere. Have you noticed?" Before either man could answer, she continued. "Nothing but goofy shit so far. All this for nothing? Inventory up and cash out what they can. Take our product and do nothing with it? We are close. And when we finish, there will be therapeutics for people dealing with the loss of loved ones. I refuse to give up now. I refuse to believe this is all for nothing. Come back for your precious inventory, but don't expect to find any because we are going to use every drop if that's what it takes. And stop staring at my tits!"

"I'm sorry," Yoshi said.

"Not you Yoshi, you can stare. But not mister inventory over here."

Jimmy's face went red. He attempted to speak, only to fall into a stutter, no words coming out. His face was full of rage. He stormed off without another word.

"Wow. Superwoman," Yoshi said.

"I am so pissed," she said. "And afraid, Yoshi. I am afraid we might fail, and what then?"

"That's the chemicals talking. You have every right to be afraid with or without the drugs, but let's be clear, we have taken a lot of drugs."

Elle noticed Yoshi's eyes darting about the room. "What are you doing?"

"Trying not to stare at your chest."

She grabbed his hands and placed them on her breasts. Yoshi yelped with surprised joy.

"Get over it, cowboy. We've got work to do." Yoshi smiled, shaking his head like a doofus. "You can let go now."

Yoshi did, dropping hands that he planned never to wash again. Elle prepped another round and injected Yoshi. In a flash, an evil witch appeared, wearing a tattered gown. She pointed an impossibly long finger at him. Deep down, he understood the finger was a hallucinatory replacement for the injector. But visions were becoming more realistic and lasting longer.

Fighting through the hallucination, if only to see Elle's boobs again (now that he had permission), he saw only the withered old witch. The longer visions meant they were on the verge of a breakthrough but there was a new pressing issue.

Yoshi needed to get to his own lab soon and needed to warn Quinn. The unlikely pair had used the product together for quite some time, never expecting to be discovered. But now they only had until Monday to alter logs to account for missing samples. Jimmy might have already visited Quinn, but it was unlikely. She would have found Yoshi to warn him as well.

Yoshi needed to break away and warn Quinn and update his own lab logs. But how to do so without upsetting the woman he longed for more than ever now that he had touched her amazing boobs?

"What are you grinning at?" Elle asked.

That he had touched them, though he simply answered, "Nothing."

"Well, knock off the goofy grin. In my current state, I see vampire teeth."

"Oh, am I more a Brad Pitt movie vampire or True Blood vampire?"

"A straight up Gary Oldman Dracula." Yoshi deflated as Elle raised the injector and a defense. "Don't worry, I find Gary Oldman sexy AF. It wasn't a slam, Mr. Fragile Ego. Now give me the shot."

He injected her. Elle jerked away in fright, brought fists to her chin, and danced in a circle before settling. She turned to Yoshi.

"The full body bunny outfit is really creepy."

"What?"

"We cannot stop Yosh. It is getting late, I know, but if we sleep, we will have lucid nightmares in place of waking lucidity. And I am not sure if I can do two days of this. I dislike this, Yoshi I am, I dislike Ink and ham," Elle babbled, losing coherence. She giggled at her own dim wordplay before growing serious. "What I like the least is the possibility that my theory is wrong."

"Only one way to find out," Yoshi said and loaded an injector. He raised it high, ready to jab her once again, but she surprised him with an enthusiastic hug.

She buried her face in his chest and murmured appreciation. "You are always there for me. Thank you so much."

"I think your theory is working," Yoshi said.

"How so?"

"Because I am lucid dreaming that a stunning beautiful and talented woman way out of my league is holding me tight."

"This isn't lucid, not yet. But if it happens, it will be because you stuck it out with me. You know you will still be in my life even if this all ends, right? I can't say that of everyone, not even people I have been intimate with."

Jealousy arose in Yoshi again and he hated himself for it. She was so blunt. That was Elle. He would have to learn to live with it if he wanted to live with her. She had been with men before, plenty, but she was right about one thing. In the end, he was the last man standing. (Except Mitch. She called him Mitch. Was she banging Mitch?)

He shook off the thought. That was the fear talking as much as the jealousy. Fear that what she said was not true, fear that it was only the drugs talking. And when their mutual trip ended, so too would their relationship.

Wham!

Something pounded on the door with tremendous force. The two held one another while turning simultaneously toward the door. A small window face high was their only view into the hallway.

Elle jerked in his arms. "Do you see her? It's a woman. Half her face is gone. She is staring through the window," Elle said.

The world had gone red. Yoshi blinked repeatedly. He saw something different.

"Actually, I see a Sleestak."

"What?" Elle asked.

"From the Retro Channel. Land of the Lost? An interdimensional lizard-like being. Super creepy. I have one of their Funko Pops, and a Pez dispenser."

"No, it is a dead woman. Super creepy," Elle said. "I have seen her before, a few times since we started taking the shots. But now she is staring."

Wham! The knock again. Intense. It was a Sleestak. Oversized eyes, the lizard like face with a mouth that needed lip balm, its lips were so dry and crinkled. It intrigued Yoshi as much as frightened him. He approached the door and opened it slowly.

"Are you okay?" Gillian asked. "You two look like you saw a ghost."

"I did," Elle said.

"I am Gillian..."

"The reporter. We know." Elle said, then introduced herself and Yoshi.

"Full disclosure time. Mitch gave me your job interview videos as background, and files with information on your histories."

"Wow. He did? I didn't know that. Two questions. Was my hair mussed up in my video? And what is Elle's phobia?" Yoshi asked.

"Sorry, not going to share personal information. You can read between the lines when the article comes out, unless some of you choose to identify yourselves. I was hoping to get everyone on the record this weekend. Not sure if this is the best time. No offense, you two look horrible. Is this because of the drug?"

"Yes/No," Elle and Yoshi answered simultaneously, contradicting one another.

"Elle, she's a reporter. Ixnay on the rugdray stuff."

"I speak Latin, both classic and pig," Gillian said.

"Nuts," Yoshi said.

Elle approached Gillian, defiant. "No. People deserve to know the possibilities of what this drug can do. It is not fair how they shut us down. Hedge funds now buy homes and apartments. That distressed the markets and made housing unaffordable for most people. They only think of money. Why can they not see the possibilities of what this could do for society?"

"And what is that?" Gillian asked.

"We will use fear as a gateway to a waking lucidity. In such a state, individuals could engage with deceased relatives. Imagine the therapeutic value of saying goodbye to a someone you never had the chance to," Yoshi blurted out.

Gillian lit up. "That is fascinating and not even in the realm of what I thought you all were working on here. The videos give me background on what got you here but have no information on what each of you is trying to do here. That is a truly a unique and visionary goal."

"So good I ditched my own experiment to help," Yoshi said, proudly.

Elle nudged him with contact as a silent thank you, but she continued sharing, excited about the plan. "Deep fear can induce hallucinations. We are using injectors today to deliver a payload of knee buckling terror..."

"You were a Sleestak when you knocked," Yoshi said.

The two women ignored him, lost in the conversation. "But imagine a controlled IV drip version. Anyone feeling alone..." Elle's breath hitched at the word. "Those lost and alone could visit whomever they desired to bring peace of mind, to feel connected."

Gillian nodded in understanding. The pair were bonding, sharing thoughts of a better world. Yoshi placed an arm on Gillian's back and shoved her toward the door.

"Too bad you have to go," he said.

"Wait, what? This is the first newsworthy thing I have encountered since arriving beyond a missing security guard," Gillian said.

"Steve? Shit," Elle said.

Elle's response surprised both reporter and lab partner. Yoshi squinted in suspicion. *What was that about?*

"Is something wrong?" Gillian asked.

"Thought I was the gossip queen, is all. I am slipping on the job," Elle said, blowing off the subject. "I think Jimmy mentioned something about it earlier, but I was too busy being creeped out to pay attention."

Yoshi's jealousy gene kicked in again. He tried to read her face. She met his gaze and nodded slightly. Yes, a conquest. Yoshi was supposed to accept Elle's history, but each surfaced name stuck a dagger in his low self-esteem heart. Ironically, he planned to sneak away to another woman, one he shared a secret with. The reporter was his ticket out. A perfect excuse to vamoose.

"We are mid-experiment. Now is not a good time to be here. You need to go to other people's labs," Yoshi said.

"I have been to several and cannot seem to find anyone," Gillian said.

"I know where to find someone. Allow me to introduce you," Yoshi said, and escorted her out.

Elle protested. "Wait, Yoshi, don't go."

Yoshi rushed back. "One more shot each while I take her to Amy. A shot will keep us on track. I'll be back in time for the next."

"No, please, stay. Just give her directions," Elle whispered to Yoshi, pleading.

"Don't want me to leave? Why? Worried I might run into Steve?" Yoshi said.

Elle blinked. She had no answer. Her silence spoke volumes. Yoshi felt rotten for throwing it out there, but his intuition was correct. Unable to control his jealousy, Yoshi needed that break for more reasons than one. He threw on his lab coat, pocketed an injector, and went back into the hall to connect with Gillian, leaving Elle alone.

CHAPTER 32

The reporter showing up when she did was perfect timing. Yoshi, already unhinged from so much Ink got so jealous of Elle's past he feared saying something idiotic to alienate her. He did not own Elle, not by a longshot, would not even if they became a couple. Her sleeping with a random Joe, Hideo, or Bob did not bother him. It was only her coworker hookups that bothered him. If she was interested in him at all, why pursue other people on the job?

If she did not like him, then fine. No harm, no foul. But Yoshi (stupid as he was in the ways of women) believed Elle was interested. He would have accepted the friend zone had she parked him there, but she never did even though he considered her a great friend. Yoshi had every intention of being there for her long after they shuttered the place.

"Don't you get creeped out here?" Gillian asked.

Yoshi led her toward his lab. "Used to get creeped out. Pretty normal now. Yikes!" A giant demonic Funko Pop blocked the door to his lab. He stepped through the hallucination. "Cool."

Gillian entered and explored the chaos that was Yoshi's lab which looked more like a comic book shop than a laboratory. Yoshi rushed over to a messy pile of papers on one of two overflowing desks, searching for something. Gillian eyed the toys briefly, then moved on to pictures hanging on a wall. Yoshi had discreetly erected a shrine to Elle under the guise of group photos.

Yoshi spoke over his shoulder. "Sorry for my actions at the door. Thought I saw something. And sorry for the mess."

Gillian turned on him. "You apologize too much."

"I'm sorry, what?" Yoshi asked.

Gillian shook her head. "I did not know what I was walking into at first, when we all assembled in the auditorium. I watched all of you there with great interest. Even in the sea of people before most had cleared out, I noticed your crush." Gillian gestured to the pictures. Yoshi cleared his throat, but Gillian raised a hand. "You say sorry, and I will crush your larynx."

"I'm that obvious, huh?"

"Yes. It's sweet. But you cannot be so timid. Save the apologies for coworkers, strangers, but not friends and certainly not lovers. You are both young. There are plenty of reasons she may or may not be into you, but you will never find out if you don't ask."

"Wouldn't she have already confirmed her interest if I am so obvious?"

Gillian nodded, good point. "That is not the same as asking. Ask me."

"What? I don't know you."

"Exactly. I am a stranger, and a woman. Pretend I am her."

Yoshi looked around for witnesses. A distraction, something to change the subject. There was no rescue to be found. He wiped his sweating palms on his pants and started.

"Elle, I..."

"Look at me when you say it."

Yoshi took a deep breath, then spit it out. "Elle. There is no science that explains what I feel about you. Trust me, I have done the research.

I know maybe you don't take me serious sometimes. I can be an aloof goof around you, but it is because I can't control my thoughts when I'm near you. When I try to articulate my words, my brain simply repeats the same thing over and over in my head: you're so beautiful, you're so beautiful, you're so beautiful. So, forgive me when I catch my breath every time that I look at you. Forgive my stuttering and acting a fool. I'm just trying to break that train of thought in my head long enough to figure out how to make a princess like you fall in love with a mutt like me."

Yoshi looked at the reporter for his grade. He worried when the woman remained silent. Finally, Gillian tapped her heart and nodded.

"You did good, kid. Now if you do not go back and repeat that word for word to her, then you do not deserve whatever degree got you here."

Yoshi leaped toward Gillian, who jerked back. He retrieved a laptop from a pile on a workstation behind the reporter. Success! He pulled away from Gillian, suddenly aware of how close he was to her. He considered saying sorry but was rather fond of his larynx.

"Got what I came for. I guess we can go."

"Sounds good, but I just realized I have yet to watch your interview. Besides fear of admitting your feelings to Elle, what is your phobia?"

"Do you follow social media?" Yoshi asked.

"No more than my job requires. Why?"

"Because if you did, you would not even need to watch my file. I came here to get my laptop for an inventory thing, but it also has a copy of a certain video. My fear went viral."

He fired up the laptop and opened a video file. He turned it toward Gillian. The video showed Yoshi sitting next to someone older than him in a nondescript living room. He paused the video to allow Gillian to take over the controls.

Gillian laughed. "Oh my God, is that you? So cute?"

"What happened, right?"

Gillian ignored his self-own and pointed to the other boy. "Your brother?"

"Yeah, haven't seen him in a long time. After college, he never really came home. Estranged, I guess you could say."

"Sorry."

"It's cool, water under the bridge. A river of tears and swirling pools of abandonment, but hey, still water under the bridge, right? My brother recorded this at my grandmother's farm. We were home alone while she was out playing mahjong with friends. His name is Jaime. I'm going to look away if you don't mind. It still freaks me out."

Gillian pressed play.

Young Yoshi and Jaime sat on a couch covered in crochet blankets. A coffee table from Japan was the only eastern flourish in an otherwise Americana living room. Framed pictures on the walls spanned generations. Yoshi and his brother were the youngest.

The boys ate popcorn while watching *Night of the Living Dead*. Yoshi crouched in a nearly fetal position, only breaking the pose to grab popcorn. Jaime watched his scared brother as much as the movie.

"Did you hear something?" Jaime asked.

"Yeah, zombies," Yoshi said.

"No, outside the window. Go check it out."

"You heard it, you check it out."

"A twatmunch says ouch," Jaime said, flicking a finger hard against Yoshi's skull.

"Ouch!" Yoshi yelled and rubbed his head.

Jaime flicked a finger again. The smack echoed through the room. Yoshi grabbed his skull again, suddenly more afraid of the living than the dead on the screen.

"Stop!" Yoshi yelled.

"Gonna' hit the same spot until you get up and check the noise."

The house had a wraparound porch that covered all but the rear of the house. Night wildlife or farm animals sometimes got onto the porch, usually in search of food. Yoshi grumbled but got up. Racoons were cool anyway and the most likely culprit.

Brass rods held up frilly white fabric curtains that looked more like a tablecloth than drapes. Yoshi jerked the curtains open and looked out into the night. The porch lights were on, awaiting their grandmother's return.

Yoshi turned to his brother. "See? Nothing."

But Jaime, eyes wide with fear, pointed over Yoshi's shoulder. Yoshi turned back and screamed. An alien with huge eyes, a massive head, and gray skin stared through the glass. Its eyes blinked repeatedly, and it swiveled its head!

Gillian slammed the laptop closed. "Shit!" She apologized and examined the device. "Sorry. Didn't mean to slam it. I was not expecting that."

"I wasn't either. That video got over a million hits. But it did not end there. My baa-baa was playing mahjong, remember? Me and my brother were alone. The thing vanished from the window. By the time we gathered the courage to go outside, we saw rustling in the cornfield. I was frightened out of my mind but wanted to see what it was."

"You should have been frightened. It looked so real. But obviously wasn't."

"We ran though the cornfield looking for it, but I caught on to something. My brother was filming with his phone the whole time. Filming me. His friend wearing the mask got lost because he did not know our fields like we did. The 'alien' eventually called out for help. It was my brother's friend Todd who made the fake head with actual blinking eyes. From the neck up and in the dark, it looked as real as real could be. He's making movies in Hollywood now. He got a job because of his early videos. Sometimes, when I wonder whatever happened to my brother, I fantasize he traveled to Hollywood to make movies with Todd."

An awkward silence filled the room as Yoshi fell into melancholy over seeing his brother again. He took the computer from the reporter. It was time to get back onto the plan at hand. Update the inventory logs on his laptop, then get back to Elle. The reporter had given him some sense of confidence, a do or die attitude. But he also needed to increase his drug intake before returning to Elle. She would have taken at least one more shot by now and Yoshi had yet to take the dose in the injector he brought with him. Yoshi planned to take extra doses to leapfrog ahead of Elle.

But the reporter was in the way so he would hand her off to Amy. After that, Yoshi would warn Quinn, then binge some Ink before returning to the experiment. Laptop in hand, he led Gillian to the elevators. Black mist poured from the elevator. Gillian looked concerned. Yoshi ignored it and stepped inside. Gillian followed.

"Place is old, dirty. No housekeeping for the weekend. The labs have good filtration systems but cannot say the same for the rest of the building. They removed all the asbestos and stuff before we moved in."

Realizing she was getting more of it outside the elevator than in, Gillian entered and took up a spot alongside Yoshi. Hands full, he pressed a button with the back of a hand. Gillian held her hands up and showed him the tremors.

"Why am I still frightened after watching that video? It was clearly a fake. What about that mist in the hall just now? Are we being exposed?"

Yoshi shook his head. "What? No. Creams, powders, liquid, pills, and gels. No particulates or gas. The closest is Mercedette's spray, and even that only shoots globule style liquid. It doesn't mean you have not encountered the product, though. Be careful what you touch. General rule? If it's black, put it back. Or don't. Can be fun in small doses."

Gillian frowned, a sign she was not down to party, so he let the conversation drop. There was a little more work to do and then he could get back to Elle. He escorted Gillian to Amy's lab.

CHAPTER 33

After waiting so long for Derrick, Amy returned to shower number two. She had left the shower much earlier and prepped her lab, but she could not shake her nerves. The water earlier had soothed her, and she could use more drying time on her clothes, so she went in for shower number two. This time extra hot.

Earlier when she left the shower, she found a note from Derrick promising to return soon. Poor guy was likely embarrassed as she was. Amy took a seat and started working on her computer. She typed at a rapid pace but eventually made a typo. When she searched the sentence to confirm the error, a dozen spiders poured from the screen onto her keyboard.

"No! Stop!"

The arachnids apparently listened. They were gone. Nothing there. Amy looked under the desk to be sure but knew better. She suddenly worried something bigger was going on. She could not control herself.

Even Derrick's absence worried her. She feared he was so embarrassed that he refused to work with her any longer. But then her fear moved beyond his absence. Amy kept thinking about failure. The powers that be refused to adopt her ideas about using filters to identify skin cancers. And now, the world at large, but especially Derrick, decided her work was so unworthy they wanted no part in it. Derrick's note was simply a ruse to escape the lab of an incompetent scientist.

Then the shakes began. Her hands danced about as if under the effects of too much caffeine. She rarely drank coffee, not like the addicts everywhere in the workplace. But occasionally she needed the boost. But she was not caffeinated, yet her hands trembled. More spiders spilled form her laptop. She slammed it close, rose and that was when she decided it was time for another hot shower.

The second shower felt good, but black silt built up near her feet. The grime was so slick it slowed the drainage flow. That seemed odd because she had already washed once. She ignored it and allowed the hot water to do its thing. Though the water was relaxing and steamy, she kept glimpsing movement out of the corner of her eyes.

Whenever she turned, nothing was there. Worse, the movement mimicked that of spiders on the loose. Nothing but folly. She was still on edge from the unexpected exposure to one of the spiders. None in the glass containers were as deadly as those in the rainforest back in college, but they frightened her just as much. Even house spiders put her in a tizzy, but usually not into the pee zone. The warm water helped calm her down, but only so much.

But the water had to stop. She was delaying the inevitable. The shower would never calm her nerves because what she feared was exposing herself to the spiders once again, even if in a controlled experience. She had every reason to be on edge.

Then there was the lab partner situation. She was a woman nude in the shower. As much as she trusted Derrick, him returning to find her still in the shower after being gone so long could be mistaken for an invitation. What other good reason would she have for still being there when he finally returned? Even if he was as trustworthy as she believed, he would probably freak and think she drowned or fell, otherwise why still be under water? He had no reason to think she had already left the shower once.

Amy turned off the water and leaped. A spider leg tall as her rose from the drain and flailed about. Amy almost tore the curtain off trying to escape. Once out of the shower she turned back and saw nothing but an empty basin. She put her bra and top back on, then reached for the panties. Dry, finally. She slipped them on. The pants remained damp, so she put the lab coat on over panties again.

The moment she returned to the lab she felt her unease grow. Why? Amy shook herself out. One leg at a time, then each arm, then the shoulders. She tried to release the tension but failed. Something was wrong. She looked around and noticed black grime covering a wall below the ceiling vent in one corner. It looked like mold. She approached cautiously. A touch of her hand would confirm if it was what she thought it was. One touch and she would feel intense fear immediately if it was their product. She reached out.

"Hi Amy, I have a guest for you," Yoshi called out.

"Christ!" Amy yelped and turned. "Yoshi? WTF?"

"Thanks for abbreviating it in front of our guest. Amy, Gillian, Gillian Amy. Knock yourselves out by getting to know one another. I must get back to my experiment."

Amy stopped him. "Wait. Have you seen Derrick?"

"No. Thought he was with you," Yoshi said, looking around and only finally realizing.

"Earlier we were working together. He has since gone missing. Like two showers long missing."

Yoshi closed an eye, tried to do the math. "Two showers?"

"A security guard is missing as well," Gillian said. "His car is still in the parking lot. Mitch thinks he stayed behind."

"Why?" Amy asked.

"Showers sounds like female talk. I will leave that all for you two. I have an experiment to get back to," Yoshi said.

"Keep an eye out for Derrick," Amy said. "Tell him I am ready to start and that I forgive him."

She was not sure Yoshi heard her. He was moving too fast. One other guy who apparently could not get away fast enough.

Yoshi was very curious about the whole shower thing, but he had no time to ask questions. Once free of the reporter, Yoshi rushed down the hall, eager to play catch up on his dual objectives. Warn Quinn and then get absolutely wrecked with Elle. But first he had to take a shot. He feared his past use made his tolerance higher. He wanted to leapfrog usage with Elle but could not tell her why. Yes, they were doing the drug together but for an experiment. She would lose respect for him if she knew he did it recreationally. Quinn had to fudge her inventory anyway, so he would take plenty when he visited her.

But he had a dose ready, so after checking no one was around, Yoshi set his laptop on the ground. Except he was not in the moment. Jealousy about the Steve revelation rattled through his mind. Of course, Elle would like a guy in uniform, one with security clearance, and in good shape. Plus, Steve had a moustache.

Yoshi took the injector from his coat pocket and ditched the lab coat. He only wore it to appear formal when escorting the reporter. Yoshi stewed over Elle's hookup with Steve even as he injected himself. *Did Elle have an affair with the man?* Yoshi wondered.

"It's called 'fucking' Yoshi. She fucked him! It isn't called an affair. No wonder she doesn't want to be with you!" Gillian yelled, appearing from nowhere.

Gillian pressed her face into his. He blinked, and she vanished. Not gone, just never there. But her words stung. The shot induced something different. The hallucinations he could chalk up to the drugs, but a growing sense of dread that weighed heavily on him came from someplace else.

The world of Ink had gone from fun to ominous. He needed to get back to Elle soon before she slid off the fun scale herself. If her dread and fears grew the equivalent to his own, she would be terrified by now. Not in the seeing things way, but existentially. He did not wish to leave her alone in such a state.

Quinn had to come first, though. His fun buddy coworker. Yoshi needed to warn Quinn about the inventory check. Unaware of what the penalties might be for misusing company assets, Yoshi assumed it was serious. So was fudging inventory logs, but that would be harder to discover than missing product. They had mostly used Quinn's stash when doing Ink together. Something about her working in the different wing raised their comfort level when pilfering the product.

Like any lab, inventory protocols were in place. A full accounting was expected before anyone could request more. He and Quinn knew they would have to fudge some documents eventually but neither expected to be shut down. They figured they had plenty of time to work out explanations for any shortages. The luxury of time would have served them well in their subterfuge, but now lack of time put both at a disadvantage. Initially the closing announcement relieved Yoshi. He figured there would be no need for further inventory checks. he was wrong.

He discarded the injector atop his coat on the floor and picked up his laptop. The world had gone red. Viagra made people see blue. Ink often made people see red. Except normally the red acted like a picture filter. This time it took the form of bloody rain. The deluge ran the entire length of the corridor. Walls dripped thick red liquid. Blood pooled at his feet. Then he heard it.

Footsteps. Not the clop of heels on tile, but heavy footfalls splashing through the gore. Halfway down the corridor stood a figure unbothered by the red rain. The individual observed Yoshi. The person wore a strange orb over his or her face.

The two stared at one another, neither moving. That nagging sense of dread weighing on Yoshi seemed related to the strange individual. Then Yoshi remembered the reporter screaming in his face. It was all a hallucination. Yoshi closed his eyes, shook his head. When he opened his eyes again, the figure had disappeared.

The elevator door opened. A bright square of light cut through the red. Yoshi entered where not a drip of blood was to be found. Yoshi blinked. Was he going lucid? Was he getting to where Elle predicted he would? He needed to hurry to Quinn. Yoshi rode the elevator to the fifth floor, got out and crossed over to the next wing.

Once there, he rushed to Quinn's floor. The effort of racing to her lab brought him back to base level. Though dread lingered, red had vanished. As he neared Quinn's lab, something sounded behind him. The figure. Yoshi could not make out the person's features because of the weird head covering. Ignoring the non-existent figure, Yoshi entered Quinn's lab.

He planned to teach Quinn how to alter logs. Unless she already knew how. Probably did, Quinn was brilliant. It only had to be good enough to be chalked up to negligence if discovered. The company already fired both, so the whole thing would likely fall through the cracks if discovered. Still, Yoshi had no desire for either of them to be called back for hearings related to missing material. Neither could know for sure how much the two of them had consumed, but the altered records would appear sloppy, not criminal.

"Quinn?"

She was not there, but the vials he knew so well were. Perfect for part two of his plan. Quinn would likely return soon. She was probably noodling up in the cafeteria. Yoshi poured some of the drug out and snorted. He closed his eyes to wait for the effects to kick in. Expecting red when he opened his eyes, he was instead greeted by the impossible.

Yoshi stood in the middle of a cornfield, back on his grandmother's farm.

CHAPTER 34

Yoshi spun in a circle in the middle of an immense cornfield. It could have been any farm, but he knew it was his grandmother's farm. The sweet odor of her cornbread floated in on the same breeze that rustled the tips of cornstalks. The cobs were heavy and ripe for picking, which meant he would have his work cut out for him soon. He and his brother worked the fields when they were younger.

His family sold the farm to a corporation once his grandmother got too old. His parents changed career paths and chose not to take over. That legacy could have fallen on Jaime, but he vanished. The adults kept everything quiet about Jaime's disappearance, speaking only in whispers about it. Then Yoshi was off to college. He returned to the farm once as an adult, but security guards turned him away. Pot was legalized, and the company converted mostly to that crop. His past became unrecognizable.

Until now. The same cornbread breeze carried with it the chill of autumn. It signaled a time of change. As a youth, autumn meant working on the farm, taking time off from high school to help pick crops. But once in college, the season meant starting a new semester out of state where he lived on campus. With so many people coming and going around school, Yoshi occasionally thought he glimpsed Jaime. But it was never him.

The chilly air brought him back in time. Churned soil at his feet gave off a rich scent, free of the fertilizer smell from early in the season. Stalks of corn towered over him, making it impossible to locate the farmhouse. He tried to remember where it was based on the sun's position in the sky, but had had no idea what time it was. Close to rising or close to setting could make a big difference.

Something rustled off to his right. The tops of the cornstalks swayed unnaturally, signaling something advancing. Yoshi fought the urge to call out, not until he knew what it was. The stalks rustled more violently. Whatever was responsible was big and getting closer. Yoshi caught a glimpse and fought a scream. A gray! One with large obsidian eyes searched for something or someone. (Him?) It bypassed him, seemingly unaware of his presence, and moved parallel to his location.

Then it turned suddenly, locking on him as if it knew he was there all along. The gray ran straight at him but never connected because something else did. Something tackled him. Yoshi went airborne and landed hard. A hand clamped over his mouth.

"Not a sound twatmunch," a voice said.

Yoshi yanked the hand away from his face and looked up at his savior. "Jaime?"

"Quiet, Yosh. They'll hear you," Jaime said instead of answering.

"Who will hear me?" Yoshi said.

"The grays, you idiot. All these years and you're still the dumbest scientist I know."

"Where have you been, Jaime? It's been so long. Hey. Shouldn't you be older?"

"I'm a timeless classic. Now how about we catch up when aliens aren't trying to kill us?"

Jaime throws his body over Yoshi as the stalks crunched around them. The brothers held their breath. Jaime grabbed a nearby fallen cob and threw it as far as possible.

More stalks crunched as the creatures chased after the noise. Creatures, plural. Jaime grabbed his brother, and they rose, running in the opposite direction of the hurled object. Yoshi quizzed his brother as they fled.

"Is this why you were gone? Are they real? Did they take you?"

Jaime stopped short, looked at his brother. "At some point, people find themselves at the intersection of Life Street and Choices Avenue. No monsters, Yosh, I simply took a wrong turn is all. We had it pretty good though once upon a time, didn't we?"

Yoshi nodded, battling a tear while finally getting a goodbye he never got. Except he did not wish to say goodbye. He wanted to reminisce with his brother, but the creatures recalibrated and headed in their direction once again. Jaime grabbed his brother's shoulders.

"It's not the little ones you have to worry about, Yosh. We scared you as a kid with the quaint version. There are others."

"Then let's run, let's get away. We can get to the farm."

"Is it still there? I came back once. Watched you sleep while I gathered some things. Didn't have the heart to wake you."

"What? Why Jaime? Why? You could have woken me. You should have woken me!"

"There we go. Poor decisions. Guess I'm full of them. Good seeing you bro. Seriously. But you need to go."

"**We** need to go!" Yoshi shouted, then swallowed his words.

A gray appeared, parting a sea of green right before them. Jaime was correct. The new version towered over them at seven feet tall. Its mouth was as oversized as the eyes were on the smaller versions. It bared needle-sharp fangs. Yoshi froze in place until his brother turned and screamed into his ear.

"Run Yoshi! Run!"

Yoshi jumped into the thick of the field, vanishing into the green, crying as he ran. He did not get far before emerging into a wide clearing. He covered his ears to stop the sound of his brother's screams in the distance. Awful snaps like popping corn brought Jaime's cries to an end.

A wooden cross rose at the edge of the clearing on which hung a scarecrow. The scarecrow's clothes appeared too big for whatever they stuffed it with. Even the sack face with button eyes barely held onto whatever made up the scarecrow's head. There was something eerie about the way the head dangled.

Yoshi understood the need to run, to escape before they found him, but the scarecrow unnerved him. He stepped forward to investigate. The grain sack head, button eyes, and mouth stitched with orange yarn seemed to stare at him. He reached up and yanked the repurposed grain sack away. Elle hung on the cross!

Ropes bound her at the wrists, torso, and legs. She appeared lifeless. Yoshi fought to untie knots, ignoring crops crunching in all directions. Hard as he tried, he could not free her. Then they appeared. The original grays, like the fake head from his youth. While still terrifying, they were not nearly as frightening as their larger cousins. The beings blinked and seemed to study Yoshi, who gestured to Elle.

"I need help. I need to get her down."

The four grays stepped forward, forcing Yoshi to step aside. Within seconds, the grays somehow freed her. Elle fell limply into their arms, and they set her on the ground.

"Thank you. Thank you!"

Yoshi bent to check on Elle and choked back a sob. Her pallor matched that of the aliens. She appeared dead, nothing but a corpse. The gray of death. Until her eyes shot open.

"Why'd you leave me?" Elle yelled in a voice not quite her own.

Yoshi fell back on his ass. The grays grabbed Elle's feet and dragged her into the field at inhuman speed. Yoshi rolled over onto his stomach, reaching out from his spot on the ground.

"Wait. No!"

Yoshi rose and gave chase, stumbling while trying to get back onto his feet. He ran out of view of the clearing, deep into the field. The clearing fell silent, the scarecrow post sat empty. It was a peaceful moment in space and time until four of the larger grays crossed the clearing heading in Yoshi's direction.

Yoshi's screams filled the air. The violent shaking of corn announced the attack. Whether it was crops being destroyed or bones turning to dust, horrific snaps filled the air. With a whoosh, something soared through the air, launched from somewhere deep in the cornfield.

A large object flew back into the clearing. It was Yoshi. His head struck the top of the scarecrow post with a sickening thud. The contact altered the course of Yoshi's flight. His body spun a cartwheel in the air before landing in a heap. His limbs no longer bothered to ascribe to anything resembling traditional human anatomy.

Once the dust settled, the clearing returned to its peaceful state. Blood fed the soil, nurturing future growth. One by one, little gray feet walked past the pulpy mess that used to be Yoshi. Only a few pairs of feet to start, then dozens, a procession of little gray feet moving along, returning to wherever they came from until soon there was nothing left.

Nothing but Yoshi joining his brother forever in the field.

CHAPTER 35

"I need my lab partner," Amy said to Gillian.

Amy opened an inhibitor jar and took a sample with a swab stick then placed it under a microscope. Gillian examined the lab while Amy did her work.

"I saw your file. Terrifying what you went through," Gillian said.

"I was against Mitch sharing those interviews," Amy said. "Is any of this off the record?"

"All of it for now. I am glad to a person everyone is aware Mitch supplied me access to the files."

"Just because it makes you feel better, doesn't mean it makes us feel better. The interview process was... Unique. Most of us decided early on to hide our phobias from one another over worries we might be perceived as freaks to our coworkers."

"On the contrary. They humanize you all."

"Wow. You put it right out there. To say it humanizes us means you never looked at us that way in the beginning, it took you watching a tape to see us as real people."

Gillian blinked. "Sorry. Did I offend? I meant no such thing. I merely meant since I do not know any of you, the tapes helped me see many of you as individuals. And yes, it evokes intimacy. We all have social media friends and IRL ones."

"Yeah, well, in real life friends know enough to leave some things unsaid. I do not know what Derrick is afraid of nor do I care. If anything in my experiment would possibly trigger him then I should know, otherwise none of my business. Another humanizing trait we might all experience this weekend is failure. If we do, what will you write?"

"Why do you assume failure? Others I spoke to are adamant the world will change this weekend. Which is it?" Gillian asked.

"The conditions are not right for any of this. Already it is late night on day one and I have not even started. Most of us won't sleep much, if at all, resulting in sloppy work. Even worse for those who do not have assistants. Which is why I need..." Amy rose and stuck her head out into the hall "Derrick!"

"You mentioned he left a note?"

"Yes, saying he would be right back. I have a different idea of what that such a time frame looks like."

Gillian eyed the jars. "What is your experiment? I understand your phobia of spiders. Does this somehow relate?"

Amy stepped away from the door. Despite her angst over her holding pattern, she lit up when asked about her work. "Yes. My hope is to stop fear in its tracks."

"Is that possible?"

"Technically no. Fear is necessary for the survival of any species. I will assume you had some partying days under your belt like most of us?" Gillian nodded, so Amy continued. "Well, we all have made some horrible mistakes under the influence of alcohol. But we made such judgements without fear. If people were no longer afraid of anything, there would be dire consequences in the real world."

"Good point. Then what are you doing?"

Amy lifted one of the green and red stickers off the jars, holding up one of each. "I grew up poor. Dental work meant tying teeth to string and slamming doors."

"Oh my gosh," Gillian said.

"It was as bad as it sounds. But what if there was only a cavity? Pure pain? No insurance to have it treated? A topical ointment from a drugstore was the cheaper alternative to provide temporary relief. That is a variation of what I hope to create. A topical ointment that offers temporary freedom from fear." She emphasized the red sticker.

"Is that possible?"

"Yes, and no. The topical part is important because once fear has taken hold of someone, I cannot un-ring that bell. My product requires a patient to be calm to start. Injections or even pills often induce anxiety in patients taking them. But creams are so unobtrusive that one can apply as if it were sunblock. Remaining calm while dosing is the start. Once applied, the cream acts quickly and blocks many of the biological pathways through which fear can take hold of an individual. There are different bodily functions that facilitate the rise of fear. Like a toothache gel, this will temporarily numb some of those functions."

"Some?" Gillian asked?

"The human brain is stubbornly effective at creating worse case scenarios from thin air. Our brains are anxiety inducing grey matter nightmare machines. Waking or sleeping, the brain is the one organ that can induce irrationality. I cannot shut down someone's brain, nor would I wish to. But taken before fear takes hold, even if the brain reacts to a situation, it has nowhere to send the signal. Other parts of the body, like the liver, involved in the physical process of fear, will become inaccessible. Despite what an individual might fear, they should be able to navigate through it.

"Like fear of flying."

"Great example. People already use various anti-anxiety meds. The problem is, they often use alcohol as a backup. Next thing you know, they turn into Karens and Kens and threaten to bring down the plane. No one goes into a situation planning on such actions. Their fight while in flight kicks in and they are no longer in control. My product would allow them to fly with some sense of calm. They could even reapply the ointment while in flight."

"This is amazing," Gillian said. "I would use this. And it is also worth writing about. I am impressed with the few experiments I have heard about so far."

"Do not fire up that keyboard yet. It is not working."

"Why?"

"As I mentioned, one must start from a base comfort level. It does not dispel existing fear, only blocks the pathways which induce fear. I am currently far from calm. Not sure how much you know, but we understood these trials were imminent. Many of us have already placed ads for volunteers. A few of us with very specific phobias always planned to test on ourselves first. We were the perfect subjects. Me, Colt, Quinn, and some others who left the island. That is why I keep arachnids on site. My intern oversaw their care, but she left."

"Derrick stepped in to help."

Amy nodded. "I could not test without him. Unfortunately, we do not share lab shorthand. Derrick accidentally exposed me to something earlier."

Amy gestured to the nearby cabinet. Gillian walked over, opened the doors, and leaped away while performing an interpretive dance that would have made those at Juilliard proud. She reached out from a safe distance and closed it.

"Heck no. I am not okay with that. I might be a good subject for your experiment."

"Not how this works. Many are afraid of spiders, but then there are those like me who suffer from legit arachnophobia. Unless someone has formally diagnosed you, I could not use you as a subject."

Gillian stepped back and looked at her hands. They still tremored. "Thank you."

"For what?" Amy asked.

"First, you made me better understand what you all do here. But you also confirmed something else. I am terrified."

"What?"

"At some point I became uncharacteristically nervous, jumpy, even saw some of those brain induced style things you mentioned. But normally I dive headlong into events without worrying about consequences. I am many things but easily frightened is not one of them. Your demeanor suggests it is not only me."

"My fear is arachnid induced," Amy said.

"Are you certain?" Gillian asked.

"What are you saying?"

"Call it the reporter in me, but there is a missing security guard. Perhaps the man remained to deal with a chemical leak."

"What?" Amy looked past Gillian to the contaminated wall. "If something leaked, it would be liquid form. My pastes and some people's powders were made in small quantities. We would know if we were exposed to any liquids."

"Drinking water?"

Amy gestured to a distant corner of the lab, which had a corporate water dispenser with the oversized jug. "Filtered. All the labs contain their own drinking water. You and I never drank from the same."

Gillian nodded. Good point, but still. "Something is going on."

"You are a reporter. You always look for an angle. As a scientist, I stick to facts."

"And the fact is you are terrified for no good reason, as am I. Have you ever used the product before?"

"No?" Amy confessed.

"Me either. How would we know if we were under the product's effects?" Something occurred to Gillian. "I am going to go check on something."

"No. Can't you stay until Derrick gets back?" Amy asked, desperation in her voice.

"Sounds like you are frightened to be alone."

The two stared one another down until Amy finally looked away. Gillian said goodbye and exited the room. There was one place that aroused her investigative instincts. She already decided it was beyond coincidence for the two men to be in the same spot earlier, and neither had a good excuse. They were hiding something. She never thought to check if the main water supply was accessible from there. What was so important about the machine room? She was not sure, but she planned to find out.

CHAPTER 36

Why did Amy lie to the reporter? Not a fabrication, but a lie of omission. Amy **was** terrified. While flattered by Gillian's excitement about her experiment, Amy did not trust the media. What should be a breakthrough could sound nefarious once talking heads got hold of something. Amy was all about sisterhood, but some sisters could go lick themselves. Amy did not have enough information to decide which side Gillian fell on.

Besides, with little warning, the woman left, off to chase a better story. Maybe the reporter was right about one thing. Two people missing seemed suspicious. Where was Derrick? Beyond the experiment, she wanted to ask someone about the contaminated wall. Amy kept a clean lab, but something foreign had formed. There was no way her working space changed that drastically in one day of shutting down. Something else had to be responsible. No matter the source, it was a contaminant. She would need to move labs, but even that thought unnerved her. Why?

"Calm down!" Amy yelled to herself, then danced in place, shaking everything out.

Dancing in a lab coat made her feel foolish. Fearful and foolish, but she was not up for a third shower. Maybe she needed food.

"Or a lab partner!" Amy waved her hands, hoping someone would hear and answer.

It was late and there was every chance Derrick simply fell asleep somewhere for the night. She was ready for sleep herself, but she wanted to give Derrick a little more time. In the meantime, she decided to move her lab, that way she could start early in the morning. Even if Derrick did return it was probably too late to start. Fatigue likely factored into her lingering nervousness.

She would take the closest lab so Derrick could find her when he returned. A puff of particulates fluttered from the vent. She coughed and stepped away. Enough was enough. She crossed the hall and entered the lab across the hall. She paused just inside the doorway.

In her mind's eye she thought she glimpsed someone down the hall while crossing over. Was there something odd about the face? No, not a face. A mask. She leaned her head back out.

"Hello?"

Nothing. *Work. Get to work.* She entered the new lab that contained two main workstations and an elaborate sink system running the entire length of one wall. A large storage room stood off to one side, its door open. A desk took up one corner of the lab by a window. Strange how Amy never met her next-door neighbor. She saw the man a few times, but they never spoke.

Several metal cabinets were open and empty. They would have held the chemicals if the scientist had any. Truth was, most had only a vial or two in their labs. Those that needed powder, or cream, or even pill form, sent their requests to Jimmy. Over time, after each scientist received their procurement of the drug, Mitch paid a visit.

The visit with Amy was a warm and inquisitive one. The employees were line cooks, and Mitch was the head chef. A boss invested in their work. Beyond that, they never saw him much, mostly coming and going from the ferry.

Mitch had shown great interest in Amy's plans, especially her efforts to inhibit common physical pathways to fear. The two acted like jazz musicians that day, riffing off one another about theoretical applications. Mitch brought up people who would like to enjoy dogs but fear them. Dogs smelled fear through enzymes in the liver, so if a product blocked those enzymes, it might minimize aggressive behavior in the animals. The possibilities were endless.

They discussed pills versus other forms of the drug and settled on an ointment. Mitch talked about the unique properties of creams designed to delay male ejaculation. There was nothing sexual about their talk, simply discussions on how effective the product might be. Amy researched the top gels on the market and found the information useful. Eventually, the inhibitor cream was born.

Lies of omission came to mind again when Amy thought of one of the reporter's questions. Gillian asked if Amy had ever experimented with the drug. Though she never tried the fear element, Amy did test her own inhibitor once. She wished to know how well it worked. There was no way in hell she was going to test it against her fear of spiders. Instead, she chose the roof.

Though unsafe, employees built a party spot up on the roof of an abandoned wing. Amy attended only one shindig to be sociable, but day drinking was not her thing, nor was pot. But she made the obligatory appearance and never returned. Until her inhibitor was born. Amy feared heights. Not to the point of a phobia, but enough.

One day, Amy took a jar with her to the roof. Early enough in the day to guarantee no one was there. Beer o'clock never began before lunch. Amy sat on the last set of steps to relax and calm herself. While sitting there, she applied the cream and waited ten minutes more.

Then she stepped out onto the roof and walked right up to the edge. It worked like a charm. She leaned over the edge with no problem.

Her knowledge of how well the inhibitor worked was the same reason it now worried her. It had been quite some time since the pee incident, and she had yet to calm down. Shortly before the reporter showed up, Amy applied some of the cream, hoping to calm herself down while waiting for Derrick. She had wondered if someone had sabotaged the jars, but the stickers seemed okay. They left paper and glue behind when she tried to remove some. There would have been signs of tampering.

Maybe it did not work this time because she was still frightened when she applied it. But even then, she should have already calmed down. There were no spiders present. But she found herself absolutely frightened. Not nervous but bordering on terrified. She searched her surroundings, trying to identify her concern.

There it was, below the new vent. At first it looked like floor to ceiling shadows, but no, it was a wall of black, like in her old lab. Was the whole place contaminated? She moved closer and saw it differed from the contaminant in her lab. The wall grime in the new lab ran thicker, bumpier like chunky peanut butter versus smooth.

Was it moving? Yes. The wall squirmed. She reached for one of the small lumps when something spindly broke through one of the dark chunks. A spider's leg! A second leg emerged, and it pulled itself free of its shadowy cocoon. The arachnid skittered down to the floor somewhere near Amy's feet. Amy did a ninja dance to avoid the small spider. It was nothing compared to the specimens in her lab, but it was a spider.

A horrific thought struck her. If one lump was a spider, then what of the hundreds of other ones? The wall came to life with movement. Arachnid legs popped into view all over the mass, like spiders escaping a wall of tar. There were hundreds. One by one, the spiders freed themselves.

Amy ran for the exit as spiders dropped to the floor behind her, but the lab door refused to open. She pushed hard only to realize in her panic it was a pull door. She yanked the door but swung it too hard. The momentum knocked her off her feet. She fell back, her coat spreading wide open where she landed. The white coat turned black as numerous spiders crawled over her.

Overwhelmed by a wave of arachnids, she realized they came from the corridor, not from behind. The ones at her back had yet to catch up to her. She leaped to her feet and tore off the spider covered coat and tossed it away. Spiders continued to head toward her position, coming from the black mass in her old lab. Amy slammed the door which thankfully ran flush to the ground. That would keep those from her original lab out but trap her inside with others.

Splat!

Something struck the door's window. The frosted glass could not hide the shape of a spider. Splayed out, it looked larger than it was. Splat, splat, splat. One by one, they leaped, covering every inch of glass. For a moment, in one small spot not covered by spiders, Amy thought she glimpsed the strange orb headed figure from earlier. But the figure vanished as spiders overtook every inch of glass.

Remembering those behind her, she turned and saw the advancing dark wave. Amy jumped atop the nearest table knowing it would only buy a little time. Spiders could climb. Hell, they were leaping outside the door. Amy grabbed a wheeled chair next to the table and shoved it away before giving chase. Her feet briefly touched the mass on the floor before she leaped into the already moving chair. Her weight propelled it faster and further away from the spider army. She rode until the chair lost momentum then she raced toward the nearby storage closet.

A thundering clicking sounded behind her, the click-clack of scuttling spiders. So many on the tile that their movements created a horror soundtrack, one that followed her wherever she ran. *Amy's Song*. She wished it would stop, screamed for it to stop.

Click, click, click. The spiders chased her. Thankfully the storage closet door was open. Amy leaped and flew into the room, smashing against its furthest wall. From her prone position, she kicked at the door, which slammed closed just before the mass hit. The closet had a rectangular window at face height and the spiders wasted no time blocking her only light.

Splat, splat, splat. Available ambient light dimmed as the spiders overtook the new window. Amy pulled her legs to her chest and rocked in place as the room fell into darkness. She was safe for the moment but needed a plan. Or weapons. Hopefully the closet contained chemicals she could use to kill the spiders.

Amy rose to her knees and felt something brush against her head. It made no sense because she was crouched. The ceiling should have been much higher. Then something tickled her neck. She turned on her cellphone light and waved it toward the ceiling. (Why did it loom so close?)

Then it hit her. It was not a ceiling. It looked like cotton clouds. Or webbing! She dropped her phone in fright. It landed so its light remained pointed toward the ceiling. What started bad got worse. Spiders descended on individual webs. Amy scrambled away as far as possible until her back hit a wall, one also covered in webbing. She could not pull free. How was it big enough to trap her? Even in the jungle, the webs were not that large. The descending spiders grew closer. Amy screamed.

THUNK!

Amy's scream turned to a gurgle when a ten-foot-long arachnid leg shot through the ceiling web and impaled her mouth! The hidden spider yanked her into the ceiling as vanishing into a cloud. Once inside the silk construct, the web shook and quivered. Amy's gurgles kept time with the frantic motions. Then, as quickly as it had grabbed Amy, it released her. She dropped back into the supply room on her back, her lips sutured shut with silk.

Her mouth and cheeks moved, but not of her own accord. Her wide-open eyes remained as still as her heart. A spider leg flittered out from inside her mouth, forcing its way through the stitched lips. Once freed, a spider crawled from her mouth. An army of spiders followed, scrambling out of the mouth of the corpse that was once Amy.

CHAPTER 37

I t all began in the electric room. With her temp office on the same floor, a part of Gilliannwanted to hit that couch and curl into a ball. Go to sleep and wait for the ferry. But it was too late. Something was going on in the facility. Gillian could not put a finger on it, but she identified roughly the place and time that her irrational fear began.

In the morning, when Mitch confronted her in the elevator, she was more angry than scared. Listening to the voice in the car as she waited for the afternoon ferry absolutely frightened her. But when she accompanied Mitch back to the building, she was no longer scared. The next time she felt nervous was at the open machine room door. Since then, things got worse enough that she imagined things that were not there.

Could it be the tapes? Was it as simple as watching others fears somehow caused the same in her? She had never felt so much goose-flesh and raised hairs as she did in the past several hours. With no good reason. That was what frustrated Gillian the most. There was no reason to be afraid that she could identify. But she could not shake it off.

Where was the security guard? That was the million-dollar question. She encountered many in that occupation with superiority complexes, so having one running around a closed facility doing God knows what was cause for concern. But what was the man's plan? Why invest time or energy in a place that was about to close?

After years of reporting, Gillian learned that tragedies almost always boiled down to a relationship gone south. Was Steve sleeping with someone on staff? If that person remained on the island, then it might explain why the guard remained.

But if the object of his affection welcomed the attention, then Steve would not have to hide. That meant there was a potential danger for someone on the staff. But Derrick had gone missing as well. Were they the couple in question? Was Derrick missing because a lover attacked him? Or had the two slipped away together?

If the two were a couple, it would answer multiple questions. The problem was, Steve had leered uncomfortably at Gillian all morning. She spoke to him when she first arrived. Steve told her to have a seat and wait for Doctor Trager, who would arrive on the next ferry. While waiting, Steve kept eyeing her. Every time she looked up, he was staring and not in a security concern manner. Based on her experience, the security guard was not gay. Perhaps Steve was obsessed with Amy and harmed Derrick because they worked together. Steve might have mistaken the scientists' relationship as something other than work partners. But what would any type of relationships have to do with the machine room?

Gillian decided to find out. Noise blasted like before the moment she opened the door. Leaving it open would give away her position, so she stepped inside and closed the door down to a crack. Then she waited for the motion sensor lights in the hall to go out. Now no one would know she was anywhere near the place unless they watched her on cameras.

She raised her cellphone flashlight and lowered her head. No more concussive head bumps, thank you very much. The main corridor shot straight through the massive space while smaller alcoves and walk-ways shot off in multiple directions. If the machinery served as the building's heart, its many pipes acted as veins. Rather than pumping blood, they delivered water, air, and sewage.

Several dusty soda cans sat nestled on various pipes, signs of engineers past. Electrical panels lined one breakaway corridor. Prominent signs warned of death. Gillian kept moving until arriving at the earlier spot. Her light proved inadequate for the task, but she had no other option. She bumped into a large metal canister, which crashed to the floor, loud enough to be heard over the already thunderous din.

Gillian leaned closer to the fallen canister for a better look. Its top had a single twist nob and nozzle like helium tanks present at far too many kids' parties. (Where everyone inquired about when she would have children.) Several more tanks stood in a row nearby.

One canister's nozzle fed into a flexible hose. Duct tape held the whole thing together. A half-unzipped duffel bag sat on the floor near her feet. Something about its shape bothered her. Gillian unzipped the bag the rest of the way and screamed.

The bag contained a head. One with long, stringy hair soaked with gore and only half a face. It's one good eye shot open!

"I'm here!" the head said.

Gillian fell on her ass. Then a light cut through the darkness and blinded her. She raised her hands to shield herself from the beam. Whoever held the flashlight appeared surprised at her presence. They froze momentarily. The flashlight beam allowed her a better view of the bag. It contained no skull, only a strange variation of a motor-cycle helmet. Was she losing her mind? The person backpedaled and extinguished the flashlight. Gillian rose to her feet and called out.

"Stop! Wait!"

She gave chase, but the door slammed ahead of her. Gillian burst into the hall in time for another door to close, that of the stairwell at the end of the hall. She took a moment to pocket her phone and allow her eyes to adjust to the bright lights of the hallway. Then it hit her.

Why skulk around in the dark? Not just now but earlier. Each time Gillian had entered into darkness it was because she had no idea where the lights were, but surely the machine room had lights. Ones not on motion sensors obviously. But why did Mitch and Jimmy skulk about in such a manner earlier in the day? Wouldn't they know where the lights were?

Maybe not. They were not building engineers. Steve would have known. In any big building, there would be plans for emergency power restoration, water shut off and such. Steve would oversee such plans. If Steve roamed in shadows, it meant he wished not to be found. Jimmy and Mitch getting around via flashlight meant stealth. They either considered Steve a threat when they were in the machine room or they themselves were up to something.

But there were not two people this time, only one. Likely Steve. Someone had returned to the scene of the crime. But what crime? There was no head in the bag. Gillian's mind had created the illusion. Just like in her office. But someone running away confirmed nefarious intentions. She stepped carefully into the stairwell to make sure no one lay in wait, then she took the stairs.

CHAPTER 38

Elle injected a shot of Ink. She would never tell Yoshi, but the initial shot thrilled her. That first time, the world changed. A chorus of voices filled the room. Guttural and raw, they murmured obscene things to her. The invisible speakers had immoral intentions. While fully understanding the inherent danger, she welcomed the obscene chorus, because many voices meant many people. That meant something important.

She was not alone.

Though able to hear the obscene suitors (oh the things they wished to do to her flesh!), she could never fully see them. Jerking her head or spinning in any direction failed to deliver them from her periphery. Whatever the talkative and grotesque beings were, they remained hidden along the edges of her sight. But she did not care what form they took as long as she had company.

A cadre of monsters (was cadre the term?) would even offer relief to isolation. Anyone or anything to keep from being alone. Never that. Where was Yoshi? She lowered the injector and popped out the spent vial. While reaching for another, she fumbled it, losing it to gravity because of shaking hands. It hit the floor and skidded. She bent to retrieve it and her foot kicked it away.

Fine. She would get another. Since Yoshi had left, she injected more quickly, too frightened, too nervous about being alone. Every injection brought forth new friends who wished nothing more than to rip her tits off and drink from the resulting blood fountain.

"Isn't that so like my invisible friends? Threatening to rip off my boobs then vanishing," Elle said.

Elle spoke when the voices stopped. It made her feel less alone. As she reached for a new bullet vial, she dropped it. That one did not survive the fall. It shattered at her feet. Something had moved in the hallway outside causing her to startle. Maybe she was not alone.

"Hello!" Elle yelled from inside the lab.

It was not a question. She made her presence known to whoever she had glimpsed through the lab door window. The image of a figure flashed quickly. Likely not a real person, especially since the head was more of a strange shiny orb than a human head. Likely a hallucination.

Hallucinations were cool. Elle enjoyed flittering and fluttering things that were not there. When she first took Ink, dead butterflies filled the lab. They flapped decayed wings and flew upside down. It was beautiful. Their wings disturbed a black mist hanging in the air. She witnessed more things after the butterflies, horrible, frightening things. But zombie butterflies made it worthwhile.

She deemed the orb head thing worthy of investigation, even though it was probably a hallucination. Or Yoshi returning. Elle stepped into the hall and looked around. No one there. Her heart beat faster. That was the part she did not enjoy about the drug. The part that made her unleash on Jimmy earlier. There was a sweet spot with Ink, then there was the heart racing part that felt highly uncomfortable. She touched her heart, willing it to slow as she searched the corridor. Its emptiness only highlighted her solitary situation.

Where was Yoshi? Why had he left her? And why did so many people leave the island? Why did everyone leave her alone? She could not take it. Easier to deal with loneliness in the lab than in the vast hallway. She stepped backward into the lab and heard a voice.

"Where have you been, Musume?"

Gooseflesh rode Elle's spine, and she could not find the strength to turn. The voice, she knew it. Fragrant odors transported Elle to another place, another time. The smells of a Japanese kitchen brought with it equal parts comfort and dread. No matter how old Elle got, the scents involved always evoked an array of feelings.

Since turning might break the spell, she simply sniffed and remembered. There was the unmistakable scent of miso soup along with the potent smell of grilled fish seasoned in sake, mirin, and soy sauce. Underneath everything was the sweet scent of rice infused with rice vinegar. She detected no hint of cooked noodles in the mix which meant the meal was not finished. Her mother would flash-cook those at the very end, so they came out as fresh after the heat as they were going in. Elle's stomach growled, but not as loud as the chef growled at her.

"I asked where you have been, Musume!"

The chef grabbed Elle's arm and spun her around. The violent motion aggravated a shoulder injury developed at a young age under the same hands that gripped her so firmly now. It could have been the same interrogation, even.

"Mama?" Elle whispered in disbelief.

The woman spit, as if disgusted by the title. Whether in defiance of her position as the matriarch, or simply hearing the word spoken in English, the woman made her displeasure known. Jerking Elle's arm into the air, the woman spun her daughter around, examining the aftermath of whatever deeds the child had been up to. And Elle was a child. She felt small, helpless.

"Where have you been?"

The woman, while small in stature, had a large presence. In her sixties, the woman's eyes remained sharp and piercing though they squinted in disgust at her child. Her voice was unwavering, her questions provided their own answers and were nothing more than rhetorical. And accusatory.

"Were you with boys?"

"No, Mama. I told you where I was. The library," Elle said in a small voice coming from a small girl.

"And are there no boys at the library?"

"Ouch!" Elle yelped as her mother squeezed her arm ever tighter before tossing the arm roughly away, as if trying to do the same to the child. Elle rubbed her arm.

"I asked if there were boys at the library."

"Yes, Mama," Elle said.

"Do they try to stick their tongues in your manko? Li-li-li-li," the woman said as she flicked her tongue in a lewd manner.

Elle scrunched her face, sickened at the sight. Yes, many men made such gestures, especially when she was on the bus or on the street. She wished she could ask her mother how to deal with such grotesqueness coming from older (much older) men. But the conversation would not sit well with her mother.

"No, mama."

"You lie! Look how you dress."

Elle could not help but glance at her pink polo shirt covered by a distressed denim jacket. Off brands, thrift store finds. Her mother preferred her to wear dresses, but the men bothered her more when she did. It was easier to be androgynous and invisible in baggy clothing. But that was too American for her mother.

"Do they push your coat aside so they can see your oppai? Not that you have any. Probably never will. If you had waited for boys to touch you, maybe they would have grown in properly."

Elle's stomach turned. The same aromas that drove her hunger in youth had long since become associated with the hurtful words. She wanted boobs. She did like boys. But she did not like men and had no desire to touch them or be touched by them. Elle's heart belonged to many teen actors and boy band singers. That was enough for her. Boys were mostly stupid, but she wanted them to like her.

Her mother frequently made it known that would never happen. According to Elle's mother, Elle was so thin, and such a tomboy that she would have no boys chasing her. Yet every boy on the planet was out to get Elle. How could Elle be with everyone at once and no one ever? Elle's head spun at her mother's angry logic. The woman was only warming up.

"Fah! Why do you think you have no father?"

Because, unlike me, he had a car and driver's license, Elle thought. Instead of saying anything, Elle simply released a tear that mapped her cheek.

"He knew the shame you would bring. With all the boys chasing you! How many more mouths will we have to feed by the time you are done?"

Elle could take it no longer. If her legs could move, she would run. Go back out the door, never come home. But then her mother had her by the hair. That meant one thing.

"Mama, no!"

Elle grabbed her head to stop the pain but also to change its trajectory. She knew where things were heading. Her resistance only caused her mother to tug harder, threatening to scalp her child. Elle had no choice but to follow her mother's path. And that path led them to a tiny closet in the kitchen. The broom closet. So small they did not even keep the garbage inside. Only the broom, dustpan, and garbage bags.

The door was thick, built at a different time, when wood was solid rather than veneer, and when paint still contained lead. The door's hinges were of a substantial size and thickness. Though the door closed tight, the thick metal created a tiny gap on the hinged side of the door. Enough for Elle to see into the kitchen during her punishment. But it also allowed her mother to watch and enjoy the show from the comfort of a warm kitchen.

It was the locks that bothered Elle the most. A triple lock, more for-tified than their front door. A small slide latch above the pull handle, then a chain lock, and a second heavy duty hinged slide latch. Elle had tested the locks before many times. There was no give. And Elle was about to be locked inside. Again. Her mother's righteous anger gave her strength. Elle could not free herself from the woman's grip.

Elle's head was on fire from the hair pulling. Her mother pushed Elle into the closet. Elle twisted, trying to turn to relieve the pressure of her hair. In doing so, she stepped awkwardly. One foot in the closet, one out. The awkward position caused her to fall forward fast. Elle's head smashed into the closet wall. Worse, with her hands occupied, there was nothing to stop her from slipping. Her face rode painful-ly down the wall. Once crumpled on the closet floor, Elle's mother kicked Elle's legs into the closet.

Click, clack, click went the locks. Crumpled in an awkward ball, Elle panicked for a moment, stuck in the position with not enough room to turn around. She finally readjusted and nursed her wounds as best she could in the tight space. The only light available to her was through the same crack that looked out at a mother she wished not to see.

Spite made Elle wish to avoid her mother until she escaped the makeshift prison. It was difficult not to listen, however. Her mother hummed merrily while prepping the meal. Nothing in the woman's demeanor suggested a war had just been fought on the very tile the woman now walked on. In stocking feet. (Shoes were forbidden past the apartment's threshold, which meant no Chuck's in the house for Elle.)

The merry tune hummed by Elle's mother suggested a copacetic home life. She kept humming while opening the oven (the metallic squeak gave it away). That meant the fish was done. Its odor wafted into the closet, causing Elle's stomach to gurgle. Next step in the meal prep meant turning down the Miso soup to a simmer. The rice cooker would shut itself off. *A miracle her mother used a modern device*, Elle had thought when her mother purchased it.

That left the noodles. Elle knew the drill. Clicking signaled the ignition of the burner, followed by the clang of a wok dropped in place atop the oven. A splash of soy sauce in the pan sizzled, creating an aroma that overtook the entire apartment. Sh, sh, sh. Her mother shook the wok back and forth while pushing the noodles round with a spatula.

Then the click of the oven being turned off. Muscle memory of the routine allowed Elle to see despite her sitting fetal in the dark. Her mother would transfer noodles from the wok to a bowl then ladle in the miso soup. Elle was as hungry as she was angry, but she would not beg for food. She understood her mother used the food to enhance the punishment. Elle vowed silence, refusing to beg for a meal.

Something scraped across the floor. That was new. At Elle's age, she could not battle curiosity. Elle pressed her face to the crack and noticed a chair in plain view of the hinged gap. Her mother arranged the seat so that it faced the broom closet. The silverware drawer sliding open sounded which meant chopsticks. After closing the drawer, Elle's mother took a seat in the chair, holding a bowl and utensils.

Her mother stirred the noodles with chopsticks, then lifted a clump high above the bowl. Tilting her head back, the woman fed herself like a bird, allowing the noodles to slide down her throat. She smacked her mouth with satisfaction while locking eyes with her daughter. The woman fed herself another scrumptious round of noodles. She wiped her mouth on her sleeve.

"Look at you. Three locks it takes to keep your filthy mind away from the boys."

Elle was enraged with a desire to fight back. She did not like boys as much as she liked books or science. Elle liked her friends of all sexes. Mostly, she liked the idea of going somewhere far away.

"Let them slurp on you? What do you do in that library all day?"

Her mother slurped again and somehow made it dirty, disgusting. Elle was losing her appetite. Elle had enough. Lean back into the dark and hide. That was the best course of action. Let her mother tire herself out. There were only so many accusations one person could make.

Then something odd happened. Her mother jolted upright in the chair with a strange look on her face. Her movement appeared involuntary. Once upright and rigid, the woman went still, staring straight ahead. Elle looked behind herself trying to see what had caught her mother's attention. There was nothing but darkness. She turned back and saw her mother's eye twitch.

Crash! The bowl fell from the woman's hands and shattered on the floor. Her mother did not catch it, and worse, did not react to the crash. Elle pressed her face against the door, suddenly concerned.

"Mama?"

After a moment, her mother followed the path of the bowl. It was not a simple fall; it was as if she thrust herself out of the chair. A hard jerk of a movement thrusting her hips from the chair and then she hit the floor, falling onto her side while landing in the spilled liquid on the floor. Elle's mother faced Elle from where she landed. The woman's eyes remained wide open and unblinking.

"Mama!"

The woman did not answer, only stared at her daughter. Eventually, a tear dripped from one of the woman's eyes. Elle's mother murmured something unintelligible, as if drunk, then went silent, never looking away from her daughter. Elle fought to open the door.

"Mama, let me help you. Please, get up, open the door!" She grabbed the handle and pulled it. Nothing. Elle slammed her body against the door, to no avail. "Mama, let me help you. Mama, please, let me get you help. Mama, please, help me!"

Elle screamed with anguish, fighting a door that refused to budge. When that failed, she screamed for neighbors, but they were an end unit. There was only the world above and the world below. No one answered. Elle screamed until her voice grew hoarse. She stomped on the floor, hoping to raise the ire of some unknown neighbor, but got nothing for her troubles except sore feet.

Time stilled. She did not know how long she had been inside, but it felt like eternity, a moment frozen as solid in time as her mother remained frozen on the floor. Elle lost count of the times she threw herself against the entrance to her wooden tomb. All failed attempts.

"No! Help me! Mama, help me, please. Somebody help me!"

But no one did, so Elle dropped to the floor and cradled herself. The scent of rice, fish, and noodles made her stomach growl. Worse, her throat ached from the screaming. Water. There was none. The predicament hit her, and she sobbed, rocking back and forth in the tight confines of her closet.

Elle grabbed the broom at one point and used the handle to pound the closet's ceiling but received no reply. She listened for footsteps above or below to signal someone was home, but all remained silent. The closet muffled the outside world to the point she could barely hear passing traffic, which meant they would not hear her either.

A mop bucket was in the closet with her, and she used it as a restroom. The mop was still damp from a recent cleaning. Elle sucked on the loose strings for moisture. The dirt and cleaning chemicals were stomach churning, but there was some water in the mix. She grew increasingly hungry and thirsty. Oh, so thirsty!

The passage of time was hard to decipher, as Elle soon fell into brief periods of sleep, though she never woke from the nightmare. With no other way to understand the passage of time, Elle kept time based on the changes in her mother's corpse. Not long after her mother fell from the chair, the woman's face turned a certain shade of blue that Elle thought was quite beautiful. But as time passed, the face grew darker and darker until the flesh gave over to gravity and drooped toward the floor.

At one point during her entrapment, Elle screamed about how she always liked boys, would touch them, and let them touch her. She said filthy things she had learned from the internet but knew nothing of in real life. She spoke the words, yelled them, cried them in the hopes it would so infuriate her mother the woman might return from the dead and tear down the door with a vengeance.

But eventually Elle's words became a croak. As her bones sought the surface of her already skinny frame, she found it more uncomfortable and painful to sit in any position. At least as she grew weaker, sleep came involuntarily. But waking brought with it tremendous pain.

Elle dry heaved frequently over the foul odors of her dead mother and rotting fish combined. Dry heaving taxed her body and cramped her stomach while denying her the sweet release of vomiting. There was nothing left in her stomach. Even her tears had dried, though her sobbing rarely stopped. She never felt so alone.

Fading in and out of consciousness, Elle came to understand her mother better. If Elle was not careful, she would end up like her mother in the end. All alone. If there was a boy who liked her, if there was a good friend, someone would come to check on her. But there would be no rescue, no one to worry about her. She was too much like her mother. All alone.

Elle remembered one of her science classes where they discussed how long someone could live without water. The answer was four days. Six and a half days later, when neighbors finally complained to the landlord about the stench from apartment 4C, first responders arrived. Unconscious through most of her mother's body retrieval, Elle cried out with a squeak. The shocked rescue crew rushed Elle to the hospital. Her heart stopped twice on the way. Though they restarted it, she was never the same.

CHAPTER 39

Elle leaped from her lab back into the corridor. She fought to breathe, battling anxiety at the thought of being trapped in the closet again. But there was no closet, merely her lab off to one side. She was no longer trapped. The long corridor helped her to breathe. She needed people. Once she found them, what would she say?

Forget the trip down memory lane. One could attribute the dark memory to lack of sleep, the drugs, or PTSD. But what to make of the odors accompanying the memory? From the aromatic rice to the rotting fish, it seemed real. Had Elle slipped into theoretical lucidity?

Unlikely. In lucidity, people could control their environment. Elle had failed to escape the closet until after she relived the horrible event. She shivered at the thought. So long ago, but always there in the back of her mind. Elle looked back at her lab where something lay on the floor close to where she injected the drugs. Too frightened to re-enter the lab and have it turn back into a closet, she pulled her cellphone out of her ass. From the back pocket.

She aimed it into the lab and snapped several photos of the large lump. Once finished, she opened a picture and finger swiped it bigger. Her heart stopped. Staring at her from the lab floor was her dead mother, frozen in place, just like in the kitchen back home.

She brought up the next and enlarged that. The image changed slightly. A woman appeared in the same prone position, but half the woman's face was gone. Had half her mother's face fallen off by the end, the skin sloughed off in death? Elle could not remember because she remained mostly unconscious at the end.

Yoshi. She needed to show him, find him. She needed someone. Elle bypassed the elevator for the stairs. Before entering the stairwell, she checked her phone. No service. Occasionally, they got service in certain corners of the building, sometimes on the roof of the dead wing where they occasionally partied. Even a text from someone she knew would help.

She stepped out onto Yoshi's wing and ran for his lab. Unlikely he would be there because he took the reporter to someone else's lab. She struggled to remember whose. She was in a haze of Ink when Gillian arrived.

"Yoshi!"

Elle yelled his name even before she reached his lab. All the rooms along the way came up empty. His proved no different. Nothing but collectibles. No Yoshi. The wall of toys rose above his desk. Under the influence of the drug, the toys' faces took on other forms.

A beast with three eyes. A screeching bat. The Gill Man from Creature of the Black Lagoon maintained its already horrific look, but with demonic, glowing eyes. The sound of plastic drew Elle's attention. Inside one box, a toy with a half-destroyed face glared at Elle with its one available eye. The figure tried to push through the plastic center of the box, trying to get out. It mirrored the face she saw on the reporter. Strange.

Foolish. Nothing but toys. Elle blinked and the dead woman with half a face disappeared. In her place stood an anime character Elle recognized but could not name. Elle would learn them all if she ever hooked up with Yoshi. In her eagerness to always be with some-one, Elle had many relationships. (Of which her dead mother would surely disapprove.) To keep people around, she latched onto hobbies of each new man she bedded down with.

None truly knew Elle because she always became who they wanted her to be, a cheerleader for their life, not her own. But most relationships reached tipping points where the other half found reasons to spend less time with her. Once the bloom was off the rose, Elle moved on to the next, anyone infatuated enough to spend more time together. During dry spells, she settled for one-night stands, including a few men at work.

Colt! They had slept together, and she knew where to find him. The lobby level lab. She did not wish to sleep with Colt again. The thought gave Elle pause. Colt would expect round two if Elle visited the man. She got angry at Yoshi, deciding his absence made her heart grow fonder for her former flame. Then it hit her. There remained one person available to her. Elle returned to the stairwell and headed toward the top floor.

She quickly arrived at Mitch's floor but came up from the longer end of the hall. The section of the building unnerved her even when not under the influence of Ink. The portion of the corridor from the western stairwell to the elevators remained under construction. Several of the original "crazy dog" rooms remained. That was the term Steve used. She felt guilty about her fling with the security guard because of his marriage. Steve had stories, though, about the history of each wing. The higher the floor, the crazier the patients, he said. That meant Mitch's level housed the most insane individuals. The crazy dogs Steve called them right before they had sex on the security office desk.

Mitch's floor was a blender of past and present. One end remained untouched, a tribute to a dark past, the other remodeled for a new century. Plastic sheeting bridged the two where construction had ceased for some unknown reason, but the plastic made the place even creepier. Behind the first sheet, a shadowy female figure appeared. Elle sped up, but the woman matched Elle's pace.

The shadowy woman kept pace, moving inexplicably from room to room, using the sheet as a transport device. Elle ran, and the woman did the same. Elle understood the form had to be her own shadow, except the woman behind the sheets appeared to wear a dress and heels. Once Elle cleared the sheeting and reached the elevator bay, the corridor segued to a modern medical facility.

Many people should have heard Elle's frantic cries and foot stomping if nothing else. The absence of any employees frightened her immensely. Why had she heard from no one since Yoshi left? And why did he leave? It made no sense. She gave him the green light. Could she be a Trager experiment? Did all her exes team up with Yoshi? Did they collectively seek revenge by taking advantage of her fear?

No. Mitch would not allow such a thing. While Doctor Trager was eager for a breakthrough with the fear element, he cared deeply about those in his care. All of whom were patients as much as employees. All of them were damaged goods and Mitch saw through that to give people a chance. Mitch had an open-door policy. It was open even as she approached, but his office was empty. She knocked on his lab door.

The hard metal hurt her knuckles and produced no discernible sound. She would not knock again. It evoked too many memories of her entrapment. If her boss was in his lab, it meant he was working or sleeping given his age and the hour. One thing to bother her boss at work, another to wake him.

Colt it was. Down to the basement to a not forever, but right now companion. It was late enough to discuss an overnight stay. Yoshi had his chance. She would spend the night with Colt and, while not planning anything physical, would not refuse it. Elle did not wish to take any more Ink for the night. Dead butterflies were one thing, a dead mother was another.

While using the stairs, she stopped at every floor on the way. The sight of each corridor empty increased her fear and paranoia. Her legs shook so much she feared tumbling down the stairs. She called out frequently.

"Hello?"

No one answered. A sound at her rear drew her attention back toward the stairwell. Head high in the square glass window of the stairwell, she thought she glimpsed a strange orb in place of a face. Staring but without eyes. Whatever it was, it vanished quickly, as if never there at all. Like the toys had never changed.

She eyed the building's grand entrance, which only enhanced her discomfort. It reminded her that beyond those doors was an island. No rescue until the ferry on Monday. Like the closet from her youth, she could not escape. Someone had to be somewhere. She called out again.

"Hello!"

The silence frightened her. She headed toward a place she knew well, the security office. Once there, she slapped the door. No response, not that she expected any. Steve hit on her often after their naked shenanigans. They screwed, but she knew nothing about him. Why was he missing? Did he stalk someone on the island? Another lover? Or was he after her? No, they had been discreet, and the man never made her feel uncomfortable.

She moved down the corridor, frantic. Keep moving, keep going until finding someone. Lights remained off on the loading dock. No surprise. But the worst revelation—lights off in Colt's lab. She entered anyway and triggered the lights.

"Colt?"

An injector lay on the floor near an overturned medical tray. That meant one thing. Sex. He found someone else. She remembered the isolation room beyond the snake pit. That was where they hooked up. Elle led him with his eyes closed past the snakes, joking about how he could not leave until he satisfied her. Elle did not care if she found the new lovers naked. She needed to talk to someone. Anyone. She raced past the snakes and burst into the empty room.

"No!"

Where was everyone? Elle rushed back through the lab and down the hall. She slapped the security door again but kept moving. She planned to exit the building and check for lights in windows from the outside. Best way to determine someone's location.

Once in the lobby, she raised her cellphone again. A bar! Enough for a text. She texted Yoshi, asking his location. No reply. Moving closer to the front door produced a second bar. Two meant enough for a call. She remained inside, too afraid to exit and lose the signal. She knew which number to call. The one she never could from the closet. Elle refused to suffer alone again. She dialed 911. Static threatened to swallow the call, but it got through. A female voice answered.

"What is the nature of your emergency?"

"I..." Elle started, unsure what to say.

"Sorry, you cut off," the voice said.

"I..." Elle struggled to articulate a reason for the call.

"What is your emergency?"

The voice refocused Elle. "Everyone is gone. I think something happened to them." Elle leaned against the wall by the exit doors, using it for much needed support.

"You're all alone?" the woman asked.

"Yes. Please keep talking to me," Elle said. "I am so scared."

"Now sweetie, no need to be afraid."

"Thank you," Elle said.

"I mean no need because you should be used to it by now. You deserve to be alone."

Elle flinched at the words, tried to shake off the Ink still in her system. It had to be responsible for what she heard. "What?"

"Who would ever want to be with you?" the voice asked. "Would anyone ever even know if you went missing? If your mother trapped you in, say, a closet, would anyone even come looking for you?"

Elle turned pale as tears built in her eyes. "No. Please, listen..."

"No. You listen. I have just now met you and I want nothing to do with you, little Ms. Princess," the voice said.

"Why? Why are you doing this?" Elle pleaded, more than asked.

Then the woman fell into a sing song full of wicked glee. "You. Are going to. Dieeeeeeee! No. Saving. You!"

"Stop, please stop."

The line fell silent. As bad as the woman's words had been, the sudden silence was worse. Nothing on the other end. Not even breathing. Elle whispered into the phone.

"Hello?"

"You're going to die. DIE ALL ALONE!"

Elle threw the phone. The voice had changed, became so loud, vicious, garbled as if it came from half a mouth. The phone skidded toward the front desk and then it began. Elle squinted, tried to understand what she saw.

White. The corridor beyond the front desk grew white. Not white as in light, simply a white void appearing to overtake the scenery like an eraser wiping out graphite. The world started vanishing. The white void ate everything it touched, and it moved rapidly, straight toward her!

The distant stairwell vanished next, closing off an escape route. A second void of white took hold there, and it too moved in her direction. The twin blankets of white threatened to merge with her as the focal point. The ding of an elevator opening sounded. Elle made a run for it, but the white grew too fast. A humanoid form with an orb head, (the one glimpsed through the door's window earlier?) appeared in the elevator before being swallowed by white.

That left one place. Outside. Elle stumbled outside. Without looking back, she ran across the front lawn to put distance between herself and the white apocalypse at her rear. Eventually, she stopped. And froze. High above, stars merged with one another into an intense brilliant white glow which made the night as bright as day.

The whiteness also advanced from the ocean in the distance, swallowing the ferry terminal before climbing the mountain. The white scaled the steep rise without effort or obstacles slowing it down.

Too fast. It all happened so fast. The blanket of white thicker than any snowstorm stretched, grew, and overtook everything it touched. Elle spun in a circle with nowhere to go. Her world shrank. The white would soon be upon her. Elle closed her eyes, crouched, and waited. When she opened them and stood, she found herself in the void. She was truly alone in the vastness of a white nothingness.

"Hello? Anybody?" Elle yelled into the nothingness.

Then she cried out in surprise and pain. A bloom of crimson appeared on her shoulder and spread over her shirt. Then her right hand disassembled with a loud pop. The hand exploded into chunks of meat and bone. She raised the hand, which had only two fingers left. Exposed bones gleamed almost as white as the void in the spots not saturated with blood.

Pure shock eliminated immediate pain. She struggled to identify what was happening. Pop! Her leg came next. A clean hole appeared and remained empty for a surprising amount of time before finally irrigating itself with blood. The source of the wounds mystified her. She struggled to stand on a leg that no longer cooperated with her central nervous system. Effects of blood loss hit, and the world spun.

"Help me?"

Unable to stand any longer, Elle dropped to the ground in an awkward heap. She felt herself floating above her own body. From somewhere above, she observed the crumpled heap of flesh in an ocean of infinite white. Blood poured from her body in all directions. The crimson tide changed the nature of the canvas, turning her injuries into a glorious painting.

Then the pain hit and pulled her back into her body. She struggled to breathe, struggled to find her heartbeat. She tried to cry out, but there was nothing left. Her strength had left her body along with the pooling blood. The ground became nothing more than a cloud. In her last moments, she realized the voice on the phone had been correct. She would die alone. She loved Yoshi, she never told him. And now she never would.

Elle's eyes fluttered and then her world turned white.

CHAPTER 40

Gillian tried to move with stealth, but she moved in a world of motion activated lights. Once the lights announced her arrival on the floor, she threw caution to the wind. She raced to her destination and threw open Mercedette's door. The view stunned her. Obscene images filled screens near the ceiling. Mercedette rested in a reclined position atop a futuristic-looking chair, wearing a VR headset and little else.

Gillian had no idea who she was chasing but did have a destination in mind. She never caught up with the stairwell person. If they entered the lab before her, Mercedette would not have known because of the VR equipment. And Gillian could not know because Mercedette had apparently turned off the lights manually, leaving candles as the lab's sole source of illumination. Gillian searched the surroundings and found signs of no one besides Mercedette whose hands fluttered around her chest.

Gillian ignored any voyeuristic guilt. She was there to protect Mercedette, not watch her. The scientist was under the influence of a drug designed to stimulate her. The drug was in R&D, who knew its potency? Only one woman. Mercedette also wore a strange skull cap that glowed with tiny lights. Other wires protruded from the woman.

Some ran to circular patches near her chest, and one wire ran to a clip attached to a finger. Mercedette looked like a cyborg.

Then the cyborg struck. With startling speed, the cyborg leaped from the chair and grabbed Gillian by the throat. The skull cap melded with the VR headset merging into a metallic cocoon. Its grin remained human and stretched too wide for the face. The smile's edges protruded to each side as if under the support of bones.

Too fast. It was too fast. Gillian could not breathe. The thing pressed harder against her throat, forced her to one knee. The cyborg tilted a head that had no discernable eyes. Yet it watched her. Its face became an orb. She recognized it. Was it something she glimpsed? The cyborg choked off her thoughts. Gillian fell to the second knee.

The pain woke her from the fugue. Mercedette remained in place, never having moved. Gillian had smacked her knees on the hard tile and held her hands to her own throat. Above her, couples moaned while having sex. Even without hallucinations, the world appeared to have gone mad. She wondered whether she had hitched a ride on some invisible crazy train.

Gillian rose to her feet and placed a hand on Mercedette's shoulder. The woman gasped under the touch and, with the speed of a cyborg, grabbed Mercedette's arm. Mercedette sat up and ripped off her headset, which knocked off the skullcap.

Mercedette's normally tight hairstyle had turned to clotted wet strings that dangled across her face. Mercedette eyed Gillian with a look Gillian experienced from many men. A look normally accompanied by catcalls.

"You should not be here. Not now. Your presence is... problematic."

"Please. I know this sounds crazy, but I cannot seem to stop shaking."

Mercedette breathed deep and tried to gain control of herself. "You do not know what I am experiencing. My thoughts are... bad."

"I understand, but I think you are not safe."

Gillian tried to free her arm. Subtle at first, then she pulled harder. Mercedette only tightened her grip but acknowledged Gillian's discomfort.

"It is not what you think. I am not an animal," Mercedette said. "I am gripping your arm at a pulse point."

"I won't pretend to know what you have gone through, what you are going through right now, and I would never interrupt. But I have felt something is wrong. There are machinations at work."

"Machinations?" Mercedette asked.

"Yes. And I believe they center on you. I believe someone exposed us to the chemical. Your chemical. Your company's chemical."

"Your pulse is fast," Mercedette said, and finally let go.

"With no reason. I have nothing to fear. My phobias are not at play."

"What is your phobia?"

Gillian scrunched her face. "What does that have to..."

"You accessed our files and read things about us. Mitch told us. I am not afraid to share who I am. But if you ask me to trust you, I ask the same. What do you fear?"

Gillian looked around the room. "This."

"That is not an answer," Mercedette said.

"It is. Subjecting yourself to this. Artificially stimulating yourself to the point of no return? I could never do this. Not even with the men in my life. I hit a wall with trust, with..."

"Losing control. You fear losing control."

Gillian nodded. "And now cyborgs."

Mercedette rose from her seat close enough for their bodies to touch. Mercedette stiffened, still lost in a lustful haze. After steadying herself, she grabbed her laptop. Wires ran from different parts of her body, and she tapped a tablet.

"My vitals are off as well. An unknown barrier has limited my ability to peak. Initially, I reached ninety-nine percent red but dropped into the eighties ever since. Exposure to the fear element would explain it, but I do not see how." Gillian's eyes instinctively eyed a nearby vent. Mercedette followed her gaze. "Does not work that way. We do not have weaponized product."

"Weaponized?" Gillian asked.

"Gas or aerosolized. Mitch thinks that is why they shut us down. The company in charge humored our valiant efforts to help people while only looking to militarize the product the whole while. Mitch is too altruistic. He kept his eyes on our prize, and it cost us all. There is no way someone could have exposed us all."

"Jimmy could have. Besides being infatuated with you, he accessed every lab while doing inventory. I worry he plans to take advantage of your altered state."

"I have already proven one thing with my experiment. Sexual desire has nothing to do with violence. While it may be powerful enough to override good decision-making skills, there is nothing in it inherently violent. After experimenting on myself, I can confirm. Sexual desire is a naturally occurring physical process. I have simply juiced it and came out with no desire to harm others. Monsters are monsters, with or without a sex drive. That will be in my study results."

Mercedette pulled off the remaining cords attached to her body. She tapped buttons to change the overhead screens. They showed the laptop camera's view of the two women. Mercedette examined their images.

"Okay. I am a hot mess. Maybe aggressive and crude right now. But there is nothing to fear. Jimmy was already here and gone. I refused his inventory request because I was in the process of my experiment. He attempted to get into my shorts. I expected no less, though he struggled to get his words out. Strange, I thought he was over his stutter. Jimmy came by to shoot his shot. I said no, and he left."

"Just like that?" Gillian asked.

"Not just like that. He was persistent. But even if he was after me, what does that have to do with your exposure?"

"Someone was in the machine room. I assumed it was Jimmy. Maybe it wasn't. But there were tanks there. Like helium," Gillian said.

"Machine room?" Mercedette asked.

"Long story. Look. I am frightened beyond belief. It has helped to transform that fright into a worry about your wellbeing. But truthfully, I am simply scared and don't understand why," Gillian said.

"I do," Mercedette said.

Gillian followed Mercedette's gaze. Jimmy stood in the observation room. The man leered at Mercedette's partially nude body.

"They're here," Mercedette said.

Mercedette stood transfixed. Gillian looked at the woman, then Jimmy. She shook her head, confused.

"You mean he's here," Gillian said.

"They are here to punish me. Punish me for my desires. Punish me for what I long to do."

"What? Are we seeing the same thing? It is only Jimmy up there."

"My temptation. Jimmy almost cost me this job once. They sent him to test me then. They know I failed at purity, so now they are here to claim me once again."

"Mercedette, there are no they. Only he. How many do you see?"

"Twelve. They travel in numbers divisible by three."

Gillian shook her head, confused. "It is only Jimmy. You see him, right?"

Mercedette nodded. "And the others. Clever trick. Jimmy was their spy all along. The upside-down men can lead me to Him."

"You are seeing things. I understand. It proves my point. You were a cyborg. A face fell on my foot."

The strange confession drew Mercedette's attention away from the window. She appeared to return to her own self. Mercedette gestured to a nearby door at the back of the lab. Gillian took the lead and rushed through it only to find an industrial washroom.

There was no secondary exit. Gillian quickly turned as a door slammed and locked behind her. Through the window, a look of mania overtook Mercedette's face. Gillian pounded on the glass.

"Mercedette, what are you doing? You are in danger. You should not be alone."

"I am not alone. They are here. All of them."

"Them? It is Jimmy. He is obsessed."

"My coworker is merely a vessel. Jimmy's obsession was driven by the Elder. Are you aware I never saw the Elder's face that day? If He is using Jimmy to get to me, I will use Jimmy for the same thing."

Mercedette walked to a nearby wall, tore off a green marker, crumpled and tossed it. She tapped the wall. "That is my code. Its removal means I need help. Mitch will eventually arrive and investigate. He will free you soon."

"Stop. This is crazy. Let me out!" Gillian yelled.

Mercedette moved to the center of the room and retrieved her self-defense device and exited. Gillian pressed her face to the glass. Jimmy vanished from above, on an intercept mission.

Gillian stepped back from the window, and her back bumped into something. Breasts? A putrid odor filled the confined space. Someone breathed in her ear. Gillian's legs turned into noodles. She could not turn around, too terrified of what she might see. Then a voice from beyond the grave whispered in her ear.

"I'm here."

Gillian bolted forward in fright and struck her head so hard against the door's glass that it cracked. A trail of blood covered the window where her face slid down its surface. She went unconscious and crumpled into a heap alongside dead grey legs.

CHAPTER 41

Mercedette raced upstairs and emerged from the stairwell into a changed world. he expected as much. What Mercedette failed to articulate to the reporter was how tremendous forces were at work in the universe. Forces powerful enough to ripple cloaks of reality. Such forces created gateways that allowed bearers of pain and suffering access to victims. She never witnessed the face of evil that day. Partly because the restraints kept her locked in place with a limited view. But mostly because she kept her eyes closed through the ordeal.

Some suggested the Elder's beauty made him irresistible. Others swore a glance meant death. Through Mercedette's pain initiation, she never opened her eyes, too afraid of fairytales. Because she never put a face to her tormentor He grew to mythic proportions in her mind. Even as she grew into adulthood and escaped into a new life, Mercedette longed to identify her attacker. Despite reclaiming her childhood religion, she could not forgive.

Now her past returned. As an adult, she vowed not to keep her eyes closed. She walked along what used to be a corridor in her workplace. Time and space meant nothing to the Elder. Therefore, the robed figures in upside-down masks holding tiki torches did not surprise her. Though only a dozen in the observation room, their numbers had grown, stretching as far as she could see in either direction.

A black mist covered the path, floating knee high. The upside-down men chanted as she neared her destination. Jimmy appeared in the distance as well and led her toward the Elder. While she pursued Jimmy, some of the robed men broke formation to follow her. Unlike the climb as a teen, her path was straight and narrow, maybe a sign that evil was more eager to appear this time. Jimmy entered a room of stone. She followed.

Pentagrams and archaic symbols covered the walls in the vast room, all painted in blood. An altar rose near the room's center. The figures who followed Mercedette positioned themselves around the altar. Jimmy stood there, no longer meek, leaning into his own version of a monster. She did not worry; she would use him to draw out the Elder.

Jimmy stripped down, taking off his clothes at a leisurely pace until he stood naked and erect. He gazed at Mercedette while disrobing. She thought he looked silly in his glasses while nude. As if realizing, he took them off and donned a robe. Jimmy placed a mask on his face. Upside down like the others.

Then he transformed.

Mercedette understood better, watching it happen to someone she knew. It was not as simple as placing a mask upside down on one's face. When Jimmy masked up, his posture changed. The eyes were blank under the mask, a hint of lips filled the space where the eyeholes were.

But with a sudden jerk, the eyes blinked at the spot where his mouth should have been, through the upturned eye sockets of the mask. Somehow, they appeared through the eye slots, sitting at mouth height. The Elder had to be close. Only the Elder had the power to contort the features of the masses in such a manner. Jimmy was no wizard, merely a horny bag of flesh. An awkward man and a more awkward lover, but she needed him to draw the Elder out.

Candles flamed to life throughout the room, lit by an unseen force. Mercedette moved forward, leaned onto the altar, and it began. Robed figures converged, pressing in on her. Moans filled the room, not of pleasure but pain, emanating from the hidden walls, housing trapped victims. In her periphery, Mercedette noticed others, all strapped down, all defiled and tortured. She recognized some by their cries, their tortured voices burned into her memory. A quick glimpse over her shoulder showed they were now adults like her. She wondered if they remained as bound and tortured into adulthood as Mercedette was.

She could not help them now. She ignored their cries to focus on her own plight. The upside-down people reached out and groped her with too many hands. They spared not an inch of her body from violation. Soon, hands moved between her legs.

Jimmy left his spot at the front of the altar and walked behind her. He lifted his robe and ripped her shorts off. She knew what was about to happen, but it was necessary to draw out the Evil One. With a grunt, he entered her. Despite everything, it caught her off guard. Gillian dropped her canister, which clanged on the stone ground. Other hands ripped off her sports bra leaving her nude, exposed. Bait.

The ground shook which had nothing to do with Jimmy. Heavy tremors signaled His arrival. She witnessed His approach in her mind's eye. Even as her former lover thrust into her, Mercedette stayed focused on the Elder. Though time and place meant nothing to such a being, He would use the easiest path to reach her. That meant the corridor. His footsteps shook the foundations.

Despite observing the Elder in her mind, she failed to lock in on a face. (Was it ever changing?) Her inability to identify Him bothered her, it was why she was there, why she tolerated Jimmy. But the face remained elusive. Her visions showed a hulking shadow so grand it filled the hallway from floor to ceiling.

Mercedette heard the lustful cries of her tormentors both in the chamber and through the ears of the Elder. Cries of misery crossing breached dimensions. The one responsible for it all drew closer, spreading His arms so wide they touched both corridor walls, scraping paint with sharp nails. It stood so tall His head brushed the ceiling (or horns?).

Mercedette ignored Jimmy to focus on the coming storm. The ground shook harder, each step a seismic shift in her life. Explosions sounded outside the temple. Not combustible, but tiles shattering under footsteps which clopped as if hooved.

The Elder proved larger than she ever imagined. She knew the Elder was a monster in actions but not in physical form. With such a long gait, it would not be long. Jimmy's moans had fallen into a chant with the other masked figures. Collectively, the group found more ecstasy in the approach of the Elder than in defiling their sacrifice.

With the trap set, Mercedette pushed Jimmy away. Despite what she subjected herself to in the experiment, she had felt nothing pleasurable during their sexual encounter. Mercedette pulled away while upside-down Jimmy fought to hold on to his prize. Mercedette struck him in the face, which cracked his mask vertically in half.

Just like that, one eye returned to human anatomy positioning while the other remained in the eyehole near his lips. Half-upside down, half upright. Jimmy cried out in pain when his mouth twisted into two locations, half above and half below.

Jimmy raged, reaching out even as the other robed figures backed away. They vanished, leaving only her and Jimmy. The bait had worked; the Elder approached. Mercedette reached down, grabbed the canister. Jimmy threw himself at her, grasping, groping, crying out, no longer a man. She sprayed. The canister sprayed a jet of liquid that covered the man's face. The pink dye splattered like diluted blood spatter.

Jimmy screamed and fell to his knees, clutching his face. The other half of his mask fell away. The man sobbed, asking why, and then the fear took hold. He struggled to right himself, waving away invisible beasts, creatures seen only by him.

The doorway shattered under the beast's sheer size when it entered. It carried with it the stench of rotting carrion. Mercedette's back remained turned away from the entrance, so the Elder was at her rear as when they first met. She gripped the canister. Designed for a double shot, but would it be enough?

"Look upon me!" the voice bellowed at a volume threatening to cause her ears to bleed.

To look upon him is death, Mercedette thought. She had survived her first encounter because she never looked back. But she always wondered. She needed to know. What was the nature of such a beast? She reached for the cross around her neck, forgetting it remained in her lab. Unprotected other than her canister, she stood up straight, naked, and afraid. A mystery at her back.

"I must see. I need to know the face of true evil," she said.

She got her wish. Mercedette turned. And disassembled.

Crick, crack, crick!

The moment she set eyes upon the Elder, her head spun one eighty with a sickening crunch. Almost simultaneously, her waist spun one eighty in the opposite direction so that her dangling broken neck faced the beast once again. The thing that had once been Mercedette fell into a pile at the foot of the altar.

CHAPTER 42

G illian was unconscious only briefly, if at all. She touched her tender forehead, and her hand came away with blood. Once she remembered what occurred, she waved an arm behind herself, relieved to find nothing but a tub sized sink. No woman stood there. But it had sounded real. And the breath! The odor was that of something buried under six feet of dirt. It was time to test her legs. Gillian stood. And nearly fell over again.

A figure filled the window. The individual unlocked the door and opened it, taking her gently by the arm. It was Mitch. He checked her out.

"You are hurt," Mitch said, eyeing the forehead wound. "Not deep. No stitches needed. Can you move? Because we must."

Gillian nodded. She was ready to get out. Mitch led her toward the lab's exit. Gillian glanced at the empty viewing booth on the way. Mitch signaled her to stop in the doorway, then poked his head into the hallway.

"Mercedette walked upstairs after Jimmy. I believe he is fixated on her. He watched her earlier, leering. Mercedette was relatively unclothed."

Seeing the coast clear, Mitch led Gillian into the hallway and toward the distant stairwell. His head was on a swivel, searching for something. He looked up and down the stairs. Once he deemed it safe, he filled her in.

"Mercedette is not the only one in danger. I will explain everything, but not here. We need to get to my office."

"What about Mercedette?" Mitch shook his head. She squinted. "What do you mean? What does that mean, shaking your head?"

"There is nothing we can do," Mitch said.

"What? She's dead?"

"Ms. McCann, please. My office."

His defaulting to formality prompted Gillian to nod. She did not know what was happening, but in her gut understood something was seriously wrong. If the answers were in Mitch's office, she would go there. They moved with stealth and were soon at Mitch's office which appeared suddenly small. In the confined space they were sitting ducks if there was a threat. Until Mitch placed his palm on the security control of the massive metal door behind his desk. It swished open like something out of Star Trek. They stepped inside and Mitch closed the door.

The surroundings surprised Gillian. Rather than a lab, she stood before a bank of security cameras, an exact duplicate of the security office setup. Beyond the alcove office rose a second door with another handprint reader.

"You have your own cameras?" Gillian asked.

"It is the same setup as the security office. A backup of sorts. I never bothered to use it until today. Events forced me to figure it all out."

Gillian eyed the various screens. One showed a woman partially out of view, stretched out on a floor, nude.

"Mercedette?" Gillian gasped.

Mitch stepped up alongside Gillian. "Yes. We cannot help her. And there are others."

"What? Other people are dead?"

Mitch nodded. Mitch took a seat alongside the control panel and urged Gillian to do the same. She dropped into a chair, relieved not to test her ever weakening legs.

"Things have escalated. That is why I was learning the cameras but too late. I witnessed Mercedette, saw…" Mitch choked on the words.

"Who is doing this?" Mercedette asked.

"Your answer is in the files. You were supposed to get them all. Who's was missing?"

As Gillian thought about it, all became clear. "Jimmy's file. His was not in the bunch."

"I asked him to give you everything. I have them all here, including his."

Mitch grabbed a nearby tablet and opened a folder on the home screen. The master list available to him was much longer than Gillian's. It included all employees, not only the stragglers who remained behind. It included jimmy's file. Mitch clicked on it.

On-screen, Jimmy, formal and buttoned up as ever, sat in the interview chair. The way he stared directly at the camera unnerved Gillian. She struggled to comprehend the idea that he murdered people.

The off-screen interviewer, a familiar voice to Gillian by now, asked a question. "You clarified in our earlier conversation that time in prison changed you. You say you are reformed. But that is not the question I asked. Again, what is your biggest fear?"

"My f-f-f-ear is I'm going to kill a-g-g-g-ain," Jimmy answered.

Mitch froze the frame, and in that frozen image Jimmy looked dangerous. Bookish on the surface, she early on spotted something more dangerous in the man. The frozen image confirmed her fears.

"Jimmy killed before?"

Mitch tapped another icon, which brought up a crime scene photo of a young dead woman. "He slaughtered his fiancé. I took a chance with him. With everybody here."

Gillian stood as angry as she was frightened. "A murderer? That is not the same as taking a chance on someone unstable. This is a murderer. You hired him and released a predator amongst your staff! You even invited me to stay, knowing a killer would be here with us."

"He reformed in prison."

"Tell that to Mercedette! And who else?"

"At least Quinn."

"Oh my God."

Something caught Mitch's attention. He leaned over Gillian and worked the controls. "Steve's office is the main hub of this system. I used my version for the first time in an attempt to locate Steve."

"Do you think Jimmy killed him too?"

Mitch stiffened and shrugged. An unknown. "The security office overrides my controls if we are simultaneously using the system. At one point my cameras shut down because someone took over from inside Steve's office."

"If not Steve, then Jimmy," Gillian said.

Mitch nodded. "Jimmy had access to Steve's office, I should have known as much. Jimmy was doing so well. I trusted him. There were circumstances behind what he did," Mitch said.

"Circumstances? How could someone like you allow someone like him here? How is what he did any different from what the homeless guy did to..."

Gillian stopped herself when she saw the pain in Mitch's eyes, but she struggled to understand how a man who lost his wife would employ a man who willingly murdered his own. Mitch finished her thought for her.

"It is not different, in the end. I hired Jimmy, took a chance, grew to care for the man. I stopped thinking about his past, focused on who he was as an employee. He was loyal, but what I did not count on was what he could become."

Mitch played with the video controls and brought up a different view of Mercedette. What appeared to Mercedette as an altar was merely a medical bed from a past century. The killing took place in one of the non-refurbished rooms from the past. On the screen, Mercedette lay deceased on the ground. The new angle inside the room rather than from the hallway showed Jimmy raging while struggling with the effects of the spray. Blood splatter covered his naked body. The pink stood out, proving Mercedette's plan worked, though it did not save her. Mitch paused the screen on Jimmy.

Another screen showed Jimmy live time. Jimmy stumbled along the corridor as if drunk. He mumbled and twitched, which made him look dangerous and unpredictable. He wore clothes loosely, but they were stained with blood and pink, soaking up that which had covered his body. Mitch switched between cameras to track the man. Jimmy reached the elevators.

"Where is he going? Is he coming here? We need to get out!"

Mitch rose and opened a nearby cabinet, which contained a first aid kit and other medical supplies. He grabbed a syringe and a vial. He loaded the syringe.

"What are you doing?"

"I am hoping to incapacitate him," Mitch said.

"Incapacitate? He has killed people. You think a needle will stop him?"

"No. But maybe slow him down."

Mitch prepared a second needle as a backup. The monitors sat atop a large desk. Mitch placed both needles on the desk in front of Gillian.

Then, with a deep breath, he slowly opened the desk drawer. Gillian eyed the gun.

"Steve left this behind. He also left a stun gun, but I did not think to grab that. When I went to investigate who was controlling the cameras, I found no one except you. But whoever was there left the door open by the time I returned from walking to Steve's car. The gun was the item I told you I was uncomfortable with. I brought it up here as a precaution. I hope you understand why I want nothing to do with it. Can you use it?"

"You can't be serious," Gillian said.

"I am. I will take my chances confronting Jimmy, but if I fail, I need to know you are safe. Can you fire a gun?"

Gillian nodded. She had fired weapons, though infrequently. Plenty of her stories over the years involved law enforcement and various gun enthusiasts. She could count on one hand the number of times she went to a range, but it was enough to handle herself. Gillian reached for the weapon but stopped upon realizing how badly her hands shook.

"They won't stop. I can't seem to halt the tremors."

"He exposed us. I do not know how Jimmy did it, but I feel it too. In the machinery room, I was simply following Steve's instructions to override timers for the weekend on the central air. You investigated an open door. There was no reason for Jimmy to be there. He was up to something," Mitch said.

That tracked. Gillian had felt something was wrong all weekend. A nagging sense that something was off. She picked up on it in that room. Whether it was Jimmy himself or something she unknowingly glimpsed in the environment, she felt a sense of doom from that moment. And then she remembered the second visit.

"There were multiple canisters."

Mitch nodded. "And hoses?"

"Yes. Flexible. Someone came in. I was frightened and gave chase. In doing so, I forgot all about what I found, did not think of it then. It sounds crazy but I saw a head in a bag and then someone ran off. Stupid that I did not link it to my condition."

"Not stupid. By then you were influenced by the fear element and hallucinating. And why question any type of hardware in a machine room. But our product is not weaponized yet."

"Yet?"

Mitch nodded. "Government wants its new toys. Frighten the enemy? Sure, let's go cowboy. It is all the investors wanted from all this. I had an agenda not in line with theirs, so they pulled the plug. We developed it in our factory though and were close. I moved Jimmy to Seattle for weeks because of his infatuation with Mercedette. He had plenty of time there to finalize the product and have it shipped. Easy for it to be off the books. We are running out of time. Can you use this?"

Gillian steadied her hands and grabbed the gun. Behind her, Mitch grabbed a lab coat and put it on. Gillian rose from the chair and bumped into the video controls. Two screens were active, one of Jimmy leaving Mercedette's murder scene and the shot of him in the elevator. Bumping the controls on the earlier video that Mitch had cued up, caused Jimmy to walk backward slowly, one frame at a time. Gillian shuddered at the strange sight, a killer returning to the scene of the crime.

But the second video commanded her attention. The live feed showed Jimmy exiting the elevator. On their floor! He stepped out of view on the screen. No reason to track him. They would encounter him soon enough. She prepped the gun as Mitch loaded one syringe into each pocket.

Gillian could not tell from the images how Jimmy killed Mercedette. If she stayed in the room long enough, the backtracking video would reveal all. As it was, Jimmy (good Lord, that was a lot of blood!) stood over Mercedette in the frame and he was totally naked.

Mitch ignored the video screen and focused on Gillian. In the distance, Jimmy called out to Mitch. The man was frantic. Mitch and Gillian shared a nod. Then each, armed in their own way stepped back into Mitch's office, ready for war.

CHAPTER 43

Gillian kept the gun hidden behind her back. Mitch left the door behind him open to allow for a quick escape if needed. Not that it would help for long. Mitch explained as they walked back into the office that Jimmy's palm print worked on the door as well which was why they could not simply ride out the weekend.

Jimmy cried out. "Doctor Trager!"

The voice startled Gillian even from a distance. The way he said the doctor's name sounded threatening. Gillian wiped sweat from her brow with her free hand. Her hand holding the gun shook so much there was a chance of a misfire.

Mitch noticed. "I am hoping I can stop him, but if not, I need to know you can do this."

"I can't just kill him."

"Doctor Trager!" Jimmy yelled, getting closer.

"We are running out of time. Can you do this?"

Gillian nodded. And then Jimmy entered. His eyes were almost as red as the blood smeared on his chest. Pink dye covered much of his face. His pants were loose, his shirt more so. Naked in the video, he had enough modesty to dress if even partially. The shirt clung to the bloody wetness on his chest. Jimmy rubbed his eyes with the back of his hand, struggling to see. He wheezed through compromised lungs.

Mitch raised his arms. "Are you armed, Jimmy?"

"W-w-w-what?" He rubbed his eyes again, too many tears to clear away. He looked up with half a pink face, like a psychotic sports fan wearing team colors. Jimmy tapped the side of his skull. "What are you t-t-t-alking about? Something is wrong with me. I can't b-b-b-reathe."

"It is mace Jimmy. Mercedette laced the fear element with mace."

Jimmy looked confused. "Why would she spray me? She wanted it, asked for it."

Mitch reached into one of his pockets and slowly approached Jimmy. "Like your fiancé did?"

Jimmy reacted as if shot. He eyed the approaching doctor. "What? N-n—no. I wouldn't do that again. You took me in because you said you understood what it was like to lose someone."

"I took a chance on you, Jimmy. On your tape, you mentioned you were afraid you might kill again. Why was that? Because you knew that you eventually would?"

"What? No. You said Mercedette would be vulnerable this weekend. You said she was using a powerful drug that would cause her to lose her inhibitions. You told me you needed someone trustworthy to check in on her. Said she would be open to sex, and that I should go to her, be with her."

The confession shocked Gillian. She eyed Mitch, who shook his head urging her to ignore the narrative of a crazy man. But did Mitch also warn her not to use the gun? Her hands shook, and she wanted to pee. Then Jimmy flew into a rage.

"You told me this weekend would be perfect, that Mercedette would wait for me. I even planned to return to the mainland with the others, but you said all these things to make me stay."

"I asked you to stay because I needed your help," Mitch said.

"Well, now, I need your help. I need to know what changed. Why are you lying?" Then he finally noticed Gillian. "Everything was going p-p-p-perfect until you started nosing around. You ruined everything!"

While Jimmy focused on Gillian, Mitch rushed forward and jabbed a syringe into Jimmy's leg. Jimmy cried out in pain and shock. The assistant looked down in disbelief before staggering back. Mitch backed away.

"Why did you do that?" Jimmy asked.

"You killed Mercedette. You killed them all, didn't you?"

"What? No. Mitch! What's happening?"

"You are a killer, Jimmy. Then, and now."

Jimmy raised his hands and pounded both sides of his skull. "No! My fiancé cheated, then admitted to the things she did with the man. I didn't mean to kill her! She came at me, and the knife pierced her eye."

"Your fiancé or Mercedette?"

"My fiancé. I would not do that to anyone again. Wait! You are trying to scare me, frighten me, that is what we do here. Right? All this is designed to frighten me. Am I your experiment?"

Then Jimmy tilted his head and looked at Gillian. (Past her?) Dead Wendy stood over the reporter's shoulder. Only the good half of the woman's face was visible, the other half hidden by Gillian's head. Dead Wendy smiled with the working half of her mouth. Jimmy pointed.

"Her. It's her. I see her everywhere. She is the one who killed everybody. We must kill her!"

Jimmy yanked the syringe from his leg and raised it like a knife. He charged Dead Wendy, but there was no distinction for Gillian, who raised the gun and fired. The shot caught Jimmy's chest. Jimmy flew back against the wall and dropped the syringe.

"Oh no. I had to!" Gillian yelled.

Mitch took the gun from Gillian and slipped it into his coat pocket. "Go," he said and gestured toward the control room.

"I need to help him," she said.

"I'm a doctor. I will help him, but you need to get away until we know you are safe."

Jimmy stepped away from the wall, a miracle he remained on his feet. His ability to still stand frightened Gillian who finally entered the control room. Jimmy staggered as if drunk. With his shirt already half open, the man's wound was on full display. Jimmy pulled the shirt open wider and stared at the new hole in his chest.

"This isn't real. I'm just scared, right?"

Then, like a faucet turning on, blood poured from the hole. After an initial gush, it spurted in time with his heartbeat. Jimmy grunted and fell to one knee. With a sudden gasp, he dropped onto his back. Mitch lowered himself next to the fallen man. Jimmy gripped Mitch's arm and eyed his long-time friend and employer. Tears filled Jimmy's eyes as it dawned on him his time was over.

"I'm scared. Really, really, scared..."

Dead Wendy appeared over Mitch's shoulder and Jimmy's eyes went wide with fear. His eyes remained open as he took only one more breath, never letting go of Mitch. Once Jimmy was gone, Mitch gently pulled the hand away and set it down on his friend.

Inside the control room, Gillian sat in the chair, head in her hands. Mitch's office had fallen into silence. That meant the gunshot had done its job. She had killed a man. Except there was no choice. She had killed someone who had killed potentially everyone in the building.

Gillian instinctively looked back at the screens. The one running backward continued to go frame by frame. Jimmy held the woman in his arms on the screen. He appeared highly distraught. But didn't he kill her?

Grabbing the mouse, Gillian hit the reverse playback button. It played backward at high speed until Mercedette shot to her feet. The woman's head became un-shot as it un-exploded. Where was the gun? If Jimmy shot her, why did he not have the gun in hand when he came to the office?

Onscreen Jimmy remained on the ground while Mercedette stood. Mercedette had turned around, had her back to the door. Jimmy was on the ground and looked in no shape to kill anyone. Gillian sped it back further, stopping at the point where the two were having sex. Nude Mercedette leaned over a hospital bed in a grungy sanitarium room. At some point, she stopped and pushed Jimmy away. Jimmy begged her to continue. Mercedette grabbed her experimental spray and used it on Jimmy. It was effective.

A gun barrel entered the edge of the screen along with a shadow, someone standing just outside the door. Then a figure entered the frame, a strange orb-headed man. It was the same strange man Gillian had seen before, though she had chalked it up to fear. An illusion. But the camera did not lie.

Gillian pushed the wheeled chair away from the desk and stood. From there, she glimpsed something below the desk. Not an orb. A helmet of some sort. Like a space-aged motorcycle helmet but with a breathing tube attached to its neck. Like the one in the bag in the machine room.

On the screen, the orb-head man stepped further into the room. A tube ran from his neck into his clothes, and the bulge of an air container strapped near the man's waist. He wore a breathing apparatus. (To avoid breathing in the fear element?) Mercedette turned, and the man fired. Mercedette's head exploded in gore, and she fell partially out of the camera's view.

Jimmy remained on the floor the whole time. Even screaming in surprise at the gunshot. Jimmy struggled to see because of the mace. But he followed the sound of her fallen body and lifted her, struggling to understand, becoming covered in her blood as he tried to revive her. His limited vision seemed to keep him from understanding the woman's face was gone. Jimmy was not the killer!

Gillian turned to run, but Mitch was already there and poked a syringe into her neck. Immediately Gillian felt a warmth overtake her body, and her legs vanished from underneath her. She vaguely felt the doctor catching her. He spoke, but his words came through cotton as her senses abandoned her.

"Do not worry. This is not the fear element. It is something else."

Her eyelids fluttered, so she only caught glimpses as Mitch carried her to the next security door. She glimpsed his hand pressing against the lock and the doors opened into a vast room. With one more blink, her eyes closed.

CHAPTER 44

When Mitch pleaded with Wendy about what to do after the visitor shut everything down, his wife answered his call. The reporter showing up answered Mitch's prayers. Everything had threatened to crumble less than a day ago when the muscle from New York arrived. But thanks to the nudge from his wife, and a surprising visit from the reporter, Mitch's long-time experiment was nearing completion. There was so much collateral damage along the way. Wendy insisted it was necessary, reminding Mitch that events of great enough importance meant breaking eggs along the way.

Mitch suffered guilt over it all. How could he not? He loved his staff like family. But any guilt over the day's events paled compared to a guilt that grew exponentially over the years. The guilt over his inability to protect his wife on that rainy Los Angeles night. She paid the price for refusing to leave his side. He could have retrieved the car and picked her up, but that was not Wendy's style. They were in everything together. Now it was his turn to be there for her.

Mitch had a long game in mind for reuniting with Wendy, but the shutdown announcement forced everything into fifth gear. When the heavy from New York appeared, Mitch feared he would lose Wendy forever. The man's words still echoed in Mitch's mind.

"Human trials just now being approved, that's the rub now in't?" the suit said.

The man tossed an envelope filled with missing people flyers. The disappearances were all over the local news, but police did little to solve the crimes given the lifestyle of the victims who were all homeless. But the New York financiers somehow linking the disappearances to Mitch, caught him off guard. The New York crew were a resourceful bunch, so Mitch did not bother to ask how they came about their information.

When it counted most, Mitch could not disguise the part he played. His face gave away the game to the unexpected visitor. Had Mitch been able to rally a vehement defense, display some plausible deniability, he might have avoided the shutdown. Once the man left, Mitch feared he had lost the chance to get his wife back.

But when Mitch asked Wendy for guidance, she responded. The shutdown frightened him so that Wendy appeared. Her perfume filled the room. Not enough to cover the odor of decaying flesh, but enough to signal she was present.

She stood behind him, reflected in the picture frame's glass. Her deceased face appeared above that of her original in the picture. Both were beautiful in their own way, Mitch thought. Fearing she might vanish, he refused to turn around and look. He waited for a signal of what she wished him to do.

Wendy leaned down and whispered in his ear. "*Kill them all.*"

Mitch knew then what he needed to do. It would be a variation of his plan that was already in motion. But it required that he act fast. There was no time to delay. Not even Jimmy (rest his soul) ever entered Mitch's lab.

No one knew what Mitch had worked on for years. Mitch wished he could show off the lab to others, as he was proud of his high-tech facility. Monitors hung throughout the room and were on remote swivels. While no employees had ever entered the space, many others had. Guests that Mitch brought along with him on rented boats, ones where no one asked questions. His special guests failed to appreciate how innovative his science lab was. He hoped his latest guest would approve of the surroundings. Gillian had become central to his plan.

Besides the occasional prostitute, Mitch had remained faithful to his wife, but he was ready for a physical reunion. He had needs. There was always going to be a guest of honor intended to complete his grand experiment. The experiment, if it worked, would solve the long-term issues of his carnal needs being met, so he took his time deciding who to fill the role with.

Prior to the sped-up timeline, Mitch had settled on Quinn, deciding she was the one most appropriate to provide him with long denied physical comfort. That was the plan until everything changed. The reporter was on the island for a reason. It was fate.

"Do you still want that story?" Mitch had asked her.

When Mitch tapped on Gillian's window, he noticed the resemblance. It eluded him earlier in the morning because he was too blind with rage. Mitch had at first failed to notice how beautiful Gillian was. He felt foolish over how he initially treated her. Especially the elevator confrontation. Mitch did not wish to hurt anyone.

Well, not most people. Some deserved it, like all the homeless who would surely kill other people's wives if given the chance. The greatest scientists never gave up. If experimental results remained elusive, it would be wise to change the conditions of the experiment, not its goal.

Mitch had changed his experiment to involve Gillian. The woman remained unconscious. He gave her time to sleep, and despite his excitement, he briefly napped as well. It would refresh him for what came next.

He would wait for Gillian to wake. His reunion with his wife had taken far too long, yet it was suddenly happening so fast. He prepped the lab, making sure everything would be ready for when the reporter woke.

G illian stirred, moaning herself awake. Whatever Mitch had injected her with left her fuzzy and warm. She struggled not to drift back to sleep. It was when she tried to move her arms and legs that her adrenaline kicked in, waking her fully. Gillian found herself strapped in one of the repurposed asylum restraint chairs.

She glanced to one side and screamed. A mummified corpse sat in an identical chair alongside her. Turning away revealed another man. While not mummified, his skin appeared frail as tissue paper. With nowhere else to look, she focused on Mitch, who stood in front of her.

Mitch pointed to one of her seat mates. "Do not worry about Charlie there. Or at least that is what I called him. He was homeless, had no ID. I call the one to your left Other Charlie."

Gillian's eyes grew wide as she noticed a sea of *Charlies* trapped in chairs for as far as she could see. The high-tech accoutrements of the room became menacing in the face of so many bodies trapped in the lab. Mitch leaned into Gillian. His sudden proximity prompted her to struggle anew against her bonds. Mitch grinned over her efforts.

"Looks like I was correct. You fear losing control."

"I fear being confined by maniacs. Let me go!"

Mitch soured. "Still defiant? That will not do. I need you scared."

"Why do you wish me frightened? Why are you doing this?"

"Because this is how I get her back."

"Who?"

"My wife, of course. You of all people know I saw my wife that day. You reported it to the papers. My employers read the report and ordered a psyche counsel for me. When I refused to refute the facts, they fired me."

"I'm sorry," Gillian said. "That was never my intention. I reported what you said, but never thought it would escalate into what it did."

"Fate. It was all fate. Had I lied, said I never saw her, I would have returned to a life of grief and eventually settled down with someone else. Led a different life, pretending that the world was okay. But I told the truth and lost my job. My collective grief led me to the ninth-floor parking garage, where I climbed out onto the ledge. Do you know who appeared?"

Gillian answered by fighting against her bonds once again. She could barely move an inch. Mitch smirked at the futile effort.

"Wendy appeared. I am terrified of heights. On that ledge, my fear brought her to me. Like my fear revealed her on the night of her death. I realized fear breaks down the barrier between our world and theirs."

"Their world?" Gillian asked.

"The deceased. This is how we reach them. Fear has always been present among people purporting to encounter ghosts. An abundance of terror tears down the walls between their world and ours. You know this. You recorded her."

Mitch raised Gillian's phone. "I wanted to listen to this ever since you mentioned it, but I had work to do first. Lots of work. While you were enjoying the drug that I injected you with, I used your facial recognition to open your phone and play it. My fear of losing Wendy that day allowed me to see her and allowed you to record her. You cannot deny what is on your tape."

Mitch pressed play. "I'm here…" Dead Wendy said on the recorder. Mitch threw it aside.

Gillian shook her head. "That can't be her voice. It's impossible. There was an enormous crowd. It had to be someone else. Yes, I wished to ask you, but I never believed it."

"Bullshit! You used the anniversary of Wendy's death as an excuse to interview me, but deep down, you needed to know if that was her voice. I can tell you now that it is."

Mitch produced a strange orb helmet with a breathing tube attached. "This device is a sign that none of this was personal. I already had this baby in the pipeline. Part of my R&D beyond that of our chemical component. I needed a shield for the toxin. I always planned to use the compound at some point, just not today. Well, plans change."

"But you said there was no gas version. You told me that, told your staff."

Mitch nodded. "If any of you knew of its existence, then the experiment would not have worked. It required stealth dosing. I was there when you found the canisters. That was me who ran off. I knew you were smart and feared you would have pieced it all together, so I sped up my work. Lucky for me, your exposure kept you from thinking straight. You were too piss-pants scared to realize what the canisters were for. It was in the air this whole weekend. No one knew I had the gas version, not even New York. It was all they wanted. Once they got their hands on it, they would have shut us down anyway. Instead, they shut me down because they figured out all the missing homeless were here in my lab. Still not sure how they knew."

Gillian's head drooped. She fought the effects of the narcotic. Tilting her head, she remembered something. "When did this start? We had lunch together."

"I had the helmets with me in a duffel bag when I hooked up the tanks to the central air. Your interruption caused me exposure I did not intend. By the time we finished our lunch together, we were already suffering the effects. Your reporting nosiness exposed me to the chemical alongside our staff. For that, I thank you."

"Why?"

"I absorbed enough to visit Wendy again."

Mitch closed his eyes and thought back to the lunch with Gillian. Gillian smiled at him during a heartwarming tale and Mitch smiled back, but not at the reporter. Wendy stood just behind Gillian's shoulder the whole time. Mitch had the conversation not with Gillian, but with Wendy. He relived their meeting with his lost love, which brought him great joy. So happy was he to see her again that his artificially induced fear soon evaporated to where Wendy vanished.

"Talking about Wendy made my fear vanish. I needed fear from the rest of you to bring her back. I retrieved one of the helmets and retreated to my lab which runs on a different air flow than the rest of the building. It was designed for minimal contamination. I detoxed here while you all got a lungful of the stuff."

Mitch wheeled a dolly over and set it alongside Gillian. The dolly held a large tank like the one in the machine room. Gillian understood what the canister contained. She defaulted to reporter mode, trying to retake control of the situation.

"Who are all these people?" Gillian asked.

"Dregs of society. They and their kind are responsible for what happened to my wife! Has anyone even noticed they are gone?"

"New York did," Gillian said, pleased that the answer bothered Mitch.

Gillian thought back to Yoshi's lab, where among his pictures of Elle hung a missing person's poster. A good-looking young man smiled on the poster, Jaime. She did not connect the poster to the video she watched until now. Gillian scoured the tragic faces of restrained homeless people stretching as far as she could see. One young homeless person was a ringer for Yoshi's brother.

"For years, I tested my theories on them. The research proved valuable. The more I induced fear, the more they glimpsed Wendy. Do you understand the scientific breakthrough that represented? They did not know who she was and yet they saw her. It proved my theory."

"You just admitted they did not know your wife. That makes them innocent. How can you say they had anything to do with your wife's death?"

The words struck Mitch. He leaned into her, raging. "If not my wife, they killed others. Stole from others, hurt others. Do not presume to judge me. I killed to bring people back. What did they kill for?"

"People are on the streets for different reasons, but killing for sport is not one of them. The man who took your wife was a criminal. His status has nothing to do with that. And before you claim altruism, what about your staff?"

Mitch pushed himself away. He paced in front of her. "Experimental collateral."

"What does that mean? You killed Mercedette. The video captured it. You said they are all dead. Jimmy did not kill them. That means you killed them all."

"I got results!" Mitch yelled in her face. His hair fell across one eye and for a moment, he looked like his dead wife. "I was running out of time and homeless people. You know how quickly they die? Already on the edge with hunger. They are too fragile for scientific work. I needed fresh recruits."

Mitch gestured to a nearby chair that Gillian had failed to notice. Mitch had Steve strapped down. The man's head hung low, with a contusion visible on his forehead. Mitch told Gillian how Steve stubbornly refused to leave, insisting he stay even without pay. Mitch explained how he used the Taser on Steve and how comedic he found Steve's fall.

"Steve's head hit the desk when he fell doing more damage than the Taser used to incapacitate him. He has been nothing but loopy since I brought him here. That meant he could not help me in the way I needed him to. He could not remain conscious long enough to tell me if he saw Wendy or not. And as you can see, my past experiments have gone mostly to rot. The place smelled for a long time, but lots of air freshener and time has minimized the odor issues. I needed fresh subjects to break down the wall for me. I needed my staff to lead my wife back home."

"This is crazy. You think she would want this?"

"Absolutely. She never meant to leave me. And she made it clear she was ready to come home."

Mitch hit the button on a remote. Multiple monitors descended from the ceiling in a circular arc surrounding Gillian. She could not help but view the screens from where she sat unless she closed her eyes. Then Mitch hooked a hose to the nearby canister before lifting a head sized object and hooking the other end of the hose to it.

"My protective mask was not the only one I prepared. I have a very special one for you. One where you can witness everything," Mitch said, lifting the helmet.

He placed it over her head. The rear half was solid black, but the entire front was an industrial plexiglass so that her entire face was visible. The hose attached at the mouth position on the mask. Something about the translucent cover highlighted the fear in her eyes. They seemed open wider than humanly possible. Mitch tested the helmet to ensure it was anchored as tightly as her arm restraints. A hint of fog covered the glass as she hyperventilated.

Mitch smiled. "Losing control. I am glad that is your phobia. Because I need you to be oh so scared."

Mitch turned on a video on the main screen in front of her. It replayed the footage Gillian already viewed, Mercedette's murder. The video showed Jimmy and Mercedette having sex before the death. Mitch watched for a moment, nodding with approval. Mitch hit another button on the remote and their grunts of pleasure filled the room, an obscene sound that completed the sense of voyeurism. The rooms were clearly mic'd as well as on camera.

"Mercedette is hot. I considered her as a replacement. The sex would be crazy. Quinn, though, was a hottie, so it was going to be her. I could bang her all day long. But then you came along. Jimmy was only a distraction, a fall guy giving me time to finish my experiment. I assume by now you have figured out that you killed an innocent man. Jimmy had reformed. The man would not kill a fly other than his fiancé."

Gillian's eyes bubbled with tears at the thought of killing the man despite his having murdered before. Gillian returned her focus to the screens to take her mind off her own guilt. Mercedette suddenly battled with Jimmy before spraying him with her device. It all plaid out in high definition.

After spraying Jimmy, Mercedette had her back turned to the doorway. When a shadow fell over Mercedette, she turned. Mitch, wearing the mask, fired one shot into her forehead. Mercedette died instantly. The shot roared through the room's speakers, and Gillian cried in fright.

Mitch produced his phone and waved it for Gillian's benefit. "Played dumb on the tech with you and Steve but I always had access to the cameras through my phone. Bluetooth. Could watch everyone from wherever I was. Also, the guns in his office came in handy. I trained with weapons after the murder of my wife, vowing never to be a victim again."

Images came to life on the multiple screens as Mitch tapped away on his phone. The unifying theme of all the scenes was Mitch stalking victims. The man looked ominous in his futuristic helmet. The other obvious connection from each scene was how the scientists fled from something that was not there. They were clearly terrified but seemed oblivious to Mitch. Whenever one seemed to notice him, Mitch leaned away into a doorway or a shadow. Mitch made no show of the gun. It was clear all the employees were frightened of something other than their boss.

Their cries of terror rose through the speakers. The man they trusted was close enough to rescue them. But he did nothing other than wait until the right time, wait until they were isolated from the others.

Mitch lowered the phone and moved to the large canister. As soon as he turned the knob, a black mist flowed through the tube into Gillian's mask. She immediately noticed the influx of particles, so took a deep breath and held it. The space between the plexiglass and Gillian's face grew dark as the mist filled the spaces in the helmet.

"Cannot hold your breath forever. I am not playing these videos for no reason. I need my audience. Are you in there?" Mitch tapped on the front of the helmet.

Gillian struggled and could not hold her breath any longer. She instinctively opened her eyes when Mitch tapped on the helmet. A black cloud awaited her. She had no choice. Her lungs were about to burst.

She sucked in air. The particles spiraled and shot into her lungs. It was as if inhaling ectoplasm from a turn of the century séance. After sucking up the accumulated gas, the view through the helmet cleared. Then it hit. Gillian shook violently and fought against her bonds. Her world turned red as hands fell on her shoulders. The person holding onto her leaped from behind and shoved his face into hers. It was Jimmy. He had a large hole in his chest. Maggots filled the bloody cavity, already going to work. Maggots also spilled from his lips as he yelled angrily at her.

"Why did you kill me? I was trying to save you from whoever shot Mercedette. Why did you kill me?"

"No! Mmm..." Gillian shook her head and pressed her mouth closed, trying not to scream.

"There we go. I won't ask if it is working. I can tell by your face. What I need from you is to tell me when you see Wendy. watch the videos. I compiled them all while you slept. Remember I promised to supply you with all the videos."

On the screen, Colt hid in a closet. Mitch opened the door and shot the young man. Then he leaned down and asked Colt a question while asking Gillian the same in the room. Gillian heard in stereo while Mitch asked Colt while simultaneously asking her.

"Do you see her?" Mitch asked.

"Yes," Gillian and on-screen Colt replied together.

"In the video or in the room?" Mitch asked.

Gillian shuddered from head to toe. The drug was taking over. She battled the restraints, trying to get away. Then something made a sound, trying to get her attention. She turned to spot mummified Charlie looking at her. The corpse spoke through a jaw barely hanging on.

"Psst. Psst," mummified Charlie whispered until Gillian turned his way. He gestured with his head, which almost fell off. His skull slipped off his neck but landed on the collar bones. "Easier if you tell him what he wants. Has a thing for little miss half-face. Just say you see her."

"I do," Gillian said.

"Where?" Mitch pressed his face against her glass and yelled. "On the screen or in the room?"

Gillian screamed at his sudden appearance and at the intensity of his interrogation. "The screen. On the screen. She stands beside Colt, smiling."

Gillian did not mention how the woman seemed to look through the screen at her. Gillian also refused to mention how she physically encountered the woman before in the storage room. The woman had been there all weekend, just out of view, somewhere on the periphery.

Mitch changed the video to another murder. Yoshi's. The poor man did not have a chance. He looked terrified in the end and so small, more a boy than a man. On-screen, Mitch leaned over the man who was already dead. "Oops. I must be more careful," Mitch said as he examined the deceased young man.

Back in the room, he repeated his question to Gillian. "Do you see her?"

Gillian again tried to hold her breath. She did not want to witness any more death. What was the doctor doing? Why was he toying with her? She needed to leave, to go away somewhere. She did fear losing control, and this was beyond anything she could have imagined. Mitch was no longer Mitch, but she refused to tell him that as well. He had become one with his strange orb mask. With each question, he held a gun to her head.

By shaking her head to clear it, the world occasionally slipped back to reality. Mitch was not an orb-head and was unarmed. But she could not hold on to reality. The orb-head man had a gun to her head. The monitor hanging from the ceiling dripped blood. Worst of all, all the dead homeless men were coming to life as animated corpses.

In the end, they were not people at all. They were simply experiments for a mad scientist. One who should have eschewed guns. His mania led him to punish those he thought were responsible—the homeless. But the weapon was responsible as well. None of the dead in the chairs (now living, now wailing in misery, now asking Gillian for help) appeared dead of gunshots. All had simply starved or perhaps were frightened to death.

"Let me go. Let me out! Help me," Gillian cried.

She quickly stopped because the sea of dead men stretched out before her parroted her shouting. They repeated her words. Mitch tapped on her glass shield again. She locked eyes with evil, but he looked away and gestured to the screen.

"Focus, and this will go quicker."

On the screen, Amy's jaw was mostly gone. Her hands were at her throat as if she could not breathe. She rested against a tile floor in a pool of blood. Mitch asked Amy if she saw the woman. Amy coughed up blood for an answer, but nodded when she realized she could not speak. Before she finished nodding, she was gone. Without prompting, Gillian nodded as well.

"On screen or off?" Mitch asked.

"On the TV," Gillian said. "Dead people on the TV, dead people everywhere. Dead, dead, dead, or is it all in my head?" Gillian laughed. A giggle at first, then uncontrollably.

Mitch tilted his head, eyed his subject. "I may have over prescribed the chemical. It took much longer for Charlie and the others to reach mania."

Gillian stopped laughing and fought against her bonds. She grunted and drooled and spit inside her mask. Her forehead was slick with sweat. She shook her head to keep from seeing the events on the screen. Her sanity slipped away, falling away as easily as a dress of silk.

"Stop, I need you to watch!" Mitch stepped behind her and stabilized her head by gripping the helmet.

Gillian stared unwillingly at the screen. Her dead friends yelled for Mitch to let her go. Mummified, Charlie protested Mitch's actions, but as mummy Charlie booed his head fell somewhere to the floor. The other dead people picked up the slack, booing and hissing at Mitch. Gillian laughed, grateful for the cheering squad.

"Go get em boys!" Gillian yelled to her dead friends.

Mitch slapped Gillian's helmet. The noise frightened her into submission. After the hard swat, he gripped her head again, and she watched another video. The video showed a scene from outside. Cameras from the exterior of the building captured the scene. Elle never got far from the front door. She fought for breath on the lawn, which was soaked in a sea of blood.

Free of the tainted interior air, Mitch removed his helmet before bending down alongside the young woman. Although her eyes had been closed, she opened them when Mitch cradled her in his arms. She responded to his presence immediately and appeared confused.

"I'm scared. I don't know what happened," Elle said.

"Do you see her?" Mitch asked Elle, who coughed before nodding. "That means you're dying."

Elle screamed and kicked with the remaining force her body allowed. "No, no, no..."

"You did good Elle. I have completed my research that proves fear opens doors."

Elle looked around at the vast yard. "I don't want to be alone."

"You're not. All of you helped me get my wife back. I'll come back for you all next. You are all my family now."

"Mama. Is that you?" Elle asked and then spoke no more.

A breeze fluttered through, carrying with it the scent of fresh-cut grass. Gillian found herself on the front lawn bleeding. She took Elle's place, suffering through the horrible cold that comes with blood loss. Mitch hovered over her, expressionless behind the helmet.

"No, no, no!" Gillian kicked and spun, riding the slick trail of blood that only carried her in a circle as she tried to find her feet, tried to move. She could not.

And then Gillian was back in the lab, strapped down. The scent of grass followed her. But she knew she had never been on the lawn. Gillian whimpered. Mitch grabbed her shoulders and leaned down to speak into her ear.

"Do you see her?"

"Yes," Gillian whispered.

"On the screen or in the room?"

Gillian stood on the lawn on the monitor. Poor Elle was a dot on the vast landscape. Dead Wendy looked away from Elle and turned to face the camera. Dead Wendy rose and walked toward the camera.

The camera shot from a high angle on the outside of the building, somewhere above the front door. Dead Wendy approached, keeping her eye focused on the lens the entire time. Eventually, she stepped out of view of its angle, only to reappear in the room. Dead Wendy stepped around the monitor and into full view, staggering on dead legs toward Gillian. Mitch asked again if Gillian observed Wendy.

Too frightened, Gillian could not find her voice. Dead Wendy leaned in and placed hands on each of Gillian's arm restraints. She leaned closer until their heads touched. Dead Wendy's head passed through the helmet.

With a loud pop, one of Gillian's ribs tore through the flesh on her lower torso. She screamed in pain. Another rib followed, then another from the other side. Her insides were coming out to play. Gillian's hands twisted and turned until they were upside down in the restraints. Her body was coming undone with loud pops of bones being displaced and flesh ripping apart as loud as Velcro separating.

Muscles burst through skin until she looked the part of a medical school anatomy skeleton. Her screams turned to gurgles as she gargled blood and gore that rose from her defeated flesh. Gillian felt the ultimate loss of control as her body betrayed her, falling apart within the confines of the chair.

She was meat, nothing more, flesh bound by sinew and cartilage. The liquid squirts and twangy pulls of tendons rose above her own screams. When she could scream no more, the dead men in the chairs took over for her.

Mitch had stepped away, releasing her head, which drooped as the neck vertebrae fought to free itself from its fleshy cage. With a sudden burst, her entire body appeared to turn inside out and back. Bones popped back into place, and flesh glopped like putty as it reclaimed its place on the outside of the body.

The re-formed Gillian screamed and broke her restraints. Her hands thrust into the air, surprising Mitch, who did not witness the bloody transformation. That remained a secret between Gillian and Wendy. Gillian's hands dropped into her lap and her head slumped onto her chest.

Mitch composed himself and walked over to the tank of gas and turned it off. He removed the mask from Gillian's face. The woman was out cold. He lifted Gillian's head. She appeared dead until her eyes shot open wide. A smile crossed Gillian's face.

"I'm here..." she said.

Outside, the sun was rising as Mitch escorted Gillian from the building. The two held hands, but Gillian walked with a strange gait. Her legs shuffled stiffly, as if she were walking on dead legs. Her head hung at an odd angle, adjusting to seeing through both eyes again, trying to adjust to the return of normal anatomy.

"I know a spot near the dock where I can get a signal. From there I can charter a boat. It might take a while, but we waited this long. I know you always wanted to try boating. Consider it the first of many gifts. Happy Birthday sweetheart," Mitch said as he helped her into the passenger's seat of his car.

Mitch raced to the driver's side and soon they were off, speeding down the winding road, heading into the sun. Lost love reunited.

CHAPTER 45

The man in the suit had just arrived in New York from Seattle. The private jet had made good time and gotten him back sooner than he expected. He was happy about that. As a man who needed to exude strength and control, it bothered him how he felt a touch under the weather. The change from warm New York weather to the cold climes of Washington State likely brought on the malady.

A car had picked him up at the airport and he tried to use the trip to recharge before reporting to his employers, but he found himself on edge. After one red light too many, he asked his driver to drop him off where they were. The driver protested, but the suited man promised it made no difference in the tip. He simply wanted out was all.

Mistake. The only thing worse than road traffic was the foot traffic. People bumped into him without even an afterthought. His unease grew, so he focused on his destination, a high rise looming in the distance. One of dozens that comprised a city block of mystery buildings. There was nothing on the outside of the buildings to hint at who the tenants might be. There were no tourist traps, hot dog stands, restaurants, or bodegas anywhere near the block. The foot traffic vanished as he neared the building.

The man leaped. As he looked up, the building grew dark. The sky behind it was red. An ink blot against a bloody sky. He shook his head, and the scene returned to normal. Something dripped on his hand. He reached out, only to realize it was not raining. Sweat poured from his brow. He used his tie to dab his forehead. Then, as he neared the lobby, he suffered shortness of breath. Sick for sure.

Get in, get out, he thought.

Security guards gave the man a wide berth. His reputation was his ID. The man made his way to the top floor. When the elevator opened, he leaped out. The damn thing had dropped about a foot when it stopped. Despite being ill, he vowed to take the stairs on the way down. No way would he go out in a falling elevator. That was a death for pussies.

But it was the corridor that made him realize that something was wrong. He slept the whole flight back on the chartered plane. A quick trip but filled with nightmares. That was unlike him. Nightmares seemed to have followed him from the plane.

The hallway stretched. There was only one office on the floor, and it was at the end of the corridor. But the corridor stretched so that the distant door grew further and further away. The man in the suit walked faster, but the ground became a treadmill. He was going nowhere. The door was getting no closer. What was going on? He ran. Then he heard the cracking.

Turning back, he watched individual checkerboard floor tiles fall away, one by one. Each fallen square showed a thirty story drop to the lobby below. The squares fell one at a time but in a progressively faster fashion so that they merged, making small holes much larger. More cracking sounded in front of him. He looked back and tiles fell away between him and the office ahead.

He ran, dodging the holes on the way until his foot caught one open square, tripping him. He fell face first and the tile below his face dropped, leaving him staring at the distant lobby. So far away. He rose and ran as more of the world collapsed. He leaped for the door as the last of the corridor vanished.

With toes barely in the conference room door threshold, he gripped the door handle as a lifeline. He stood precariously while his heels dangled over the immense drop behind him. Carefully, he opened the door and leaped inside onto carpet and relief. The world was normal inside the room except that all eyes were on the man making love to the floor.

The man in the suit stood, dusted himself off, and straightened his tie. He looked at the group of executives. Everyone knew one another. The man's unstable entrance was anathema to his normal composure. He refocused, uncertain of what prompted his actions.

"Seattle was a success. I shut it down…"

"Very good," the group said in unison.

Speaking as one was strange. Even more strange was how the combined voices came out as a single voice. Despite a mix of female and male executives, a single male voice sounded out. The suit studied the faces in the room. It creeped him out the way they stared. The suit backed away into a corner. Unwell, he needed to finish his job and get out.

"Well done, Baker," the CEO at the head of the table said.

The CEO then grabbed the back of his own hair and pulled as if slipping a Tee-shirt over his head. As he did so, the man's hair came off! Baker stiffened, stunned at the strange display. Upon closer inspection, it was not only hair that came off but the entire face! Skin and hair dangled in the man's hand.

The others around the table followed suit. Each grabbed their own hair and pulled until the skin and scalp ripped away. Through the group's blood covered heads, the faces took on demonic features with red eyes and mouthfuls of canine teeth. A contagion of smiles overtook the room. The group rose and advanced on him. Baker backed up against the wall. He had nowhere to go. His fight or flight kicked in.

He chose flight and grabbed a chair. Baker smashed the window and leaped. On his way down, as he fell, the man had time to remember the office earlier. The only portion of his life that flashed before his eyes was Mitch preparing the coffee and handing it over.

"Cream or sugar?" Mitch had asked.

"Black," Baker said.

Baker took the cup and failed to notice how dark the liquid in the cup truly was. It was almost as dark as the world became when he hit the ground with a sickening thud.

In the high rise, the board sat around the table, never having moved since Baker entered. The smashed window carried with it a chilly wind, but the assembled group paid no mind.

The CEO broke the silence. "Looks like it's time to increase funding. All in favor?"

The *ayes* had it.

About the Author

P aul Carro is a horror author who came onto the scene with the hit novel *The House*. He also writes and edits *The Little Coffee Shop of Horrors Anthology* series as one half of an uncle/nephew writing duo with author Joseph Carro. Paul has sold and optioned multiple screenplays and has served as a producer in film and reality TV. He is an active member of the Horror Writers Association and lives in Santa Monica, California.

Also By Paul Carro

The day began when Sheriff Frank Watkins discovered two bodies and three heads. Then things got strange. When a mysterious house appears form thin air in a field, the town of Tether Falls, Maine will never be the same. Doors open throughout town and people are transported into a terrifying world beyond their understanding. Soon residents find themselves trapped together. Nine strangers with nine secrets so dark they wish to take them to their graves. One house is willing to accommodate them all.

Strap in for a pulse pounding horror thrill ride from acclaimed horror author Paul Carro. A member of the Horror Writers Association, Paul has created a terrifying world where nothing is at it seems. The House is now open. Enter if you dare!

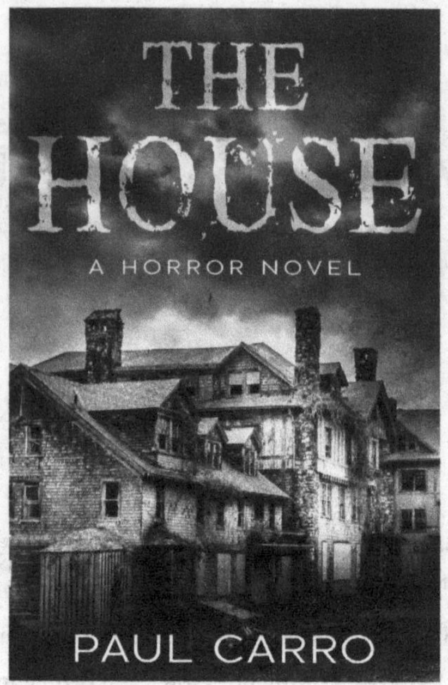
THE
HOUSE
A HORROR NOVEL
PAUL CARRO

Also By Paul Carro

2 authors from 1 family visited 12 coffeeshops to craft 12 single sourced cups of terror!

Authors Paul and Joseph Carro the only known uncle/nephew horror writing duo visited twelve coffeeshops around the country and used the location to inspire twelve unique tales of terror. Each story is prefaced by the coffee shop we worked in and what inspired us. Volume two even adds drink recommendations. If you love naked zombies. killer hill people, and aquatic horror, you will love The Little Coffee Shop of Horrors Anthology. Volumes 1 and 2 available now!

PAUL CARRO
JOSEPH CARRO
WHERE THE SHAKING IS NOT FROM CAFFEINE
BUT FROM THE TWELVE TALES OF TERROR
THE LITTLE
COFFEE SHOP
OF HORRORS
ANTHOLOGY

FOR THOSE WHO LIKE THEIR COFFEE DARK AND THEIR STORIES DARKER
The Little
Coffee Shop
of Horrors
Anthology 2
PAUL CARRO
JOSEPH CARRO